ALSO BY MN WIGGINS

The Sugarfield Sugar Cookie
Sweet Southern Drama

Magical Arkansas Tales

Clinical Optics Made Easy: The Fabled
Second Edition

Letters of the Arkansas Traveler

Lost in Time

[A Novel]

MN Wiggins

ACT TWO
Arkansas Traveler Series

DSP

DAVIS STREET PUBLISHING
Florida

Letters of the Arkansas Traveler

Published by
DAVIS STREET PUBLISHING, LLC
14260 W. Newberry Road #117
Newberry, FL 32669
www.Davisstreetpublishing.com

Cover design by MN Wiggins
Cover illustration by Wesley Goulart

ISBN (paperback) 979-8-9861503-4-5
Library of Congress Control Number: 2023911371

This novel is dedicated to the hard-working people in all facets of healthcare. Thank you for all that you do for us.

I would like to thank the Arkansas Historical Society, as well as the individuals who lived in 1950s Arkansas and graciously agreed to speak with me, and the authors of the beautiful books on the landscape of downtown Little Rock in that decade, making it easy to visualize what our characters would have seen.

Thank you to the multitude of friends who kindly served as beta readers for this work. Your feedback was invaluable.

Lastly, I'd like to thank the long-ago physicians who took the painstaking time to author the brilliant medical textbooks from this period providing such clear and valuable insights into the practice of 1950s Ophthalmology. You did so much for so many with such little technology. You are my heroes.

2004

Hi, my name is Dr. Melvin Napier.

Welcome to Little Rock, Arkansas, circa 2004. That nice-looking young man in the suit down there is me. I'm a private practice ophthalmologist about to fly to Jonesboro to serve as an expert witness. My whole life, lucky breaks have fallen my way, first college, then med school, residency, a beautiful wife, wonderful kids, and a great job. Take this side hustle, for example. They chartered me a private plane, for crying out loud. How cool is that? But deep down, I've always known that the universe would turn on me one day.

I just didn't know it was today.

Chapter 1
The Flight
April 30, 2004

How does a salad start a meeting? Let-tuce begin." Dr. Melvin Napier smiled as his young sons giggled over the phone. "Okay, that was the last one. Put Mommy back on. I'll see you two little monsters tonight. Yes, you are. That's what Mommy calls you. Ask her later. I love you.

"Hey, sexy. Yeah, I'm at the airport. Nothing. Just sitting. They said the pilot would find me." Melvin glanced around the private terminal of the Little Rock airport. "Can you believe they chartered a private plane for one person? Just so you know, this is now the lifestyle to which I've become accustomed." He shook his head. "Why would I be nervous? I get on the stand and answer a few questions—in and out. But after this, my expert witness days are over." He shrugged. "Because I had to rush through clinic to make this flight. You know how hard it's been to find patients. I can't afford to lose anybody." He paused. "But I have to say, a private plane's pretty sweet. I wonder if we could divert to the Bahamas?"

Melvin grinned and held the phone away from his ear. Nearby passengers briefly glanced at the angry voice spewing out of his cell. "Baby, honey, sweetie, I would never leave you. It's not like I packed a bag, got a passport, and hid money for months to slip off to an exotic island where I change my name and live off my hidden talents. The thought never crossed my mind." Melvin frowned. "Wow. That's harsh. I have talents—they're just hidden. Hey, seriously, what are we having for dinner?" He grinned. "Mmm, I love me some Palak Paneer. Is it your Nani's recipe?" His expression soured. "Come on, Alexis, it's my birthday. I don't want take-out. I want home cooking." His smile returned. "Thank you, honey. You're now my favorite half-Pakistani wife . . . in Arkansas . . . this week. And since it's Friday, I like your odds." Melvin jerked the phone away from his ear once more. "Language, dear. There are small children in our home. If your math was correct, one or two of those could be mine."

An older lady sitting opposite Melvin looked up from her book with disgust. Melvin muffled his phone and grinned. "Just go back to your book, sister. What is that, anyway? *Magical Arkansas Tales?* Sounds like a kid's book."

He put the phone back to his ear. "A surprise? Did you get me a 1984 Ferrari? Because if you did, you're now the coolest wife on the planet." He sighed. "Yeah, but do the kids *have* to go to college? It's Magnum's Ferrari. Uh-huh, uh-huh. Well, what if they get athletic scholarships? Then we saved up for nothing." Melvin nodded. "Half my DNA. True enough. Well, here's hoping they're mathletes. So, what's the surprise then?" He shook his head. "Fine, don't tell me. Just promise me it's not tickets to another Russian ballet. That's five hours of my life I'll never get back. Well, it felt like five. Okay, uh-huh. And after the kids go to bed? Mmm, that sounds promising. Wait, what kind of movie? No, this is my birthday, not yours. We are not watching the *Accommodating Emmetrope* for the umpteenth time. Because it's boring as hell. The point is to keep me awake. Well, I realize that, but why can't *Top Gun* or *Red Dawn* put you in the mood? Those are love stories. Oh, Grandma's on the other line. I don't know. Maybe six, depending on traffic? No later than seven. Did you order me a cake? You're so sweet. How did a dorky white guy from Sugarfield get so lucky? Don't answer that. Yes, the minute I land. Love you, too. Bye."

"Hi, Grandma. I was just chatting with my mistress. Who's Alexis? Oh, right, the lady I married with those kids she claims are your grandchildren. Tell you what, until she produces an actual blood test, I'm not so—yes, she's fine. Yes, I'm here now. No, I can't drive to Jonesboro. There's not enough time." Melvin sighed. "Why would you say that right before I get on board? Airplanes are perfectly safe. No, I haven't met him yet. I'm sure he's fine. They rented an entire plane for me. They're not going to hire some kid to fly it."

Melvin glanced up. A teenager dressed as a pilot stood over him. Melvin held up a finger to ask for a moment. "Look, I need to—well, maybe, but I have to—uh-huh, uh-huh." Melvin looked at the pilot and rolled his eyes in apology. "Grandma, listen to me. If the man was alive to tell you the story, then his plane didn't really explode. Plus, that was over fifty years ago." Melvin shook his head. "Just because he was a doctor doesn't mean my plane will crash, too. The universe doesn't work like—Grandma, I need to—I have to—call-you-later-bye." Melvin flipped his phone closed and stood. "Sorry about that."

The pilot's face remained expressionless. "No problem, sir. Your time is important. I'm just the hired help."

"I wouldn't say that. How about we start over? I'm Melvin Napier." Melvin held out his hand, but the pilot turned his eyes to his clipboard.

"Good, because my docket says I'm to fly one Dr. Melvin Napier 102 nautical miles to Jonesboro, Arkansas on April 30th, 2004, with a noon departure. Sir, my name is Leonard McCoy, and I'll be your pilot for the day."

Melvin's eyes widened as he grinned. "Like the doctor on *Star Trek?*"

The young man's brow furrowed. "I'm not sure what you're referring to, sir. I'm a pilot, not a doctor. Shall we board?"

Melvin followed McCoy out to the tarmac. *This kid can't be more than nineteen.* He considered how responsible he'd been at nineteen. It wasn't reassuring. *He's older than he looks. If Grandma asks, dude's pushing forty.*

"Been flying long?" Melvin shouted over the noise of the other planes.

"Ever since I was a kid."

"You mean, like, last month?"

"What was that, sir?"

"Nothing."

"They said you're a surgeon?"

Melvin nodded. "Ophthalmologist."

"Is that eyes?"

"Yeah."

"Live around here?"

"Over the river in Maumelle. We love it."

McCoy nodded. "Nice area, if you can afford it. Got a wife, kids?"

"Two. Children, that is. I couldn't handle two wives."

"I'll get you back to them safe and sound, sir."

McCoy opened the door to his single-engine, red and white, six-seater prop plane and helped Melvin onto the step stool as if he were an old man. A little offended, Melvin climbed into the back where two passenger seats faced forward, and two faced the rear. He buckled into a forward-facing seat and then unbuckled to remove his suit jacket in the hot, stuffy cabin air. Melvin wiped the sweat from his brow as he watched Not-a-Doctor McCoy take an eternity to review the checklist on his clipboard. Finally, the engine whined, cabin airflow came on, and off they went.

Melvin closed his eyes and enjoyed the smooth acceleration of takeoff. It took him back to his teenage drag-racing days on the stretch of highway just south of Sugarfield, back when he was stupid, back when he was McCoy's age, the kid who now held his life in his hands, the only person on the planet who'd never heard of *Star Trek*.

Once they leveled off, Melvin unbuckled and switched seats. McCoy pointed out the plane's amenities, and Melvin helped himself to the snacks. Munching on one after another, he gazed out the window. The long, straight Interstate 40 stretched out forever, with cars moving like ants to a picnic. Endless farmland lay on either side, like a map with rectangles and squiggly lines where creeks worked their way through the dirt.

Melvin felt a rumble and put a hand on his stomach. *Did those snacks have dairy?* By the second rumble, he realized it was the seat beneath him. *Crap.* Melvin smiled, proud for thinking the word crap. He and Alexis were making a concerted effort to clean up their language. Just last week, their four-year-old had uttered, "She's a real bitch." Alexis had sworn he didn't get it from her, but the evidence wasn't in her favor. Now, they substituted words. This morning, she'd uttered such obscenities as *cheese and crackers* and *son-of-a-biscuit-eater.* It was stupid, but they were trying.

Melvin felt a larger rumble. "Hey, McCoy!" he shouted over the engine's roar. "What's going on up there? Are we in a storm?"

"No, sir. Clear skies. Just a patch of rough air. We apologize for any discomfort."

We? Melvin wondered. *It's just him. Does he have a tapeworm?*

McCoy turned around and winked. "I'll try to make this as smooth as possible, sir, but damn it, I'm just a pilot, not a miracle worker!"

Melvin nodded. *Okay, a typical smart-ass teenager. I can relate.* Melvin shouted back, "Yeah? I've never felt rough air like that." The plane suddenly dropped, ramming Melvin's head into the ceiling. "Ow! Rough air, huh?" The plane jutted hard sideways, throwing Melvin into the fuselage wall. "*Son-of-a-bitch!*"

"We recommend you buckle up at this time, sir. There could be some turbulence."

"Could be? Just what the fu—?" The plane threw Melvin backward and then shook like a jackhammer.

As if speaking through a fan, McCoy shouted, "Well, sir, there does indeed seem to be some degree of turbulence. We're going to do our best to pull above it. Please remain seated with your seat belt fastened at this time."

5

Melvin struggled to buckle in as the plane tossed, tilted, fell, and shook. His face now green, he mentally counted the snacks he'd eaten. McCoy managed to pull up, but the turbulence worsened at the higher altitude and the cabin pressure shot up. Melvin put his hand on his chest, struggling to breathe. The plane was thrown backward, Melvin's seatbelt nearly cutting him in half. The next moment, the plane thrust forward, slamming him into the metal plate behind the worn seat padding. Melvin's eyes widened in pain.

A voice from the cockpit called back, "I don't know if she's going to hold together, sir. I predict we'll have you on the ground shortly."

No longer able to reply, Melvin closed his eyes and clenched his fists. He saw Grandma shaking a finger over his grave, saying, "I told you so." The violent movements and suffocating cabin pressure reached unbearable limits, and Melvin focused on his shallow breathing. *This is it. This is the day I die, on my birthday, at only thirty-three.* A thought washed an eerie calm over him. *The pain of death is temporary.* The plane shook and jerked, but in that moment, he felt peace. *Whatever's on the other side, I'm about to find out. I'll finally get to meet my grandfather.* Thoughts of Alexis and his boys flashed through his mind, triggering more sweat on his brow. *They'll have to get by without me. Why didn't I get more insurance? Why didn't I listen to State Farm? Wait, aren't they just homeowners?* Once more, the plane tossed him forward and back like a rag doll. Once more, he felt the pain of the seatback. It was the last thing he knew before the darkness.

Melvin felt the warmth and softness of a mattress and pillow. He adjusted in the bed and stopped, pain stabbing his ribs. Struggling to open swollen eyes, he made out the cast on his right leg elevated in a sling. His left shoulder was in a sling, too. He could see the large room with five other patients and stared in disbelief at the white metal tube frames of old-timey hospital beds with hand cranks at the foot.

A nearby nurse came over. "There you are. We were wondering when you'd decide to join us."

"Where am I?"

"You're in the University Hospital. Can you tell me your name?"

"I'm where?" Melvin closed his eyes and shook his head. "How long have I been out? What day is it?"

"It's Wednesday."

He forced his eyes open again. "I've been out for almost a week? What happened?"

She smiled. "Why don't you just rest for now? No need to worry. You're getting the best care 1950 has to offer."

1950? Son-of-a-biscuit-eater.

1950

Chapter 2
A Room, A Girl, and a Ceiling Tile

Melvin carefully watched the nurse and thought, *She's screwing around. Probably pissed they made her wear that old uniform.* She injected something into his IV. "What's that?" he asked.

"Just a little something to make you comfortable. For a fella who almost died, you sure ask a lot of questions. We don't even know your name."

Before he could answer, the warm and fuzzy feeling of waking up on a cold winter morning and snuggling under the covers washed over him. A goofy smile spread across his face as he stared at her nurse's hat. *Is it Halloween? I can't remember. Is this a party? Am I drunk on someone's couch? I love this couch.* He grinned as the darkness returned.

Melvin awoke to pain. *Where am I? Where's Alexis?* The plane, hospital, and the nurse's costume came rushing back. *Did she say this was University? I'm in Conway? How did I get here?* He looked around the room as much as his swollen eyes would allow. *This is a ward. University only has private rooms. Where am I?* He looked again. *I've been here before. But when?*

Melvin felt around for a call button that wasn't there. He started to shout, but his ribs said otherwise. It was just as well. Alexis was an R.N., and he knew darn well never to yell out for the nurse. *The trial,* he thought. *Guess I missed that. Stupid private plane. I'll never get on one of those again. Where's Alexis?*

A Dean Martin song floated in from the hallway outside, and Melvin turned his head. *That's appropriate. This whole room could be straight out of a black-and-white movie.* A cross breeze climbed through the open windows and meandered across the ward, bringing tidings of stench.

Melvin winced. *Somebody's a smoker. Why aren't they running the A.C.?* He glanced at the tiled ceiling. *No vents? No air conditioning?* His eyes turned toward the floor. *Spiral floor heaters. Wait, is that a two-pronged outlet? How old is this place?*

The nurse returned. "Welcome back," she said cheerily. "Are you hurting? I'll give you a little more morphine. Do you know where you are?"

Melvin nodded. *That explains it.* "The morphine's snowing me. Could we switch to a high dose non-steroidal?"

"A what?" she asked with a smile. "What are you, some kind of doctor?" Melvin nodded. "Oh, I'm so sorry, doctor," she said, standing more erect. She grabbed his chart off the end of the bed and flipped through it frantically. "No one gave me that in report."

Melvin's eyebrows rose. *Why is she showing me so much respect?* Then he nodded. *Must be a new grad.*

"We don't even know your name, sir, just that you were brought in after being hit by a truck outside of Jonesboro. I hear you're lucky just to be alive. What's your name, doctor? Is there any family I could call? I'll go get Nurse Rachel. Just wait here."

Melvin pointed at his leg in the sling. "Not a problem." *Am I in Jonesboro? This must be an old community hospital affiliated with the med school.* He released a deep breath. *Makes sense. But I swear I've been here before.*

He rolled his head and looked out the window at the sizeable grassy park below. *That settles it. No park like that around University.* He noted a large brick building with a hexagonal third-story turret in the distance. *That looks like the McArthur Museum in Little Rock. How weird.*

Melvin glanced at the other patients in his room. They didn't appear ill. He ran his hand over his cast and felt the tight bandage around his ribs as he shifted. *Why did they put me in a low acuity ward? Why am I not hooked up to a monitor?* He closed his eyes. *I bet I lost my wallet in the crash, and they assumed I was indigent. Homeless or not, I should at least be monitored. No wonder Alexis hasn't found me. Who would think to look in a*

10

small Jonesboro hospital? She must be going nuts. I've got to call her. Where's that nurse? Is she on break?

A nurse appeared with a breakfast tray for the guy at the far end of the room.

"Would you like a pack of cigarettes, Mr. Dewitt?" she asked.

"Yes, ma'am."

She noticed Melvin's stare. "Don't worry, doctor. You'll get yours."

Melvin's mouth fell open as she passed smokes to Mr. Dewitt, who lit up without regard for anyone. Melvin braced himself for the odor. He glanced at the other patients, but no one seemed to mind. Melvin bit his tongue. *I just woke up and will not be the one jerk in the room who says something.* Then he noticed the ashtray next to his bed. *Where the hell are we—Kentucky?*

After delivering food to the other patients, the nurse finally came over. "I'm Nurse Rachel. I hear you claim to be a doctor. Is that on the up and up or just a line to pick up women?"

Melvin sighed in relief at the familiar snark of an overworked, underappreciated nurse. "I'm Dr. Melvin Napier, and it's not a line. I'm married."

She rolled her eyes. "Marriage doesn't mean much to the doctors I know."

"I need to call my wife. Could I use the phone?"

She tapped on his cast. "You're bedridden, genius. You think the cord stretches that far?"

Melvin took a deep breath. "Could I borrow a cordless phone?"

Rachel put her hands on her hips. "You want me to bring you the phone without the cord? You know it won't work that way, right? You sure you want to stick with the story you're a doctor?"

Melvin closed his eyes. *What's with these Jonesboro nurses? I was so hoping this one was normal.* "Could you at least tell me which hospital this is?"

"You're at University Hospital."

"And what city are we in?"

She nodded. "Not from around here, huh? This is Little Rock, partner. The hospital's part of the University of Arkansas Medical School. You're in good hands. Well, good enough."

"Little Rock? The med school's now in Little Rock, *Arkansas*?"

Her eyes narrowed. "Most days, the University of Arkansas is located in *Arkansas*. That's why they call it that, honey." Rachel checked his pupils. "I think we need to examine your head wound again." She tapped her foot. "No, I think you're messing with me. You know what? I'm going on break. Nurse Cathy can deal with you. She's real special—bless her heart. I think you two deserve each other." As she walked out, Rachel called back, "Get some rest, *doctor*. Maybe you'll sound smarter tomorrow."

Melvin's head pounded. *I'm back in Little Rock? But there's no med school here. How could they build a hospital, and I not know it?* He shook his head. *They didn't. They converted an old building. But if I'm home, where's Alexis? How could she not find me?* He nodded. *Without my name, they couldn't have contacted her. How long have I been out?*

A drop of water hit the top of his head. Glancing up, he noticed water accumulation in the ceiling tile. Another drop hit him, and then another. Stuck in bed with a broken leg, he tried to time the movement of his head with the fall of each drop. Melvin watched the ceiling tile slowly sag with saturation. It was just a matter of time. *Where's that nurse? What was her name? Cathy?*

Several water droplets later, a nurse in her late thirties burst into the room carrying a tray of bacon, eggs, pancakes, sausage, coffee, and a side of biscuits and gravy for dessert. She almost dropped it twice as she made her way to Melvin.

Melvin smiled as she placed it in front of him, the pancakes now christened with coffee. *Hmm, nutritionist on vacation?* Then it struck him he'd never seen a nurse deliver food.

12

She smiled and said in a thick New York accent, "I'm so sorry I'm late with your breakfast, sweetie. It was change of shift, and we had report, and then we ran out of sausage. I had to go out and catch a whole other pig. Do you know how hard that is this time of day?" She winked. "Can you tell me your name? Are you really a doctor?"

"Yes. I'm Dr. Melvin Napier. I'm an ophthalmologist."

In a chipper voice, she replied, "Nice to meet you, Dr. Melvin Napier, the ophthalmologist. I'm Cathy from Buffalo, but everybody calls me chatty Cathy, always have, always will. Started saying that when I was just a little girl. I have no idea why. My mother says I popped out three weeks early just because I had a lot to say. I've lived here for six years now, maybe seven. Let me think about it"—she looked up and counted with her fingers—"four, five, nope, six years. But just because they say I'm chatty doesn't mean I go around repeating gossip. Nope, if you want to hear it from me, you'd better listen up the first time."

Melvin grinned. "I've heard that somewhere. Hee-Haw, right?"

"What's Hee-Haw?"

"It was my parent's favorite show like a hundred years ago. They never missed it."

"Funny, I've never heard of it. I think I've listened to every show there ever was. Maybe it didn't reach Buffalo. Have you ever been to Buffalo? You should go. It's a marvelous place. Very beautiful. You're probably wondering why I moved down here if it was so great. Well, it all started one day when I was looking at some orangutans at the zoo. Then, all of a sudden—hey, Dr. Napier, your hair is wet! Are you running a fever? Your pillow's all wet, too. Well, would you look at that? There's a leak in the ceiling. Did you know there was a leak? I'm so sorry, Dr. Napier. This is not acceptable. No-siree-Bob. This is not the way we do business in *this* hospital. I'll have the boys fix that up in a jiff, good as new. So, you're just an ophthalmologist, huh? Not an EENT? Do you practice here in Arkansas? I love Arkansas, don't you? Have you ever played the ponies in Hot Springs? Oh, it's marvelous!

13

And the mountains going up the pig trail to Fayetteville? Oh, my heart almost stops. But not like my Aunt Ethyl. Her heart stopped for real. So tragic. She was so young and beautiful. Everything else just paled in comparison—except maybe the mountains around Fayetteville. They are gorgeous. Have you ever been? Because if you haven't, you should. And don't even get me started on Eureka Springs! You don't say much, do you, Dr. Napier?"

Melvin smiled. "I would appreciate it if you could address the leak. And yes, I have a practice downtown."

"Really? Then you must be brand new. Dr. Thomas is the only EENT I know of in Little Rock. Are you joining him? You must be joining him. What a terrible way of moving here, getting hit by a truck and all. Do you remember it? Was it awful? I can't imagine. But if I could, I would imagine it would be awful."

Melvin nodded. "Could I speak with the attending?"

"Oh, of course, doctor. He's already been by early this morning, but now that you're awake, I'm sure he'll want to see you again. In fact, I'm sure he'll be rounding shortly. Get it? He'll be rounding your way because he's rounding?" She laughed with a subtle snort.

"Yes, I get it. Thank you. I don't have a phone at my bedside. Is there one I could use to call my wife?"

"Phone at the bedside!" she cackled and slapped his arm in the sling. Melvin winced. "Like it could stretch that far. That's a good one, Dr. Napier. You're funny. You're a funny doctor. Not all doctors are. No, some doctors are not funny at all. But you are, and I like that. I'll put in a call to her, no problem. I'm sure she's worried sick about you. What's her number?"

"Her cell number is 555-867-5309."

Cathy's eyes widened as her hand covered her mouth. "Oh my, I am *so* sorry. Why is she in prison? What did she do? Oh, that's really none of my business. Did she kill someone? How awful for you. My cousin robbed a bank once. Don't know why I just told you that. It

14

wasn't even a bank. It was a Piggly Wiggly. Are you going to divorce her? No one can blame you for divorcing a murderess."

"Prison? What are you talking about?"

"You said we could only reach her in her cell."

"No, *on* her cell. Anyway, please just make the call. Her name is Alexis."

"But doctor, that's too many numbers. Is she overseas? Is that why? What's the name of the city? I hope it's Paris. Paris, France, not Paris, Arkansas. Not that I have anything against the one here." Cathy put her hand over her heart. "Really nice town, with this cute little grocery store next to a theater as you drive in. And from there, you can go up to this lodge on Mount Magazine. It's so beautiful. Before the war, I always wanted to go to Paris—the one in France. I've been to the one here. Oh, are you French? You don't look French. Is she French? Does she speak French? She'd better if she grew up there, right? Oh, just imagine, she's thousands of miles away, and you're in this horrible accident. She has no idea whether you're dead or alive. Oh, how sad! I think I'm going to cry. But listen, you have to be thankful. Know why? Because she's not in prison. That's such a blessing for you!"

Melvin nodded again. "I'll just wait for the attending. Who is it?"

"It's Dr. Miller. You'll love him. Everyone does. He's such a wonderful doctor. He's not from France, but he did fix your leg. I'll bet you'll be up and around within twelve weeks."

"Three months? Did he say that?"

"Yes! Isn't it great?"

Melvin sighed. "Yeah, great. I don't know Miller. Is he new?"

"Is he new?" Cathy laughed and snorted again, slapping the grumpy patient next to him. "Get a load of this guy! He gets run over by a truck, rolls into town half-dead, and wonders why he doesn't know everybody already. You're a hoot, Dr. Napier. What's your brand?"

"I don't know. Samsung?"

"I've never heard of those. Are they French? We only have a few different ones, but I'd be happy to send a kid across the street to find your smokes."

"I'll pass, thanks."

"Really? You feeling okay? Want some morphine?"

"No," Melvin said. "I'm fine. Maybe you could have a T.V. installed on the wall?"

"A TV on the wall!" She closed her eyes as her laugh boomed. "Please stop with the jokes. You're going to make me pee!" Cathy wiped her eyes. "You know, you're now my favorite patient, Dr. Napier."

"Thanks. Just try to get a hold of my wife, please. If you can't, let me know, and I'll give you the number for my partner, Dr. William Harper."

"Okeydokey, I'll see what I can do, doc. Here. If you don't want smokes, at least take a magazine."

Melvin tossed the magazine on his bed and sighed as three more drops hit his head. *She could at least have given me a towel.* He picked up the news magazine and opened his eyes as much as the swelling allowed. He didn't know the baseball player on the cover, but that didn't mean much. Other than golf, Melvin was the farthest thing from a sports fan. However, he was keenly interested in what was printed in the top right corner: April 10th, 1950. *Old uniforms, cigarettes, and fifty-year-old magazines?* Melvin shook his head. *No doubt now. I'm in Kentucky.*

Flipping through, he saw articles about the military's concern over decreased spending on defense, the ongoing search for a cure for cancer, tensions between Pakistan and India, Congress not showing enough bipartisanship, and the President running the White House from his vacation compound in Florida. Melvin rechecked the date on the cover. No, it wasn't current.

One hour and three soggy pancakes later, the wife of a patient arrived. Melvin flipped back to page 39. The model in the ad wore the same dress style and hairdo. *Holy granola. No thirty-year-old woman would be caught dead with a fifty-year-old haircut. What the hell is going on?*

Three men entered the room with a ladder. Two men moved Melvin and his bed over a few feet while the third disappeared halfway into the drop tile ceiling. Like Melvin, he was well versed in the art of profanity, which was required in abundance to repair the leak. Not having another tile immediately at hand, he put the wet one back in place. The men pushed his bed back under the bull's eye of the sagging tile. Melvin stared at the inevitable.

Fortunately, the ward's cross breeze picked up and dried the tile, leaving a water stain. Melvin watched as the stain took the shape of the Golden Boot, a college football trophy designed to resemble the state of Arkansas connected to Louisiana. Melvin had seen it once while channel surfing for an episode of Magnum, P.I.

He stared at the stain with his mouth open. *It's a coincidence. It can't be. It just can't.* His mind shot back to a night eleven years ago when he was a first-year medical student and picked up a girl in a Little Rock bar—long before Alexis. Melvin recalled it with crystal clarity. She was a law student named Rebecca or Rachel or Raelyn, or maybe Christy, and was from Lake Charles, Louisiana, or somewhere like that. After several drinks, she'd taken him for a tour of her school at two in the morning. Melvin never asked why a student would have keys to the main doors, but in his defense, he didn't care. She'd led him to a study room on the third floor and soon had him on his back on a large table. That's when he'd first seen the ceiling's Golden Boot stain. Even in a drunken haze, he'd appreciated the irony of staring at Arkansas on top of Louisiana while a girl from Louisiana was on top of him.

Melvin closed his eyes. *If I'm in Little Rock, that's McArthur Park out there, and this is the law school building.* He glanced around. *The table would have been right about here. How could I witness the formation of something I saw*

17

over ten years ago? He shook his head. *I was drunk, it was dark, and I was being attacked by a law student with nothing on but a floor lamp.* He sighed. *This is it, though, same building, same room, and that's the stain.*

He closed his eyes again. *It's just a dream. I'm at home, in bed with Alexis, and I'll wake up any minute. Just need to wake up.* Melvin shook himself hard and stopped, his ribs declaring the painful truth.

His eyes grew wide. *Holy crap, I'm trapped in an episode of Happy Days.* Melvin's breathing turned quick and shallow as the room spun and faded from view. He forced slow breaths until his vision returned. *So, this is University Hospital from years ago, a hospital before it was a law school? The med school was here before it was in Conway? I went to that school for four freaking years. How come no one told me?* He paused. *Maybe if I'd gone to class.*

Melvin frowned. *This isn't fair. I step on a plane and get transported over 50 years into the past? That's some bullshit right there.* He was correct. Arkansans didn't do that sort of thing. Sure, it might happen in Victorian England, or just about anywhere in California, but not around here. He intended to speak with someone about this. But whom?

Where's that attending? It's been hours. Melvin picked up the magazine again. This time he read about Senator Joe McCarthy looking for Soviet spies, and other articles echoing the threat of communism and depicting the USSR as evil incarnate. But a different kind of story caught his eye, a story about the horrible living conditions inside institutions for the mentally ill. He'd heard stories in med school but had blown them off. No modern society could've treated people that way—yet this article stated otherwise. *If I tell anyone who I really am . . . Damn if I'm going to be mistaken for mentally ill in 1950.* Sweat beaded on his brow as he recalled his conversation with Chatty Cathy.

Had he said too much already?

Chapter 3
The Canadian Miracle

Lunchtime rolled around, and Melvin bit into his chicken-fried steak as he tried to put Cathy out of his mind. *I'm alone—no identity, no friends, no family. It's just me and the eventual MI from this food.* He used his spoon to create an opening in Mashed Potato Dam and watched the horror of brown gravy flowing down to demolish the sleepy little town of Fried Okra. *So, how do I get home? First, I need to figure out how I got here.* Melvin sipped sweet tea and considered every time-travel movie and TV show he could recall. *There's always a machine or a portal.* He paused. *Except for the Land of the Lost. The Sleestacks had a crystal.* He glanced around the ward. *Not a Sleestack situation. Portal it is. I just need to find it.* He looked at the cast on his leg. *Good luck with that.*

Melvin turned and looked down at the children in the park playing ball in the afternoon sun. In his mind, he saw his two boys chasing after them. *I wonder what they're doing right now? Do they even know I'm gone? Does time stand still in 2004 because it hasn't happened yet? What if it doesn't?* Melvin's heart rate increased. *What if time passes there the same as here, and they think I'm dead or ran out on them? How did Alexis break it to them? Was there a funeral?* Sweat soaked his bandages as images of Daniel and Jake without a father flashed in his mind. *She'll have to sell the house and go back to work. Daniel starts school next year, but Jake will grow up in daycare. He'll forget me.* Melvin's heart pounded against his chest wall. *I'll just be the man in the pictures beside his mother.*

Melvin forced deep breaths. *I'll get home. I'll heal up and charter another flight to Jonesboro along the same route. If there's a portal, I'll find it.* He stared at the far wall. *That'll take cash.* This was a problem. He'd put everything in his briefcase to get through security at the airport: wallet, watch, keys, even his wedding ring had been tucked in his wallet when he'd scrubbed in for surgery that morning. He'd forgotten to put it back on. Those things were long gone now. On the flip side, the date on his driver's license would have been hard to explain. He nodded. *I'll get a job. I'll walk up and say, I'm an ophthalmologist without a license or credentials, but only because my training institution hasn't been built yet. What could go wrong?*

I'll need a place to stay. He looked up at the tile. *Grandma's over in Sugarfield. Dad won't be born for a couple of years. I can see it now: "Excuse me, Mrs. Napier. I'm sorry your first husband died. Would you mind heading to California to meet my grandfather and get knocked up with my dad? As you can see, that makes me your grandson."* Melvin shook his head. *They'd shoot me.*

There's always Mom's family here in town. He smiled. *I'll just stride up to the doorstep of the DeChambeau mansion and say, "Hi, I'm the future son of your unborn daughter who, by the way, one day gets knocked up by a farm boy from the sticks. Mind if I live with you for a while and borrow some cash?" They'd have me arrested.* He sighed. *What's the upside here? Elvis is still alive. So is Buddy Holly. That's cool.* He paused. *How the hell am I going to pay for this hospital stay?*

Before dinner, a tall, thin physician in worn cowboy boots came around, leading a small army of white coats. In a friendly Texas drawl, he said, "Well, looky who decided to join us. I hear you're an EENT from France come here to join Dr. Thomas. John's no spring chicken, so I'm sure he's happy to get ya. I'll tell you, though, getting hit by a truck is a hell of a way to be welcomed to America." He stuck out his hand. "Harry Lane's my name."

Melvin's eyes narrowed as he shook his hand. *So, now I'm French? Damn Cathy.* "Melvin Napier. Good to meet you. I heard Miller was my guy."

"Naw, Frank headed out this morning. Taking the wife to Tahiti or Bermuda or some such place. I'll be masterminding around here for a while. You don't sound French. What are ya, Canadian?"

Now I'm Canadian? It wasn't the worst idea. "Why? You have a problem with Canadians?"

"Oh, hell no. We got nothing against you guys. Now, if you was from Oklahoma, we'd have a problem. Those bastards stole one down at the Cotton Bowl last fall. I'm not one to point fingers, but it came down to questionable calls from the officiating crew." He pointed at Melvin. "Every damn one of them was from Tulsa. So, as you can imagine, treating a Sooner would raise one of those ethical dilemmas I've heard so much about."

Melvin nodded. "They say not all's fair in baseball."

Lane chuckled. "Napier, if there was any damn doubt you were Canadian, it's gone now." He pulled out his half reading glasses, leaned over, and inspected the cast. "Move those toes for me, Canada." Melvin wiggled his toes. "Good! Now I want you to do that for five minutes every hour. Every hour, now," he said, pointing his finger. "I want you to get real religious about it."

"No problem, Harry. How long do you think I'll be in this cast?"

Lane's eyes brightened, and a devilish grin spread across his face. "Thurkowski, get your Polish ass up here!" A young man in a white coat slunk to the front of the group. He didn't look thrilled to be there. "Uh, my name is Thurman, sir. And I'm not Poli—"

"Man asked a question, Thurkowski. Make your people proud."

"Well, sir, the patient—"

"Patient has a name, son! Show him some damn respect, even if he *is* Canadian." Lane turned and secretly winked at Melvin.

"Yes, sir. Dr. Napier had an open fracture of the left tibia and fibula."

"Thurkowski!" Lane yelled in a drill sergeant's voice. "Stand next to the patient. Hold up *your* left leg. Go on, get it up a little higher. Now, do you still think it's his *left* leg that's busted? I'll give you a hint. The broken one's got a cast on it. It's no damn wonder we had to rescue your people in the war."

21

"It's his right leg, sir," Thurman said as he tried to maintain his balance. "And my people are from Omaha?"

"Well, hot damn! You do know your right from your left. Next week I'll teach you how to distinguish your elbow from another anatomical structure. Continue."

"Dr. Miller reported he easily set the fracture. The post-casting X-rays indicate good alignment. Therefore, a wedge cast may not be necessary, indicating the primary cast might be removed in three weeks and replaced by a secondary cast up to the groin."

"Correct!" Lane said as he snapped his fingers and pointed. "You do know something, Thurkowski. I've changed my mind. I'm not gonna fire you today. So, who's it going to be? What about you, Holman? You look like you're slacking!" Another young man in a white coat looked uneasy as Dr. Thurman quietly melted back into the group, safely out of the line of fire.

Lane turned back to Melvin. "I figure we'll plan on changing out that cast in three weeks. If things go well, the second one can come off in 10-12 weeks, depending. I've seen some of these breaks heal real slow and take up to a year. We'll know more as we go. Your rib and collarbone fractures should heal up by the time you go home, but I wouldn't get in too big a hurry. These things take time. Sit back, relax, and we'll keep you comfortable. Maybe read a book. Based on all your injuries, I'd suggest *War and Peace*." He grinned and winked again. "See you tomorrow, Canada. I'll let John know you're here. Wiggle those damn toes. Holman! You're up, son. And you'd best be better 'n yesterday. Damn if I ain't stepped on cockroaches smarter than you."

Melvin's mouth hung open as the team walked out. *Three months to a year? I don't get to see my family for three months to a year?* Sweat formed on his brow as his heart pounded again. *And after that? What if I can't get home? I'm just destined to live out my life in American Graffiti? Is this what the universe planned for me, to die alone and forgotten, lost in time?* Melvin wiped his eyes and shook his head. *Bullshit. I'm making it back. First, I need to survive, to blend in.* He picked up the magazine again. *I need to learn everything there is to know about April 1950.*

The evening nurse removed Melvin's head bandage and handed him a small mirror. Melvin tugged on his bruised, swollen eyelids and examined himself. Tilting the mirror, he discovered only minor scrapes on his forehead. The nurse didn't bother rewrapping it. *Why did they even bandage it in the first place?*

Without morphine, his rib pain stabbed away any hope for sleep. His worries didn't help. Who was this EENT everyone assumed he'd come to town to join? Lane was going to contact him. The guy would know it was a lie. He'd have to assume Melvin was a con man, insane, or worse. Melvin thought about those magazine articles. This was the era of McCarthyism. Here he was, a stranger in town with no identification and no past. What would tomorrow bring: police, psych eval, or FBI?

👓

The next morning, a tall, silver-haired gentleman in a sear-sucker suit and bow tie came to see Melvin. He reached out his hand and, in a melodic, Bing Crosby voice said, "Greetings, friend. I'm John Thomas. I see you've got a little eye trauma, but I'm sure you know all about that."

Melvin's brow furrowed as he shook his hand. *Is he screwing with me?* "Yes, sir, I do know a little something about eyes. I'm Melvin Napier."

"I hear you're an EENT with a practice in the French section of Canada. Québec, was it?"

"Word travels fast. I only practice Ophthalmology, though."

Dr. Thomas paused and looked Melvin in the eye. "You know, I've had that magazine ad out for a partner for over two years. You're the first to respond. Most people don't want to live in Arkansas, I suppose. No idea why. I've always found it beautiful. It's curious you would just show up for an interview." Melvin remained silent.

Dr. Thomas's eyes narrowed. "Most people, most Americans anyway, would have wired or telephoned or sent a letter of inquiry first." A bead of sweat trickled down Melvin's temple. The older gentleman smiled. "Now, I don't mean any offense by that. You and I are from slightly different generations. Perhaps that's the custom up North. Nothing wrong with it, I suppose." He paused in thought. "No, nothing at all. And I'm so sorry you were in an accident. That's certainly not the way we prefer to make a first impression. Now, as long as I'm here, let me take a look at you. Your orbital X-rays were negative. Seen many blow-outs in your practice?"

He's not here to turn me in. Holy cheese and crackers—this is a freaking job interview! "Yes, sir, I've seen more trauma than I cared to. Fortunately, my vision is at baseline, EOMs are full, and there's no diplopia."

Dr. Thomas's expression lightened upon hearing the appropriate lingo. "Do much surgery?"

"Mostly cataracts and some plastics." Melvin was hesitant to say more. Who knew what procedures were around in 1950?

"Plenty of cataracts for you here in Arkansas. Plenty of trauma, too, with all the farming, fighting, and football. Why are you leaving your practice back home?"

"Weather in Arkansas sure beats Canada, and sometimes you need a fresh start."

Dr. Thomas flashed an embarrassed shade of red. "I heard about your wife's incarceration. I understand wanting to get away from all that. Do you have children?"

Without thinking, Melvin replied, "Not yet. But I'll have two sons one day."

"Melvin, if I may call you that, I admire your positivity." Dr. Thomas reached out for another handshake. "I think you'll do fine here."

"Really? I mean, thank you, Dr. Thomas."

"Dr. Thomas was my father's name. Please call me John. Now, as long as you're stuck in bed, we might as well get your hospital credentialing done."

Credentialing? Here it comes. I don't even have my driver's license. What's it going to be? Police or feds?

"I know what you're thinking," John said. "It's written all over your face."

"It is?"

"You're wondering how you're going to get credentialed. Don't worry, Melvin. We know you lost everything in the accident. You focus on healing up. I'll talk to George in the front office and get things going. We'll get your letters from Canada later. And don't worry about the hospital stay. Now that you're on faculty, we take care of our own. When you get out, you can stay with me and Mrs. Thomas until you find a place."

"I don't know what to say. Thank you."

"Not at all. I have to take care of my new partner now, don't I? Anything else you need in the meantime? Maybe a novel or two?"

Melvin's pulse quickened. *Partner? He expects me to practice here in the Stone Age. How the hell do I do that?* He paused. "It may sound boring, but I prefer journals and textbooks to casual reading. Do you have anything I could borrow?"

John smiled. "Of course. We'll send them over today."

As John walked out, Melvin shook his head. *What just happened?*

By early afternoon, a young student arrived carrying the 3rd edition of Gifford's *Textbook of Ophthalmology*. "Greetings, sir. Dr. Thomas sent over this textbook. He said he was still gathering up his journals."

Melvin smiled and noticed the kid wasn't making eye contact. "Thanks. What year are you in school?"

"Oh, I'm not in medical school yet, sir," he replied with his head down. Then he looked at Melvin with conviction. "But I will be

25

someday. And I already know what I want to be, an EENT, just like Dr. Thomas. He's amazing!"

"That's great. What's your name?"

"Billy Rock, sir."

Melvin's expression went blank as he stared, making the kid uncomfortable. Until his retirement in 2001, Dr. Rock had been the longest-serving chairman of Otolaryngology in the Medical University of Conway's history. He was world-renowned and had personally been the ENT for three US Presidents. Melvin had been a third-year med student on his rotation when the sitting President personally sent cufflinks with the Presidential seal on Dr. Rock's birthday. Now, here he was, just a skinny kid. "Trust me, you keep hanging out with Dr. Thomas and working hard, and you'll get into med school. You'll make a fine EENT one day, *Doctor* Rock." Billy blushed at the title, smiled, and hurried away.

Melvin sighed as he looked at the textbook. *Today's as good a day as any to start. Whatever today is.* He asked the guy in the bed next to him for the paper. It was Friday, May 5th, 1950, five days since stepping on a plane in 2004, five days since his family had last seen him. Melvin could only recall the past two. He wondered what Alexis and the boys were doing as he cracked open the textbook to re-learn Ophthalmology, 1950s style.

Halfway through the first paragraph, Melvin drifted as he considered the magnitude of the undertaking. A technological explosion during his residency had changed modern-day Ophthalmology overnight. But here, none of that existed. How would he make diagnoses? Even if he could, how would he treat? His heart rate shot up. All of his cataract training had been on machines. He'd once seen an old-fashioned cataract surgery as a second-year resident but couldn't recall the steps. All he could remember were a lot of sutures. How long had it been since he'd thrown a stitch? He couldn't recall that, either. Did they even have sutures in 1950?

Melvin took a deep breath. *Relax. You've got this. Lane said you're laid up for almost a year. More than enough time to figure this out. Residency in 1950 was probably only a year anyway.* He restarted the first paragraph, then drifted off again. Could he learn all the old surgical and diagnostic techniques physicians had used for centuries but he'd never needed? He shook his head. *So many questions.* Melvin began to read in earnest and hoped Gifford's *Textbook of Ophthalmology* held the answers.

The next evening, Nurse Rachel arrived at his bedside with two men in white. She pointed at Melvin. "That's him, fellas."

Melvin raised an eyebrow. "Cathy's not on this evening?"

Rachel smirked. "Chatty Cathy called out—again. Now we get to do her work in addition to our own. We just love her to death. Bless her Yankee heart. Tonight, you're stuck with this ole southern girl."

"That's fine by me." Melvin watched as the two men placed white cloth panels around his bed. "What are these for?"

"They're for your privacy for what comes next."

Melvin's eyebrow shot up again. "What comes next?"

Rachel wrinkled her nose. "Let me put it this way. I've come across week-old catfish that smelled better than you."

Melvin nodded. "I can't argue. I haven't exactly hit the showers with my leg in this contraption."

"That's one reason I'm here. I'm also here for number two, or lack thereof."

"Not surprised about that either. You guys pumped me with enough morphine to constipate a horse."

"Not recently. I hear you've been refusing pain meds. Isn't that a little stupid, even for a doctor?"

"Opiates can become addictive even with short-term use. I'll take the pain."

Rachel's eyes widened as she put a hand on her chest. "Opiates are addictive? I had no idea. Look at you, teaching me something. Imagine, a high-flying doctor wasting his precious time and knowledge on a lowly nurse. I might just pass out from the shock of it all." Her hands went to her hips. "Do you seriously believe nurses don't know morphine causes constipation and dependence? Who do you think cares for the patients after you scribble orders and run away?"

"Have I offended you in some way?"

"Not yet, but give it time. You're joining the staff here, right? I'm sure you'll fit in with those other idiots. Now, let's get you out of that gown. I have patients other than you. Here's the sponge. I'm not touching that."

After she finished, Melvin offered, "I don't have an appreciation for all the negative experiences you've had, but on behalf of physicians, please allow me to apologize."

Rachel stared at him for a moment, then her expression softened. "You're the first to say that. Maybe things are different in Canada. Do me a favor. The next time you're in the doctor's lounge or out on the golf course smoking cigars and all that talk is going on, remember, just because a nurse goes on a date with a young surgeon doesn't mean she's a hardboiled street hooker."

"No, it certainly does not. And I would say something to that effect."

"Thanks. I almost believe you."

"You should. I don't lie."

Her eyes narrowed. "You don't?"

"Well, I don't tell lies about other people."

She finally smiled. "So, you only tell lies about yourself?"

"Don't we all?"

"Alright, it's time to address number two."

Melvin's eyebrows shot up. "Do you mean Mag Citrate? Stool softeners?"

Nurse Rachel shook her head.

"Suppositories? Enema?"

She smiled as she gloved up and waved at him with her index finger.

"Oh."

"Look on the bright side. A couple of years ago, we didn't even have gloves. Lucky for you, I trim my fingernails. We can't roll you over, so the boys will lift your bottom."

After recovering from being violated and the brown stampede that followed, Melvin picked up his textbook again and tried to regain his dignity. As he immersed in the study of antiseptics, caustic agents, and diagnostic exam pearls, the days melted away along with his eyelid swelling. He finished the textbook and sent word to Dr. Thomas for more.

👁 👁 👁

Not long after, Melvin looked up from his third book to find three young women smiling at him. His eyes narrowed and anus tightened as he tried to recall his last bowel movement. "May I help you?"

"Oh, we just wanted to know if you needed anything, Dr. Napier."

"Yes," another added, "we're awfully sorry to hear about your divorce."

The first girl slapped her arm. "Shut up, Veronica! You weren't supposed to say that."

"Well, *excuse* me, Susie! How am I supposed to know? I've never met a divorced man before. Have you, Annette?"

Annette nodded as she chewed her gum and gave him the eye. "Uh-huh. His first name initial is M. Isn't it grand?"

Melvin smiled. "I don't need anything, ladies. I'm fine. But I appreciate you checking on me." He resumed reading, then glanced over his book again to their smiling faces. "Is there something else?"

"Well," Susie said, looking away, "we read all about you."

"Yeah," Veronica added, "and we heard about Nurse Rachel. Is it true what she said?"

29

"Actually," Susie said, "it wasn't what she said. It's what she *didn't* say."

Veronica put a finger to her lips. "I'm skeptical, though. The whole thing sounds a lot more like Nurse Margaret than Rachel. What do you think, Annette? Margaret or Rachel?"

Annette nodded and smacked her gum. "Uh-huh. Yeah. He's a looker, alright."

Susie rolled her eyes. "It's Rachel. You heard how far she went with Dr. Holman on their first date."

Melvin's brow furrowed. "Rachel and Margaret?"

Six eyes suddenly widened. "Rachel *and* Margaret? Is that how they do it in Canada?"

"Do what?" Suddenly, his eyes were as wide as theirs. "No, no, no. That's not what I meant. What did you mean, you read about me?"

"What are you girls doing in here?" Cathy demanded, whisking them away. "Leave this man alone. If you don't have anything better to do, I'll find you something."

Melvin's cheeks flushed. *Were they checking me out?* He smiled and tried to recall the last woman before Alexis to show any interest. The only one that came to mind was a focused young law student from Louisiana. But she hardly counted. She'd gone to that Little Rock bar with a premeditated agenda packed into her tight-fitting jeans.

But the fact remained, three young lionesses had just eyed him like a slab of meat, as if he were someone else, as if he had transformed. He picked up the small mirror next to his bed. *What's changed? Am I the bomb in 1950?* He shrugged and returned to reading, oblivious to the birth of a reputation and what would follow.

When he'd finished the last chapter, Melvin realized he'd completed three textbooks in the same number of weeks, including a book on Canada. Reading in medical school and residency had seemed a herculean effort, but this felt easy. Melvin shook his head, chalking it up to situational motivation. He had to come off as a seasoned 1950s surgeon. *Dr. Thomas seems like a southern gentleman, but I'll only get one shot at this. Fail, and I'm on the street with no means to charter that plane. That can't happen.*

The cast on his right leg was removed around three weeks as planned. A replacement cast was scheduled for that afternoon. His ribs and collar bone healed, Melvin was sitting up and chowing down on chicken and dumplings when a team of white coats appeared, led by a middle-aged man with solid white hair.

With a big grin, the attending physician said, "Howdy. I see you survived the clutches of my partner from Texas. You can rest easy now, son. You've got a good ole' boy from Oklahoma looking after you. I'm Frank Miller, and you're the famous Dr. Napier."

Melvin shook his hand. "I don't know about the famous part."

"Oh, but you are. Everyone knows about the doctor who was hit by not just one, but two trucks, lost several pints of blood, and still refused to let that stop him from making his way to Little Rock to become our next EENT. It was in all the papers. My wife and I read about you down in Pensacola. They're calling you the Canadian Miracle. And they're not wrong. By all accounts, you should be dead. Do you feel dead?"

Melvin shrugged. "I'm dead tired of being laid up in this bed."

"I'll bet you are." Miller grinned and folded his arms. "But I've heard you've found ways to occupy your time, reading textbooks and your extracurriculars."

"Extracurriculars?"

Miller turned to his group. "You hear that, fellas? A true gentleman doesn't talk. That's a lesson you should learn, Dr. Holman."

"Dr. Miller," Melvin said in a serious tone, "I would like to get out of here."

"I might be able to do something about that if you can explain something to me first." Miller held up an X-ray to the window light. "Dr. Thurman, what do you see?"

Dr. Thurman studied the film in detail with a concerned look.

"Before I retire, Dr. Thurman?"

The young resident continued to stare, then leaned in closer.

Miller rolled his eyes. "Just a tip, son. Leaning in closer only makes what you don't know look bigger."

"I'm confused, sir. Dr. Napier's plain films are completely normal."

Miller turned to Melvin. "Dr. Napier, do you have any explanation you'd like to share?" Melvin shook his head. Miller pivoted back to the group. "Anyone care to speculate?" No one cared to do so. Miller glanced at the film. "There can only be one explanation." He clapped his hands once and raised them for the group to examine. "Gentlemen, as far as you know, I've never claimed these hands to be miracle workers. I've never asked you to look upon them in awe. You should— but I've never asked. That would be arrogant. That would be wrong. As always, I prefer to take the high road and allow my numerous, *numerous* miracles to speak for themselves." The team erupted in laughter. With no need for another cast, the Miracle Hands from Oklahoma prophesied two weeks of rehab before the Canadian Miracle would be set free to stick his fingers in the eyes of strangers.

Chapter 4
Circa 1950

On Monday, June 5th, 1950, Melvin thrust open the main hospital doors, the same ones Louisiana-what's-her-name would unlock for him in the future. Breathing non-hospital air for the first time, he closed his eyes and felt a late afternoon breeze caress his face.

When Melvin opened his eyes, his shoulders slumped. *Hollywood lied. This is supposed to be 1950. Where are the leather jackets and poodle skirts? Where are the teenagers drag racing for pinks? And check out that kid over there. I'll bet he doesn't even fight with his parents over rock and roll. What a total square, man.*

Melvin bounced up and down and felt the tightness in his calves. Despite being laid up for five weeks, he felt good, athletic even. He'd somehow dropped fifteen pounds on the chicken-fried gravy diet and felt energized. He rubbed his abs. They might not be a six-pack, but they were no longer a pony keg. He tugged on the shirt Nurse Rachel had given him from her church's charity bin and lifted his knee to gauge the stretch in his jeans. He looked up and down the street with a strange desire to go for a run, a new sensation for the couch-potato video gamer. *Aw man, that's right. No video games in this decade. Good thing I won't be here long.*

Dr. Thomas tooted the horn as he rolled up in his flashy metallic green 1949 coupe with white sidewall tires and shiny chrome bumper. Melvin smiled and nodded. *It's no Ferrari, but it'll do.* He climbed into the comfortably wide passenger seat. "She's a beaut, John. Business must be good."

"Thank you. Picked her up in Conway last summer. One of our employee's family has a dealership there. I've worked hard and felt I deserved some indulgence. She's got all the bells and whistles: radio, heater, even a mirror over there on the passenger side."

Melvin smirked. "A passenger-side mirror, huh? Word on the street is: objects may be closer than they appear."

John's brow furrowed. "It is?"

"Yeah, because it's a convex mirror. You know, the image is upright, minified, and virtual?" Melvin paused. *How do I know that?*

John smiled. "Someone's been reading optics. I can't tell you much about the mirror, but she's got a doozy of an engine. Listen." The V8 had a deep soothing rumble as he revved her up. "Ready to go? Sure I can't talk you into spending a few nights with the missus and me? The loft over the clinic isn't much."

Melvin shook his head. "I'm sure it's more than enough. Thanks again for the offer. Until I get a car, it just makes sense to live where I work."

"You're quite welcome," John replied as they pulled onto McAlmont Street. "The office isn't far, but I can show you a little of your new city along the way. Something got your eye?"

Melvin turned from his stare of where the interstate would one day be. "Uh, no. I was just looking for my seatbelt."

"Seatbelt? This car wasn't built for the track. I'm afraid she didn't come with any type of harness."

Melvin nodded. "Yeah, right. I was just joking. Say, how much does a beauty like this go for, if you don't mind my asking?"

"She wasn't cheap. Before the add-ons, the tag was just over a grand and a half. It's a lot, but you shouldn't be ashamed if you're honest and work hard."

Honest? Melvin's eyes narrowed. *What did he mean by that?*

"See that tall structure? That's the old Army tower building from the early 1800s. It's a museum now, dedicated to General McArthur. And next door is the Museum of Fine Arts, a wonderful place. Not ashamed to say, Mrs. Thomas and I played a small role in supporting her construction."

"Impressive," Melvin said, pretending he'd never seen it. "When was she built?"

"Twelve or thirteen years ago. And she's built to last. Wouldn't surprise me if she's still standing fifty years from now."

"Wouldn't surprise me either." Melvin pointed at the surrounding homes. "My wife loves these old Victorians. Too bad she's not here to see them."

John opened his mouth but thought the better of it. "The office is just down this way."

"On DeChambeau? How about that?"

"You're familiar with the street?"

Melvin's cheeks reddened. *You're supposed to be from out of town, idiot.* "I'm familiar with the family name."

John smiled. "Is that so? The story goes their ancestors first settled this area and discovered gold down by the river. French trappers, I believe."

"Yup, that's the story my mom told me growing up." *Stop talking, dummy.*

John raised an eyebrow. "How did your family hear of the DeChambeaus up in Canada?"

"In general, Canadians are very well-read." Melvin closed his eyes. *Stupid, stupid, stupid.*

As they turned down DeChambeau, Melvin wondered how far John's office building would be from his in 2004. The closer they got, the wider Melvin's eyes grew. *It can't be.* But it was. John parked in the alley next to the same building where Melvin would practice over fifty years later.

John led him around to the front. "Welcome to the beautiful old Adams-Napier building, circa 1925. It's befitting a Napier has finally returned to the old girl." He patted the brownstone arch over the doorway. "I think she looks happier already. Let me turn on some lights and give you the nickel tour."

Melvin knew the building's history well. In 2001, Bill Harper had given him a detailed account of the structure when Melvin had joined the practice. It had been a ladies' boutique and then a realtor's office before sitting empty for years until Bill bought it. Melvin couldn't wait to see it a half-century younger.

Melvin noted the familiar, polished hardwood floors imported from Lebanon as they entered. The first floor was divided into two large sections by an ornate Italian black metal spiral staircase that led to the second floor, looking just as it would in the future. An impressive Egyptian sandstone inlay encompassed the base of the staircase.

"These hardwoods are outstanding," Melvin remarked as he bent down, pretending to examine them. "Based upon the density, I'd guess this wood is from somewhere in the Middle East?"

"Impressive, Dr. Napier. It's actually from East Africa."

"And this stone, I'm thinking, Egyptian?"

"Very close, again. Imported from Greece. I pause each day I walk in and consider the skill of the artisan who shaped and installed it. Simply beautiful."

"Oh, and what a great-looking staircase. Is this Italian craftsmanship?"

John shook his head. "No, it was imported from France. But I agree, it's exquisitely made. You wouldn't have found anything like it in the States back in those days. This place was owned by a friend when I first started practice, the same fellow who designed and built our house. I never knew him to be an extravagant spender, but he spared no expense on this building." John pointed. "He had a psychiatry practice here on the left, and his partner did eyes over on the other side. He sold it to us after the market crash in '29." He put a hand on the staircase railing. "We have two lofts up here. Yours is on the left."

36

They ascended the stairs carrying textbooks, plus linens and groceries Mrs. Thomas had sent. John turned the knob and used his shoulder to bump open the door. "She sticks a little."

"I'll take a little sandpaper to it," Melvin replied as they entered the tiny one-bedroom apartment.

John sighed. "It's not much. A little kitchen area, a breakfast table, and in there is a small bedroom with a mattress and box springs. It's not the Ritz."

Melvin smiled. "It's great, John. Exactly what I need."

John shook his head and swatted at a cobweb. "I suppose it will get you by until you find a more suitable place. I almost forgot." He disappeared downstairs and returned with a suit. "This was my son's. I hope it fits. Here are your keys to the loft and a set to the main door downstairs. Are you sure you wouldn't rather stay with us until you get settled? Mrs. Thomas is making liver and onions tonight."

Melvin cringed. *Is that what people ate in the fifties?* He forced a smile. "Wow, as tempting as that is, you've already done too much. I couldn't impose further."

John nodded and stepped out onto the landing between the two lofts. "A man needs his privacy. I respect that." He pulled a small envelope from his suit pocket. "Here, you'll need this."

"What's this?"

"Just a small advance on your earnings. Before you say no, consider that you can't wear the same suit every day. I'll introduce you to my tailor after work tomorrow. Well, I should get home for supper. Are you certain you want to stay here tonight? It's awfully Spartan."

Melvin smiled and shook his hand. "Please thank Mrs. Thomas for the linens and groceries."

"Will do. I'll show you the rest of the office in the morning. If your social calendar allows, how about joining Mrs. Thomas and me for breakfast Saturday morning? I'd like to introduce you at our country club."

"Sounds great. Thank you again."

Melvin closed the door, alone for the first time since his arrival. He'd been in the loft dozens of times in the future, packed to the ceiling with old records, unused equipment, and Christmas decorations. But today, it felt different. Today it was empty. Today, it was home.

Home, he thought. *No loving wife, no kids running to meet me at the door, nothing but a tiny kitchen table, a couple of chairs, and an old bed.* He sat in one of the wooden chairs and reached into the sack Mrs. Thomas had sent, pulling out jars of homemade soup. Melvin searched the bare cabinets in the tiny kitchenette. *Nothing to heat the soup in or matches to light the stove if I did.* He grinned. *Literally, I don't have a pot to piss in.*

Melvin sat and stared at the wall, the loft's only form of entertainment. As he did, the emptiness of the room enveloped him. In 2004, he had a beautiful wife—maybe a smart mouth—but still, a beautiful and loving wife with two fantastic kids he loved more than anything. After years of medical school and residency, they finally lived in a lovely home in a nice neighborhood. He was a partner in a thriving practice. He'd had it all. Staring at the wall, it hit hard how much stepping onto that plane had taken away. Now, he had no one. Now, he had nothing.

Melvin's eyes welled up. *The last thing I told her was that I hated the Russian ballet and her favorite movie. All she wanted was to share what she loved. But that wasn't good enough for me, selfish prick. And I told Daniel and Jake they were monsters. They're four and two, for Pete's sake. They aren't going to understand I was joking. The last memory I gave them was their dad being an asshole.* He wiped his eyes on his sleeve. *Don't cry. You do not cry.* He stared hard at the wall, willing the tears to dry up. "Screw this." Melvin shoved his chair backward and stormed out, pausing only to lock the door. He stared at the doorknob and shook his head. *What's anyone going to steal, soup?*

He aimlessly wandered the aisles in the grocery market down the street, thumbing John's cash in his pocket. *Flour, baking powder, I can't use any of this crap. Why can't they have Pop-Tarts like a normal grocery store?* He picked up a can. *What the hell is hominy? It looks like murdered corn, dead in the river for a week.* Melvin glanced down the aisle and dropped the can. There, a few steps away, down on the third shelf, was a wondrous sight. Walking as if in a trance, his eyes widened with each step. *Could it be?* He picked up the rectangular box and stared at it in wonder, cradling it like a newborn. *Is it real? And only thirty-nine cents?* He grabbed a bottle of milk and rushed home with his box of Sugarfield Sugar Cookies and a dented can of hominy—whatever the hell that is.

With no cups in his loft, he searched the breakroom downstairs, snatching a silver coffee mug with a blue lion on it. Soon he was at his kitchen table, dipping one cookie after another into his milk, allowing it to soak just long enough to soften but not so long as to become soggy. Melvin closed his eyes as the sugary goodness danced in his mouth, flooding back sweet childhood memories of his dad bringing home these world-famous delights from his job at the Grable Cookie Alliance. Melvin dunked another. This time he could hear his two boys sitting across from him, giggling as they dunked their cookies like Daddy—milk everywhere. He could hear cartoons in the background. It was Saturday morning, and Momma was still asleep. This was their thing. Melvin slowly opened his eyes to find himself alone, lost in time in an empty room. The cookie slipped from his fingers and plummeted into the mug. *Damn.*

Melvin got up and rummaged through the kitchenette drawers. *No spoons? You've got to be kidding me.* He slammed the drawers shut. Melvin dug his finger into the mug, but the soaked cookie fell apart. Turning the mug up to let the pieces flow into his mouth, a gush of milk spilled down his neck. "Son-of-a-bitch!" he shouted, slinging the mug at the wall—shattering it. Melvin stared at the pieces and saw his life. His head fell to his chest, and he cried.

Chapter 5
The Girl Next Door

Melvin put on his borrowed suit the following day and headed downstairs.

"Good morning," John said. "I trust that old mattress was serviceable?"

"I slept great," Melvin lied. "Thank you."

"I don't want to rub it in, but you missed some tasty liver last night. We have a full day ahead, so let me give you a brief tour. We've done some remodeling over the years." John pointed left. "Our optical shop is over there. You can see our reception area here, and our lanes are back around the corner on the right."

An attractive woman with blonde hair sat erect behind a wooden check-in desk in front of a generic-looking waiting room. She smiled and gave Melvin a small wave as John led him around the corner to a long hallway that smelled of disinfectant. Melvin glanced down at the familiar square tiled floor. "You like the flooring?" asked John. "We had it installed last month."

"Yeah, it's so white. I mean, of course, it is. It's brand new."

Just as it would in Melvin's day, the hallway had six exam rooms, known as lanes. John led him into the first lane on the right side of the hallway. Melvin noted the exam chair, desk, and bulb-style projector. But what caught his eye was the slit lamp, the workhorse of his field. It was a design he'd never seen.

John's eyes lit up. "Like our new slit lamps?"

"Yes, it's different than the ones I've used."

"I should hope so. These just came out. Dr. Littman made some nice additions. See here? You can rotate this and change magnifications. It works on the principle of Galilean telescopes. Having read optics, I know you'll appreciate that."

Galilean telescope? Melvin thought. *One more thing to look up. Damn you, 1950.* Melvin fiddled with the slit lamp switches without a clue how they worked. "It's a beauty. Can't wait to try it out. Do you still have the manual?"

A broad grin spread over John's mouth. "You're a manual man? So am I. Our receptionist filed it. I'll have her pull it for you."

A bead of sweat ran down Melvin's back as he glanced around the room at the foreign-looking instruments. He took a deep breath. *Chill out. The techs will do this for you anyway.* "Your equipment is impressive. Doubt I'll have any trouble adjusting to it," he lied.

"It may not be what you had in Canada, but everything in this room is top of the line."

As they stepped back into the hallway, John said, "So, we have three lanes on the right to see patients. The ones on the left are for special testing. Let me show you."

"This is great," Melvin said with a smile as John showed him more equipment that he had no idea how to use. Melvin's pulse quickened once more as they exited the final lane. *That was it? No visual field machines? No cameras? No lasers? How do you treat anyone?*

As they passed the door to the basement, Melvin played dumb. "Is that a closet?"

"No," John replied, opening the door. "This leads to our basement we use for storage. I'll show you." As they went downstairs, this room, more than any other, looked just as it would 54 years in the future. The only difference Melvin could see were three black metal pipes hanging from the ceiling. In 2004, two were black, and the middle one was galvanized—replaced after the basement flooded decades ago. Melvin reached up and tapped each one. "You know," he lied, "my dad used to own a hardware store where I worked as a kid. He taught me all about pipes. This one here in the center is about to fail. I'd replace it before you have a flood on your hands."

"Your father was in hardware?" John asked, tapping on all three. "That's interesting. I can't tell any difference, but I trust your expertise. I'll have a plumber check it out. Thank you, Melvin."

Melvin noted the familiar black discoloration at the top of the brick walls near the basement ceiling. "Did you have a fire?"

John nodded. "You have a keen eye. Around 1925 or so, an electrical fire broke out from faulty wiring. They had to replace some original flooring on the south side and a couple of interior walls, but the old girl survived."

Back upstairs, John presented Melvin with his new office in the back hallway. A crammed file room in 2004, today it sported an empty wooden bookshelf, two brown metal filing cabinets, and a gray metal desk trimmed in rubber. Melvin noted the gray all-weather carpeting and bare white walls, reminiscent of his loft.

Two cardboard boxes sat in a corner, along with a coat rack hosting three sweater jackets. John quickly snatched the jackets. "I'm sorry, Melvin. This was our storage room before we knew you were joining us. I thought we had everything ready for you. I'll have those boxes moved out of here today. Well, that's the tour. I have some patients ready but make yourself at home. We have coffee in the break room. Feel free to look around our optical shop on the other side. Sally will let you know when you have a patient."

"Thanks, John." Melvin took a seat behind his new desk and stared at the wall. *Who's Sally?*

Melvin examined his new desk chair, a short-back gray swivel. His dad had one just like it in his office. As a boy, Melvin had spun in it like a merry-go-round. He rubbed his hands across the smooth plastic gray handles and slowly turned in a circle, wishing he could talk with his dad now.

Melvin stepped into the hallway to introduce himself to the rest of the staff. But as he walked around, he couldn't find any. So, he introduced himself to the one person he could find, the receptionist. "Hi, I'm Melvin Napier."

"Well, *hello*, doctor," she replied with a sultry, breathy voice entirely inappropriate for that hour of the morning. She sashayed around the desk and stood before him, brushing her hair away and smiling. "I'm Sally. Did you say your last name was Napier or Wonderful?" She stared for an uncomfortable amount of time.

Melvin stepped back, tugged at his collar, and looked away. *Isn't this decade supposed to be repressed?*

Sally laughed, revealing a smoker's cough. Gently touching his arm, she said in a more natural Arkansas voice, "Relax, I'm just teasing. People always say I look like Marilyn, so I figured, why not sound like her? To see the look on your face. It was darling."

"Yeah, you had me going there, for sure. First time meeting someone, some might feel that was a little inappropriate. Not me, though. I love a good joke. But others might, you know, like, for example, everyone else. But yeah, you sounded just like her."

"I look just like her, too, don't you think? Not just in the face and hair, but also her figure?" She slowly twirled for him.

Melvin nodded. "Again, feels inappropriate having just met you, but yeah, spitting image. You two could be sisters."

"Well, aren't you as sweet as you are handsome." She stepped in a little closer and caressed his biceps. "And feel those arms. Dr. Thomas never mentioned you were an athlete. You must practically live in the gymnasium." She winked. "I get the feeling you and I are going to spend a lot of time together after dark."

"What?" Melvin swallowed hard as he glanced at the patients in the waiting room staring at them.

"Calm down. You're so uptight. I just meant that we're neighbors. I live upstairs in the loft across from you. I wanted to introduce myself earlier this morning, but Dr. Thomas was so excited to show you around that he forgot all about me. We've waited a long time for a new doctor." She moved closer and looked up into his eyes. "We're so happy you're here."

Melvin took a step back to regain his personal space. "Thank you," he replied, turning his head to avoid her smoker's breath.

Sally took another step forward. "So, I hear you're from Canada. Is it true what they say about Canadian men?"

Melvin's eyes narrowed. "I don't know. What do they say?"

"Oh, I've heard a few things. I'm so excited to meet someone new. The people around here are so stuffy and boring. You're the first foreigner I've ever met. It's not like Little Rock is the international capital of the world. It's not the capital of anything."

"Except Arkansas."

"What?"

"Little Rock is the capital of Arkansas."

She rolled her eyes. "Well, of course, it is. You know, if you're going to move to our country, you should really learn a little about us first."

"I'll take that under advisement?"

Sally playfully brushed her blonde locks over her right ear and resumed her beauty pageant pose. "So, where in Canada are you from? Anywhere I would've heard of?"

Remembering his town across the Arkansas River wouldn't incorporate until 1985, Melvin offered, "I'm from Maumelle."

"Is that so? We have a Maumelle here, too."

His eyes widened. "Really?"

"Yeah, over by Pinnacle Mountain. There's the Big Maumelle River, the Little Maumelle, and Maumelle Station, and then on the other side of the river is a small town called Maumelle, somewhere near the Army base. That's quite a coincidence that you're from a town with the same name."

"Yeah." Melvin looked away. "What are the odds?"

"I know. It's like you just looked at a map of our area and picked out a name to say that's where you're from."

"What?"

She laughed and gently touched his arm again. "I'm just messing with you. Hey, if a good-looking doctor wants to work here, he can be from wherever he wants: Maumelle, Piggott, Timbuktu. I do *not* care."

"I really am from Maumelle."

She continued to stare. "Uh-huh. I like your eyes."

"Thank you? So, what time do the techs get here?"

"What's a tech?"

Melvin considered their title might be different in this decade. "They're the people who do refractions, measure eye pressure, take history, and so on. You know, that kind of stuff."

"Oh, I see," she nodded. Her eyes narrowed. "Well, Dr. Napier, in the United States of *America*, we call those folks—doctor."

"Gotcha," Melvin replied, trying to recall how to perform eye measurements. "Dr. Thomas mentioned you filed away the manual for the new slit lamps. Could you get it for me?"

Sally raised an eyebrow. "Nope."

"No, you won't, or no, you don't remember where you filed it?"

"Oh, I remember because I have a system." She twirled her hair. "I only file patient charts. Everything else I throw away." Sally shrugged. "Say what you will, but it's a system that works for me. The beauty is in the simplicity. Besides, nobody reads instruction manuals anyway."

Melvin folded his arms. "So, exactly *how* long have you worked here?"

Over the next several minutes, Sally happily launched into a spill about how she was single, in her early twenties, and had grown up in Conway, a city not too far away, yet far enough to be on her own, and that her father owned a local car dealership there. After high school, she spent a couple of years at the Teacher's College of Conway but felt teaching wasn't right for her. Sick to death of living at home with her parents, who aren't modern *at all*, she moved to Little Rock with a girlfriend, and they rented the loft upstairs.

As she carried on, Melvin felt the stares of the patients in the waiting room and raised a finger to ask if everyone was checked in, but Sally showed no signs of pausing. "Then I found a job at Suzanne's, this upscale dress shop. It's just a few blocks from here. And I was good at it. I sold more dresses than the other girls—bunch of hags. But to earn extra cash, I filled in here when the full-time receptionist went on vacation. Her name was Clara, by the way. When Clara got married to this farmer a couple of years ago, who was clearly beneath her, they moved to Greenbriar, which is this little town north of Conway where nothing exciting ever happens, and that's when Dr. Thomas offered me this job. It paid more than Suzanne's, so *obviously*, I had to quit and take it. And it's a good thing I did because last year, my roommate, Barbara, married a mid-level manager at the dairy factory, who's a little boring but still kind of cute. But get this—he's a widower with a ten-year-old daughter. Can you imagine? I was left all alone to pay the full rent. Anyway, I'll have you know that I've made it all on my own and don't rely on my parents or some man to take care of me. In fact, since college, I haven't accepted any support from my parents except for the new car I get each Christmas. As a personal rule, I never turn down a new car. And did I mention I was single?" She primped her hair. "I know that's hard to believe with everything you see here, but the last ring I got from a man was the one I stole from a magician when I was six."

Sally's eyes narrowed. "I'm sorry to hear about your wife's imprisonment and the divorce."

Melvin looked away. "The whole thing was very sudden."

"I can't imagine. What's your ex-wife's name?"

"Alexis."

"That's a pretty name. I'll bet she's beautiful. Do you have a picture?"

"No, actually, I don't."

"No, I guess not, now that you're divorced. How long were you guys married?"

"Five years."

"Wow. Do you have children?"

"No, not at this time."

She winked. "Not at this time? Is that a sly way of saying, not that you know of? Are you a man about town, Dr. Napier? A girl in every port? I wouldn't be surprised. Rich and powerful men do that all the time. Is that what happened? Your wife murdered one of your lovers? I'm not judging. I've been so jealous before I could have just killed someone, too. I get where she's coming from."

"You have an active imagination, Sally."

She shrugged. "So, I've been told."

"And you ask a lot of questions."

"I like to know a lot of things."

"Maybe you should stop asking."

"If you're politely telling me to mind my own business, I've been told that, too."

Melvin smiled. "*Am* I being polite?"

She took his arm. "Let me introduce you to Ronny Roberts, our optician." More patients trickled in and lined up at her desk. Melvin turned and pointed to them, but Sally rolled her eyes and led him to the optical shop.

"Ronald, this is Dr. Napier. Be nice." Leaning close to Melvin, she whispered loud enough for Ronny to hear, "Watch your back. Ronny loves practical jokes. I can't tell you the number of messages I've gotten from "the clinic" reporting I was with child—or worse."

The short, forty-year-old potbellied man grinned widely and shook Melvin's hand. "It could happen."

Sally shook her head. "With the men in *this* town, it'd be an immaculate conception."

Ronny's grin grew wider as he released his slow southern drawl. "Well, that could happen, too. Some of us still believe in that sort of thing. But I don't think you quite fit the profile."

"As you can see," she said, pointing to his stomach, "Ronny sports his own profile, courtesy of his momma's biscuits and gravy, chicken and dumplings, and tea cakes on Sunday. They live together, not far from here in Cabot. Next, he'll show you pictures of his mangy dog. Who in the world wastes photographs on a dog?"

Ronny put his hands on his hips. "We don't talk about Ringo that way. And he looks a damn sight better than anything you've drug home."

Sally looked at the ceiling and nodded. "There might be some truth to that."

As Ronny engaged in polite small talk, Melvin repeatedly nodded at Sally to thank her for her time and indicate it was okay for her to step away and get back to her job. He guessed that, even in 1950, patients would be grumbling by now. Sally disappeared, only to return with three cups of coffee.

"Ronny, did you hide my Detroit Lion's mug?" She asked. "You know it means the world to me. It was a gift from my uncles."

"Was it the ugly silver one with the blue lion?" Ronny asked as he winked at Melvin.

Sally frowned. "I'm telling you, whoever took it, there will be hell to pay. There *will* be suffering."

"Considering where your lips have been," Ronny replied, "I'd say that mug has suffered enough."

Melvin swallowed hard. "I should really get back my office and, you know, do some doctor-things. It's over that way. Just past the glaring patients waiting to be checked in. Hey, great to meet you guys."

Ronny folded his arms and grinned as Melvin left. "Sally Davis, are you smitten?"

"Don't be ridiculous," she scoffed. "He's hardly my type."

"Are you kidding? You have two standards: available and breathing."

"Shut up, you smarmy bastard, and find my damn coffee cup."

Thirty minutes later, Melvin heard a knock on his office door. "Dr. Napier?"

"Yes, come in, Sally."

She glanced around and nodded. "Nice office. I love what you haven't done with the place. That bare wall just goes swell with that other bare wall. Didn't you bring at least one picture or a plant or something?"

"I lost everything in the accident. Are you here to give me interior design tips, or is there something I can do for you?"

She raised a seductive eyebrow and leaned on his desk. "Depends. Are we still talking about work?"

"Yes, we are."

The eyebrow dropped. "Oh. Then I came to tell you that your first patient is ready in room three, *doctor*."

The time had arrived. He'd read the antique textbooks, but there's reading, and then there's doing. It'd be hard enough to see patients without a technician, but to do it in 1950? Like a dead man walking, Melvin slowly rounded the corner and approached the exam lane. He stood outside and pulled the thick chart from the door. As he thumbed through it, his heart sank. Every page was nothing but three-line entries of indecipherable scribble. Shoulders slumped, he took a deep breath and knocked on door number three.

"Come in?" replied an older female voice. "You startled me."

"I'm sorry, ma'am. I'm Dr. Napier."

"Mrs. Mary White. I've never heard of a doctor knocking on his own door before. It's peculiar."

"Well, I'm Canadian, apparently. What can I do for you?"

"Oh, how nice! I've never met anyone who wasn't American."

"I'm from America."

"I thought you said you were Canadian?"

"Canada is part of North America."

"What?"

"What can I do for you, ma'am?"

"I'm just here to check on my condition, doctor."

"And what condition is that, ma'am?"

She pointed at the thick chart in his hand. "Isn't it all right there?"

Melvin plopped the chart onto the desk. "I'd prefer to hear it in your own words."

She waved dismissively. "Oh, that's just silly. What would I know about such things? I just came here to be taken care of."

Melvin sat on the exam stool in front of her. "Okay, let's see. Are you on any eye drops?"

"Well, I was, but then I wasn't."

"Do you remember which eye drop you were using?"

"Of course. It was that eye drop in that plastic bottle with a green label. Or was it a white label with green letters? Now that I think of it, it could have been red. Is there a red one?"

"Do you remember the name of the drop?"

"No, but then I don't think it had a name. I remember it had a top that you twisted on and off."

"Do you remember what the drop was for?"

"No, not really. It's just whichever one my sister gave me. She makes the best medicines and salves in her kitchen."

"So, it wasn't a prescription medication from a drugstore?"

She leaned forward and shook her head. "Was that important?"

He smiled. "I suppose not. How about we just start by checking your vision?"

"Whatever you say, Doctor Napier. What church do you go to?"

"Uh, huh. Please take this paddle and cover your left eye." Melvin measured her vision, hoping for 20/20, but no such luck. *Crap, now I have to remember how to refract.* He opened the briefcase and found the trial frames. As he built her prescription into the bulky frame and fiddled with the knobs, she asked, "Are these going to be my new glasses?"

Melvin smiled. "Oh, yes, ma'am. They're the latest fashion from Paris—Paris, *Arkansas,* that is."

She reached over and slapped his knee. "Oh, you're a jokester, aren't you, doctor? I like you. Are you married? You know, I have a wonderful granddaughter. She's an excellent cook. She's not doing anything this weekend."

"Now, as I change the lenses in these frames, you tell me if things look better or worse."

Thirty painful minutes later, Melvin found a reasonable prescription and was ready to move on to the rest of the exam, still with no idea why her chart was so thick. He rolled the slit lamp table up to her and positioned her in it. He found the on-switch, but everything else was a crapshoot. He messed with the levers and knobs and wondered at what point the TARDIS might take off.

Mrs. White smiled. "This is the most thorough exam I've ever had. The other doctor was so quick. I'm not even sure he was looking at anything. You're a good doctor, Doctor Napier."

"Thank you, ma'am. Now we need to check your pressure."

"Oh boy, you won't be happy after that."

"Really? Eye pressure's been a problem for you?"

"Not for me, but it sure bothered that other doctor."

Without the usual eye pressure device on the slit lamp, Melvin rummaged the desk drawers and found a box. As he pulled out a silver metal instrument, Mrs. White winced. "Please go slow when you lay me back. I have the vertigo."

Fortunately, the Shiotz tonometer manual had escaped Sally's filing system and was still at the bottom of the little box. Quickly scanning the instructions, he looked around and found a bottle of cocaine solution to numb her. Laying her back slowly, he added weights to the instrument until he got the reading, then looked at the chart. He sat her back up. "Your pressures are 32 in the right eye and 38 in the left. Have they ever been this high?"

"Oh, those are good numbers, Doctor Napier. I was worried they'd be worse."

"I need to look deeper inside your eyes." He looked around for a 90 or a 78-diopter lens, but no such luck. Recalling an optics lecture from years ago, he stacked trial lenses together to form an 80-diopter lens and managed to examine her optic nerves.

"Mrs. White, did you know you have glaucoma?"

"Oh, my. Is it serious?"

"Well, it can be. We'll need to start some eye drops."

"Whatever you say, doctor. I'll call my sister this afternoon."

"No,"—he held up a finger—"No-no. We need medication from a *pharmacy*." Melvin could think of at least four choices that didn't exist yet and settled on one of the two that did. "I'm prescribing pilocarpine. I want you to take it four times a day. Do you think you can do that?"

"Whatever you say, doctor. Do you like casseroles? My granddaughter Ruth is a pip at making casseroles."

Finally getting her out of the room, Melvin slumped on his exam stool with his head in his hands. Sally poked her head in with a grin. "So, how did it go with Mrs. White?"

"On the positive side, I got invited to Sunday dinner to meet her granddaughter."

"Ruth? You're not going, are you?"

"No, I politely declined."

Sally nodded. "You catch on fast. Her granddaughter's a hag. She doesn't know how to talk or dress. Doesn't drink. Doesn't even *smoke*. I heard she's never even been out of the stable, if you know what I mean. What would she do for you, anyway? Cook dinner, then have you sit and watch her knit? Pretty *boring* if you ask me. So, how's her grandma doing, anyway?"

"I can't discuss it."

"I understand. How's her glaucoma?"

"Does Dr. Thomas discuss his patients with you?"

"No."

"Then what makes you think she has glaucoma?"

"It says so in her chart, see? High-pressure glaucoma, not using her pilo, IOP worse. And the one after that says, "Glaucoma worse, refused surgery again.""

"You can read that handwriting?"

She shrugged. "I figured it out a while back. There's not much else to do around here other than deal with these *people* who keep demanding to be checked in and out."

Melvin's eyes lit up. "You're beautiful!"

Sally's cheeks flushed. "Thank you. For a while there, I thought maybe you didn't like girls."

He looked into her eyes. "I need you, Sally."

"You do?"

"Yeah, I need you to help me read these charts. You're a lifesaver. Let's do the next one."

"Uh, yeah, sure. I'd love to. Anytime."

Chapter 6
Welcome to the OR

On Thursday morning, John invited Melvin to surgery at University Hospital. Stepping back inside the hospital just three days after his release, Melvin rubbed the lapel of the suit he'd purchased with John's advance and straightened his tie.

Melvin smiled with the familiar comfort of putting on fresh scrubs and stepping into the operating room. The world outside might not look like 1950s TV, but the OR did. It was every bit an episode of MASH—minus the tent. The scrub nurse even sounded like Major Houlihan. Melvin took a deep breath. "What's our first case, John?"

"We're removing a cataract."

Melvin breathed a sigh of relief. *Observe a surgery everyone assumes you know how to do? Yes, please.*

A heavy-set gentleman rolled in on a stretcher. No one in the room resembled an anesthesiologist, and apparently, John wasn't waiting. "Good morning, Mr. Bridges. This is my new partner, Dr. Napier. Can you tell us which eye we're working on today?" Mr. Bridges pointed at his left eye.

Melvin's eyes widened. *Holy smokes, did he just do a time-out?* He'd been certain this was invented around the late nineties, yet here was John doing it decades earlier. John leaned over and whispered, "Don't want a lawsuit from carelessness, now do we?"

Melvin's shoulders slumped. *Malpractice suit in 1950? That was a thing? I thought these were the good ole days?*

"I'm feeling dizzy, Dr. Thomas," Mr. Bridges complained.

"You didn't respond to the blood pressure medicine this morning, and we had to bleed you down to a safe range to operate. Don't worry. Everything will be alright. Cindy, what's his BP now?"

"140 over 90, Dr. Thomas."

"Thank you, dear. Do you have the collargol drawn up?"

"Yes, doctor."

"As you know," he explained to Melvin, "if we don't get his systolic below about 180, we could have an expulsive choroidal on our hands. Naturally, I never exsanguinate more than 300 to 400cc's. I'm sure you understand why."

Melvin nodded. "Of course." He had no clue.

John pointed to the left eye. "See here? His cataract is completely white. You can see the nucleus floating around in it. And why is that, Mr. Bridges?"

"Because I took a few weight loss pills."

"You took *a lot* of weight loss pills," John corrected. "Prolonged use of heavy doses of dinitrophenol. Which I believe is also illegal in Canada."

Melvin nodded again. "Yup, sure is." *Dinitro-what?*

"And what will we do the next time Mrs. Bridges encourages you to shed some weight, Mr. Bridges?"

"Find a new wife?"

"Mr. Bridges?"

Mr. Bridges rolled his eyes. "I'm going to the gymnasium and cutting back on pie."

"That's correct. Now please roll over onto your side and put your knees into your chest."

Melvin's eyebrow rose as he watched John lift the patient's gown and slip something into his rectum. Melvin took a step back, confident one of those 1950s lawsuits was now on the table. "You know, in Canada, we tend to work on the other end of the patient."

John smiled. "That was just a little tribromethanol. Works great. What do you guys use?"

"Topical mostly. A few retrobulbar blocks, but not many."

John raised an eyebrow. "Cocaine or Pontocain?"

"Both," Melvin lied.

John nodded. "Normally, that's what I use as well. Mr. Bridges was somewhat less than cooperative when I did his other eye. Lesson learned."

Topical cataract surgery in 1950? Melvin's eyes widened. *That didn't start until 1998.*

Soon the patient was dozing, and John gave him a shot deep behind his eye. "This is Novocain and adrenaline. I assume you use the same?"

"Pretty much," Melvin nodded.

John held out his hand. "Collargol, dear." The nurse passed him a syringe. He pulled down Mr. Bridge's lower eyelid and squirted. John glanced up at Melvin. "Just a little makes all the difference. Don't you agree?"

Melvin nodded. *Note to self: find out what the hell collargol is.*

Drapes were applied, and John handed Melvin a retractor. "Could you elevate the upper lid for me and hold his lower with your fingers?"

"You don't use a lid speculum?"

"A blepharostat?" John asked as he effortlessly passed a 1-0 silk suture to stabilize the eye. "I've tried it, but nothing beats a good assistant like yourself. Here, hold this." He passed the suture to Melvin, who fumbled a little, but then figured out how to hold it along with the retractor to keep the eye in position.

John stuck out his hand. "My cataract knife, Cindy, if you please." He put the knife to the edge of the eye, paused, and looked up at Melvin. "Steady as she goes. This is the most delicate part." Melvin made darn sure the eye wasn't going anywhere as John entered the eye with a smooth motion and created a large wound.

He looked up at Melvin. "Once, when I was just a young house officer, I inserted the knife upside down. I didn't realize it until I'd already made the counter puncture on the other side."

"What did you do?"

"Of course, if you withdraw to flip it over, you'll lose the chamber. My attending had me cut inferiorly instead, and we did it that way. Worked just fine and saved a young Dr. Thomas a good deal of embarrassment." John smiled under his mask, then went about finishing the case.

After performing four more the same way, John announced the last case was a Seton operation for advanced glaucoma.

Seton? Melvin wondered. *What the heck is that?*

John made two incisions and called for a white silk suture. He threaded it in one side and out the other.

Melvin watched intently. "John, I didn't know you were a glaucoma guy."

John looked up. "What do you mean?"

"You're a glaucoma specialist, right?"

"I treat glaucoma, but I don't understand your meaning."

Melvin subtly shook his head. *Freaking 1950s people.* "Let's say another EENT had a patient needing glaucoma surgery. They'd send it to you, right?"

"No. Why would they?"

"Let me ask it another way. What would you do if you had a patient with a retinal detachment?"

"I'd fix it."

"And if they have a bad corneal ulcer?"

"Melvin, we help whoever comes through our door."

"You don't ever refer?"

"No, that's just not done. Patients are referred to us. We're the specialists. How does it work where you're from?"

"Well, some ophthalmologists are fellowship-trained in a particular area. For example, we have glaucoma guys, retina guys, cornea guys, and so on."

"And that's all they do, care only for patients with glaucoma?"

"Well, yeah, mostly."

"That's an interesting system. I've never heard of fellowships. I knew Canada was different, but I had no idea. It'd never work here in the States."

Melvin shrugged. "Time will tell."

John smiled. "I'll say this, your country sounds fascinating. I believe I'll take a trip up there this summer. I'd like to visit the hospital where you trained and see if I can observe. Maybe visit with a few of your mentors."

"Yeah," Melvin replied, looking away. "That'd be great."

"Oh, and by the way, I wanted to thank you for your excellent diagnosis on Tuesday."

"My diagnosis?"

"You were spot on about that pipe in the basement. The plumber said we dodged a bullet by catching it early. Please give my regards to your father. He must be quite a fellow to teach his son such useful skills."

"Yeah," Melvin replied as he looked down. "I'll let him know next time I see him."

Chapter 7
Leisure: 1950s Style

On Saturday, June 10, 1950, John picked Melvin up for breakfast. After four straight days of homemade soup and sugar cookies, he didn't have to twist his arm.

When they reached West 9th street, Melvin saw a vibrant African-American business section destined to disappear with the building of the interstate. He had heard stories of racial tension in the 50s and was curious about his new partner. "Do you and Mrs. Thomas shop here?"

"On occasion. You have to be careful."

"Oh?" Melvin replied innocently. "Do they overcharge?"

"No, that's not what I mean."

"Is it a high crime area? Pretty unsafe?"

"No, it's perfectly safe. How do I say this? Spending time here is not looked upon favorably by certain segments of our society. I will say relations have improved over the last twenty years with all the deaths from Narsus syndrome."

Melvin nodded, knowing the disease all too well. A widely used cure-all drug in the 1930s had caused devastating genetic defects in children, defects that were passed on to their children if they survived. If John thought the number of people killed by Narsus was terrible now, he should see things fifty years later.

"Socially speaking," John asked, "are things a little different where you're from?"

"I'm still not sure what we're talking about," Melvin lied.

"That answers my question. The more we chat, the more I like Canada. I've forgotten. Where exactly are you from, Winnipeg?"

Melvin's eyes narrowed. *He's testing my story.* "No, Québec. Technically a little town outside the city, but pretty much Québec."

John took him by the State Capitol building and later pointed to the Colonial Bakery plant. "See that large bay window? A friend of mine named Benny Craig broadcasts minor-league baseball games from there. He reads a ticker and makes sound effects. Fascinating to watch him."

As they headed west down Highway 10, the road curved around a neighborhood Melvin didn't recognize. He'd traveled this road a million times on his way to work, but this curve and that neighborhood didn't exist in 2004. "What's this neighborhood on the left?" he asked.

"It's called West Rock. People who live here work in the area."

"That's interesting," Melvin replied, wondering what happened to the families living in a neighborhood destined to vanish.

"I suppose you've done your research before deciding to come here," John said. "The Federal Housing Act passed last year, and people are talking about relocating neighborhoods like this one to the east."

"Do you mean black neighborhoods?"

John kept his eyes on the road. "Did I hear you're a golfer?"

Melvin nodded. *Struck a nerve. Interesting.* "Yes, I've been known to shank a ball or two."

"I don't know much about the game, but that sounds pretty good to me. Down that road on your right is a first-rate golf course."

"You mean Rebsamen?"

"No, the Riverdale Country Club. The development down there is rather impressive, considering the flood wiped everything out in '27. Interesting you would mention Mr. Rebsamen. Last I heard, he was pushing city planners to build a public course in this area." John turned and looked at Melvin. "Now, how would a fellow from Québec know that?"

"I heard about it when I was in the hospital."

"And you knew they were talking about right here? Impressive."

They crested a large hill, and John pointed right. "Down that street is the Pulaski Heights Country Club, just a stone's throw from ours. Beautiful facility. Top-notch."

"Yeah, I've always wanted to play Pulaski Heights. I mean, I've always wanted to play somewhere as nice as what I hear Pulaski is."

John smiled. "Already heard about that, too? You had an informative hospital stay. Well, our club is no slouch, either. I think you'll like what you see."

John pulled into the driveway of a beautiful two-story rock home adjacent to the Westfield Country Club. Mrs. Thomas came out smiling. "We're so excited you're here, Dr. Napier. Please, come right on in. Breakfast is on the table."

"Thank you, ma'am," Melvin replied, stepping inside. "And thank you for the soup and the linens."

"You are most welcome. Well, this is our home. It's not as much as some, but it's far nicer than anything we've ever owned. We're happy here."

"It's a beautiful place, ma'am."

"As I mentioned earlier," John said, "she was built in '24 by a good friend and mentor. I played many a card game right over there as a young physician and got a lot of advice sitting out on that patio. That's where he convinced me to get up the courage to ask for Ms. Lane's hand in marriage."

"Lane, as in the surgeon from Texas?"

John nodded. "Harry's my brother-in-law. Their family's been in Little Rock for years. Her father's a retired neurologist. Harry claims he's a Texan because he studied down at UT, but he's as Arkansan as they come. We all grew up together." John winked. "I'll let you in on a little secret. His exaggerated drawl is something of a put-on. Before he went to Austin, he never wore boots or dipped tobacco. And as far as I can remember, he never uttered the word, ain't."

Melvin's mouth watered as he sat down to a vast spread of pancakes, biscuits, ham, bacon, eggs, and sausage. "This all looks so good. And before I forget, thank you again for allowing me to borrow your son's suit. I hope he didn't mind."

John and Mrs. Thomas traded glances. "He didn't mind at all," she replied with a forced smile. "Please, eat. Oh, and I've cooked something exotic. John, before you turn your nose up, I'd like you to at least try it. They call it Canadian bacon."

"Thank you," Melvin replied as he helped himself. "We had this nearly every Friday night growing up."

"Your mother made this for you?" She smiled. "How nice."

Melvin nodded as he chewed and quickly swallowed. "It's my dad's favorite topping, along with hamburger, pineapple, and pepperoni."

"Well," she replied, "Canadian cuisine sounds so . . . interesting."

Melvin crammed another bite of the best maple syrup-soaked pancakes he'd ever had. Then he devoured two biscuits and gravy, six strips of bacon, four sausage patties, a side of ham, and three servings of scrambled eggs.

John smiled. "I've never seen anyone put away food like that. I wanted another biscuit, but frankly, I was afraid to get my hand anywhere near you. Come on, let's head over to the club. After all that, you could use the walk."

Strolling through the Westfield Country Club's ornate iron gates, John led him to the pro shop. "Melvin, this is Joe Campbell, our head professional. Joe, this is Dr. Melvin Napier. I believe you will find him somewhat of an expert at golf. I'm made to understand he can shank a shot with no effort at all."

"Greetings, Dr. Napier. It's a real pleasure. As you can see, Dr. Thomas's knowledge of golf is something to behold."

John shook his head. "No need for compliments, Joe. Say, I need a word with the judge. Is he around today?"

Joe winked at Melvin. "Yes, sir. He's in the locker room. Ask him about his score this morning."

"Thanks, I'll do that. Would you mind giving Dr. Napier a tour of our little club? I'd like to sponsor him for membership."

"Of course, sir."

As soon as John was off, Melvin asked, "Any relation to Dr. Anthony Campbell, discoverer of Narsus?"

"No, sir. I get asked that all the time. I read about him though—amazing guy. Speaking of which, we've heard quite a bit about you from Dr. Thomas over the last few weeks. I'm sorry to hear about your accident and your shanks. If you decide to join, I could help with at least one of those."

"Thank you, Mr. Campbell, but in full disclosure, I don't just deal in shanks. I like to push, pull, hook, and hit it fat. I'm an equal opportunity golfer."

"Sounds like you'd fit right in. Let's step outside. We have one of the nicest practice facilities around." Joe opened the door for him. "By the way, call me Joe." He paused. "You're the first prospective member ever to address me as Mr. Campbell. Thank you."

Standing just off the ninth green, Melvin said, "This is beautiful. What do you have growing in the fairways?"

Joe shrugged. "It's just grass."

"Yes, but is it Bermuda or some variant?"

"I honestly don't know, Dr. Napier. Crabgrass, maybe? It's just whatever grows here. Whatever it is, we keep it mowed."

"Oh."

Joe grinned. "I'm messing with you, sir. When it comes to course agronomy, we take things very seriously. The fairways are Zoysia-based, and our greens are the latest variant of Bermuda. We aerate at least four times a year and have a professor from the University come down twice a year for soil testing."

Melvin nodded. "Impressive. I'd love to try the course at some point."

"Why not now? Drs. Miller and Lane are teeing off in about twenty minutes. You can play a few holes, and then we'll finish the tour. I'll let Dr. Thomas know the plan."

Joe took him to the locker room and sized him into golf shoes. "A caddy will meet you outside with clubs and a dozen brand-new balls that just came in. Let me know how they play. Supposed to be longer, easier to work off the tee, and hold the greens better."

Melvin smiled. *Guess golf ball marketing doesn't change.*

Outside, a caddy greeted him with a thin canvas bag filled with a beautiful set of steel-shafted persimmon woods, blade irons, and a bull's eye style putter. The young man walked him to the practice range, where the surgeons were warming up.

"How about that!" Harry Lane exclaimed as he stuck out his hand. "Easy money is here. Don't put too much pressure on that leg today, Canada. Remember, Miller fixed it."

Frank Miller shook his head. "What he means is, thank goodness someone from Oklahoma was here to do things correctly. Good morning, Melvin."

"Morning, fellas. Thanks for letting me tag along. I'll try not to slow you down."

Harry grinned. "Doubt you could play any slower than Miller. Hey, speedy, why don't you give us something to do during your fourteen practice swings, like lighting up those Cuban cigars you've got tucked somewhere in that bag?"

Frank opened his bag. "If you like 'em so much, why don't you bring some?"

Harry winked at Melvin. "Now, why the hell would I do that?"

Frank cut a cigar, handed it to Melvin, and lit it. The two men laughed as he coughed.

Harry patted Melvin's back. "That's okay, Canada. Maybe they don't have cigars in the Great White North. Let's see, since you're a rich eye doctor, how about $20 a hole?"

Frank's eyes widened. "Twenty? Don't let this goat fool you, Melvin. The cheap bastard wouldn't spend 20 bucks if his wife were ransomed."

Harry winked. "If you knew my wife, you wouldn't hold it against me. But typical for an Okie, Frank's missing the point entirely. I'm not spending—I'm collecting. With my draw, it ain't even gambling."

Frank folded his arms. "The only thing your drawl is good for is making people say, Huh?"

"Gentlemen," Melvin interrupted, "I'd love to see the course. Shall we go?"

"I ain't never taken money off an eye doctor before," Harry jabbed. "Feel's right, though." As they approached the first tee, Harry gestured toward the tee box. "Why not go first, Napier? May be your only chance today."

The caddie handed Melvin a new ball from the bag. Just as he did for his large 2004 driver, Melvin teed it up high and well forward in his stance. The two surgeons watched in amusement as Melvin took a healthy swing and severely undercut the ball—sending it nowhere.

"Hot damn!" laughed Harry. "That tee flew farther than your ball. It's not your fault, Napier. Maybe Frank made your right leg a little shorter than your left. You just need to compensate. Squat a little to one side like this."

"Stop being such an ass, Harry," Frank said. "Nobody likes a Harry ass. Now, Melvin, I don't know what equipment you're used to, but with these, you need to tee it low, put it in the middle of your stance and swing with good tempo. He gets a Mulligan off the first, right Harry?"

"Sure, sure."

Red-faced, Melvin re-teed as Frank suggested. He released a deep breath, relaxed his grip, and slowly took the club back on plane, building significant torque between his upper and lower body before releasing in an aggressive forward motion. With a loud crack, the ball launched two hundred and ninety yards down the center of the fairway.

"Son-of-a-bitch," said Harry, with no drawl at all.

Frank's toothy grin spread ear to ear. "Bring your wallet, Harry? I hope it's as big as Texas."

One hundred eighty dollars and a string of profanities later, Harry walked off the ninth green and announced he was done. He opened his wallet to Melvin, offered to buy lunch, and then marched on ahead, mumbling as he went. The term "Canadian sandbagger" was heard multiple times.

Once seated in the elegant dining room, Frank commented, "I've never seen anyone swing that way. It looked painful."

"I'll tell you what's painful—"

"Shut up, Harry. You bet the man. Now act like one."

Harry stood up. "Napier knows I'm just screwing around. I'm hitting the shitter. Don't order the lobster while I'm gone. I'm already in the poor house."

After he'd gone, Frank asked, "So how about it, Melvin? Where did you learn that swing?"

"That's how they teach it back home. I've never known anything different."

"Well, it was a pleasure to watch you play and a pleasure to see Harry lose for a change. That's something I would've paid money to see. Maybe not $180."

Melvin wrinkled his nose. "He got a little heated, didn't he?"

Frank shook his head. "Not at you. He knows his old lady will skin him alive when she finds out. Hey, want to have some fun? Watch this." He motioned for the waiter.

"Yes, Dr. Miller. How may we serve you today?"

"We'll be on the Lane account today."

"Very well, sir."

"Three lobsters, please. And your best chardonnay."

Throughout lunch, Harry gave Frank the stink eye and ranted over the price of lobster which "must have been flown in by Lindberg himself." As they finished off their apple cobbler, Joe arrived to continue the tour. The two surgeons stood and shook Melvin's hand in a gentlemanly fashion and expressed the desire to do it again soon— but not too soon, per Harry.

Following Joe into the main foyer, Melvin noted the dominating club crest over the fireplace sporting a large D in the middle, just as his mother had described countless times in stories about her family founding the club and adding the letter for DeChambeau.

"That's impressive," Melvin commented as he pointed at the crest. "What does the D stand for?"

"Oh, it stands for our motto here at Westfield, diligence, dedication, and discipline. The club started as purely equestrian with the intent to breed horses." Joe shook his head. "But based on what goes on around here now, that should really be a big ole F."

Melvin's eyes widened. "And F stands for . . . ?"

"Family, fun, and folly, what else?"

Melvin's eyes narrowed. "Yeah, I can't think of anything else."

"Come on, the main attraction's this way." Joe opened two French doors revealing a large patio full of people lounging around an Olympic-sized pool.

"Nice, huh?"

"Incredible."

"It's the largest pool in town after they filled in the one at Forest Park. We've even installed a heater so you can do laps year-round. And if exercise isn't your thing, you can just hang out at the poolside and let our first-rate staff take care of you. Why not jump in today?" Joe pointed left. "You'll find a dressing room with showers over that way, along with a selection of swimwear. We also have a steam room and massage service."

An attendant whispered something into Joe's ear. He shook his head. "I'm afraid I'll have to leave you at this point. Dr. Lane is demanding a golf lesson. Dr. Thomas gave strict orders for you to stay as long as you wish and enjoy yourself. Anything you require will be placed on his account. If I can answer any other questions, please don't hesitate to ask." The two men shook hands. "Oh, and this evening we're having a concert out on the first fairway. Rose Jackson is a local singer with an amazing voice. Hope you can come out and join us."

Still sweaty from golf, Melvin strolled over to the dressing room to see just what a selection of swimwear meant. Sure enough, an attendant showed him new trunks with the club's monogram in various colors.

"How much are they?"

"It's taken care of, sir."

"I prefer to pay my own way," Melvin replied as he felt the roll of Lane's cash in his pocket.

"These are complimentary to certain prospective members, sir. Orders of our club president, Mr. DeChambeau."

"Is that so?" *Would that be my grandfather or great-grandfather?* Either way, it was family. "In that case, I'll take the red ones." He tipped the attendant. "And give my compliments to Mr. DeChambeau."

"You've given me too much, sir."

Melvin looked him in the eye. "Do you have a family?"

"Yes, sir. Four boys and two girls."

"Then, here." Melvin doubled the amount. "You need it more than I do."

After a shower, he donned his new swim trunks, slipped into a lounge chair under a large umbrella by the pool, and ordered a scotch. After a long, satisfying sip, Melvin leaned back with his hands behind his head, closed his eyes, and listened to the happy bustle of children splashing in the pool on a warm June afternoon. *If I have to be temporarily stuck in the past, it could be worse.*

Perfume attacked his nostrils as someone plopped into the lounge chair beside him. "Don't you just love sitting and watching all the privileged children splash around while their parents ignore them, mingling over business deals and engaging in who knows what else?"

Melvin cracked opened his eyes to a tall, fit, attractive girl in her mid-twenties wearing a navy one-piece bathing suit that accentuated her figure. She shook her head. "All the while, never giving a thought to the poor people who live down the hill? People who don't know where their next meal's coming from?"

"I'm sorry. Who are you?"

"No need to apologize," she said as she playfully removed her sunglasses and looked into his eyes. "I didn't think you'd mind if I joined you." She picked up his scotch. "You looked so relaxed sitting there." She took a sip, never breaking eye contact. "I just had to know what you're thinking." She stretched her shoulders back, highlighting what her mother had given her.

"I was thinking how pleasant it is here," Melvin replied, rubbing his finger where his wedding band used to be.

"It is pleasant, isn't it? Of course, it's always pleasant when you're in the upper one percent. Do you know what's not pleasant? The ninety-nine percent who aren't. Where's their fair share? When do they get a piece of the American dream?"

"Believe me. I'm not wealthy."

She shrugged and finished his scotch. "Doesn't matter. You're here, and that makes you complicit by association."

Melvin's eyes narrowed. "Who are you, exactly?"

"My name is Francis Guinevere Moore." She flashed a coy smile. "Thank you for asking."

"That's a nice name. I had a grandmother named Francis."

Primping her hair, Francis sat a little more erect. "Surely, I don't remind you of your grandmother."

"I couldn't say. She died before I was born. I've never even seen a picture of her."

"Oh, that's tragic." She reached over and touched his arm. "How did she die?"

"Boating accident. It was grizzly."

"That's horrible. I love boating. I spent two years cruising the Mediterranean on our yacht after college. It was lovely."

"Well, this wasn't."

"What happened?"

"Engine exploded. Fire killed everyone on board."

"Holy smokes!" She put a hand on her chest. "I didn't even know that could happen. I may never get on a boat again." She paused and smiled. "You haven't even told me your name. Some might interpret that as rude behavior."

Melvin nodded. "As rude as sitting down uninvited?"

"Yes, don't you just hate when people do that?" She winked. "I won't take offense because I already know who you are."

"You do, huh?"

"Um-hm." She looked into his eyes again as she dabbed a finger in the scotch glass and sensually traced her red lips. "I read all about you in the papers. You're practically famous. And I have a girlfriend at the hospital who told me a thing or two about you. I must admit, she wasn't exaggerating." Francis felt his bicep. "You must spend all your time in the gymnasium. Those red trunks suit you. Do you think I'd look good in red?"

Melvin pulled his arm away. "So, you believe the world has a lack of social justice? That the privileged get to come to places like this while others don't?"

Her eyes lit up. "That's right. And that's why I've enrolled in law school this fall. A smart woman can do anything she sets her mind to.

70

I'm going to be the most successful public defender this town has ever seen."

"Good for you. We need do-gooders in the world. I do have a question for you, counselor."

She waved her hand dismissively. "I shall allow it. You may proceed, kind sir."

"You speak of the injustice of the wealthy partaking in the club, yet you're here, too."

"Only out of protest, I assure you. My parents forced me." She leaned in with a devilish grin and whispered, "But I don't always do what they say."

"Maybe you should."

Francis leaned back. "You're such a cad. What fun would that be?" She slid over as close as she could. "So, Dr. Napier, what I really want to ask is: Have you seen everything our fair facility has to offer?"

He scooted away from her in his chair. "Yes, I believe I have."

She smiled and subtly regained the lost ground. "I'll bet you haven't experienced the *full* tour. If you'd like, I'd be happy to show you."

Melvin returned a stern look and removed her hand from his thigh. "No, thank you. I doubt you can show me anything I haven't seen before."

Francis's expression soured. She slid back into her chair, and her chin sunk to her chest. "I don't know what to say. I'm so embarrassed."

Melvin's countenance softened. "Look, you're an attractive young woman, and I'm sure—"

"No one has ever given me the brush before."

"It's nothing personal. It's just that—"

"Certainly not men, not women, no one."

"You seem to have a lot of experience for your age."

"This just doesn't happen."

71

"I would think, statistically, it would have to, you know, sooner or later."

Francis wiped her eye. "I just wanted a little fun before I'm forced into a loveless marriage. And who do I hear is at our club but the Canadian Miracle? And he's just as good-looking as they say, but he thinks I'm hideously atrocious."

"Well, those are big words, so I'm pretty sure I didn't think them. They say I'm good-looking, huh? What's this about being forced into marriage?"

Francis shook her head as she looked down. "Just another of my awful parents' business deals. I'm just political capital—you know, a bargaining chip, a means to an end." She looked up at Melvin with sad eyes. "They forced me to leave the one true love of my life and take up with an old man just because of his last name."

"That sounds awful. How old is he?"

"Twenty-seven. He's dull as mud and only half as smart. His name is John. Even the sound of his name is dull—*John*."

"You know, I'm older than that."

Her eyes brightened. "But you're exciting! You should've died but refused. You demanded more out of life and *got* it. Every day must feel like a victory to you. I've never known anyone like that. And they say you know how to treat a woman. I heard the stories of what went on in the hospital."

Melvin's eyebrow shot up. "What stories?"

"Come, doctor, no need to be coy." She slid toward him once more. "We're both adults here."

"Some more than others. Nothing happened in the hospital."

"We both know I could round up witnesses to counter that testimony. Seven, to be exact."

"No, we don't know—*seven?*"

"From the accounts I've heard, those witnesses would have no problem with recollection. So, now you understand my enthusiasm for our little rendezvous today. I'll be married pretty soon, and life will be over."

Melvin shook his head. "Life is just beginning for you. If you don't love this man, then stand up for yourself and tell your parents."

"I've tried, but it's too late. He already proposed over a dinner between our families. You should have seen it, Dr. Napier. He used note cards. A note card for a one-sentence question! Have you ever heard of such a thing? And to top that, I didn't even get a chance to respond. My mother answered for me. Then his family insisted I not attend law school after I'd studied so hard to get in. Apparently, such a pedestrian occupation isn't dignified enough for his fiancé. I'll have you know, though, I stood my ground. I announced I'd been accepted into that school and was going. My mother was fashioning the tablecloth into a hangman's noose when John stood up. He said my accomplishments should be recognized, and we could wait. So, I'm off to Fayetteville in September. After that, it's to the gallows."

"Well, maybe this John isn't so bad."

Francis rolled her eyes. "A pet fish isn't bad, but I wouldn't want to kiss one, let alone bear its children."

"You can still say no. As you said, a smart woman can do anything she chooses. You're not a second-class citizen. You have the right to lead your own life. Isn't that in the Constitution? Something about the pursuit of happiness?"

A faint smile came across Francis's lips. "Declaration of Independence. Well, maybe that's how things are in Canada, but it's a man's world down here, and we just try to survive. But you're sweet to say such things." She innocently leaned over to kiss his cheek but grabbed his face and planted one on him, forcefully leaning into him. Melvin pushed her off as she bit his lower lip. He held pressure on his mouth and glanced around the pool area. Thankfully no one noticed. "What the hell was that?"

Francis sat back with a satisfied grin, licking his blood from her lips. "Well, I had to know what all the fuss was about. Now I do. Sure you don't want a tour of our more private rooms? Maybe later tonight?"

"Very sure."

"Suit yourself." She put her sunglasses back on. "I guess one day I'll tell my grandchildren how the famous Dr. Napier tried to make it with me, but I slapped his face and turned him down cold."

"Is that an appropriate story for grandchildren, Francis?"

"Who knows? Maybe I'll be the fun grandmother who might say anything. For now, I'll settle for telling it to my girlfriends." She pulled down her sunglasses and winked. "Of course, I'll alter the ending."

"I had no idea 1950s women were this way. You're the second one this week."

"What do you mean, 1950s women?"

"That's what we call American women in Canada."

"What did you think we were like?"

"Like the women on TV: well-dressed, pearls, polite and reserved."

"So, you are wealthy."

"What? No."

"You are if you have a TV. You thought American women were a bunch of sexually repressed squares? Who was this other woman?"

"Just the receptionist at our practice."

"Sally? Figures she'd pounce on you at first sight. Well, if you want something in common with most men in this town, making it with her will do the trick. Hope you don't mind if it burns when you pee."

"I'm not making it with her or anyone."

"Why not? Don't you like girls? Or is it just Americans?"

"Can't a man just do his job, be respectful of women and get the same in return?"

Francis wrinkled her nose. "That doesn't sound like any man I know, thank goodness. Are all Canadians this uptight, or are you just

74

playing hard to get?" She leaned in and whispered, "I've played every game there is—except this one. How *exciting*." Pulling away before he could, she stood up. "Well, I'm sure my father's looking for me by now. If you change your mind, I'm not hard to find. Just don't wait too long. Before you know it, I'll be Mrs. John DeChambeau."

"That's funny. My grandfather's name was John De—"

"What was that?"

Melvin wiped sweat from his brow. "Nothing. Nothing at all. Nothing happened."

"I know," she replied, sashaying as she walked away. "And that's a crime."

Melvin sprinted to the dressing room, changed, and booked it back to John's house. He entered the living room panting. John looked up from his reading chair and smiled.

"Have a good time? Did you get the *full* tour?"

Melvin's eyes widened. "What? No—I mean, kind of. Is that a thing?"

John's grin got larger. "By the look in your eye, I'd say you did. And you're sweating. That's natural, of course. In full disclosure, I had a hand in setting up that little meeting."

Melvin slumped down on the couch. "You did?"

"Sure. You've been cooped up in that hospital for over a month. You needed to get out and stretch your legs, so to speak. A young man needs a little companionship now and then. An older man needs it, too, by the way. So, I called in a favor to ensure you were properly cared for, a welcome to the neighborhood of sorts." John winked. "Have to look out for my new surgeon."

"I don't know what to say. If you only knew *who* it was."

"Well, of course, I know. My goodness, you should see the look on your face right now. Look, I understand what you're feeling."

"I seriously doubt it."

John raised a hand to stop him. "A man feels uncomfortable asking for certain things, especially when he's new in town. I was in your shoes once. There's no shame in accepting a little charity."

"Oh, there might have been some shame to it."

John continued to smile. "Hogwash. If you enjoyed it, that's all that matters. I'm curious to know how she compares to your experiences in Canada. All the boys here say she's an absolute pleasure. They say there's none better."

Melvin looked down at the rug. "*All* the boys say that?"

"Well, sure. From what I can tell, she's in excellent shape, with just the right amount of curvature for interest, not flat and boring. Wouldn't you agree?"

Melvin cringed. "I swear I didn't notice."

John nodded. "I must admit, looking at her, I'm tempted."

Melvin looked up. "You are?"

"Yeah, but who are we kidding? At my age? I wouldn't have the first idea where to start. Unless you wanted to come along and give me pointers?"

Holy shit! Beads of sweat raced down Melvin's back. "Yeah, that's never going to happen."

John sighed and looked away. "I understand. You wouldn't want to babysit a novice golfer."

"Golf? You're talking about—" Melvin released a long breath. "You set up the round with Harry and Frank."

"Naturally." John cocked his head. "What else was there?"

Melvin leaned back and crossed his leg. "Nothing. I'd love to play golf with you, but you should learn from a pro like Joe. You don't want my bad habits."

John nodded. "Sound advice. Speaking of which, could I offer you some? Man to man?"

"Sure."

"Stay away from Francis Moore."

Melvin's eyes widened. "What?"

"I understand she's pretty, you're a young man, and we sometimes fall prey to our baser instincts. Maybe that sort of thing is acceptable in Canada, but down here, especially in the South, we don't thrust ourselves upon innocent young women. We present ourselves with the comportment of gentlemen and show a degree of restraint and decorum in the presence of the fairer sex."

"John, let me explain—"

He held up his hand. "Please let me finish. As physicians in our society, our community will tolerate nothing less than morality beyond reproach. Additionally, you should know Francis is the daughter of a powerful family and engaged to a man in an even more powerful family. If you must persist in this dalliance, I must insist you exercise discretion. Pornographic groping in the pool area in full view of everyone is simply unacceptable. If not for your moral well-being, Melvin, then at least for the children's sake. Think of the children!"

Melvin stood and held out a hand. "You have my word. I'll treat Francis Moore like a three-foot rule at a strip club. From this day forward, I'll only think of her as if she were my grandmother."

John smiled and shook hands. "That seems odd, but I appreciate your understanding. One question, though. What's a three-foot rule?"

Melvin grinned. "According to my buddies—total BS."

Chapter 8
Journey Home

By August 7th, 1950, three months had passed since Melvin's arrival. Squirreling away every penny to find a way home, he'd furnished his loft as sparely as possible, reminiscent of his freshman year of college—except for the sobriety. Living downtown meant most things were within walking distance, a good deal for a guy with no car or 1950s driver's license.

He continued to read textbooks and muddled through his first technology-free surgeries. Clinic was going well, too. Even without technicians, he saw a good number of patients each day, although their demographics had changed. Back in 2004, his patients were sixty-year-old men and women with significant eye disease. Here, they were 20- to 30-year-old well-dressed women with little to no ocular problems. And they were all single. Occasionally, he saw a 60-year-old grandmother, who invariably brought along her twenty-something-year-old granddaughter, who invariably was available. And while his 2004 patients complained of their eyesight, these patients were more interested in how Melvin was getting along and why he wasn't eating enough.

On this morning, Melvin sat in his office perusing the Little Rock paper as he waited for his next patient. Governor McMath had just won the Democratic nomination for his second term. There was a photo of a large group of Marine reservists gathered at War Memorial Stadium waiting to ship out to Korea for a police action. He nearly spilled his coffee as Sally's voice boomed throughout the clinic, "GET OUT AND DON'T COME BACK!"

Melvin sprinted around to the waiting room. Sally stood behind her desk with her arm outstretched, pointing to the door as three young women slunk out, head down. Sally mumbled, "Keep walking, bitches."

Melvin's eyes widened. "What's going on?"

"Oh, nothing," she replied nonchalantly as she sat back down. "Just doing my job."

"What did they want?"

"They were trying to make an appointment with you. Can you believe that? Don't worry. I handled it."

Melvin shook his head. "You do understand we're in the business of seeing patients, right?"

Sally rolled her eyes. "They didn't need to be seen."

"How do you know that?"

"Because I told them you were completely booked for a month."

"Am I completely booked?"

"No, but when I offered them an appointment with Dr. Thomas, they said they wouldn't mind waiting—every last one of them. So, I kicked them out."

"How do you know they didn't just want an examination?"

She folded her arms. "Oh, they wanted to be examined, alright."

"Sally, you can't just turn away patients because you think they're here for reasons other than medical care. You can't *know* that."

"Of course, I can. Don't worry. This happens all the time. You'd be amazed how many messages you get in a day."

"You haven't given me a single message since I started."

"I know. I file them all." She smiled. "I have a system."

"You throw away every message I get?"

"No," she replied with indignation. "Just the ones you don't need. It just so happens that all the ones you've received required filing." She shook her finger at him. "You should thank me. Your time is way too valuable for that kind of nonsense."

"Do you trash every message you take for Dr. Thomas?"

"Of course not. That would be irresponsible. I take my position here seriously. I am nothing if not professional."

"If you've been blocking female patients from my clinic all this time, why is it full of single young women and their grandmothers?"

"I can't catch every fish in the stream, Dr. Napier. I'm only one woman. You have a patient ready in room three."

Melvin pointed at her. "We will discuss this later." As he turned, he noticed a patient glaring in the waiting room. He looked back to Sally. "Have you not checked Ms. Carter out yet? I finished her exam thirty minutes ago."

Sally shrugged. "I needed coffee."

Melvin loudly sighed. "Will you *please* check her out? She needs to come back in a year."

"Of course, doctor. That *is* my job. Come on up, Rosemary. We don't have all day. So, was there anything wrong with you, or were you just faking?"

Melvin's eyes widened. "Sally, you can't ask that. It's inappropriate. My apologies, Ms. Carter."

"But it's my job to ask, Dr. Napier."

"No, it's not."

"It is. I have to make her appointment, and her answer will determine whether or not we're all booked up. By the way, I love that skirt, Rosemary. Where's the rest of it?"

Melvin shook his head as he went to see his next patient. *I know this decade is different, but I do not get these people.*

That evening, Melvin pulled down a coffee can from the drop tile ceiling in his bedroom. Nine weeks of wages for a single man in a one-bedroom loft had it stuffed with cash. It wouldn't take much more to charter a plane. It helped that the University had written off his stay as professional courtesy. Curiously, they'd never asked anything more about his credentials, nor did the state medical license committee, who'd given him a temporary permit to practice. Melvin assumed a full and unrestricted license would be granted when the permit expired— if he were still around.

Along with his finances, Melvin's physical conditioning had improved, too, but he'd had little choice. Almost dying upon arrival here, logic dictated equal or worse injuries on the return trip. To survive, he'd need to be in the best shape of his life. He'd started jogging a couple of months ago, only to learn jogging wasn't a thing in 1950. A grown man running through the streets for no good reason raised the eyebrows of business owners and law enforcement. Next, he tried hopping a bus to the outskirts of town to jog the rural highways. But that didn't work either, with every car stopping to help him in his emergency. Ultimately, Central High's head coach allowed him to use their track after hours. The coach had been unable to refuse. Melvin was his daughter's favorite eye doctor.

In addition to exercise, Melvin tried to eat low sodium and low cholesterol. It was no small feat for 1950. On many days, as Ronny and Sally chowed down on cheeseburgers and chili fries, he munched on apples or raw carrots he'd cut into slender rectangles. *Carrot sticks*, he'd thought, *French fries of the damned*. But the sacrifices had paid off. Now in top form with cash in hand, Melvin Napier was ready to go home.

Ditching the textbooks, he now focused his evenings on flight plans for the 102 nautical miles between Little Rock and Jonesboro. He'd chatted with pilots at the airport bar and learned the most common routes taken by single-engine planes, the kind he would board in 54 years.

Still, questions remained, questions that awoke him in the middle of the night. *Do small planes in the 50s travel at the same altitude as they do in the future? Does the time-of-day matter? What about the weather? It was sunny the first time around. Should I wait for a sunny day? What about the plane's velocity? I have no idea what that was. And even if my plane gets near the same location, it's stupid to believe it will happen again. Even if it does, why would it work in reverse? Can I survive it twice?*

Look, dummy, who cares about risk? Do you want to get back to Alexis and the boys or spend the rest of your life here? Melvin shook his head. *I cannot live through the 70s again.* He paused. *What if I'm the trigger? What if just getting in the air sparks it? What if this whole thing is some kind of aberration, and time is looking to correct itself? Yeah, it's looking for a way to send me back to re-balance its chi or some shit.* He nodded. *This could work.*

By Sunday, September 24th, 1950, everything was set. After five months of separation from his loved ones, Melvin finally had a noon flight to Jonesboro on a single-engine prop plane.

As he waited at Adam's Field, he marveled at the smallness of the future Little Rock Airport. Commercial and private flights shared a terminal. There were no metal detectors, screenings, or pat-downs, and everyone was dressed like they were going to church. Melvin glanced at his watch, *Twelve forty-five. Where is this guy?*

Finally, the pilot appeared. His three-day-old five o'clock shadow paired nicely with his partially untucked Hawaiian shirt. He moseyed over to Melvin with a hitch in his step. The pilot reached out a hand with a smile that sent the rough wrinkles of his sunbaked face upwards, hoisting the edges of his handlebar mustache. "Howdy! I'm Ted from Texas."

No last name, just Ted? Melvin winced at the smell of booze and shook his hand. "I'm Melvin Napier. We had a flight scheduled for noon. An on-time departure was important to me."

Ted's smile didn't fade. "Just keep your shorts on, partner. It'll still be there when we land. We'll make up time in the air. Where are we going again?"

"Jonesboro. You don't know the details of the charter?"

Ted patted Melvin's shoulder. "I do now. You ready to go?"

Melvin turned to avoid his breath. "Yeah. Here's the flight plan I'd like to use."

"Brought your own flight plan, did ya? Well, how about that?" Ted glanced at it for half a second. "Alrighty then, El Capitan. It's your dime. I'm just the hired help."

"No offense. I have my reasons."

"Of course, you do, boss man." Ted winked. "I don't offend easy, anyhow. I just g-o-o-o with the flow."

Melvin nodded and took a step back. Ted might not be easily offended, but his body odor could offend anyone. Melvin felt the heavy September wind as they walked onto the tarmac. "How strong do you think that is?"

Ted stuck his finger in his mouth and held it up. "About 12 knots."

"Does that worry you?"

"Naw. Does it worry you?"

"If it doesn't worry you, then it doesn't worry me, Ted."

Ted grinned. "You know, that's what my first wife said when we started dating. Next thing you know, she's knocked up."

"How many children do you have?"

"Total or per wife?"

Despite the crisp 66 degrees outside, Melvin climbed into a hot and humid passenger compartment, eerily similar to the one he'd boarded in 2004. Aside from the exterior pinstripe, it could have been the same plane. As he sat in the stale air and thought about returning to the scene of the crime, a wave of nausea washed over him. *This isn't going to work. Suppose it does. I have patients scheduled for Monday. I have surgeries on Tuesday. John's been good to me, and I'm running out on him.* Melvin sighed as he waited for takeoff. *Doesn't matter. I'm not meant to be here. Maybe by going back, none of it ever happens. Maybe no one misses me because I was never here. Yeah . . . maybe.*

Once airborne, Melvin switched seats, trying to re-create his actions. He crunched on carrot sticks to mimic the snacks he'd eaten the first time through. Like a kid in the backseat, he repeatedly pestered Ted for updates on their altitude.

Melvin closed his eyes and tried to recall his original flight. *Was I descending when it happened? No, I don't remember that. So, if the flight plan was an arc, it must have occurred somewhere on the flat part of the curve. But where?* He looked out the window as he had the first time to see the ants on I-40. But I-40 wasn't there. Not yet.

The plane leveled off, and Melvin adjusted in his seat. Then he leaned forward and stared at Ted. *Is he looking down at something, or is that bastard asleep?* The plane began to rumble. Ted's head snapped up along with Melvin's heart rate. Melvin put a hand over the pressure in his chest. *This is it!* He braced himself as the rumbles intensified, flashing back to when he was eight at a southern Missouri theme park. His father, Raymond, had convinced him to go on an indoor ride, promising it was slow. But once strapped in and moving, Raymond confessed it was a roller coaster just as they plummeted into pitch-black nothingness. As the plane plunged several feet, Melvin heard his father again, "It's too late now!"

The plane began to shake just as it had five months ago. Melvin clenched his fists. *I'm going home to my family. I don't care how much it hurts. Don't care if it almost kills me.* Then his eyes widened. *What if it sends me the wrong way? What if I end up further back in time? What was I thinking?* He grabbed his seat.

"Better buckle up," Ted yelled in his Texas drawl. "Getting a little rough up here. Storm popped up out of nowhere. I'm going to treat her like I should have done my third wife and steer clear."

"Don't you dare!" Melvin yelled back.

Ted turned his head around. "You know Clarissa?"

"No, you son-of-a-bitch! Stay on the course I paid for."

Ted from Texas mumbled unflattering words as the afternoon sky turned pitch black. The shaking intensified, and Melvin was tossed so hard his seat belt broke. *I'm not going to make it. We have to turn around.*

The 50s aren't that bad—No! I'm going home. The plane dropped several more feet, sending Melvin's stomach into his throat. *This is stupid. I can't get home if I'm dead.*

As Melvin squeezed his eyes and thought of Alexis, everything calmed. He opened his eyes to a bright light. No, not that one. It was the sun through the window of the plane. *I made it!* He felt all over his body. *No broken bones, no hospitals, just heading home. But is it the right date? No way to know until we land.* He sat back in his seat and released a deep breath. It was over. *Wait, if we're back, then we're still headed to Jonesboro. Screw the trial.* He leaned forward to tell Ted to turn around but paused. He'd just transported Ted fifty-four years into the future against his will. Melvin hadn't considered that. Ted from Texas now owed some major back alimony.

"Uh, Ted from Texas, let me start by saying you're one hell of a pilot. Do me a favor and radio the tower and get a check on the date and time, would you?"

"No need there, El Capitan. Far as I know, it's still September 24th, and my watch says thirteen thirty-five."

"What?"

"One thirty-five, partner. And gracias on *el complimento.* I steered clear of that puppy at the last second."

"You did *what?*"

"No need to thank me. We were about to get into this weird green fog in the middle of that storm. Reminded me of my second wife. I met her down in Tijuana. Or was it Pensacola?"

"You turned *out* of the storm?" yelled Melvin.

"Yup. You know, my second wife was a lot like that fog. You think you're getting into one thing but turns out you're getting into this whole other deal. And trust me—you don't want it. Then there was this one time in El Paso, me and this buddy of mine found some peyote, only it wasn't regular peyote, and the next thing you know—"

"You purposely turned the plane out of the storm."

"You don't want to hear my peyote story?"

"No, I don't want to hear your damn peyote story."

"You sure? Because it put us into a green fog like that one back there. No, sir, that wasn't regular peyote at all. It all started when I got drunk and thought I was making it with a beautiful senorita. But it turned out someone had left their coat on a barrel. Next thing you know, I've got splinters in my—"

"Ted, listen to me carefully. Turn us around and fly into that green fog."

"No can do. Not for you, not even for the Gipper."

Melvin reached for his wallet. "I'll double your fee. Triple even."

"Naw. After all I've been through, I have a zest for living and an aversion to the contrary."

"Shit," Melvin said, leaning back with his arms folded. "So close."

"Yup, don't know where that storm came from. Just popped up out of nowhere. Like it was hunting us."

"Looking for me," Melvin muttered.

"Only 42 miles to Jonesboro as the crow flies. Should have you safely on the ground in no time."

"Take us back to Little Rock."

"Aw, come on, should be smooth sailing from here. Just like slipping a nightgown off your lady."

"*That's* your analogy of smooth sailing?"

Ted turned and grinned. "Well, if it ain't smooth sailing, then maybe she's ain't your lady."

"Just take me home."

Home. Is that what this is now?

Chapter 9
Don't Forget to Breathe

After a week of moping around the clinic, Melvin sat alone in his loft, pondering his next move. He polished off the last of Sally's chili macaroni. *Maybe there's a silver lining. The storm appeared out of nowhere. I must be the trigger. It's just a matter of getting back up there. Damn, that girl can cook.*

He counted the cash in his coffee can. *Just enough if I don't buy anything. What's a little more sacrifice?* He rubbed his chin as he nodded. *I can swipe toilet paper from downstairs.*

Melvin hired a pilot the following weekend and walked him through the flight plan. Unfortunately, the trip went as smoothly as slipping off a Texas nightgown, and they landed safely in Jonesboro. Over the next two weeks, Melvin lived on oranges until Sally brought him tuna casserole, the most delicious thing he'd ever inhaled.

By mid-November, Melvin had managed four more flights, all as smooth as sliding off four more Texas nightgowns. He sat at his tiny kitchen table and poured through his notes again. *What am I missing? Was the first flight an aberration? Was the storm random?* He scratched his head. *Every flight was identical: same course, same distance, and the same type of plane.* He snapped his fingers. *The pilots were different. Ted's the key. I'll bet that bastard fell asleep and veered off course. If he did it once, he could doze off again.*

Melvin arrived at the airport bar that weekend just in time for Ted's wake. Airport personnel packed the room to toast the good-natured Texan who was "the best damn pilot they'd ever seen" and "could outfly anyone, even with his eyes closed," which, in the end, had done him in. Melvin joined them, giving condolences to three of his six ex-wives and more children than he could count. He raised his glass. *Here's to the drunk son-of-a-bitch who could've gotten me home, the only one who stumbled onto the right spot. But where?*

Melvin slowly sipped a watered-down scotch. *The sky's too big to search randomly. But if I start with the crash site, physics could predict the rest. I need to know where they found me. Why didn't I think of it before?* The place to start would be his ER records. But pulling his own file could raise flags. He put his glass down and headed out of the airport. *It's time this decade worked in my favor.*

Returning to the Adams-Napier building, he found a generic white coat and rummaged through clinic drawers until he found a stethoscope to complete the ensemble. He headed over to University Hospital and walked down to Medical Records. Staffing would be minimal on a Sunday afternoon. Melvin strutted up to the desk clerk and put his palm on the counter. In an authoritarian voice, he ordered, "I need the ER chart on Melvin Napier."

The young lady smiled, nodded, and retrieved the manila chart. "Here you go, Dr. Napier. Hey, what's wrong with your voice? You sick?"

In a baritone voice, Melvin replied, "Yeah, just a cold. Thanks."

"Your cheeks look a little flush. By the way, these glasses you gave me work great. I think you're a wonderful doctor. Did you like my pineapple upside-down cake?"

Melvin flipped through his chart. "Yeah, it was great. Thank you again . . . uh . . ."

"Marci. Golly, I hope you feel better soon. You know, why don't I bring you some soup tomorrow? I wouldn't mind. Monday is Sally's afternoon off, right?"

He handed the chart back and smiled. "I just need a good night's sleep. But thank you, Marci."

The chart recorded he'd arrived in the back of a delivery truck, but no mention of the driver. He couldn't make out the nurse's name on the note, but it was clearly written that Dr. Nelson had been on duty. It wasn't much, but it was a lead.

Despite Melvin's attempts to keep his aerial excursions on the down-low, it was a hot topic around the office. At first, they speculated a Jonesboro hospital was trying to poach him away. Then, it was generally accepted the flights were social calls. Ronny purported he was proud of Melvin for "getting his share of the field." John announced it wasn't anyone's business to discuss, though privately, he was pleased Melvin kept his womanizing out of town. Sally grumbled about the stupidity of going all the way to Jonesboro with fine young women right here in Little Rock.

Despite her claims not to care, Sally worked hard to get details out of Melvin, casually mentioning a cute scarf or a lovely perfume at the department store some young woman might enjoy, or she'd comment about going through Jonesboro soon and would ask Melvin if he knew any cozy restaurants. When her subtleties yielded no results, Sally cut to the chase. "So, Dr. Napier, what are your thoughts on the local dating scene?"

Melvin's eyes narrowed. "Why so nosey?"

She smiled and touched his arm. "I'm not nosey, just neighborly. You wouldn't understand the difference. You're a man."

He shook his head. "Dating? Wow, I couldn't say. I haven't been on a date in so long. For me, though, it doesn't matter. I've already found my soul mate. You could say she doesn't know it yet, but one day she will."

Sally's pupils dilated as she stood speechless. Clearly, Melvin had just professed a secret love for her. What other explanation could there be? As she watched him walk away, a voice behind her said, "Don't forget to breathe, bitch."

"Shut up, Ronny!"

"Do you need a napkin? You've got a little drool on your chin. Why don't you just get it over with and—"

"Shut up, Ronny. I swear, if you had any balls, I'd neuter you!"

After his last surgery on Tuesday, Melvin went to the Emergency Ward to find Dr. Nelson, but no luck. The staff guessed he'd been a moonlighting fourth-year medical student that the hospital frequently used after hours. Melvin went to the office of the Dean of Medicine, but the senior class had since graduated. To their knowledge, Dr. Nelson had taken a job somewhere in Florida and left no forwarding address.

Back in his loft that evening, Melvin heated up the last of Marci's chicken noodle soup. He carried the bowl into his bedroom, sat on his bed, and gazed upon his newest purchase, a large cork bulletin board displaying all the research he'd collected since his flight with Ted from Texas. Melvin nodded as he looked it over. All the detective shows had a board like this, revealing critical information right after the third commercial break. And not just police: time travelers, stalkers, and serial killers all had a pin-up board of some kind. Why not him? Melvin slurped his soup as he re-read notes and tried to make new connections. The key was somewhere on this board. The way home had to be right in front of him.

Hearing something at his loft's door, Melvin sprang off the bed. If anyone stumbled across this display of present and future knowledge, he'd be committed for sure. Opening his front door, he found no one. He sniffed for the lingering smell of cigarettes, but there was none. Hearing Sally clanging pots and pans next door, he quietly closed his door. No need to alert her that he was out here.

Keeping his neighborly, not nosey, next-door receptionist out of his loft and away from research had been no easy task. It had started innocently enough. "Could I borrow some coffee? If you like, I'd be happy to come in and make a pot." But as time went on, her innuendo had grown less subtle. "I had a terrible nightmare and don't think I should be alone right now," or "My hot water is out. Can I borrow your shower?" as she stood in his doorway wearing a towel.

Other times, Sally's knocks were sadness over a date gone sour, a phone call not returned, or dragging up the stairs at 5 A.M. and needing to talk about what a mistake she'd made. She wasn't one to sit home on a Saturday night, so there was always a story to tell. During her confessionals, she'd delve into more graphic detail than Melvin claimed to want to hear, but he always listened. Curiously, he never noticed anyone coming or going from her loft, and she never gave names.

But no matter what excuse she gave to enter his loft, Melvin politely declined. In step, Sally would invite him to her loft instead, where wonderful leftovers lived in her fridge and a variety of alcohol inhabited her cabinet. Dinner, booze, and conversation with Sally were never dull. She drank, smoked, and cursed more than any woman he'd met in either time, and he found her smart, funny, a damn good cook, and enjoyed the unfiltered connection between her brain and mouth.

As time went on, Sally became more than just wining, dining, and entertainment. Her insistent companionship provided a connection to a world that wasn't his, demanding he accompany her on picnics, matinées, concerts, and plays, prying him out of the solitude of his secret after-hours project. And, of course, she'd taken him to McKeen's.

Just down the street from the Adams-Napier building lived an old bar named McKeen's. The heavy oak doors creaked as they opened, revealing a beer smell that permeated the well-worn hardwood floors, coffered ceiling, and dark wood-paneled walls decorated with the McKeen tartan, a twelve-point buck head, and photos of fishing expeditions in the Gulf.

Walter McKeen had grown up a couple of hours outside Little Rock in Paris, Arkansas, and opened the bar in the fall of 1918, just before Prohibition. Like others, he survived the draught by turning it into a members-only social club serving concoctions of fruity drinks with Walter's secret ingredient—alcohol. And while Little Rock sported several not-so-secret places to drink in those days, McKeen's was the only place you could get Caribbean rum. His cousins smuggled it to him in fruit trucks up the Mississippi and Arkansas highways hidden under watermelons and cantaloupes. But by 1950, Prohibition had long vanished, and patrons like Sally and Melvin enjoyed walking down the street to exercise their freedom.

But they were more than mere regulars at the bar. Back in July, Melvin had performed Walter's cataract surgery, Melvin's first in 1950. Fussing over every little detail to avoid screwing up, he'd given Walter the VIP treatment. Walter was so pleased that he'd proclaimed Melvin his adopted son and honorary American, at least within the four walls of the bar. He even planted a miniature Canadian flag near the register in Melvin's honor.

Walter loved Sally, too, especially when she flirted and pestered him to dump his old lady and marry her, carrying on about her dream to marry a man who owned a bar. Walter always smiled and replied she was more woman than a man his age could handle, and he could never leave his bride. Then he'd point to a picture of his wife and say, "I don't know what I did to deserve her,"—then he'd wink—"but it must've been something pretty awful!"

When Sally couldn't drag him away, Melvin's evenings were dominated by his research. He read every physics book he could find at the Little Rock library on Seventh and Louisiana. When he wasn't doing that, he attended physics lectures over at Little Rock College and was soon on a first-name basis with the professors. One of these was David Brown, a tenured associate professor with a knack for explaining things.

"Welcome back, Melvin," David said as he wiped chalk from his hands at the end of his lecture. "I'm still so pleased with your interest in Physics. Was it a favorite of yours in college?"

Melvin shook his head. "I avoided it like the plague."

"Too intimidating?"

"No multiple-choice tests."

David slowly nodded. "I find that answer disturbing. What did you think of tonight's talk?"

"It was fascinating but a little contradictory to Einstein's special theory of relativity."

David's eyebrows shot up. "Oh? How so?"

"After a glaucoma surgery, if the pressure in the eye becomes too low, tissues inside the eye can swell and touch each other, forming an adhesion. Similarly, if we believe that space could be folded and form an adhesion, then based upon the relationship between time and space, we could have a point where one could travel in time without requiring the speed of light."

David cocked his head to one side. "You did attend *my* lecture, correct? Because it had nothing to do with Einstein or the folding of space. Absolutely nothing." David rubbed his chin. "Curious. Well, at least you're thinking about physics and not hamburgers or the movies like most of my students." He turned back to the board and raised his chalk. "Okay, let's talk for a moment about what Dr. Einstein's really saying."

Melvin smiled. Here was the impromptu lecture he'd wanted. As he listened, he nodded. *Dude has a board. He's legit.* But his head hung as David ended by saying, "Practically speaking, meaningful time travel is pure science fantasy, more suited for Saturday matinées than the classroom."

Chapter 10
3rd Sunday of the Month

On November 19th, 1950, the Sunday before Thanksgiving, Melvin awoke to movement downstairs. Still hungover from McKeen's, he descended part-way down the spiral staircase and saw a waiting room full of patients. *Monday already? How much did I drink?* He glanced at the waiting area and rubbed his eyes. Today everyone in the waiting room was African-American. Melvin quickly dressed, came downstairs, and headed to his lane. John came around the corner and stopped him.

"I'm sorry if we disturbed you, Melvin."

"Not at all. What's going on?"

John ushered him back toward the staircase. "I'm seeing patients. There's no need for you to be here."

"I'm not racist, John. Where I come from, society is more integrated. We work to rise above our differences. At least, we try. Let me help."

John shook his head. "This is a delicate matter. As you know, I am the only EENT in the area. I open our doors on the third Sunday of every month to provide this care. The other townspeople will be at church this morning, turning a blind eye to this clinic. They assume it's charity and never speak of it. It is not. These are paying patients like everyone else. It sounds wonderful where you're from, but here, if we had a mixed clinic during the week, our doors would close."

As John spoke, Melvin wondered how he hadn't known about this clinic. He'd slept in most Sunday mornings and then worked on his board. It was just in the last three weeks that Sally had been suggesting, demanding, really, that he accompany her to the Episcopal Church down the street where he'd uncomfortably sat with another woman in the church where he married Alexis. Melvin figured if he wasn't already bound for Hell, this punched his ticket.

John put his hand on Melvin's shoulder. "Look, I appreciate your offer. You are a good man, Melvin Napier. But it's taken me years to earn this community's trust. I don't think they'd accept a white doctor who isn't from around here, someone who isn't even American."

"For the last time, Canadians *are* Americans, but I get it. If you change your mind—"

"I know where to find you." John winked and pointed up the stairs. "Besides, it appears you have a prior engagement."

Sally stood at the top of the stairs where she'd been listening. She gracefully descended, took his arm, and softly said, "Come on. Let's go to church."

Melvin awoke on Thursday, November 23rd, as he did every day, thinking of his family. But this was Thanksgiving, his first without them. Would they sit and watch the parade on TV? Would they go to Sugarfield for dinner at Grandma's or drive up to Missouri to see Alexis' parents? He sighed and pulled himself out of bed. Whichever they chose, it would be a heck of a lot better than what awaited him today. Sally had invited him for Thanksgiving with her parents in Conway. Invited wasn't quite the word. She absolutely refused to allow him to stay in his loft like a hermit on Thanksgiving, not when he had options. Ronny had invited him for dinner with his mother, but Sally had pulled him aside and described a meal with Ronny and his mother in vivid detail. John had also invited him to a large get-together he was hosting with extended family, which Melvin had also declined. Sally was his friend and just looking out for him. Besides, how awkward could one meal with her parents be?

It was bitterly cold as her cherry red convertible sped down highway 365, colder than Melvin could remember for that time of year.

It didn't help that his window was partially open. Sally's smoking left him little choice.

"Do you have to drive so fast?" he asked. "It's only thirty-something miles. Conway isn't going anywhere."

"Sorry, mother," she replied with a smile as she took a drag. "Are you chilled? Can I get you a sweater? Would you like to knit one?"

"I am a little cold. Thank you very much. Could you stop smoking so I can roll up this window? You smoke more than this car."

"New cars have to burn off a little oil while they break in." She grinned at him. "Aw, does my smoking bother you?"

"Yes, it does."

She shrugged. "Maybe it bothers me that you don't smoke. What's wrong with you, anyway?"

"I don't think we have enough time today to answer that fully."

She smiled and crushed her lipstick-stained cigarette in the ashtray. "Since you asked nicely."

As they neared the city limits, Melvin glanced at his watch. "Looks like you got us here in record time, Mario."

She glanced at him. "Mario?"

"Famous race car driver back home. Almost as fast as his brother, Luigi. Say, how about we drive by the school?"

She shrugged. "I guess. It's on the way."

Curious to see his old alma mater in 1950, Melvin leaned forward as they passed through the main entrance. Only it wasn't the University, at least not yet. Today it was the Teacher's College of Conway. As they drove through campus, he shook his head at familiar landmarks next to open areas where buildings would one day stand.

Sally sighed. "Two years of my life right here. I should have stayed in school. Why did you want to see this place?"

"I remember you mentioned it," he lied. "Naturally, I wanted to see it."

She cut her eyes at him and smiled. "That's sweet."

Her white-walled tires pinged gravel as they continued, passing neighborhoods with familiar street names until she turned onto Davis Street. Melvin's eyes narrowed. *I know this street. But why?* "I didn't know you grew up on Davis," he said.

"Why would you? You could've guessed, though, right? After all, it's my last name. My family's been here for generations."

"Your last name is Davis?"

Sally made a sour face and slapped his arm. "Don't be an ass. At least not until after we leave."

Melvin grinned. "Aw, are you worried I'll embarrass you in front of your family?"

"Well, I am now." She slowed and pulled off the road.

"Is this it?"

"No," she said in a somber tone. "There's something you need to know."

"Oh?"

"My parents are old-fashioned. I mean, not modern *at all*. So, if they say anything about me that doesn't sound right, just be cool, okay?"

Melvin raised an eyebrow. "Like what, for instance?"

She gave a look that she wasn't joking. "I'm already twenty-four."

"I thought you were twenty-six?" he asked with a smile.

"See? There you go again, being an ass. Fine, I'm already twenty-six. According to them, I should be married, barefoot, and pregnant with my third kid by now. I'm a major disappointment. And they *will* bring it up."

His eyes narrowed. "You weren't worried about me being alone on Thanksgiving. This is about you. Your parents think we're dating, don't they?"

"Noooo!" She hung her head and rolled her eyes up at him. "Maybe."

Melvin frowned. "Oh, hell, no. Take me home, *now*."

97

"Come on, Melvin. *Please?* I've told them all about you. Frankly, it's gone on so long that they no longer believe me. Do you know how much that hurts? My own family thinks I'm lying."

"Because you are."

"Not the point. My dumbass brother even accused you of being an imaginary person like the ones I used to talk to."

Melvin's expression softened. "You had imaginary friends when you were a kid? That's kind of cute."

She looked away. "Yeah, sure . . . as a kid."

"Sally, I can't go in there and lie."

She waved her hand dismissively. "Of course, you can. I believe in you, Melvin. You can do anything you set your mind to. Look, you'll never see them again, and it won't mean anything to you. But it'll mean the world to me. I'll do anything for you in return." She raised an eyebrow. "*Anything.*"

Melvin sighed. "Fine. I won't say we're together, but I won't deny it either. They can think what they want. In return, I borrow your car any time I need it."

She threw her arms around him and squeezed. "Oh, thank you! They'll be so thrilled to see you're real. You are so much better than the last boy I brought home. *So* much better."

Sally turned onto the gravel driveway of a blue wooden house with a large concrete porch and immaculate landscaping. A solitary medium-sized oak stood in the middle of the yard. Melvin's head cocked to one side as he stared.

"What's wrong?" she asked. "Were you expecting a mansion? Daddy does well, but he's cheap. He grew up in that house."

"No, it's a nice-looking home," Melvin replied. "It's just . . . nothing. The flowers are beautiful."

"Yeah, Momma's flower beds have to be perfect. See that oak? Daddy planted it the day I was born."

"Why did he plant one tree in the middle of your yard?"

"Because it symbolizes family unity. He may be a car salesman, but he's a poet at heart. You're still staring. What is it?"

"You ever get the feeling you've been somewhere before?"

"I promise you've never been to my parent's house. If you had, you wouldn't be back." She gave him an evil smile and laughed. "I'm mostly kidding. But if Daddy makes a motion like he's going for his gun, run like hell."

"Now, who's the ass?"

Sally grabbed Melvin's arm before he opened the car door. "One last thing. You're a *Democrat*, right?"

Chapter 11
Thanksgiving 1950

They were barely out of the convertible when her parents descended upon them, hugging Sally. A partially-gray bearded man in a flannel shirt and unbuttoned overcoat stared at Melvin with cold, piercing eyes. "I'm guessing you're Dr. Napier," he said with a southern accent. "You look familiar. Have you been by the car lot?"

Melvin noted his firm grip. *Must be his shooting hand.* "No sir, Mr. Davis. And thank you for having me over for dinner."

"No problem. Call me Cole. I'm the dad around here, and this is my wife, Kate."

Kate shook his hand a little too enthusiastically. "It's so nice to meet you, Dr. Napier. We've heard so much about you. Now here you are, all real and everything!"

Melvin glanced at Sally. "I can only imagine what she's told you."

Sally blinked several times. "Momma, why don't we get out of this freezing weather and go inside?"

"I'm all for that!" Cole exclaimed.

Melvin reached into the car for Sally's sweet potato casserole. As they headed for the front door, he overheard Kate whisper to her, "He's every bit as handsome as you said. Now, your brother's here, and he's had a few. I don't want a scene. Not on Thanksgiving."

Sally's smile melted. Melvin slipped up behind her. "The brother, huh?"

"Not much of one," she mumbled as her mother shot her a fierce look.

Melvin paused as he stepped into a wood-paneled living room. *This is so familiar.* Four little kids ran various patterns through the house as they yelled. Between their screaming and the unvented gas floor

100

heaters, Melvin's head immediately throbbed. He forced a smile and calculated the odds of what would happen next: a kid wiping out and getting burned on a heater or the entire family dying from carbon monoxide. Right now, it was even money.

Oblivious to the children, a man lay on the couch with one leg on the coffee table, drinking beer and watching football on a tiny black and white TV.

Melvin nodded. *The brother—our entertainment for the evening.*

Cole walked over, kicked the man on the couch, and held out his hand. The man glanced at Melvin, grunted, and handed Cole a five-dollar bill.

"Daddy?" Sally asked in a disappointed tone. "You bet on whether or not Melvin would show?"

Cole held up his hand. "Now, sweetie, that's not strictly true."

"He's right," said the man on the couch. "We bet on whether or not you made him up."

Sally gave her father the stink eye. "We love you, honey," Cole said, "but you have to see it from our side. You tell us about your amazing boyfriends, but they never materialize. Like the fighter pilot you dated, who couldn't meet us because he had emergency training on the Fourth of July. Or that boy who was JC Penny's heir who got called away to open up a new store on Christmas. Or the senator who had to cancel because of an emergency session on Easter Sunday."

"Technically, he was a state senator," Sally corrected.

"You see my point. Now you're dating some rich doctor? What were we supposed to think?" Cole winked at her. "But I always bet on you, pumpkin."

"No, you don't, Daddy," said the man on the couch. "I had to give you five to one odds."

"Shut up, boy!"

A woman in an apron appeared from the kitchen and exclaimed, "Sally!" as she hugged her. "And you must be Dr. *Wonderful.*" Melvin spun around as if she were talking to someone else. She laughed. "Oh, he's a doll. And funny, too. Just like you said."

Melvin shook her hand. "I'm Melvin. A pleasure to meet you."

"I'm Norma," she said, brushing flour off her apron and out of her hair. "Sorry about my appearance. Kate and I've been cooking all day. We're glad you're here, Sally. Could you start the potatoes? Oh, and Melvin, this is my—Stacy! Get off that couch and meet Sally's boyfriend."

Stacy gave a what's-up head nod and turned back to the game.

Norma's eyes narrowed. "And that's my husband, Stacy. And these are our children, Hersh—STOP RUNNING THROUGH THIS HOUSE!" She shook her finger. "If one of you boys trips and falls into those heaters, you'll be sorry. And if I have to tell you again, I'm gonna cut a switch. Don't you give me that *look*, Tom! Sorry, Melvin. That's Hershel, Jim Bill, Tom, and the little one under the chair is Ted."

Melvin smiled. "Four boys? That must be a handful. They look like great kids."

"You'd think that, wouldn't you? Just don't turn your back on them."

With the ladies and Cole disappearing into the kitchen, Melvin grabbed a chair opposite Stacy. "Who's playing today?"

Stacy stared at the screen and took another drink. "It's *Thanksgiving.*"

Lucky to recognize it was football, Melvin had no idea how to respond.

Stacy audibly sighed and grunted, "Lions and Yanks. Not that it's much of a game. Damn it, New York! Tackle that son-of-a-bitch! I swear he's gonna run for two hundred yards today." He finally looked at Melvin. "Detroit hasn't won on Thanksgiving in 12 years. And I haven't won a bet in just about as long. Who the hell knew they'd show up today?"

Melvin had never heard of the New York Yanks, but that wasn't saying much. He only knew of the Lions after shattering Sally's mug.

Cole walked back into the room. "Cold today, isn't it?"

"Yeah," Melvin nodded. "Coldest Thanksgiving I can remember."

"Doesn't it get colder than this in Canada?"

"Well, yes. I meant for Arkansas. I've never heard of you guys ever having it this cold."

"Yup, the newspaper says a lot of snow is headed up to the northeast tomorrow. Could be a blizzard."

"Glad I'm down here, then."

Cole's eyes narrowed. "I'll just bet you are. You know, I love it here. I'm not going anywhere. Know what I'm saying?"

"Sometimes you don't get a choice," Melvin replied as he watched TV. "I was happy somewhere once, but fate had other plans."

"Fate?" Cole scoffed. "Fate's an excuse for people who don't take responsibility for their decisions."

Melvin looked at him. "Surely you agree there are things we can't control in this universe."

Cole's cold gray eyes stared through him. "Everything can be controlled if you have the knowledge and the will. Take that tree I planted in the front yard. Over its lifetime, it's seen drought, pestilence, and disease. By all rights, it should have died years ago. That tree wanted to survive. Look at it now, healthy as ever."

"Some would say the universe wanted the tree to survive, and so it did."

Cole pointed at him. "That kind of thinking gives credit where it's not due and removes blame when we fail. A man accounts for his actions. If I say I'm going to stay here, then that's what I'm going to do, universe or no universe."

Stacy turned his head around. "What the hell are ya'll yammering about?"

Before anyone could philosophize further, Kate summoned everyone to the table. A bustle of activity ensued as the women wrangled the children to the kid's table. As the adults stood around the big table, Cole asked the blessing. Melvin gazed at the pure Norman Rockwell spread, everything you could imagine on Thanksgiving Day. Cole carved the plump turkey, turning his head to the side so that ashes from his cigarette fell clear of the bird. Everyone took their seat except Norma, who hovered over the children.

Melvin closed his mouth around a fork full of Sally's casserole. His eyes rolled in pleasure as it melted in his mouth. Every other dish was just as good, and it was clear where her cooking talent originated and why Cole and Stacy had potbellies.

Not long into dinner, Kate noticed Sally reaching for more mashed potatoes, and the evening's entertainment officially commenced. "Are you enjoying those, dear?"

"Yes, they're delicious."

"Well, go easy on them. You're not as fit as you used to be. If a girl doesn't watch her figure, no one else will either."

Melvin cut his eyes to gauge Sally's expression as she put the bowl back down with authority. He could almost hear the profanities in her head as she reached for salad instead. She turned to Melvin and asked, "Do you think I'm fat?"

"Whoa, whoa, whoa!" Cole said, his hands shooting up as if telling him not to steal third. "Now, Melvin, I know you two aren't hitched yet, but I'm gonna tell you my rule for a happy marriage. No matter what she asks, and I mean no matter what, your *only* acceptable responses are one of the following:

Yes, dear, you're right.

Yes, dear, I'll get right on it.

No, that dress doesn't make you look fat.

Or number four: You're right, honey, she *is* a bitch."

"Daddy, you're horrible," Sally snarled. "Don't go teaching him bad habits. I don't know why Momma puts up with you."

Cole looked lovingly at Kate and replied, "Because, number one: we're a team. She was there when I needed her most. Nothing could ever tear us apart." He took Kate's hand and smiled. "And number two: the turkey's not the only thing getting stuffed tonight."

"Cole!" Kate slapped his arm. "Not in front of the children."

"What? They're old enough. Hell, one of them has four kids of his own. I'd say he's figured it out."

"The *grandchildren*," she pleaded. "Now, you kids don't pay any attention to what Grandpa's saying."

Three of the boys kept their heads down and continued to eat. Ted looked at his grandmother and grinned. "Gobble, gobble, gobble." Quick as lightning, Norma covered his mouth, her cheeks beet red.

Stacy leaned back in his chair and cracked open another beer. Noticing Sally's disapproval, he defiantly turned to Melvin. "You want one? They drink in Canada, don't they?" Sally's left eye twitched as she stared at Stacy, her ears turning red.

With no dog in the hunt, Melvin grinned. "Yes, we do, and yes, I would." Sally's dirty look then shot his way along with a swift kick under the table.

Kate laughed nervously. "Normally, I'd ask how you two became a couple, but Sally's told us all about it."

"She has?" Melvin's shins got kicked again. This time Ted saw it, laughed, and kicked Tom under the kid's table. Tom retaliated with a handful of mashed potatoes into Ted's face. The next thing Tom knew, Norma was dragging him into the bedroom. The other boys could hear his wails over the whipping. Ted licked potatoes from his face and giggled.

"Why yes," Kate continued, ignoring the surrounding theatrics. "She told us how alone and friendless you were moving to America, so she invited you to church. You started attending together regularly, and sparks just flew."

"Wow, sparks just flew?" Melvin repeated with a smile. "Who could argue with a story like that?"

"You see, Stacy," Kate said proudly, "good things happen when you go to church. Maybe you should think about that."

Stacy belched. "You want me to be just like my dip-shit little sister?"

Cole's hand shot up as if he were about to strike him. "Watch your damn language, boy! There'll be no profanity under my roof. And don't talk to your mother that way."

Stacy's head hung as if he were ten. "Sorry, Momma."

In the awkward silence that followed, Melvin inquired, "How about you guys, Kate? How did you meet?"

"Oh, it's such a great story," Sally cooed. "Daddy was on leave during the war and met Momma at a USO dance. They looked into each other's eyes, and that was it. Right, Momma? I just love that story."

"Uh, huh," Kate replied, shifting away her gaze. "That's the story."

"So, it was love at first sight?" Melvin asked.

Kate raised an eyebrow. "Well—Sally, honey, you've dripped gravy on your dress. You should know, Melvin, she's decorated her clothes with food her whole life. She absolutely can't wear white."

"Is that the reason?" Melvin asked.

Sally kicked him hard under the table. "What other reason could there be?"

"I can think of a couple," Stacy replied with a grin.

Sally pointed at her brother. "Shut up and drink your beer."

"Now you *want* me to drink? Make up your mind, girl."

Cole slammed his palm on the table. "I respect you, Melvin. Not many men are willing to consider Sally on account of her age and what she is."

Sally's cheeks burned red. "Daddy, please stop."

Melvin glanced at her, then back to Cole. "What do you mean?"

Sally quickly interjected, "He means a young Democrat, right, Daddy? It's okay because Melvin's one, too, aren't you?" She gritted her teeth. "Melvin, I said, *aren't* you?"

"Aren't I what?"

Sally smiled nervously. "A Democrat, silly."

Melvin took a sip of his beer. "Oh, you'd best believe it. I'm a, you know, Canadian Democrat. Yup. Hardcore."

"Your father's right, dear," Kate said. "Like it or not, you're no spring chicken. I'd like a granddaughter to spoil someday."

Norma's voice arose from the kids' table, "Don't look at me. After having these little monsters, my downstairs looks like a moon rocket blew up." Ted giggled and made explosion noises.

Kate moved her finger side to side like the pendulum of a biological clock. "It's all up to you, then, dear. Tick-tock."

Sally hid her face in her hands as Cole continued. "Melvin knows what I mean. There's no reason for Sally to be ashamed. Momma, what did you call it? A lifestyle choice?"

Melvin's ears perked up. *This is still 1950, right?*

"Sally's a,"—Cole snapped his fingers, looking for the word—"a *T-totaler.*"

"T-totaler?" asked Melvin.

"You know," Stacy added, "she don't drink, smoke, cuss, or nothing. Basically, she's the dullest damn person on the planet. That don't stop her from judging *you*, though. Because it's wrong to have fun and live your life the way you want."

Melvin's mouth fell open. *Have they ever met their daughter?*

Kate sat a little more upright. "Well, Melvin doesn't think she's dull. Or else he wouldn't be here. Right, Melvin?"

He nodded. "Dull is a word I would *never* use to describe your daughter. As for being a T-totaler, well, I just accept her for who she really is."

Sally exhaled as Cole and Kate smiled at his answer. Stacy folded his arms. "Whatever."

As Melvin accepted another beer from Cole, he noticed Sally staring at the can like a lion eyeing a wounded gazelle. He'd also noticed her smack her lips with each cigarette her mother lit. He grinned on the inside. *She can't keep this up. Sooner or later, she'll explode into profanity and make a grab for those cigarettes. Any minute now.*

Sally raised an eyebrow at Stacy. "Maybe you *should* be a little more like your sister. If you didn't drink so much, maybe you could hold down a job for more than a week."

Several beers in by this point, Stacy snorted, "I got a job."

She leaned toward him. "Doing what? Sitting on your tail? Who'd be dumb enough to hire you?"

"I would," said Cole.

Her eyes widened. "Oh, Daddy, why? You know he can't sell cars. Most days, he can't figure out how to shower. He's lucky just to show up. And anything he makes just goes to booze. That's why you and Momma have to keep giving them money."

Norma looked down and said nothing.

"You let me worry about my business, young lady."

"I can sell cars," Stacy said as he fought to stay awake. "I'm not stupid, you know."

"Could've fooled me."

"You're stupid."

"Am not."

"Are too."

The children listened intently from the kids' table. Soon, a biscuit flew from one boy at another. In retaliation, Hershel punched Jim Bill in the arm, who, in turn, hit Tom, who hit Ted, who then cried. Norma, who had yet to eat anything, dragged Tom back to the bedroom for another whipping. The instant she had him around the corner, Ted's tears evaporated, and all three boys giggled at the wails.

Norma returned and shoved Tom into his seat. "I'm exhausted! You kids are going to drive me to the nut house. Any minute now, a white van's gonna pull up, and men are gonna drag me away to a padded room." Hershel kept his head down and continued eating while Jim Bill and Tom went to the window to look for the van. Ted giggled and chanted, "Nut house, nut house, nut house."

Norma turned to Sally with a solemn face. "Take a hard look, sister."

Kate laughed nervously. "You know she's just teasing, honey." She put a hand on Melvin's arm. "And I want *you* to know, Sally and Stacy don't usually behave this way. Sometimes they think they're five and seven again, not 30 and 32."

Melvin turned to Sally and silently mouthed, "Thirty?" She shrugged with a weak smile.

"When they were little," Kate said, "she'd follow Stacy around like a puppy. If he went hunting or fishing, she'd go, too—such a tomboy." Kate sighed. "We worried she wouldn't be ladylike enough to be married someday. She didn't show any interest in the boys until she started over at the college. That was the last time she brought a boy home until today."

Melvin's eyebrow raised. "Really? I feel honored."

"Don't be," Sally muttered.

"I know she's met others at her church over the years," Kate continued, "but she never brought them here."

"Well, Momma, can you blame me?"

In a motherly tone, Kate replied, "It would have been nice to meet the people you were spending time with." Then she turned to Melvin, "After a while, she wouldn't even tell us their names. Who knows which astronaut or senator it was."

"He was a *state* senator."

"Maybe we were a little hard on the last boy she brought home. After all, he did have a neurological condition. What was that boy's name? Was it Wesley or Walker?"

"No, it was Joey," Cole said.

"Joey?" Kate asked. "Joey was that little boy down the street who followed Sally around. Remember? She whacked him on the forehead with a 2x4, and then his mother dragged her down the street by her ear to tell me. How could you forget that?"

Melvin gave Sally a look of horror. She shrugged. "We were playing bugs. He had one on his forehead. What was I supposed to do?"

Melvin's eyes remained wide. "Not hit him with a 2x4?"

She smiled. "I killed the bug."

"That's right!" Stacy exclaimed, waking up. "I remember that day. Momma, you cussed that lady up one side and down the other."

"I did no such thing."

"Yes, you did. You used all kinds of words I'd never heard before. And you told her if she ever grabbed your child again, you'd kick her ass up and down the street and let her dumbass kid watch."

Kate's cheeks turned a brilliant red. "That is *not* what I said."

Stacy folded his arms. "Then why did she call the police on you?"

Kate folded her arms. "We may have exchanged a few unpleasantries, but everything else was a misunderstanding. Now, enough about—"

"Yeah, I remember that now," Cole interrupted. "They up and moved to Lake Charles right after that."

"Well, I'm sure that was purely coincidental," Kate replied. Then she muttered, "Didn't bother anybody when that old hag moved."

Sally smiled. "What was that, Momma?"

"I was asking, whatever happened to Walker? Did he ever get over his condition?"

Sally rolled her eyes. "His name was Wiles, not Walker. And he didn't have a neurologic condition."

"Are you sure it wasn't Walker?" Kate asked.

"I dated him, Momma. I should know."

"She's right, Momma," Stacy snickered. "His name *was* Wiles, remember? He had that girl's name."

"Really?" Melvin asked. "A girl's name—*Stacy?*"

"Yeah," Stacy replied with a bewildered look. "A girl's name—*Melvin.* And he had some kind of twitch."

"No," Cole corrected. "It wasn't a twitch. It was more like a tic. Like this." Cole forcefully blinked one eye. "Isn't that what they call it, Melvin?"

The anger in Sally's voice climbed in step with her volume. "He didn't have a neurological condition, and he didn't have a tic. You all just badgered him to death with your endless questions and threats, showing him all your guns. And you, Daddy, telling him you could shoot the balls off a squirrel at a hundred yards if he was ever inappropriate. When's a squirrel *ever* inappropriate? And ya'll making fun of his name. It was cruel and uncalled for. He never twitched once until he met all of you. And ya'll wonder why it's taken me ten years to find a man willing to come over here! And I'll tell you something else,"—Sally drove her finger down into the table—"The *only* reason Melvin agreed to come was because I didn't tell him diddly *squat* about any of you!"

A palpable silence fell over the room, even at the kids' table. Kate said softly, "Well, whatever his name was, all *I* know is that poor boy with the neurologic condition never came around here again."

Cole and Stacy turned red, fighting to hold it in until tears rolled down their cheeks. When beer and laughter spewed out, Sally threw down her napkin and stormed off down the hall. Family pictures in the hallway rattled with the slamming of the bathroom door.

Cole stood and wiped his eyes. "She's gonna be in there for a while. Hope nobody has to pee. Come on, Melvin. I want to show you something." They went down the hall and into a bedroom. "This was the kid's room when they were little. Now it's Kate's sewing room and where I keep these." He opened a gun cabinet. "Ever hold an 1873 Winchester?"

Melvin's eyes lit up. "You mean the one Jimmy Stewart had in Winchester '73? I loved that movie."

As Melvin gently examined the pristine weapon, Cole smiled. "You look like a fellow who's held a gun before." He winked. "Now it has your prints on it. That could be handy."

Melvin chuckled and passed it back. *What the hell did that mean?*

"Yeah, she's a beauty," Cole said, checking the lever action. "Something every fella would like to get his hands on, but not every man would know how to handle. Yup, no matter how old she gets, you still see her as your pride and joy. You just don't know how far you'd go if you ever saw her mistreated. Know what I mean?"

Melvin nodded, knowing exactly what he meant.

"She's quite a gun," Cole continued. "My great-grandad took her off a dead Indian in 1874. It's been handed down ever since. I'll give it to my grandsons one day." He looked Melvin in the eye. "Family is everything. It's worth sticking around for. A real man sees it as the most important thing there is. A fella like that would be willing to stop anything or anybody that tried to tear it apart."

Melvin held up a hand. "You should know I have a past. Did Sally tell you I was married?"

"She did. Said your ex-wife's in prison. Told us not to mention it."

"It wasn't a planned separation. You could say it was forced upon us. Now that I'm here, I don't have plans to rush into anything. I want to be upfront about that."

"I can respect that." He handed Melvin a pearl-handled derringer. "Life is a chess game. A smart man looks at the whole board. Never know when you might have to move backward to get to where you need to be."

Melvin pointed the pistol around the room.

Cole nodded. "And sometimes, even when you're being real careful, some little thing winds up getting you in the end. Take that pistol, for example. Do you know what makes it so dangerous?"

Melvin stopped playing and inspected it a little closer. His eyes widened. "It's loaded?"

Cole smiled. "What's dangerous is what you don't see. There's no safety, and it's got a hair-trigger. Life can be like that, too."

No longer listening to Cole's life-daughter-gun philosophy, Melvin used two fingers to hand the gun back before accidentally shooting himself.

Despite the cleaning rags in the gun cabinet, Melvin noted Cole didn't wipe the prints off either weapon as he put them away. Cole patted him on the back. "The pie ought to be out by now. Want to hear how I can shoot the balls off a squirrel at two hundred yards?"

"So, now it's *two* hundred yards?"

"I bought a scope."

As Melvin and Cole entered the kitchen, Stacy exclaimed, "Look at that! He ain't twitchy. Boy, you might just make the cut after all." Stacy tossed him a can of beer. In a smooth, one-handed motion, Melvin caught it mid-air, pulled the tab, and started drinking. It might have been the most athletic move he'd ever made. As Stacy raised an impressed eyebrow, Melvin knew his street credit had just gone up.

Seated once more at the table, Melvin took a bite of pumpkin pie so moist and smooth it dissolved in his mouth. A second helping later, he looked up to see Sally had emerged from the bathroom and was signaling it was time to go. Kate quickly wrapped leftovers for them while Melvin shook hands and thanked everyone. Cole walked him out while Sally stayed behind to hug her mother and Norma. As Melvin stepped out of the living room into the freezing night air, he heard Stacy tell his sister, "He'll do. Don't screw it up."

As Cole and Melvin stood on the front porch rubbing their hands for warmth, Melvin examined the dinner bell hanging on the wooden column. "That's cool." He leaned closer to read the engraving. "To Sally, with love on her 35th. I'll always take care of you." He squinted. "I can't make out the name below it."

Cole blew into his hands and shuffled his feet. "That's been in our family for generations. It hung on the original cabin that sat on this spot before it burned. That bell's all that's left."

"Sally's a family name, then?"

"Yup, her great-great-grandmother. Her husband was Leonard, but his name faded off years ago. When I was a kid, Momma rang that bell for dinner, and we'd all come running. Twenty years ago, where all these houses are now, that was nothing but our farm. Hey, what kind of car do you drive?"

"I don't have a car. I walk or take the bus."

"Take the bus?" Cole spit off the porch. "Every man, even a Canadian, deserves a set of wheels. Come on down and see me at the lot. I'll take care of you."

"Thanks, Cole. That's generous."

"We're just happy you're around. We worry about Sally in that city. Since she's been talking about you this summer, I can't remember seeing her happier. You're a good man, Melvin. Drive safe."

"Thanks, but I won't be driving. You're daughter's pretty particular about her car."

Cole's eyes narrowed as Sally emerged onto the porch. "Sally, you let him drive home."

"No, Daddy. After all the beer you guys poured down him, I don't want him falling asleep."

"Those beers were nothing, sweetheart. Look at him. He's fine."

Melvin shook his head. "There's no arguing with her, Cole."

"Well," he smiled, "at least you figured that out early. Come back and see us." He shook Melvin's hand again and hugged his daughter. Everyone waved goodbye as Sally's convertible made a grinding noise, followed by a small backfire before backing out onto Davis Street.

Barely a block down the road, Sally lit her first cigarette. She took a long, satisfying drag as the car's heater kicked in. Blindly, she reached between Melvin's knees, popped open the glove box, and pulled out a bottle of gin. Wedging it between her thighs, she unscrewed the cap as she sped down narrow Conway streets on the dark and cold Thanksgiving night. With a cigarette in one hand and a bottle in the other, she unfurled a string of profanities as she shifted gears.

"That lazy, damn, son-of-a-bitch, dumbass, drunken, good-for-nothing, shit-for-brains is working at the car lot? How stupid can Daddy be? He blows every dime on alcohol and cigarettes. Does it matter they have four kids and can't afford groceries? Momma and Daddy pay for *everything*. And poor Norma has to work part-time down at the bank just to make ends meet. His *wife* has to work. Can you imagine? It's so embarrassing! How can someone drink and smoke their life away?" Melvin watched her light her second cigarette off her first as stop signs became mere octagonal suggestions.

"Maybe you should hand me that bottle. It's dark out, and you're upset." He wrestled the gin from her hand.

Sally frowned. "Don't be ridiculous. I'm perfectly fine." She fished under her seat and came up with a bottle of rum, pulling the cork with her teeth. As she smoked, swigged, and swerved to miss mailboxes, Melvin glanced around, wondering how much more liquor could possibly be hidden in the tiny convertible.

He pried away the rum. "Stacy aside, you kind of drink and smoke a lot, too."

Sally's eyes and mouth opened wide as her head turned on a swivel, her cannon of fury receiving new coordinates. "How can you say such a thing? Who are you to judge *me*? And how the hell can you take his side? Besides, it's completely different! I drink *socially*. You and me sitting in this car? That's social. And I only smoke when I'm nervous." She gave him the stink eye as she lit her fourth cigarette off her third. "See? Right now, you're making me nervous. Besides, we're not talking about me. We're talking about my dumbass, shit-head brother. He's the drunk. He's the one who shows up shit-faced at work. If you want to judge somebody, he's your guy. Sure, I may show up sleepy, but who doesn't? Have you ever seen me miss a day? Have you? I've never missed a day of work in my life—as far as you know. He's missed plenty."

Melvin shrugged. "In all fairness, you just have to throw on a shirt and walk down a flight of stairs." Even as the words were coming out, Melvin knew he'd screwed up. Sally slammed on the brakes, coming to a complete stop in the middle of highway 365.

"I fix *my hair*, Melvin! Do you know how much damn work that is? All this doesn't just happen. You don't know because you're a man. Admit it. You don't know what the hell you're talking about!" She threw the car into gear just as a honking car zipped past, nearly taking her side mirror. "Shit!" she screamed. Sally pulled off the road and put her head on the steering wheel. Melvin caressed her shoulder and apologized until she agreed to let him drive.

He rubbed his arms and shivered as he ran around the car and slid behind the wheel. As he looked down, his head cocked to one side. There were three pedals instead of two. "Uh, Sally, is this an automatic transmission?"

She wiped her eyes as she settled into the passenger seat. "You mean one of those hydra-matics? No, nothing fancy like that, just a regular old on-the-column five-speed."

Awesome. Standard transmission . . . standard transmission. I think you push down on that one and pull the handle thingy? The car lurched and died.

Sally wiped her eyes once more and smiled. "Are you trying to impress me by popping it into third? Stop fooling around and take us home." Melvin nodded. The car jerked forward again and died.

Sally shook her head and took a drag. "You're doing it all wrong. Give it gas smoothly as you let it out." Melvin tried again—then again. Each time she laughed a little louder as she chugged gin. "Shit, do you even know how to drive?"

"Stop laughing. It's just been a while. Why won't this pedal work?"

"It's called a clutch, and it gets stuck. Just work with it." A sly grin spread across her face. "Daddy says those automated transmissions were invented in Canada. Guess now we know why."

"Shut up. You're not helping."

"Come on. It's like riding a bike."

"Something else I've never done," Melvin muttered.

"You've never ridden a bicycle? Every kid's been on a bike."

"Not me."

She gave a sad face. "Your parents never bought you a bike?"

"Oh, they did. I just refused to get on it."

"Aw, poor baby." She caressed his arm. "Were you scared? Did you fall and skin your knee?"

"Nope. I literally never got on. Just didn't want to."

"How did you get around as a kid?"

He shrugged. "Didn't. I just stayed at home."

"Were you sickly?"

"No."

"Then what did you do all day when you weren't in school?"

He fiddled with the gear shift. "Sat on the couch and played video games."

"What's a video game?"

"It's sort of like a board game—very Canadian."

"Huh. You know, you should stop talking because it makes you seem odd." She winked and took another swig. "It's a damn good thing you're cute."

The car jerked again and died, prompting Melvin's own string of obscenities. Sally covered her mouth to stop laughing, but it only made her laugh harder. Soon, tears were streaming down her cheeks until—

"B-U-R-R-R-P!" Her eyes widened as she covered her mouth with both hands. "I am so sorry, Melvin. That was so un-ladylike. I'm completely embarrassed, yet"—she smacked her lips—"I'm tasting something. What is that?"

Melvin threw up his hands. "I'm *trying* to get this piece of shit moving. I'm not playing, What did the girl next to me just belch up?"

"Huh. I'm going with mashed potatoes. What do you think?" She leaned over and blew in his face.

He turned his head. "You may be the one who's drunk, but I'm the one who's about to vomit."

"Yup, mashed potatoes." She smacked her lips in satisfaction. "Guess I got that second helping after all."

"And it's a good thing *I'm* cute?"

She leaned over and put her head on his arm. "Know what I'm going to do? I'm going to teach you how to ride a bike."

"Uh, no."

"I am. I could teach you a thing or two, Melvin Napier. If you'd just let me."

With a loud grinding noise, Melvin got the car into gear and on the road. Sally swapped the empty gin bottle for rum. When the rum was gone, she pulled down the passenger-side visor and slid out a flask of scotch. Melvin slipped off his coat, but she was gone before he could tuck it around her. He reached over and pulled the dangling cigarette from her mouth. As sleet fell, he quietly drove them home in fourth gear, praying he didn't have to shift and wondering how the hell to stop once they got there.

118

Chapter 12
Six-month Review

Eleven days later, all incoming reports indicated Melvin had been a success at the Davis house, and Sally was walking on air. He was excited, too, having had an epiphany over Thanksgiving that would surely get him home. Seeing Cole's potbelly had triggered an idea, radius of curvature, something he'd once learned in optics class but had forgotten—until now.

After surviving the horrors of a standard transmission, he'd tucked Sally into bed that night and returned to his loft to find his map. Spreading it out on the kitchen table, he'd used the map's scale to measure his shoestring the length of 45 miles and tied it to two pencils. Placing one on Jonesboro, he'd drawn a semicircle west of the city. Melvin had rubbed the goosebumps on his arms as he stared at it. This was it. Ted from Texas, bless his drunken departed soul, had said they were 42 miles from landing just past the storm. Their position must have been somewhere along the curved line on this map. If the storm was waiting for him, all he had to do was fly that line. With his last paycheck in hand, Melvin had just enough. Now, nothing else mattered.

Melvin emerged from his exam lane on this December 4th Monday morning and escorted his patient to Sally's desk. "Let me know how the new glasses work, Ms. Randel. You might not notice much difference as the prescription barely changed. Frankly, you see pretty well without glasses. I'm sorry I can't make it to brunch with you on Saturday, but I appreciate the offer. Thank you again for the pound cake. It looks delicious."

He slid the cake behind his back as they turned the corner. As a rule, Sally refused to schedule follow up when baked goods were involved. But instead of her suspicious eye, Melvin found a short man in a plain black suit with a plain black tie over his white collared shirt standing in front of Sally's desk, tapping his foot with an impatient look. Melvin glanced over the man's shoulder and met Sally's eyes. She shrugged and looked on with interest.

"Dr. Napier, I presume?"

"Yes, may I help you?"

"That would certainly be in your best interest."

"One moment, please. Sally, could you schedule a one-year for Ms. Randel?"

"Yes, sir, Dr. Napier. Step right over here, Josephine. Pound cake, huh? Such a classic."

The man opened his wallet and flashed his credentials. "William J. Smith, agent of the Medical Licensing Committee."

Melvin felt the room spinning. *The MLC? Why did they send someone? Do they know? Oh, shit. They had agents in the 50s? Wait, I'll be out of here this weekend.* He exhaled. *Screw this pencil pusher.* Melvin smiled as Sally said, "I'm sorry, Josephine. We're all booked up for next year. You might try the eye doctor over in Memphis. He's married, a little hairy, and has a hump, but I hear he's the best. Want his number? By the way, I love your outfit. I bet you could make all kinds of money if you wore it at night."

"Dr. Napier?" the agent asked, his voice rising in irritation.

"Oh, yes, sorry. My office is right this way. You say your name is Will Smith? That's cool."

"Hardly. I'm on the premises today to inquire about your delinquency in producing letters supportive of your education and credentials to practice medicine in our state."

"Thank you for saying that in earshot of my patients. Perhaps we could wait until we reach my office? Say, would you like some pound cake? It has a lemon glaze."

The agent held up his hand. "I am obligated to inform you that any attempt to fraternize with an agent in the form of flattery, gifts, or the offer of favors will be duly noted in the report and will generate charges of bribery and obstruction of a state official in the discharge of his duty."

Melvin opened his office door. "So, that's a no, then?"

Agent Smith took a seat. "Failure to produce supportive documentation of your education and credentials to practice medicine will result in a criminal investigation and charges of practicing medicine without a proper license, a felony charge that carries stiff fines and jail time." He produced a manila folder from his briefcase. "My records indicate your six-month temporary medical permit will expire as of today."

Melvin chuckled as he plopped into his desk chair. "Seriously? You're giving me my first notification of this *today*?"

Agent Smith's expression didn't change. "By ordinance, the onus of keeping up with the expiration date of a temporary medical permit falls to the practitioner. Thus, prior notification is not an entitlement, and I am not required to contact said practitioner until which time delinquency occurs. My sole purpose today is to investigate and report to the Committee on the circumstances surrounding your delinquency. After reviewing my report and recommendation, the Committee will decide upon conversion to permanent licensure or outright rejection and filing of criminal charges. I will tell you that the Committee has followed my recommendation in every case I've investigated."

"Every case? Well, aren't you impressive?" Melvin winked. "How long have you been an investigator for the MLC?"

The agent again held up a hand. "May I remind you that any attempt to fraternize with an agent in the form of flattery, gifts, or the offer of favors will be duly noted in the report and will generate charges of bribery and obstruction of a state official in the performance of his duty."

"Yeah, I caught that the first time. Say, Agent Smith, do you always talk like a VCR instruction manual? How about when you're on a date? Do you say, You are entitled to order one entrée off the left side of the menu only, but I'm obligated to inform you that under title 36, subsection c, the selection of lobster will result in certain obligations to be named later this evening?"

Agent Smith's nose tilted up a few degrees. "Sir, I don't pretend to know enough medical parlance to know what a VCR instruction manual is, nor do I understand your reference to lobster. I *can* tell you I'm allergic to shellfish, and therefore your comments have no significance to me whatsoever. What *is* significant is your flippant tone, and for that, I thank you. You are making my job easier."

"You're quite welcome. That *is* why I came to work this morning. And, for the record—" Melvin pointed at Agent Smith's breast pocket. "Are you writing this down?" Agent Smith pulled out a small notepad and licked his pencil. Melvin continued, "I recant my prior statement that you are impressive."

Agent Smith's eyes narrowed. "In that, Dr. Napier, we share a common opinion."

Melvin put his hands behind his head and tilted back in his chair. "So, you agree that you're unimpressive?"

"No, that is not what I—you know, Dr. Napier, I've been doing this a long time. I've never met an alleged practitioner with such disrespect for a representative of the MLC. Not that it matters. As a rule of thumb, practitioners trained outside the United States are woefully inadequate. I've never found one worthy of recommending permanent licensure. In fact, I've advised the Committee to cease issuing temporary permits. How you managed to finagle one is a mystery I look forward to solving."

"So, you're saying your statement regarding the Committee following every one of your recommendations is false?"

"I say nothing of the sort. I don't make false statements. Speaking of which, Dr. Napier, if you legitimately hold that title, where are your letters of support?"

Melvin yawned and stood up. "Not that I don't enjoy a good back and forth with a government agent dressed in black, but as you can see, I have several patients waiting on me. Perhaps we could have this discussion over the lunch hour?"

"By my watch, you no longer have the legal authority to see patients. You may produce your letters of support, or you may leave the premises, but what you may not do, Dr. Napier, is continue seeing patients today without my authorization."

Melvin shot him a look of concern. "So, you're saying they *haven't* sent letters to your office yet?"

Agent Smith tapped his foot. "Do I look like a man who enjoys wasting time?"

"Well, Agent Smith—by the way, may I call you J?"

"You may not."

"Frankly, J, I'm as surprised as you are. I will call and inquire forthwith."

Agent Smith revealed a partial grin. "No need, Dr. Napier. *I* will call."

"You want to call Canada?"

"That's how we handle things at the MLC." He stuck his hand out. "Give me the number."

"Well, I don't have it on me."

"I can look it up," he announced, pulling out his notepad again. "Tell me the institution's name."

"No, I have it. It's just filed away in my office. Should I phone you when I find it?"

A thin grin spread across the man's face. "I'll wait."

Sally stepped inside the door. "Excuse me, Dr. Napier. I have that number."

Melvin raised an eyebrow as he and Agent Smith stood up. "You do?"

"Yes, sir," she answered in a high-pitched, innocent voice. She brushed back her hair, smiled at the agent, and stood in a beauty pageant pose. "You gave it to me when you arrived. I know you've been so busy helping the proud citizens of our state that you must have forgotten. You asked me to call and make sure they didn't delay sending the paperwork to the MLC. But I can be so dizzy sometimes!" She touched the agent's arm. "I get so overwhelmed in my job here that I must've forgotten to do it. If I didn't have my head screwed on, I'm sure it would come right off. Most mornings, I'm lucky if I remember to button up my blouse. Can you imagine what that would look like?" She subtly thrust her shoulders back. "Agent Smith, I'm afraid this misunderstanding is all *my* fault. I'm very sorry, sir. You traveled all the way down here just because of *me*." She lowered her head and looked up at him with puppy dog eyes.

Agent Smith blushed. "It wasn't all that far. Everyone makes mistakes, dear."

"Sally," Melvin scolded as he shook a finger, "don't ever let this happen again. You're dismissed. Well, Agent Smith, shall we make that call? I have patients waiting."

"Certainly, Dr. Napier. The sooner we resolve this, the sooner I can go about my business. You don't have anything to hide, do you?"

"Other than the fact I'm a fully licensed Arkansas ophthalmologist from the future who's traveled back in time to pose as a Canadian ophthalmologist seeking full licensure in a foreign country—no, sir."

"A sense of humor is not part of my job description, Dr. Napier."

"I know it's not, J."

Sally disappeared as Melvin began dialing the number she had provided. The agent put his finger on the receiver and cut the line. "I'll make that call if you don't mind."

Melvin shrugged. "I'm impressed."

"Well, this is hardly my first day on the job. I'm wise to all the tricks you people play. Our motto is, Trust no one."

Melvin folded his arms. "That's a terrible motto. You don't even trust each other at work?"

"Well, of course, we do. That is not what I—"

"What *I* meant, Agent Smith, is that you're calling the French section of Canada. I just haven't run into many Arkansans who speak our language. I'm impressed."

"They don't speak English there?"

"Not at my institution. English is a second language in Canada. Many don't speak it at all."

The agent grimaced and handed him back the phone. "Well, I speak American, and that's the only language I need to know. Make the call."

Melvin nodded and dialed several random numbers. "Bonjour. Yo soy Dr. Melvin Napier. Ah, Mademoiselle Croissant, cumma sum laude? No, no, no. No esta Chanel number five. Es necessito para *medical degree*. Sí, soufflé." Melvin looked at the agent and nodded as he continued. "Excusez-moi, *medical license* en Arkansas. Rapido, oui, maura mi? Oh? Lo siento, no me gusto. Muy bueno. Au revoir."

"Well?"

"She apologizes. They had a fire a few months ago, which caused the delay. She remembers me and will have the papers drawn up and signed. Said it should be here soon. Of course, in the French culture, soon doesn't always mean the same as it does here."

"Is that so? Correct me if I'm wrong, but some of your French sounded like Spanish."

"Oh? Do you speak Spanish?"

"I've heard enough in the cowboy movies to recognize it."

"Well, I'm impressed you picked up on that. It's part of our local dialect. Did you know Canada was originally a Spanish settlement?"

"I did not."

"Well, it was. And when the French arrived, they lived in harmony as the French and Spaniards have done for centuries."

"I'm not here for a history lesson, Dr. Napier, and I know when I'm being had. I am not—"

Smith stopped in mid-sentence as Sally appeared in the doorway with three buttons of her tight blouse undone. "Excuse me, Dr. Napier, but your patients are asking about you." She fanned herself and tugged on her shirt. "My, but the boiler has the office toasty today. Mr. Smith, would you mind terribly if he returns to work? I'm afraid I'll get fired if he doesn't. And then I'll be out on the street with nothing but the clothes on my back."

"Well, we can't have that," Smith replied, wiping his forehead with his handkerchief. "I suppose I don't have any direct proof that everything's not in order here. Just know that I'm watching you, Dr. Napier. And those letters had better arrive soon—*American* soon. You'd better give me your number, miss. I may need to bring you in for questioning."

Sally flashed him a smile. "Oh, of course, sir. It would be my civic pleasure."

Chapter 13
Three Boxes of Weather Equipment
December 16th, 1950

At 11:25 A.M., Melvin shivered in his seat, attempting to shake off the cold while waiting at Adam's Field for his noon flight. He'd wanted it sooner, but options were limited. *At least I'll make it home for Christmas,* he thought.

He smiled as he'd done it right this time, subtly saying goodbye to everyone, including the woman who'd recently committed a class C misdemeanor by lying to a government official to save his job. He'd given Sally a long hug knowing she'd get the wrong idea—which she did. But no matter, he was going back to where he belonged. He'd left a note on his office desk about a family emergency and instructions to donate what little he owned to charity. It wasn't a complete lie.

His thoughts drifted to Ted from Texas. *I'd already be home if he hadn't chickened out at the last minute. Who knows how many more times that storm will appear? Today may be my last chance.* Melvin needed a pilot willing to fly into bad weather, and now he had one.

Captain Mort Hardwicke had the reputation of a consummate professional. Former Army Air Corp with combat experience, his no-nonsense demeanor exuded someone who got the job done. In complete non-Ted from Texas fashion, he arrived well-groomed, on time, and with no hint of alcohol. He introduced himself to Melvin in a matter-of-fact manner.

Melvin claimed to be an experimental meteorologist with the National Weather Service named Tom Bonner, the name of his mother's favorite weatherman from the future. Melvin spread out his map on a nearby table. "There's a high probability of a unique storm developing along the curve I've indicated here. Our mission today is to locate and fly into the storm so I can take measurements."

Hardwicke looked him over sternly. "Is that so? And your name is Tom Bonner?"

Melvin nodded. "*Doctor* Tom Bonner, actually. You know, grad school and all."

"And you expect a storm today. What kind?"

"A class double A cumulus stratosphere mesmerizer."

Hardwicke put his hands on his hips. "Well, Dr. Bonner, I've flown in every kind of weather. Perhaps you could explain to me, with all that graduate education, why I've never heard of such a thing?"

"Do you subscribe to the Weather Channel?"

"No. Is that a magazine or a radio station?"

"Scientific journal. All us meteorological types read it. Last month, they had a great article on class double A cumulus stratosphere mesmerizers. I'd be happy to lend you my copy. Few of these have ever been witnessed." Melvin pointed at him. "And none have ever been measured."

"Is that so? Well, I've never backed down from a mission. Let's discuss some ground rules." Captain Hardwicke explained what he was and was not willing to do, the dangers of flying into a storm, and the fact that if they got into any real danger, the captain was the captain. He assured Melvin that his prior military aviation experience should allow them to get far enough inside to take measurements safely if the storm was present. Hardwicke methodically took notes as he looked over Melvin's map and finalized their flight plan.

He pointed at Melvin's bag. "Is that your weather equipment? Looks small."

Melvin smiled. "I didn't pack the big equipment because I didn't feel the need to overcompensate."

Hardwicke stared at him, his square jaw not budging.

Melvin took a breath. "Alrighty, then. Shall we go?"

Hardwicke nodded and led the way with a brisk pace. Melvin slung his bag of Sugarfield Sugar Cookies over his shoulder and followed.

They boarded a six-seater, single-engine prop plane, and Melvin settled into a forward-facing passenger seat. He slipped a sugar cookie while watching Captain Hardwicke go through his preflight checklist, something Ted from Texas hadn't done. Soon the engine roared, and they were up and on their way with an on-time noon takeoff.

Hardwicke set course for the most southerly portion of the curve while Melvin sat back and devoured another cookie. *The stories I'll have to tell. No one will believe it. I should have brought newspapers or souvenirs or something. I didn't get anything for the kids, not even a My Dad traveled back to 1950, and all I got was this stupid T-shirt.* He dug around in his pockets and fished out some change. *Well, at least they can have these coins. Might be worth something in about an hour.*

He grabbed another sweet cookie from Heaven. *It's been eight months since I've seen Alexis. Eight months of fending off attractive women.* Melvin nodded. *I am one hell of a husband.* As if in answer to his modesty, the plane shook briefly, then dropped several feet before leveling off. He put a hand on his stomach. *It's way too early. Can't be anywhere near the curve yet.* He peered out the window—clear sky in every direction.

"Just some turbulence," Hardwicke called back. "Did it register on your equipment?"

"Let me check." Melvin looked at the boxes of cookies in his bag. "Yup, sure did." He grabbed another one. "Let me know if you anticipate any more." Melvin sat very still. *Hmm, no nausea. Cookies must be helping.* He ate three more of the Grable Cookie Alliance's finest.

The plane smoothly arrived at the curve's southern point, and Hardwicke gently banked to a northerly heading. Melvin scanned the horizon, munching hard in anticipation. *This is it. The storm has to be here.*

Hardwicke called back, "How's your equipment holding up back there?"

"Doing fine, as I expected. This is the best they make at GCA."

"GCA? Why do I know that name? No matter. Get it ready because here we go."

The sky darkened. Melvin bent down and clenched his fists for the inevitable shaking, a shaking that didn't come. The sun reappeared, revealing nothing but the horror of a delightfully clear blue sky.

"That was a heck of a dark cloud," Hardwicke said. "Thought maybe we'd found your storm, but not to be. By reckoning, we've arrived at your curve's completion. All in all, you couldn't have picked a nicer day to fly."

Couldn't have picked a nicer day? Melvin folded his arms. *Asshole.*

Captain Hardwicke glanced out the side windows. "We've got ten miles of visibility in every direction. Maybe your class double A cumulus stratosphere mesmerizer took off for the holidays. Can't say I'm surprised. We don't get thunderstorms this time of the year. What do you want to do now?"

Melvin cocked his head to one side. *He's right. Does this all hinge on temperature? When I went up with Ted, it was at least thirty degrees warmer. Damn.* Melvin cleared his throat. "My weather model must have been off. We'll try again in the Spring. Let's head home."

"Roger that. Tell me, Dr. Bonner, did you say you worked for the Weather Bureau?"

"National Weather Service," Melvin replied, wondering if it existed yet.

"Never heard of it."

"Uh, yeah, it used to be the Weather Bureau, but it's about to change names. You'll hear about it soon."

"Is that so? Where are you guys based?"

Melvin smiled. "Everywhere you find the weather, my friend. I work out of the Little Rock office."

"Interesting. You stay pretty busy with meteorological research?"

"You have no idea."

"Must make it pretty difficult to see your eye patients, then."

Melvin's cheeks reddened. "You know about that?"

"My kid sister's a patient of yours. Told me all about you. We might have met sooner, but you turned her down her invitation for brunch. Broke her heart. Cried for days."

Sweat formed on Melvin's brow as he gripped his bag tightly. He had no reply for the man who now held his life in his hands, the overprotective brother.

"Plus, I can spot a liar. Especially when he claims he's carrying weather equipment in a bag barely big enough to hold a box of cookies. Syd from the flight desk pointed you out. Said you've chartered several flights. Said you were using another name because you go womanizing in Jonesboro. I don't care what today's stunt was about or what your sick perversions are, Napier, but I'm going to see to it that you never get another flight out of Adams. One thing more. I know six ways to kill a man with my bare hands. If you ever speak to my sister again, I won't need the other five."

Choosing not to ask which one his sister was, Melvin leaned back. *Getting murdered over declining pancakes and mimosas? Ain't that about a bitch.* He shrugged. *Sally probably refused to schedule her follow-up anyway. Guess I'll try this again in a few months.* His eyes widened. *A few months? Why did I go and screw with Agent Smith? A guy like that lives for his job. He won't stop.* Melvin's thoughts turned to 1950s prison. His respiratory rate shot up, and his breathing shallowed. The plane's interior cabin started to dim, and a horrific pain arose in his stomach. He grabbed his belly and broke out in a full sweat. He put a hand to his forehead and then checked his pulse. *Tachycardic, diaphoretic, acute abdominal pain—it's a ruptured appendix. He'll never land in time to get me to the hospital. This is it.*

Hardwicke turned his head around. "What's going on back there? You look pale. What's that all over your mouth?"

Melvin wiped his mouth and saw fingers full of sugar crystals. He looked in his bag. Three empty boxes of weather equipment looked back.

1951

Chapter 14
Anniversary

It was April 30th, 1951, exactly one year since Melvin had arrived. After surviving his flight with Captain Hardwicke, he'd feigned illness to turn down Sally's invitations to Conway for Christmas and McKeen's for New Year's Eve. Instead, he'd spent the holidays barricaded in his loft, wallowing in self-pity. None of it had been his finest hour.

But since then, Melvin had redoubled his efforts to get home, saving for more flights and hiring a PI to track down Dr. Nelson in Florida. Unfortunately, Nelson could only recall the Good Samaritans had been a husband and wife on their way back from Memphis.

Getting home wasn't his only priority. The man in black was still out there, somewhere, filling out forms, reviewing regulations. He hadn't made contact yet, but every day was a day closer to that eventuality. Melvin's first thought was to discredit Agent Smith somehow or distract him by finding a bigger fish. But now, he'd settled on another, slightly less immoral plan, the subtle art of forgery.

But 1951 had no personal computers or printers, and forgery was no easy task. Plus, without the internet, Melvin didn't know the proper appearance of a fictitious Canadian medical school letter. But it would undoubtedly contain contact information, including a phone number. This time around, Agent Smith would have someone who spoke French call it. Melvin needed someone to answer that call in French, someone who wouldn't mind breaking the law. Where do you find someone like that?

Then he had it. All he had to do was take a trip to Québec. Surely a city that size had a medical school. He could woo or bribe a secretary into forging letters and answering the verification call. The letters

133

would look official because they'd be official—well, official-ish. The phone number would be legit, and the person on the other end would sound French, or at least not Arkansan.

He'd decided to talk with John after work about some time off. Today was his birthday, after all. What could be nicer than a trip home to see your folks? But the more Melvin had thought of it, the more he'd sweated the thought of trying to woo the school secretary. Single women down here lined up for an exotic, foreign doctor and potential husband, but he'd be nothing up there. The last woman he'd wooed was Alexis. For the life of him, he couldn't remember how he'd done it. Maybe she'd wooed him. He looked in his coffee can. *Here's hoping bribery works.*

As he headed downstairs to clinic, he paused. *Wait, how do I get a passport to Canada? I still don't have any real form of ID.*

By noon, he'd settled into his office for a Spam sandwich and a bag of Fritos. As he ate, he perused his mail and found a letter from the Medical Licensing Committee. Melvin swallowed hard. This was it. It had to be a summons or something worse. He took a deep breath. *This was going to happen sooner or later. I'm surprised Smith isn't delivering this in person—smug, tie-wearing bastard. What if I don't open it? What if it got lost in the mail? I need a lawyer.*

"Dear Dr. Napier,

It is with great pleasure that we are converting your temporary permit to permanent unrestricted licensure to practice medicine in the State of Arkansas. As such, you are bound by the laws and regulations thereof, and . . ."

"Holy shit!" Melvin shouted, slamming his sandwich on his desk and launching Fritos skyward. "How the hell?" He stared at the letter and took a bite of his mangled sandwich. Obviously, Mademoiselle Croissant hadn't sent anything to the Committee. And where was

Agent Smith in all this? Suddenly, Melvin's joyous expression soured. *Sally. Did she go out with him? What did she do? What did that little asshole make her do? She hasn't said a word.*

Sally bopped into his office without knocking and plopped down on his sofa. "Geez, what did that sandwich ever do to you?"

"Nothing, I was just—"

"Hey, it's April 30th. Isn't that your birthday?"

"How did you know? I haven't told anyone."

She smiled. "We have our ways."

"Speaking of which," he replied, "I just got a letter from the MLC. Full license, no questions asked. Know anything about that?"

In a high-pitched, innocent voice, she replied, "I'm just a little ole receptionist, Agent Napier. What would I know about such things?" A devious smile spread across her face as she slowly unfastened her blouse. "My, but the boiler has the office toasty today."

"Button your shirt back up and tell me what happened."

"Oh, you're no fun. Nothing happened, at least not what you think. But I like that you're jealous. It looks good on you."

"What happened?"

She leaned back on the couch. "Nothing, really. Daddy took Agent Smith hunting a little while back."

"What do you mean, hunting?"

"Daddy can be persuasive. When he takes someone hunting, they don't come back until they see eye to eye. It's no big deal."

"And if they don't see eye to eye?"

Sally shrugged. "They don't come back."

Melvin's eyes widened. "Did Agent Smith come back?"

She put a finger to her lips in thought. "You can get lost in those deep woods and never be seen again. Hunting is dangerous, you know."

"Your dad's not from Chicago, is he?"

"Don't be silly. He's as Arkansan as you can get. We do have family in Detroit, though. Well, not real family. That's just what we call them. They're more like my uncles."

"Family, but not related, and they're from Detroit?"

"Yeah, they're harmless. I've known them ever since I was little. They come down a couple of times a year to check on their businesses and go hunting with Daddy. Momma cooks a big dinner, and then they sit around and smoke cigars. They've been good to us. They help Daddy get the best inventory prices for the lot."

"What does your dad do for them in return?"

"Nothing much. He takes them around to visit."

"Visit who?"

She shrugged. "Local officials, business owners, you name it. The best part is, they want to meet you. You'll love them. They're always cracking jokes. Like the last time they were here, Uncle Jack said if you ever did me wrong, he'd fit you in concrete shoes. Isn't that hilarious?"

Melvin blinked twice. "When did you say they were coming?"

"They'll be down around duck season. They love their shotguns."

"And you're joking about Smith, right? He came back safely?"

She smiled. "Sometimes these things just have a way of working themselves out."

Melvin swallowed hard. "Please thank your father for speaking with him."

"Oh, it was nothing. Daddy likes you. We all do. Now, what should we do tonight to celebrate your birthday? Dinner and McKeen's?"

"No, thank you. I have work to do. Maybe another time."

"Another time won't be your birthday."

"I can't drink tonight anyway. I have surgery tomorrow."

"What's that got to do with anything?"

"Everything, if you're my patient. Let's celebrate this weekend."

Sally wrinkled her nose and left. He knew she wouldn't take no for an answer, not for long.

Chapter 15
Comfort Care

Sally knocked at Melvin's door early that Saturday morning. In tears, she collapsed into his arms. "My grandfather's dying."

"I'm so sorry. Is there anything I can do?"

She sobbed a little more, pulling a large handkerchief tucked inside her blouse, and vigorously blew an impressive amount of snot. "Would you drive me up there? I don't think I could go alone."

"Of course," Melvin replied, positioning himself so the handkerchief didn't touch him. "Where do they live?"

"Eureka Springs. It's only a little more than a couple of hours from here. Thank you so much. You'll want to pack a bag because it might be for the whole weekend. Is that okay?" She blew into the handkerchief once more, then looked up with sad eyes.

"Yeah, we can do that, I guess."

"You're such a good friend." She kissed his cheek and skipped back to her loft to pack. Melvin shook his head. *Grief affects people in strange ways.*

They headed north up Highway 65 in her new sea-foam green sedan, and Melvin once again struggled with the standard transmission. Too distraught to drive, Sally had no problem cozying up to him on the bench seat for instruction and encouragement. "Now, go easy with this foot and give her some gas," she explained with her hand on his thigh. "When you shift, you need to push a little more because the clutch sticks."

"The clutch stuck on your last car."

"It sticks on a lot of cars."

It made a painful grinding noise as he shifted. "This is a new car, right?"

"Of course, it is. See the odometer?"

"Your last car was brand new, too, right?"

"Yeah, it just needed to be broken in and have the clutch fixed and radiator patched."

"Uh-huh. And your dad gets these cars from Detroit, from your uncles?"

Her eyes narrowed. "What's your point?"

Melvin shrugged. "When's duck season?" Finally getting the hang of it, the motor purred along. "So, you never said. What's going on with your grandfather?"

Sally looked away, then turned back. "Let's not talk about that right now. Tell me about your grandparents. You never talk about your family."

"Nothing to tell. My mom's mom died in a boating accident, and the lawn guy killed her dad."

"Geez, Louise." Her eyes widened. "What about your dad's folks?"

Melvin shrugged. "Grandma's first husband died in the war. She met my dad's father on a trip to California, but he died before they made it home. Dad came along a little after that."

"Oh, that's awful. What happened? Heart attack?"

"Nope. Avocado. Choked to death. To this day, my grandmother will not touch guacamole."

"What's guacamole?"

"I don't know. Mashed up avocado and some other stuff."

Sally wrinkled her nose. "Well, I've never seen an avocado, but they sound dangerous."

Melvin reached over to change radio stations, and she slapped his hand. "I like this song."

"It's melancholy. I know you're worried about your granddad, but let's listen to something a little more upbeat. It'll help you'll feel better."

"I feel better just having you with me. But maybe you're right. Let me see if I can find some Sinatra."

"I was thinking rock and roll."

"What's rock and roll?" she asked. "Is it a game?"

"No, the music. You know, like the song, Rock Around the Clock?"

Sally stared at him blankly.

"They play it at sock hops?"

"What's a sock hop?" she asked.

Melvin almost stopped the car. "Seriously, you've never been to a sock hop, where girls wear poodle skirts?"

"Girls wearing dogs on their skirts, hopping around in socks? You're just making that up."

"But you've heard of Elvis and Buddy Holly, right?"

"No. Are they friends of yours?"

"What about Chuck Berry?"

"Yes! I *do* know him. We went to school together. No, that was Bill Berry. So, this music you're talking about, it's Canadian?"

Melvin rubbed the back of his neck. "Yeah." *Well, shit. I've only been back here a year, and I've already erased rock and roll. Bon Jovi's going to kill me.*

"I'd like to hear it," Sally said. "Sing me a rolling rock song, you know, something really Canadian."

He shook his head. "It's rock and roll, and I don't sing."

"Oh, come on. It's just us. I'm sure it'd cheer me up. Sing for me, please?" She batted her eyes. "Sing Rock and Roll Around the Clock?"

"It's Rock Around the Clock."

"That one doesn't roll?"

"You want to hear it or not?"

"Yes, please."

Melvin performed his best a cappella of the theme song to Happy Days while Sally sat wide-eyed and smiled. "That was amazing!" she exclaimed as she clapped. "I love that happy sound. And your voice! You should be on the radio."

"I should be on medication. I can't believe I sang out loud. I've never sung for anyone, not even my wife."

Sally looked down. "Maybe you're changing, Melvin. Maybe I bring out a side of you that you didn't know you had. Maybe I bring out something she couldn't."

After lunch in a roadside diner, they arrived in the beautiful little town of Eureka Springs. Sally's spirits had improved, and she seemed happy. Melvin felt good, too, glad he could be there for his friend in her time of need. Familiar with the area, she directed him down a road that turned steeply uphill and eventually led to a mountain cabin with breathtaking views.

Melvin climbed out of the car and noted the absence of vehicles, the unmown grass, and the cobwebs on the front porch. "Your grandparents live here?"

"Who? Oh, no. This is my parent's cabin. We can stay here during our visit."

"Oh, I thought we were—"

"Oh, we are,"—she popped the trunk—"but I thought we should freshen up before we go over."

"Let me help you with those."

Sally shook her head. "I got the bags." She tossed him the key. "Get the door."

Melvin unlocked the log cabin door, but it wouldn't open. He leaned into it, but it refused to budge.

Sally put the bags down on the porch. "Yeah, it sticks sometimes. There's a trick to it. Stand back." She lowered her shoulder and rammed it, knocking the door open. "See? The trick is, you have to be a man."

Melvin picked up the bags. "You're hilarious."

She held the door for him. "Mind the step there. Don't trip on your skirt."

Melvin stepped into a living area covered in dust and cobwebs but otherwise nicely appointed. Sally opened a couple of windows and began to clean. "Daddy brings my uncles up here a couple of times a year. He started bringing me when I was 10. Used to drive Momma crazy with worry, but I loved it. They taught me how to track, shoot, and skin things. Do you hunt?"

"The only thing I hunted as a kid was chocolate Pop-Tarts."

"What are Pop Tarts?" she asked as she beat the dust off the couch cushions.

"It's a flat rectangular pastry designed for a pop-up toaster. Very popular in Canada."

"That's wild. So, you would toast the pastry?"

"Actually, no. Nobody toasts them. You eat them cold."

Sally's eyes narrowed. "You're putting me on. You make tarts for the toaster, but nobody toasts them?"

"Nope. I mean, you might toast it once, just to see what it tastes like."

Sally disappeared into one of the two bedrooms to shake out the linens. "Why?" she called back. "Do they taste bad toasted?"

"No, actually, they taste great toasted. We just prefer not to."

She poked her head out. "Canadians are stupid."

"We are not. If you had a Pop-Tart, you'd understand. Growing up, my mother gave me Pop-Tarts for breakfast almost every morning."

"She didn't make you biscuits and gravy or sausage and bacon or ham and eggs?" Melvin shook his head. Sally's brow creased in concern. "Not even pancakes?"

"Nope. Occasionally, she'd serve little chocolate donuts. Sometimes the white ones with powdered sugar."

Sally looked at the floor. "Well, I'm sure those tarts were difficult to bake. Your mother must be fantastic in the kitchen." She grabbed his hand. "Come on. I want to show you something." She led him to the back porch, where the views were more spectacular than the front. She pointed out the various mountains and Leatherwood Creek below. She snuggled up and pulled his arm around her. "Isn't it romantic up here? I never get tired of that view."

Melvin stepped back. "Shouldn't we be going over to your grandparents?"

"Of course. I'll call and let them know we're coming."

"Aren't they expecting us?"

"Yeah, but I need to let them know we're here." She motioned to a wooden bench. "Have a seat and enjoy the view. I'll be right back." She opened the patio door and called back, "Oh, be sure to check before you sit. We have brown recluse spiders." Melvin blinked twice and decided he was just fine standing and inhaled the sweet mountain air.

She returned, smiling. "Great news! Granddad's doing much better. They think they may have jumped the gun, saying he was on his deathbed. Right now, he's too tired for visitors. Isn't that wonderful?"

"That's great. Maybe we should go by the store and pick up some groceries for them."

"Uh, no need. They've had neighbors doing that all morning. Plenty of groceries."

"I thought he was too tired for visitors?"

"Well, yeah, all the neighbors wore him out. The doctor said he just needs some peace and quiet. It's the best thing."

Melvin took a step toward the cabin. "So, we're headed back to Little Rock, then?"

"Golly, no." She pulled on his arm to turn him back around. "We've come all this way. Check out that view again. We should enjoy the cabin and see them tomorrow."

He nodded. "It is nice. Let's go back to town and pick up something for dinner."

Her eyes lit up. "Yeah, let's go to the market. I'll cook for you. It's the least I can do. I hope you won't be disappointed if it's not as good as your mother's."

Melvin smiled. "I like your odds."

That evening, Sally served up the best steak, potatoes, and carrots Melvin could remember. Afterward, she built a fire and uncorked some wine. They wrapped in quilts and sat on the rug, watching the flames and listening to the crackles. Feeling the wine, the warmth of the fire, and a full belly, Melvin's worry about getting home faded. Sally appeared to be enjoying herself, too. She no longer mentioned her grandfather. Melvin's eyes grew heavy by the end of the second bottle. He thanked her for the pleasant evening, stumbled into one of the bedrooms, checked under the bedsheets for spiders, and passed out.

He dreamt of a purple frog and a talking cat sitting on his chest smoking cigarettes. He swatted at them as they tried to touch his face. Melvin opened his eyes to find Sally on top of him, kissing his neck. He pushed her off. "What are you doing?"

"What are we doing? What do you think we're doing? You're the absolute worst signal reader in the history of men."

"What?"

"I take you to a romantic cabin in the mountains, cook for you, sit in front of a fire drinking wine with you, and you don't make a move? You *force* me to sneak into your bed like a thief in the night? Frankly, it's embarrassing. All I want is a little attention." She leaned in to kiss him again, but he pulled away.

Sally frowned. "Is the thought of touching me that horrific?"

"No, of course not. You know I'm married."

"You're divorced, and your wife's in prison."

"Still, I took a vow."

"Of celibacy? Come on, Melvin. I stopped smoking for you."

"When?"

"Earlier today. Doesn't that make you happy?"

She leaned in again. Once more, he pushed her away.

"I'm happy you put down the cigarettes."

"I can make you happier if you'd just let me."

"I can't."

"Damn it!" She sat up against the headboard and folded her arms. "Why are you pining for a woman whose picture you don't even carry? You don't have one picture of her in your *whole* loft."

Melvin's eyes widened. "When were you in my loft?"

"What?"

"You just said I don't have a picture of my wife there. How would you know that?"

"Did I say that? Well, let's be clear. She's not your wife. She's your ex-wife. And we've been in your loft before."

"No, we've been in *your* loft several times. You've never been in mine."

Sally's eyes went wild. "What are you saying? Are you saying I broke in? You think that while you were out one day, I somehow picked your lock, went through all your things, tried on a couple of shirts, and then laid in your bed, smelling your pillow? How dare you accuse me of something like that? How could you even think that?"

"I didn't. I just couldn't remember you being in my loft."

"Oh. Well, good. Now stop trying to make this all about me. We're talking about you here." She pointed at him. "I've seen the way you look at me. You can't expect me to believe you don't find me attractive or at least care a little for me. Why else would you come up here?"

"I came up here for you. Your grandfather's sick, and you needed a friend."

"Granddad's not sick. Why would you think that?"

"Because you told me."

"I did *not.* You just needed an excuse to let go of the guilt of your sorry ex-wife. I brought you here for your birthday."

"So, you lied about your grandfather dying?"

"Noooo. He *is* dying. We're all dying, Melvin. It's just a matter of when—which I never technically specified."

"I can't cheat on my wife. Divorced or not."

"Well, shit. I can't believe I quit smoking for you." She laid back down. "If you won't get frisky, will you at least hold me until I fall asleep?"

"Yeah, I can do that. Would you like to put something on? Shirt, nightgown—anything?"

"No."

As they started to doze, Melvin kissed her cheek and whispered, "Just for the record, you're very attractive." She smiled, drifted off to sleep gently, and snored like a freight train.

Chapter 16
A Star is Born

Melvin awoke the next morning to the sizzle and aroma of grilled ham. Still groggy from wine and lack of sleep, courtesy of the Midnight Express, he stumbled into the kitchen. Sally was in an apron at the stove. She turned and smiled. "Well, good morning, sleepy head. Coffee's right over there. Sleep okay? I don't normally get up this early, but I just woke with all kinds of energy. Can't remember much about last night, but it was the best night's sleep I've had in years. Who knew it was so chilly this early? I built a fire and made you ham, eggs, and silver-dollar pancakes. I hope you like it. I know it's not the toaster tarts your mother used to bake, but it's all we have."

Melvin rubbed his head and yawned. "I suppose it'll have to do." He winked. "Just kidding. This looks amazing." And it was.

She grabbed a cup of coffee and sat down across from him. "You know, I've never made breakfast the next morning for someone I didn't sleep with. My goodness, Dr. Napier, you've just got me doing all sorts of new things."

"Well," Melvin replied, "if you cook like this, you can make my breakfast anytime." Sally's eyebrows shot up. He quickly added, "You know what I mean."

"Yes, unfortunately. Speaking of trying new things, I want to show you the real reason we're in Eureka Springs today."

"I thought it was all about last night?"

She sighed. "Well, there was hope. No, the real reason we're here is to try something new, something to get you out of your dull drums. Look at *this*." She plopped the newspaper in front of him.

Melvin's eyes widened. "Twenty percent off baked beans at Warner's Market? No way. It's got to be a misprint. Well, that was certainly worth the three-hour drive up here. You know, I heard about some macaroni in Kansas City they're practically giving away as a two-for-one deal."

Sally's eyes narrowed as she tapped on the paper. "Look right here, smart ass."

"Hmm, they're making a movie here. That's interesting."

The pitch in Sally's voice skyrocketed. "And they're casting extras today. Let's go try out. Please?"

Melvin wrinkled his nose. "Be in a movie? What's it about?"

"Who cares? It's a movie! Don't you want to be in the movies? Don't you want to memorialize yourself somehow? Don't you want people 100 years from now to see you and wonder, Who was that person? What were they thinking?"

Melvin raised his hand to dismiss the idea but paused. It was 1951. Alexis loved old movies. If he could get on film, he could signal her somehow. She'd know where he was and when. At least she'd know he was still alive. It was a long shot, but his best so far. Melvin was all in.

After waiting an eternity for Sally to get ready, Melvin drove into town. She'd always kept her hair just the way she wanted, but Melvin had never seen her primp this much. Once in the car, Sally was like a ferret after a triple espresso. She cracked the window, turned on the heater, rolled up the window, turned off the heater, checked herself in the mirror, and made Melvin swear six times on his ex-wife's grave that she looked alright.

The movie was shooting in downtown Eureka Springs, using the massive old Victorian hotel as a backdrop. By the time they parked, Sally couldn't speak and could barely breathe. She held a death grip on Melvin's hand as they walked to the outskirts of the set. A small crowd of locals had lined up in front of a tent. As they waited their turn, Sally furiously fanned her face despite the crisp 60-degree morning air.

"Oh, there's too many people," she panted. "We're never gonna get picked."

"Relax," Melvin replied. "The flyer says the scene calls for extras walking on the street and standing in the background. That's a lot of people." He glanced at the paper. "The movie's called, All About Emma. Doesn't say what it's about. Huh, I've never seen it."

Sally slapped his arm harder than intended. "Of course, you haven't seen it, dummy. They haven't made it yet. Does it say who the stars are?"

"No," Melvin replied, rubbing his arm. "I suspect it's someone named Emma."

The assistant casting director hurriedly formed everyone into a long line, shoulder to shoulder. Sally's knees buckled as they got into position. Melvin put his arm around her to prop her up. The man walked down the line saying, "Yes, no, no, yes, no, yes." Unfortunately, Sally and Melvin were a no. A fierce scowl spread across Sally's face as he went farther down the line. She took a step forward. "Hey, buddy! You can't tell us no. Do you know who this is?"

Without turning, the assistant replied, "Don't care."

She shouted back, "Well, for your information, pal, this is *Doctor* Melvin Napier!"

Melvin lowered his chin and took a step back. The fellow immediately turned around and came back.

"You a real doctor?"

Sally put her hands on her hips. "As real as they get, buddy boy."

The assistant casting director nodded as if he'd just solved a riddle. "One of our actors requires your services, Doc. We could find a small role for you in return for a little discretion."

"Well," Melvin replied as he wrapped his arm around Sally, "my wife's a nurse. We're a package deal."

"Yes, sir. Follow me."

As they followed behind, Sally reached up and kissed his cheek. "Look at you," she whispered. "Big liar."

"I didn't lie. My wife *is* a nurse."

"Ex-wife, and maybe she's good for something after all."

As the assistant led them up to the top floor of the old hotel, Melvin wondered what awaited. Here's hoping it was an eye problem. He'd been through the ordeal of an Internal Medicine internship and rotated through the Coronary Care Unit twice back in the day. What could be worse than that?

He glanced at Sally. Her confident strides signaled she had complete faith in his ability to handle whatever this was. Then he recalled it was 1951, and to most, a doctor was a doctor.

At the door to the suite, the assistant hesitated. "Normally, we'd have you sign a non-disclosure before going in, but as a doctor, I know your oath keeps you from saying anything."

Melvin nodded. "We're just here to help."

"Great. Keep that in mind."

Upon entering, Melvin's eyes trained to the two large, intimidating men in suits standing like statues against the wall on either side of the fireplace. A third man in a bathrobe was curled up and sobbing in a corner. Melvin's first impression was that the two men had beaten him, but as he entered the room further, a fourth man was face down on the floor. Melvin rushed over to him and ordered Sally, "Go see to the other man. Check for injuries." Sally shot him a What-the-hell look but did as she was told. As Melvin reached the man on the floor, he said aloud, "Shit, he's not breathing."

An older, well-dressed, rotund man entered the room. In an authoritarian voice, he pronounced, "Your assessment is spot on, doctor. I believe that's been the case for the last few hours. His condition is what your profession might call, stable."

"Did you call an ambulance?"

The assistant casting director and the two statues shifted uneasily. The older man, whom Melvin now suspected was the film's director, pointed to the man in the corner with Sally and said, "You're here for him, doctor. That's your patient."

Melvin attempted to examine the sobbing man, but he refused to leave the fetal position. Melvin looked up. "What happened here?"

The assistant answered, "Now look, doc, you don't want to know more than—"

Melvin's back straightened. "If you want my help, cut the bullshit and answer my question! What's going on?"

Sally backed away, her pupils dilating as she stared at Melvin.

"No need for colorful language, Dr. Napier," the director said. "Let's start again. I'm Henrik V. Porter, the third, ringmaster of this one-ring circus. And this sobbing little clown is our main attraction, in other words, the major star of our motion picture." Then he pointed at the dead man on the floor. "That gentleman is, or rather *was*, a great admirer of our major star. An admirer who provided a certain brand of entertainment in return for reimbursement of his effort."

Melvin grimaced. "He's a hooker?"

The assistant grinned. "No, Doc. He *was* a hooker. Now, he's a dead hooker."

Melvin stopped short of asking if anyone had called the police, deciding it wasn't in his or Sally's best interest.

Porter continued. "We can't get our investment over there to stop boo-hooing. The longer he's off the set, the more money we lose. The film industry is not in the business of losing money. We don't know if the prostitute gave him anything to ingest or if he intends to hurt himself. Our rather large security advisors over there didn't find anything useful on the body. Would examining it tell *you* anything, doctor?"

Careful not to leave fingerprints, Melvin briefly examined the dead body, noting the ligature marks around the neck. "I believe I have all I need." With that, Porter made a slight hand motion. The two muscular men suddenly became animated. In a flash, the body was gone.

Melvin examined the trembling actor again. *This guy looks familiar.*

Henrik V. Porter, the third, tapped his foot. "How soon will I have my actor, doctor?"

Melvin wondered what sedatives were available in the 1950s. Then he had an idea. "Give me an hour."

"I'll leave you to it, then. You have 30 minutes."

After the director had gone, Melvin turned to the casting assistant. "I need marijuana."

"What?"

"Weed, grass, Mary Jane, whatever you call it. Bring me some."

"Doc, only musicians mess with that stuff. You're not going to find it up here in Bible land."

"Go to your guys who build the sets, transport equipment, things like that. They'll have it. And be quick about it. And, hey, don't forget the papers."

The assistant hurried out the door mumbling, "Papers? What kind of doctor are you, anyway?"

Sally was still staring at Melvin with big eyes. In a small voice, she said, "You're so calm. I'm falling to pieces inside. And now you want to smoke dope? What else don't I know about you, Dr. Napier?"

He gave her a comforting smile. "Well, if you've been around long enough, you learn a thing or two."

Sure enough, the assistant returned with some marijuana. Melvin rolled a joint effortlessly, lit it, and put it in the actor's mouth. He coughed a few times but soon settled down. "What is this stuff?" he asked.

Melvin replied, "In this case, it's medicinal. And it's okay to keep inhaling. You're not running for President." As the actor continued to calm down, Melvin thought, *I've seen this guy. Alexis would know. She's gonna freak out when she hears this story.*

The actor stood up and said, "I've never felt this good." He shook Melvin's hand and was hurried off by the casting assistant, who said something about Melvin being a miracle worker.

Not long after, one of the massive security advisors escorted them to a tent in front of the hotel. Soon a gentleman came in and shook their hands. "Hi, I'm Dan, first assistant director. You must be Dr. and Mrs. Napier."

Sally thrust out her hand. "That's right. I'm Mrs. Napier. So nice to meet you."

"The pleasure's all mine. You're both heroes around here as far as we're concerned. When Almar gets into those fits, we have to shut down for days. The company loses a fortune. But you had him back on his feet in no time. He's out there right now, giving the performance of a lifetime. I've never seen him so confident, so relaxed. It's like he's a different guy. He's hitting every mark, getting along with the other actors, and even being nice to the crew. And something else." He shook his finger. "He's normally picky about what he eats, calls it veganism or something. But a little while ago, he ate half the food table, including the brisket. He's a new man."

"Well," Melvin replied, "we're just happy we could help." *Almar? I know that name. Did he say vegan? In the 50s? No way.*

Dan continued, "I understand you want to be in the movies."

Sally nodded enthusiastically. "And how!"

"Okay. We have a small part for each of you. It's not much, but you'll get to shout at a taxi, and the director promises not to cut it. How does that sound?"

Sally's knees began to buckle again, and Melvin steadied her. "Sounds great. Just tell us what to do."

Soon after, a girl whisked them away to makeup. It was a whirlwind of activity as another girl handed them a script to read while another took measurements for their costumes. Sally reveled in the attention while Melvin read the script. "This makes no sense," he complained a little too loudly. Henrik V. Porter, the third, overheard.

"Oh? Do elaborate, good doctor."

Melvin pointed at the script. "Right here. Your character, Emma, goes completely blind from a near target, only to magically regain her vision later?"

Porter folded his arms. "No. She has lost her forbidden love and stares at his picture so long her eyes go bad, and she's forced into a lower station when her family discovers her infirmity and disowns her. Her eyesight is regained when her true love returns to rescue her."

Melvin laughed, "Yeah, right. Exactly how does that work, medically?" Sally glared from behind the director, flashing Melvin every hand signal she knew to shut the hell up.

"Whatever do you mean? Our technical advisor tells us this could happen."

"Yeah, no. The whole thing is kind of hooey."

Henrik V. Porter, the third's upper lip curled at these words. He stormed off, saying, "I'll have you know that hooey has paid for my three mansions in Beverly Hills." After a few steps, he stopped and turned back. "Normally, I would have you thrown off my set, but we do owe you a bit of debt, and this *is* the lynchpin of what will surely be a most forgettable film. It couldn't hurt to be a bit more believable. You say you know a little about the eyes, doctor?"

"That's a fair statement."

"Then, as our new technical advisor, would you be so kind as to rewrite the scene to be a bit less hooey, as you so elegantly put it?"

"Sure, but we'd still want to be in the film."

"Oh, we can do better than that. Instead of hailing a cab, you can be the eye doctor. Do you think you could play an eye doctor, Dr. Napier?"

Melvin and Sally shared a smile. "I think I could pull it off."

Dan raised a finger. "We have Kincannon for that role? He's going to be pissed."

Porter waved his hand dismissively. "Is he under contract?"

"Yeah."

"Then tell that despicable lazy drunk he's fired. We'll use him in the next one. And tell him if he ever goes near my wife again, our security advisors will prepare him for his next role in *The Severely Beaten Man*."

"Yes, sir. Which wife was that?"

"Astute question. I believe it was ex-wife number three, but I can't be certain. Just tell him to steer clear of them all." Porter turned and addressed the crew. "Ladies and gentlemen, we have a new doctor." Obligated applause arose from the tent. "Someone retrieve the head writer, pronto."

Soon, an overly thin, balding man with a goatee arrived. Porter put his arm around Melvin's shoulder. "Jay, this is Dr. Napier. He says your vision loss scene is pure *shit*. He said his nurse could have written it better, and English is not her first nor second language."

Jay took a long drag off his cigarette as he stared at Melvin. "That so?"

Porter's eyes lit up as he stepped back to watch. "Go on. Tell him, Dr. Napier. Tell him you can smell the caca from his scene all the way over in the next state. Heaven knows what state that would be—Alabama?"

Melvin's chin dropped. "I just said a little tweaking could make the scene more medically accurate."

Porter snarled, "Tweaking? Poppycock! I believe the word *hooey* was bantered about."

Jay stroked his goatee. "What'd ya have in mind?"

"I have a thought on why she would get blurry from staring at a picture too long. It would start with her refraction."

Jay's brow furrowed. "Her what?"

"Sorry. Does the character, Emma, wear glasses?"

Jay nodded. "Yeah, she does."

"No, she doesn't," Porter corrected. "Eve absolutely refuses. Says it covers too much of her face, which she purports is her greatest feature."

Jay released a long sigh. "Now it's the glasses? From what I hear, it wasn't her face that landed her this role."

"Well, that's neither here nor there. Emma has *no* glasses."

Melvin nodded, "So, you're saying she's an emmetrope."

"No," Porter said. "I believe she is supposed to be a Methodist."

"An emmetrope is a medical term for a patient who doesn't need glasses," Melvin replied. "Now, it's possible that prolonged staring at a picture held too closely could stimulate her accommodation and theoretically send her into an accommodative spasm."

Porter's eyes grew wide. "A spasm, you say? How delectable."

"Yes, from accommodating."

Porter thought for a moment. "So, forgive my layman's grasp of the medical vernacular, but as I understand you, you're saying the script works if she's an accommodating emmetrope? Say, I do like the sound of that."

Melvin nodded. "You could put it that way. And she could be instantly cured if her lover gave her atropine eye drops."

"Did you hear that, Jay? Instantly cured by magical eye drops!"

"Well, atropine isn't magical, you see—"

Porter raised his hand. "Tut, tut. Don't bore me with mundane details, doctor. We have a movie to make. Jay, rewrite the script to incorporate what the doctor ordered. I'm done with this film being *All About Emma*. From now on, we're making *The Accommodating Emmetrope*."

Melvin's mouth fell open. *Alexis's favorite movie? I knew I recognized that guy. She'll see me for sure. What if she doesn't believe it? She'll need proof.* He turned to the director. "I have one request."

"Oh?"

"Will Sally and I be in the credits?"

Porter and Jay had a good laugh. "Good heavens, no, my boy. The union would have our balls for that. The film would never leave the can."

Melvin looked disappointed. "Well then, could we name our characters?"

"Well, you could," replied Jay, "but they don't have names in the script."

Melvin noticed an equally disappointed look on Sally's face. "What if instead of saying, Pass me the instrument, nurse, I say, Pass me the instrument, Sally?"

Jay rubbed his goatee. "Can't see any harm."

"Nor can I," Porter chimed in. "Make it happen. Consider it payment for services rendered. And be happy for that, because we wouldn't have paid you otherwise. We're completely over budget as is!" And off he went.

Sally kissed Melvin's cheek. "Thank you for sticking up for me. I won't forget about you now that I'm a star." She dramatically brushed her hair from her face. "And tell my people, I'm not to be referred to as Sally when I'm on set. Call me by my stage name, Alexis."

"You to be called by my wife's name?"

"Ex-wife, and if she's keeping you from *me*, then I want something from *her*. Her name will do nicely."

A chill shot down Melvin's spine as he suddenly recalled why Alexis had fallen in love with this movie as a little girl. One of the characters had her name.

Before they knew it, Melvin and Sally were in a mock-up of an eye lane. He was instructed to examine Emma without putting his shadow on her or blocking her face from cameras one or two. He was to sternly look her in the eyes and announce she suffered vision loss because she was an accommodating emmetrope. Then, in a voice of doom, he was to raise his finger and proclaim, "There is no cure!" After this, the starlet would break down and cry as Sally comforted her. Cheesy as it was, Melvin did as he was asked and referred to Sally as Alexis every chance he got. When Emma delivered her lines, he was directed to sit and compassionately listen to her with his fingers interlocked. Instead, he subtly moved them into a heart shape to signal Alexis.

It had grown dark by the completion of shooting, and Melvin and Sally walked to a small restaurant to celebrate. She glowed as Melvin assured her this would become a major film and millions would view her performance over the next fifty years. She grinned ear to ear, never asking how he could know such things. Her dinner grew cold as she went on about how she was now an actress, and there was no telling where it might lead. Melvin listened and smiled.

After a little too much wine, they made their way back up the mountain to the cabin. Between the alcohol and the day's adrenaline, Sally didn't make it past the couch. Melvin built a small fire, pulled off her shoes, tucked her in with a quilt, and kissed her goodnight. Soon, the freight train was rolling once more. He closed the bedroom door and looked forward to a sound night's sleep, knowing there'd be no repeat of last night. The purple frog and the talking cat would have to invade someone else's dream, putting down their cigarettes just long enough to touch someone else's face.

Chapter 17
Going Home

On the drive back to Little Rock, Sally chatted the whole way, but Melvin didn't hear a word. *Will Alexis recognize me under all that makeup? She's watched that movie a thousand times. Why notice me now? Even if she does, will she connect the dots? I've got to do more than just signal her. I've got to communicate. But how?*

He thought back to movies where letters had been delivered through time. *Does that really work?* Maybe so. There had been a cryptic old letter delivered from someone named Sam when Melvin's first son, Daniel, was born. He still hadn't figured out who Sam was or how he'd managed to do it. Next, he considered movies where they communicated through newspaper ads. *Why would she pick up a fifty-year-old paper?* Then he thought about movies where people communicated through a book or a diary. *That'd never work. How would she know which book to read?* The only thing Melvin knew for sure was that he watched a lot of movies.

Over the next month, Melvin racked his brain while Sally did her best to distract him. She dragged him to movies or plays at the Robinson Center, claiming she needed to hone her craft by observing other actors, and, as a star, it wouldn't do to be seen alone. And since Melvin had launched her career, she insisted he was obligated to accompany her. And, of course, she couldn't be alone at McKeen's. There was no craft honing at McKeen's. They just went there to drink.

It was at that very establishment on a June evening the answer presented itself. Sally was in the lady's room as Melvin sat at the bar, polishing off his third beer. Walter brought him a fourth.

"What's the worry, son?"

"Do I look worried?"

"You look like a man with a lot on his mind. I can't imagine why. You have a steady job and the prettiest girl in town on your arm. You shouldn't have a care in the world."

"Sally and I are just friends."

Walter smiled. "Uh-huh."

"I was just thinking about . . . It's complicated."

Walter sighed. "What's her name?"

"How do you know—?"

"I always know, son."

"Her name is Alexis, and I need to communicate with her. I just don't know how."

"You mean, you want her to scram before Sally finds out, but she doesn't get the picture?"

"What? No, I mean, like, I want to send her a letter. I just don't know how to get it to her."

"Post office not good enough?"

"She doesn't exactly have an address right now."

Walter nodded. "I know the type. You never know when or where they're going to show up."

"What was that?"

"I said the problem with women like that is you never know where they'll show up."

"But I do know. Walter, I know exactly where she'll be. You're a genius!"

Walter wiped the bar. "Genius? No. Amazingly successful and dangerously handsome for an old man? Maybe. But seriously, son, you should drop this Alexis and appreciate the beautiful woman you have. You'll never regret it."

"Thanks, Walter."

"What lies are you telling my future husband?" Sally asked as she sat back down.

Walter grinned. "You talking about him or me? Because I'm married, sugar plum. Some days even happily. Mostly Tuesdays."

Melvin stood up. "Walter just gave me some great advice. I've got to run. Oh, and I'm going to need to borrow your car. Thanks—bye."

Sally sat with her mouth open as she watched her date run away. "Walter! What the hell did you tell him?"

"Beats me, sweetheart."

She shrugged and downed Melvin's beer. Planting her elbows on the bar with her chin in her hands, she leaned toward Walter with a twinkle in her eye. "Now, tell me all about Tuesdays."

✉

Melvin high-tailed it to his loft. It was so simple. Why hadn't he thought of it sooner? His house in 2004 wasn't there yet, but the *land* was. All he had to do was locate his backyard, bury a letter, and Bob's your uncle. Workers had started an extensive landscaping project just before his original flight. Surely, they could find a container buried at the correct depth. They'd naturally give it to Alexis if it had her name on it. Melvin nodded as he smiled. Not only could he let her know he was alive, but she could stop him from ever getting on the plane—foolproof!

Melvin spread his map across his tiny kitchen table. He tapped his fingers. *Our street isn't there yet, and the main roads through Maumelle are different.* He snapped his fingers. *The hills haven't changed. I'll have a hike, but I could find it.* He paced in his loft. *What to bury it in? The letter has to survive 53 years underground. I'll need something more than a coffee can.*

The following evening, Melvin approached David after his physics lecture. "Great talk tonight. I enjoyed it."

"Thanks, Melvin. Glad to see you're still coming around. I don't see many amateur physicists. Counting you, I've only ever seen one."

Melvin nodded. "Thanks—I think. Hey, your talk tonight got me thinking of building a time capsule, something to last a long time. How could I construct that?"

David stroked his chin. "Newtonian movements made you think of building a time capsule? It's as if you aren't even listening when you come to my lectures. Still, the construction could be fascinating. How long would you expect it to be underground?"

"I don't know. Let's say, 53 years?"

"That's oddly specific. So, you're expecting people in 2004 to dig this up? I've often wondered what the world will be like that far into the future. At the rate we're progressing, I suspect we'll have flying cars and conquered war, famine, and most diseases."

Melvin shrugged his shoulders. "Or not. So, how would I go about building it?"

David scratched his head and then brushed dandruff off his corduroy blazer. "Your best bet would be the guys over in Engineering, but let's conceptualize it first. Will this be placed in concrete, like in the corner of a new building?"

"No, I'm going to bury it directly in the ground."

David nodded. "What will the capsule contain?"

"Papers, mostly. Documents, maybe pictures."

"In that case, it'd need to be watertight. Airtight would be better."

"Like in a zip lock?"

"What's that?"

"Nothing, just thinking out loud."

"If you have documents, you might try a large pickle jar. You can seal those quite adequately, hermetically even. However, I've never understood what hermetically sealed means. Pretty tight, I imagine? Perhaps we should look that up. Now, where did I place my encyclopedia collection? Oh, yes, back in my office. Now, we're going to need volume H."

"David, focus. The time capsule?"

"Oh, yes, of course. You'd risk ground shifts breaking the glass jar over the years. The ground will move due to saturation, temperature changes, insects, roots, and earthquakes."

"Earthquakes?"

"Yes, Arkansas occasionally has them. More in the eastern half than here, but it's not out of the realm of possibility over the next, did you say, 50 years?"

"53 years."

"Right," he smiled. "Exactly 53 years. Perhaps you should consider placing the jar in an exterior container. Something that could stand up to all those forces."

Melvin shook his hand. "Thanks, David. I knew you were the guy."

"No problem. Bigger questions, though. Why a time capsule? Where will you bury it, and how will you notify the future of its location?"

"You know," said Melvin as he walked away, "those are all logical and relevant questions. But like those Newton particles, I have a bus to catch. Good night!"

David shook his head. "Nope. Didn't listen to a darn thing."

The next day, Melvin went to the hardware store and bought tall mason jars, but no luck on a container. He tried the five and dime, but nothing fit the bill. With his head down, he started home and spotted an Army/Navy store. A rectangular, green, metal ammunition box sat on the shelf, the perfect size for two thin jars, and sported a lid with a clamp. He snatched it up and returned to the hardware store for a soldering kit.

That evening, he sat at his kitchen table, trying his hand at soldering. He inscribed to please give the box to Alexis Napier and the importance that she receives it promptly. But his words were too small to be legible, not to mention running out of space and melting two holes through the container walls to boot. Melvin slammed the solder pen onto the table and stared out the window. Soon, he smelled smoke. Melvin jerked the pen off the table, burning his left hand and yelping in pain. Within seconds, someone knocked at his door.

162

"One minute!" he yelled as he thrust his hand under the kitchen faucet and tossed a damp dishtowel to cover the smoldering table.

"What's that smell?" Sally asked from the other side. "It's all the way over in my place."

He cracked open the door. "Sorry, I was cooking."

Sally tried to peek around him. "Really? What-cha cooking, good looking?"

"Tuna fish?"

She covered her nose. "Was it dead when you started? It smells like wood burning."

He shrugged. "It's called wood-plank cooking. It's very Canadian."

She nodded. "They do say foreign food tastes better than it smells. I didn't know you cooked. I'd love to see you handle a spatula."

"Oh, I have moves—in the kitchen."

She winked. "I'll bet you do."

"But to appreciate Canadian cooking, you have to see the process from the beginning, and it's late in the game. Another time?"

"Hey!" She frowned and grabbed his hand. "How did you burn yourself?"

"Uh, I tried smoking? I'm not very good at it."

"And how! You want *me* to quit? You're the one who needs to stay away from cigarettes. Geez-Louise."

"Couldn't agree more. I'll stop today."

Her eyes narrowed. "Cooking and smoking. You're acting odder than usual. What's going on?"

Melvin looked down at the floor. "I didn't want to admit it, but I'm a little homesick. Just need to work through it on my own."

She gently blew over his burn. "I understand. I appreciate you being honest with me. You know you can tell me anything, right? Alright, I'll leave you to your tuna, but if it burns up or swims away, I'm making pot roast. And put some iodine on that hand." She kissed his wound and left.

Dang, he thought as he closed the door. *I can't go over there now. What the heck am I going to eat?*

The next day after work, Melvin bought two more containers. The guy behind the counter gave him the eye. "That makes three. Got a lot of ammo on hand?"

Melvin glanced around. "No, just an art project."

The man folded his arms. "Sure, pal. Cause I know a guy."

"Okay?"

"You know, a guy with a little something-something to put in those containers."

Melvin shook his head. "I'm good, thanks."

"Suit yourself, but those Russians didn't want to stop in Berlin. Trust me, I know. A little extra firepower never hurts, in case those boys decide to come around here."

Melvin smiled. "I promise you, sir. Soviets will never step foot in Arkansas."

"That's the spirit, son!"

By the third container, Melvin had legibly written in large letters, Give to Alexis Napier ASAP. It would have to do.

On Saturday, June 16th, 1951, Melvin borrowed Sally's new navy-blue coupe and drove across the river to Crystal Hill Road on his way to his future neighborhood in Maumelle. He passed a road sign for Marche but none for Maumelle. *What the hell is Marche?* he wondered. Melvin drove on with dense woods on either side, scanning for anything familiar. Soon he approached barbwire fencing with prominent signs: No Trespassing, Property of the United States Government. He nodded, recalling a golf buddy telling him that Maumelle had been an artillery range in WWII. Surely, it was abandoned by now.

164

Melvin parked alongside the desolate road. He scanned both ways before slipping through the barbwire and into the woods. Working his way uphill through dense forest brush, he reached the top of the ridge. Like the road, the view was nothing as he'd remembered. Even the banks of the Arkansas River looked different. He walked along the ridgetop until he came across a familiar outcropping of rocks. He sat upon them and gazed at the river below. With his eyes closed and smiling, he could hear his two boys playing here and nearly falling. *Thank goodness Alexis never saw that.* Melvin let go of a long breath. It felt like the first in over a year.

Using the rocks as a reference, he pushed through brush until he found a small oak starting to split at the base not far from three small boulders he knew well from his backyard. Melvin sat on the forest floor and wept. He was home.

This is the perfect place to bury a letter, he thought. *Nobody but hunters have any reason to be here until they develop it in 2000. Being fenced off as government land is just added insurance.* He worked his way back to Sally's car and rushed home to start writing to his wife.

Chapter 18
The Letter of the Arkansas Time Traveler

As Melvin sat in his loft that evening with pen in hand, the words came quickly.

Dear Alexis,

I don't know where to begin. I love and miss you like crazy. If you're reading this, the landscapers have discovered the ammo box, and hopefully, I'm still there with you. You're not going to believe what I have to tell you, but on April 30th, 2004, I got on a small plane that never reached Jonesboro. I survived the crash but somehow ended up in 1950. As strange as it sounds, I've been stuck here for over a year. I've put a paper in the box with an ad I took out last week with our names and wedding date to prove it. You'll think it's a joke, but look up old papers in the library, and you'll see it's true. Plus, I played the eye doctor in The Accommodating Emmetrope just for you. Look carefully. It's me.

Oddly enough, I'm working as an ophthalmologist in the same building. And if you still think this is all a put-on, I clipped out a story they wrote about me in the paper about my injuries, recovery, and joining the practice. Everyone assumes I'm Canadian (no idea why), but I've been called worse.

I miss you so much. Not a moment goes by I don't think about you and the kids and finding a way home. I've learned as much about time travel as I can and have befriended a physicist to help. I've done some experiments and will keep trying.

I pray you've gotten this in time and can stop me from getting on that plane. But if I'm already gone, know that I'm alive, and no matter what, I'll find my way back to you.

Hug and kiss the boys for me. Let them know their father loves them very much. I can't stand being apart from you. I love you so much.

Melvin

June 16th, 1951

The letter was perfect. The plan was perfect. For two solid weeks, he sat perfectly frustrated in his loft each evening, staring at his letter while Sally's new car was in the shop after throwing a rod. On Wednesday, July 4th, the car was back. His hand was on the doorknob to go over and ask to borrow it for Saturday morning when a knock came from the other side.

"Wow, you opened that pretty quickly," Sally said with a grin. "Do you just stand there, hoping a pretty girl will knock? That's adorable, and a little sad."

"No, I was just—"

She grabbed his hand. "Come with me. I want to show you something. And don't say you're too busy."

She led him into her loft and climbed out her window onto the fire escape. "You're not afraid of heights, are you?" she asked, already halfway up the ladder.

Melvin peered over the railing. "I'm not particularly fond of what happens after you fall. Plus, it's dark out here."

"The sun hasn't even set yet," she called down from the roof. "Stop being such a chicken."

"Chicken? What are we, twelve? Are you leading me down the tracks to see a dead body?"

"A what?" she hollered. "It's a two-story building. The fall won't kill you unless you hit something in the dumpster down there. At most, you'd break a few bones, no big deal."

He shook his head. "I don't like the sound of any of that."

"Just grow a pair and come up here."

"You know I almost died in a horrible plane crash, right? Emasculating me for a little fear of heights is not cool."

"It was a plane? I heard it was a couple of trucks. I'm sorry. I'll be more considerate of your feelings. Hey, *Melvina*, try not to get your skirt caught on the ladder. How was that? Better?"

"You're an ass," he proclaimed as he slowly climbed. Sally helped him onto the roof.

"Hey, what's all this?" he asked.

"It's my garden. I started it a couple of years ago. Did you think all those great tomatoes came from the market?"

Melvin put his hands on his hips and nodded. "It looks amazing."

"All this heat hasn't helped. Going to have to start over from scratch if it doesn't rain soon."

"How did you get all the wood and dirt up here?"

"Wasn't easy."

"That's a sturdy-looking bench. How did *it* get up here?"

"I built it last spring."

"She cooks, smokes, drinks, gardens, and does woodworking on the side. There's more to you than meets the eye, Sally Davis."

"If you only knew. My garden isn't the only reason I brought you up here. Come and sit with me."

"Will it hold us?"

"You want me to throw you off this roof?"

As they sat atop the Adams-Napier building, the sunset's last rays faded into darkness, and fireworks ignited over the river. She pulled his arm around her and put her head on his shoulder. Melvin smiled. *I'll have that letter in the ground this weekend. Won't be long now.*

On Saturday, July 7th, Melvin drove her car back to Maumelle. He parked alongside the road and pulled a shovel, ammo box, and garbage bag from the trunk. Taking a step toward the fence, he noted a light green pickup heading his way. Quickly tossing everything back in the trunk, he tried to think of an excuse to be there. *Maybe I broke down? No, they'll want to help me fix it. Why do people have to be so damn neighborly in this decade?* All Melvin could think to do was smile and wave as the truck approached. An older man in a straw hat and his wife gave a weak smile in return and accelerated on by, onward toward Marche, wherever that was. Melvin coughed in the hay-littered air from the truck's wake. *Finally, some good luck.* He grabbed his things and ducked through the barbwire fence.

Six paces east of the three boulders, he pierced the dirt with his shovel, immediately hitting rock. He moved over a few inches and found more rock. *Should've brought a pickaxe.* Melvin worked through the rocks to a depth he hoped could withstand the weight of a landscaping bulldozer.

He carefully inspected the ammo box one last time, running his finger down the edges, sealed watertight with glue. Inside were envelopes containing his letter and newspapers tucked inside mason jars. He'd placed cotton balls inside the jars to wick moisture and placed each jar in a sock to absorb vibrations and outside moisture.

He tied up the ammo box in a small garbage bag and carefully lowered it into the hole as if it were a bomb. "You know what this is?" Melvin asked the trees and the brush. "It's a time bomb." Melvin rolled his eyes. "Come on, guys. Get it? *Time*-bomb?" The trees said nothing. "Geez, tough forest."

He lifted a shovelful of dirt to fill the hole and paused. *If I'm right, and Alexis finds this, I'll be home the instant I fill this hole.* He took a deep breath and watched the dirt slide off the shovel into the hole. He shoveled in a second and a third. *Should I have left a note for Sally and John? No, I barely got rid of the last note before they found it. Too much to explain if this doesn't work.*

He filled the hole and carefully covered the area with pine straw. Taking a seat on a boulder, he gazed at where his house would stand. *I guess time doesn't change instantly.* He walked over to where his boys' rooms would be and imagined tucking them in. Then he walked to the master bedroom, kissed Alexis in his mind, and promised he'd return.

Wiping tears as he headed down the hill toward the car, Melvin heard someone shout, "Stop right there!" Two distant figures in green barreled toward him as quickly as the brush would allow.

Who are these guys? Am I in their favorite hunting spot, or are they growing something out here? Either way, Melvin scampered through the brush with his shovel and hastily through the barbwire, slicing the back of his left hand. He jumped in the car and sped away as the two men emerged onto the road.

Melvin held pressure on his hand. *Who were those guys?* He checked the rearview three times, took a breath, and slowed down. It was no time to get pulled over as he hadn't bothered to get a driver's license. In his defense, though, he didn't own a car.

Safely back in his loft, Melvin gently unwrapped his hand and washed away dried blood, revealing a minor scratch. *Not as deep as I thought. Weird it bled that much. It's not like I'm on aspirin.*

The next morning, Melvin and Sally walked to church. In the vestibule, everyone was speaking in hushed tones. The energy level was palpable. Sally tapped an elderly lady on the shoulder. "What's going on?"

"Didn't you read the paper this morning?" she replied.

Sally waved her hand dismissively. "Heck no. I was *way* too hung ov—up. I was too hung *up* reading my Bible this morning. You know, that's *God's* newspaper. Who cares about the other? Why? What did it say?"

"We've been attacked. Right here in Little Rock. Can you believe it?"

"Attacked?" Melvin asked. "By whom?"

"Those dirty Russian communists. We should've taken them out when we had the chance."

Sally's eyes widened. "What did they do?"

"They tried to blow up the ordnance works over near Marche yesterday! We're lucky to be alive. Here, read for yourself."

The paper reported the pursuit of an unknown person by military personnel guarding the grounds of the Maumelle Ordnance Works. The individual was carrying a weapon and seen getting into a dark blue coupe. Local witnesses reported seeing a man in the area getting out of a similar-looking vehicle around that time. The man was described as sinister-looking with a deranged smile and holding a long-range rifle, an ammunition box, and a body bag. He is suspected of either espionage or sabotage but was routed by local troops before any damage could be done. Citizens are to be on the lookout for any strangers in town or other forms of suspicious behavior. A contact number for the authorities appeared below the article.

Churchgoers were in disbelief. Even the morning sermon revolved around the story, with the minister calling it troubled times.

But Melvin never heard the sermon. As they sat in the pew, thoughts flooded his head. *Those guys were soldiers? Why was the Army patrolling an abandoned base? What the heck is the Maumelle Ordnance Works? More importantly, they saw the car. Did they get the license plate number? Holy shit! Probably shouldn't think swear words in church.* His face grew pale as sweat beaded on his brow. Sally squeezed his hand and whispered, "Relax. We're all scared, but it'll be okay. If the FBI doesn't get him, the locals will. Then he'll *wish* the FBI had found him first."

Holy shit!

As they walked home, Sally squeezed his arm. "I'm scared, Melvin. Communists right here in Arkansas! Do you think they were trying to blow us up? Do you think they'll try again?"

"Little Rock holds no strategic value to the Soviets. Besides, I don't think he was a spy, probably just a hunter. A lot of deer in that area, I would guess, never having been there."

She shook her head. "A hunter? It's not deer season. That doesn't make any sense."

"Exactly. The guy was a poacher. Probably why he ran."

"I'm still scared." She looked into his eyes. "I don't think I should be alone tonight."

He patted her hand. "Don't worry. I'll be right next door."

"Gee, *thanks.*"

By Saturday, October 6th, the letter had been in the ground for three months. Every morning since, Melvin had awoken, hoping for a miracle. And every morning since, he'd only found 1951. On this morning, he sat at his tiny kitchen table, racking his brain. *Did someone dig it up? The soldiers would have scoured every inch of the woods. I must have left tracks.* He shook his head and poured a cup of coffee. *If they had the letter, they'd have my name and occupation. I'd be in custody. But if it's still buried, why am I still here?*

He sipped as he stared out his window. *What if someone else digs it up in the future, before 2004? Or what if the workers never found it? Maybe I buried it too deep—or not deep enough. If the bulldozer's weight crushed it, it'd be mangled junk. Or maybe they found it, but I didn't seal it well enough. Maybe it decomposed and is unreadable. I should re-seal it and bury it in a different spot.* He nodded. *Maybe at a different depth.*

Not that it mattered. He couldn't get anywhere near the area with military, state, and federal investigations in full swing. And with the locals on patrol, anyone caught in those woods right now would never be seen again. Melvin paced in his loft, talking to himself well into the early afternoon.

"What if Alexis got it but not in time? Or maybe she does. What if I'm wrong about everything? What if she gets it, stops me, and creates a new timeline?" Melvin's expression went blank. "Everyone assumes the old timeline vanishes. What if it doesn't? What if the old timeline just goes on? What if I'm the old timeline? What if there's now another me in the future with my family? Even if I do get back, the other guy's not just going to step aside, not if he's me." Melvin's eyes narrowed. "He's going to do everything he can to keep tucking in *my* children and screwing *my* wife! I'm going to kill that son-of-a-bitch." Melvin looked in his mug. "How much caffeine have I had?"

He stared out the window once more. "I'm pissed at a guy who may or may not exist." He raised an eyebrow. "I created him with the letter. I can un-create him by destroying it. What if I'm wrong? What if all this just takes a little longer to work? Or maybe it didn't work because I'm the one who destroys the letter?" He put his cup down. "I need something stronger." He stormed across the landing and knocked on Sally's door.

She opened the door with wide eyes. "You scared me." She primped her hair. "You've never knocked on my door before."

He scowled, "You want to have a drink with me at McKeen's?"

She glanced at her watch. "It's a little early." Then she shrugged. "Who am I kidding?"

Melvin put his hands on his hips. "Is that a yes?"

"You're a little wound up today—but a date's a date. Yes, I'd love to."

"Call it what you will. Let's go."

They walked the short distance in silence. In heels, Sally was barely able to keep up with his pace. She sat down at a table and caught her breath while Melvin got them drinks. "Alright, Jessie Owens, what's got your goat?"

Melvin pummeled his scotch and slammed the empty glass down on the table. "I think someone's sleeping with my wife, and I need to decide what to do about it."

Sally's eyes narrowed as she sipped her beer. "Ex-wife. She's out of jail?"

"She's definitely not *in* jail."

"She murdered someone, and she's already out? Canada officially sucks eggs."

"The point is, this guy's sleeping with her and taking care of my two—"

"Your two what, Melvin?"

"Dogs. I have two dogs that I love more than anything, Daniel and Jake."

"I like those names. When I was little, I had an imaginary friend named Jake. Daddy always teased me and said he was a ghost. That always made me so mad."

"Are we here to talk about your problems or mine?"

She put her hand on his arm. "You're right. Why didn't you bring your dogs with you?"

"They couldn't make the trip. It's killing me."

"A lot of rules with crossing the border, huh? I'm sorry about your dogs, but screw that bitch! She could have come down here after she got out. But did she? No, she's with another man."

"Well, he is the love of her life."

"Don't make excuses for her. She married you, not *him*."

"Well, actually—"

"Oh shit!" Sally covered her mouth. "She divorced him and married you? You were the other man?" She slapped his shoulder.

"Ow!" He grabbed his arm. "What was that for?"

"For being stupid. I can't believe you married a woman who cheated on her husband. That should've been your first clue. And now the hag crawls right back to him instead of looking for you? You can't trust her, Melvin. You probably never could. I say good riddance. They deserve each other."

Melvin looked down and swirled the ice in his empty glass. "Maybe they do."

"Of course, they do. Screw 'em." Sally got up and returned with a glass of bourbon and another beer. "You're not thinking about going back, are you?"

Melvin downed the bourbon. "Thought about it. I could get rid of him so easily. With just one small action, I could make him disappear. No one would ever know."

Sally's voice dropped to a whisper. "You mean like with just a phone call? I've seen Daddy go through that. It takes a toll, Melvin. It sounds good now, but once you cross that bridge, that's it."

"I guess so." He reached over and polished off her beer.

"I get it. She meant a lot to you, and now some asshole has taken your place, and you're hurt. Yeah, you *could* take this guy out, but is that who you are? She made her choice. Maybe you need to accept that she's with him and you're here with people who care about you. I've been through it. Sometimes you just have to move on. You have to count your blessings."

"Maybe you're right. Maybe I should be happy for her." He smiled at her. "Gardener, carpenter, and philosopher. You never cease to amaze."

"Stick around, kid," she winked. "It only gets better from here. I'll grab us the next round. What sounds good? You've had what, one scotch, one bourbon, and one beer?"

Melvin nodded. "Yeah. That'd make a cool song."

Sally winced. "A song about three drinks? Good luck with that." As she rose to go to the bar, she spotted a man in a dark suit speaking with Walter and looking her way. She quickly sat back down. "Melvin, listen carefully. We were together last Wednesday—the whole night. Got it?"

"What?"

"Excuse me, ma'am," said the man in the suit. "Are you Sally Davis, owner of a dark blue coupe with Arkansas plates?"

"Who's asking?" she replied without looking up.

He flashed his ID. "The Federal Bureau of Investigation is asking, ma'am. Would you please confirm your identity?"

She glanced at him. "I've seen badges like that in the five and dime."

Melvin put his hand on her arm. "Sally, just answer his questions."

She rolled her eyes. "Yes, I'm Sally Davis, and I own a car. Some might say it's blue. So what?"

"And are you still in possession of said vehicle?"

"Yes, I still own *said* vehicle." She looked at Melvin. "Who talks like that?"

"Ma'am, can you verify your whereabouts on the afternoon of July 7th, 1951?"

"That was three months ago. I can't tell you what I had for breakfast."

"Sally," Melvin said, "that was the day people saw the guy over by Marche—remember?"

She raised her eyebrows. "Is that what this is? Why didn't you say so? I had my hair done that day."

The agent nodded and wrote on his pad. "And you drove your vehicle to the salon?"

"No, it's just a couple of blocks. I walked."

"Did you drive your vehicle at all that day?"

"No, it was parked in the alley."

"Did you lend your vehicle to anyone that day or any day before that day?"

Her eyes cut to Melvin. "Nobody drives my car except me."

"And no one else has ever borrowed your keys for any other reason?"

"What did I just say?"

"Have you seen anyone new hanging around? Anyone suspicious or who appears out of place?"

"Other than you?"

"And when you next drove your car after July 7th, 1951, did you notice it was parked differently in any way or disturbed in any way?"

"My car wasn't disturbed, but I am. I'm disturbed by a stranger asking a lot of questions while I'm trying to have a drink with my date."

"Are you always this belligerent, ma'am?"

Melvin nodded. "Dude, you're catching her on a *good* day."

The agent wrote something on his pad. "And what is your name, sir?"

"His name is Jedidiah," Sally interjected. "He's my cousin from Alabama."

"I thought you said he was your date?"

"That's right. You have something to say about it? You're not from around here, are you?"

"No, ma'am. I'm from Connecticut."

"Well, Connecticut, before you disparage our customs any further, consider that one way or another, I'm related to everyone in this bar. And everyone in this bar is better armed than you are."

"I think I have what I need. Good day, ma'am."

Once the agent had left, Melvin remarked, "No love lost for the FBI, huh?"

"Those bastards have harassed Daddy and my uncles for as long as I can remember."

"Thank you for not mentioning that I borrowed your car."

"I wasn't going to tell him shit, even if I thought you *were* a communist spy."

"You know I'm not, right?"

"Don't be silly. If I'd thought that, Daddy would've taken you hunting."

177

Chapter 19
Thanksgiving 1951

By November, the Red Scare had faded. Investigations had failed to uncover evidence of espionage in the Wonder state, and Melvin was itching to get back to Maumelle to either check on or destroy his letter. He still couldn't decide which. He was reluctant to drive Sally's dark blue coupe again and wondered when Cole might give her a new one.

It was Thanksgiving Day, November 22nd, 1951, and Sally mandated that Melvin go back to Davis Street after skipping out on Christmas, New Year's, and Easter. As they sped down highway 365, the car made a grinding sound each time she shifted.

"That doesn't sound good," Melvin said. "How old is this car again?"

"Six months. That sound's probably nothing."

"I don't know. Should it already make noises? Maybe you should get a new one."

"You think so? I'll talk to Daddy. I saw the prettiest canary yellow sedan the other day. It was trimmed in wood and just as cute as can be."

"Bright yellow? I don't know. Gray or black might be the way to go. Something that would blend in."

Sally shook her head. "A pretty girl deserves to be noticed. She does *not* want to blend in."

As they turned onto Davis and neared the house, Sally again pulled over a few houses short. "Okay, let's talk before we pull in."

"Oh crap, here we go again. What did you tell them this time? Are we married with children? Do you have kids stashed in the trunk you bribed to play along?"

"Remember last year when I asked you not to be an ass? Momma and Daddy might be under the impression you've been out ring shopping but haven't popped the question."

"Son-of-a-bitch, I knew it."

Sally shrugged. "Half of it is true. You haven't popped the question. And before you get all huffy, you should know I did it for you."

"For me?"

"Well, yeah. We've been dating for over a year now. I didn't want you to appear indecisive."

He shook his finger. "We are not dating."

"You're not getting into the spirit of this, Melvin. Yes, we've been dating for quite some time. You don't want my mother to think you're getting the milk without buying the cow, do you?"

Melvin threw up his arms. "There's been no dating, no milking, no cow. How about this year we try honesty?"

Sally scoffed, "Don't be ridiculous. I just need you to play along. Please? Now, remember, you're about to propose, but I'm not supposed to know anything about it, but I really do. Got it?"

"Am I still a Democrat?"

As she pulled into the driveway, two other cars were there.

"You didn't mention anyone else coming to dinner."

"Those are Michigan plates," she replied in excitement. "My uncles are here!"

Melvin lost his appetite. "You didn't say they were coming."

"I had no idea. How wonderful. You're going to love them."

"Hey, I don't feel so well."

"Relax, you'll be fine. Just agree with whatever they say, don't let them get you alone, and don't make any sudden movements."

Melvin noticed no one was outside to greet them this time. Sally pulled back the screen door and knocked, but no response. As they entered the house, Melvin's head was again assaulted by unvented floor

179

heaters and the noise of four slightly older children running throughout the home with reckless abandon. Stacy lay sprawled out on the couch watching a television twice as large as last year.

"Hey, Stacy," Melvin said. "New TV? That screen is huge. What is that, 17-inch?"

"Yup, they'll never make one bigger. Think fast!" Suddenly a beer was hurled at Melvin's head. With a quick sidestep that exposed Sally to the projectile's path, Melvin simultaneously reached out in front of her face, caught the can, opened it, and brought it to his mouth, all in one smooth motion.

"Damn!" Stacy exclaimed as he sat up. "You're my new hero."

"What the hel—*heck*, Stacy!" Sally shouted. "Throwing that fuc—*full* beer can at my head? Stupid ass—stupid *as* an idiot!"

"Go on, lil' sis," he grinned. "You can say a bad word. I know you want to. I'll bet you want a beer, too. Admit it."

"You don't know anything, and that's your problem."

"Melvin!" Kate exclaimed, giving him a big hug. "We were worried we'd scared you off last time."

"Not at all. I appreciate all the invitations. Life's been busy. Thank you for having me today."

"Well, we're just so happy to see you again!"

"I'm here, too, Momma," Sally said.

"Of course, you are, dear." She gave Sally a partial hug. "And you brought Melvin!"

"Momma, you didn't tell me the uncles would be here."

"Well, dear, they surprised us this morning. Hopefully, we'll have plenty. Did you bring the green bean casserole?"

"Yes, Momma, right here. I've been holding it this whole time."

"Is that my little girl I hear?" a northeastern voice hollered from the kitchen. "Come on in here!"

She handed off the casserole and took Melvin's hand, leading him into the kitchen where her dad and five other men sat at the table.

"There she is! Doll, you're the prettiest thing I've seen since we left Michigan. Give me a hug!"

She hugged all six men and then pushed Melvin in front of her. "Everyone, this is my special guy, Dr. Melvin Napier. Melvin, this is Uncle Jimmy, Uncle Frank, Uncle Jack, Uncle Donnie, and Uncle Larry. And, of course, you already know Daddy."

"This is the guy?" Jimmy asked. "Have a seat, Melvin. Sally, honey, be a doll and grab me a beer. Then we're going to need a moment with your boyfriend. Man talk, you understand."

"Now, Uncle Jimmy, don't do anything to him. I don't exactly have a line of good men knocking at my door, you know."

"Relax, sweetie. Whatever happens is entirely up to him. Ladies, could you please give us the room?"

"The gravy will burn," protested Norma. Kate took her arm and escorted her out.

Melvin sat down to stern looks, including Cole's.

"Sally's our girl, Dr. Napier," Jimmy began.

"Her happiness means more to us than, say, the well-being of other people," added Jack.

"How long have you two been seeing each other?" asked Donnie.

"I've known her for about a year and a half."

"And you haven't asked her to marry you? You think you can just keep getting the milk for free?"

"There's been no milk," Melvin protested, glancing at Cole.

"What's the matter? She's not pretty enough for you?" asked Larry.

"No, she's a beautiful woman."

"You just don't like blondes?" asked Jack.

"I like blondes just fine."

"It's just you like other blondes," Donnie said.

"No, it's not like that."

"You don't like women. Is that it?" asked Larry.

"No, I like women."

181

"So, what's your deal?" asked Jack. "You got a busted pipe?"

"No, I've just been respectful. I've treated her like a lady."

"So, you take her to church and pretend to be her man while you run around behind her back?" Donnie asked.

"No, that's not happening either. I've been faithful."

"Faithful? To a woman you've never *had*?" Larry asked.

"That's right."

"But you want to, right?" Donnie asked.

Melvin glanced at Cole and didn't know how to answer.

"I mean, all things being equal, you'd like nothing better than to bend her over like a shotgun."

Melvin rose with fiery eyes. "That's enough. I don't care who you are. Talk about Sally like that again, and I'll come across this table."

The room fell silent as a bead of sweat ran down Melvin's temple. Finally, the uncles cracked smiles and filled the room with deep-seated laughter.

"Sit down, kid," Frank grinned. "We're just screwing with you. Seriously though, when will you make an honest woman out of our girl?"

Melvin cracked a grin. "You don't think she's honest now?" A thunder of laughter followed.

"Hell, I hope not," Frank said. "With all the dirt she knows, we'd all get the chair. This kid's all right, Jimmy. He's got balls."

"Yeah," added Larry. "He just doesn't know what they're for!"

Once the laughter faded, Melvin said, "Great to meet you guys. I'm going to join Stacy and catch the game."

"No, you're not," Jimmy said in a serious voice. "You're going to sit here and talk plans. Have a cigar. I'm thinking a June wedding in Detroit. We'll take care of everything. What do you think, boys? That'd be alright with you, Cole?"

"Sure, but you fellas all know how Sally gets when you make decisions for her."

Jimmy dismissively waved his hand. "Sally's a good girl. She'll do what she's told. It's time she had a strong man to keep her in line. Melvin's the guy. She's nuts about him, and he's the first man willing to stand up for her. Done and done."

"Lots of advantages being a part of this family, kid," Frank said. "How's that medical license of yours?"

"Just fine, thanks."

"Nice when things work out, isn't it?"

"Speaking of medical, doc," Donnie said, "You ever patch up a gunshot wound?"

"He's just an eye doctor," Cole said.

"A doctor's a doctor," Donnie replied. "You do any plastic surgery?"

"Yes, a little."

"So, if a fella needed a new nose, face, or eye color, you could do that?"

"No. I could fix a droopy eyelid. You'd need a plastic surgeon for what you're describing. And current technology doesn't allow us to change someone's eye color."

"But when you operate, you use a lot of supplies, right?" asked Jack.

"Yes, of course."

"So, who's your supplier?"

"I don't know. The hospital handles all that. I'm sure they have a procurement manager."

"Now we're talking. You could introduce me to this manager?"

"I suppose so. I mean, sure."

Excused from the table, Melvin quickly headed into the living room while the women rushed back into the kitchen to remake the gravy.

Sally jerked him into the hallway. "You okay? I didn't hear anything, and then I heard laughter. When I didn't hear anything else,

I was afraid they'd taken you to the garage. Let me see your hands. Good, nothing missing. They left everything alone down *there*, right?"

Melvin's eyes widened. "Yeah, everything's intact."

"Oh, thank goodness! I know Momma's keen on another grandbaby, so I didn't think Daddy would let them do anything permanent. Were you scared?"

Melvin shook his head. "Not until now. What the hell have you gotten me into?"

"Nothing, it's all fine. I just worry about the little things."

"Little things?"

"I didn't mean it that way. I mean, you're not. At least, I don't think so." She put up her hands. "Not that it would be a problem if you were. It's just that at the cabin last year, it felt—adequate."

"Adequate?"

"I mean more than adequate. I mean, I really can't say. You'd think after seventeen months I'd be able to sketch that thing out like a street artist."

"Feel free to stop talking."

"I'm just glad you're okay." She leaned in and hugged him tightly. Melvin could tell the hug included tactile reconnaissance.

"Hey, get a room!" came a voice from the couch.

"Get a brain!" Sally retorted.

Finally able to sit in the living room out of harm's way, Melvin glanced at Sally, sitting on the ottoman beside him. June was only seven months away.

"Go, go, go! Yeah, man!" yelled Stacy.

"You're rooting for the team playing Detroit?" Melvin asked.

"They're called the Packers, dipshit."

"Don't talk to Melvin that way."

"He's dating *you*, isn't he? If the shoe fits . . ."

"Oh yeah, I've heard of the Packers," Melvin proudly announced. "Aren't they good this year?"

"They're three and six, *genius*. Happy, Sally?"

"I heard they had a great quarterback," Melvin said.

"Rote's having a great game *today*. Already threw a touchdown and rushed one in. And it's only the first quarter."

Melvin nodded. "And those are good things, right?"

"Good for me. It's fourteen to ten, baby. I got a C note riding on them. Screw the Lions. It's finally my day!"

Cole emerged from the kitchen. "You want to give me the twenty now?"

"Daddy!" exclaimed Sally, "You didn't bet on Melvin showing up, did you? I told you he was coming. I told you like a month ago."

Melvin's brow furrowed. "You just invited me last week."

Sally put her hand on his arm. "Hush, Melvin. Not everything is about you."

"No, sweetheart," Cole replied. "Out of respect, we didn't bet on your boyfriend this year."

Stacy winked. "He didn't get the odds he wanted."

"Shut up, boy. Today's wager is all football. Your brother took Green Bay for some reason. Son, do you have twenty to lose this month? Detroit's got Doak Walker and Leon Hart, who's over 250 pounds."

Sally folded her arms. "Stupid also bet a hundred with the guys downtown."

"Stop being a rat, Sally. Yes, yes—yes!" he yelled, spilling beer as Rote connected a 48-yard pass to Dom Moselle for Green Bay's third touchdown. "Who's stupid *now*?"

"You are," Sally replied. "Betting money you don't have. What are you going to do if you lose, genius?"

"You're just a girl and don't know diddly. I got the Packers and fourteen points. I *can't* lose."

A voice arose from the kitchen. "Cole, did I just hear your boy bet against Detroit?"

"Just a friendly wager, Jimmy," Cole hollered back. "Nothing personal."

"Lots of money on that game," the kitchen voice warned. "No way the Lions don't make the spread. You should have taught your son better."

A few minutes later, Detroit responded with a 33-yard touchdown pass to Leon Hart, narrowing the gap to 21-17. Cole shook his head and got up to attend to his guests in the kitchen. "Lot of football left, son. I want my twenty before you pay those yahoos downtown."

"We'll see who's paying who, Daddy."

As soon as Cole left the room, Sally snipped, "It's whom, idiot. Who's paying *whom*?"

"You know, you're just a ring-tailed bitch. What the hell's the matter with you, Melvin? Don't they have women up in Canada? You got to come down here and settle for our leftovers?"

Melvin looked down and bit his lip as Sally's Why-the-hell-aren't-you-defending-me stare burned into the back of his skull. "Uh, nobody like your sister up in Canada. She's one of a kind."

"Well, you're right about that," Stacy conceded. "If there were two of them, I'd just shoot myself. Well, son-of-a-*bitch*!" he shouted as Detroit scored again off a fumble.

Laughter came from the kitchen, followed by, "Hey Stacy, next time you want to make a bet, call me first. I'll take your money."

Kate called for everyone to eat and directed Melvin to the main table, where all eight men sat while the women joined the children around the card table in the corner. After Cole asked the blessing over the bountiful spread, Melvin glanced over at Sally. She appeared entirely accepting of her seat and chatted with Kate and Norma while they fussed over the boys.

"So, Dr. Napier," Larry began, "ever kill a man?"

Melvin choked on his food. "Excuse me? No, of course not."

"You operate, and anything could happen. Things happen, right, Cole?"

"Yeah, Larry, things happen."

"No, no one's ever died during my surgeries. Why?"

"Just asking. Never know."

"Let the man eat, Larry," Jimmy admonished. "He's got things to do and a question to ask. He'll need his strength for what comes after." The five uncles chuckled as one made a corresponding hand gesture. Cole and Melvin sat uncomfortably, drinking their beer, careful not to lock eyes. In a buzzed tone, Stacy asked, "What're ya'll talking about?"

"Just eat, boy," his father directed.

Motivated now more than ever to get the hell out of 1951, Melvin angled for a new ride for Sally. "Cole, did Sally tell you about the noises her car's been making? I'm worried she might get stranded."

"What do you have her in?" Frank asked in a concerned voice.

Cole continued to look at his food. "She's in a coupe from the March shipment."

"The *March* shipment? Aw, Cole, you can't have her drive around in that. Doc's right. Those cars are a piece of shit. Give her one out of the September batch. Those are premium."

"Cole," Melvin said, "I didn't mean your cars were faulty. I—"

"He's looking out for your daughter's welfare like *you* should, Cole. The March shipment. Are you dense? What were you thinking?"

"Yeah, sure, Frank, I'll look at what I've got left from the Septembers."

"Give her a nice big sedan. She'll need it to haul kids around. What color do you like, sweetheart?"

"My car's fine, Uncle Frank," Sally replied from the kid's table. "Even if I broke down, I can take care of myself."

"Girl, I asked you a question. What color?"

"I like yellow."

"I don't think any yellow sedans came in that batch," Cole stated, the tension in his voice rising.

"Not a problem. Donnie here will bring down a nice yellow sedan next week. Right, Donnie?"

Donnie sighed. "Yeah, Frank. No problem."

After pie and more cigars, Melvin signaled Sally it was time to leave. He shook everyone's hand, politely declined an invitation to go duck hunting in the morning, and made tracks for the door.

"Good night, Stacy," Melvin said.

Stacy followed him outside and down to the car. "Damn Lions. Who knew they would come back and beat the spread? Hey man, I'm in a little jam here. Can you float me a hundred? Or maybe just fifty?"

"No, he can't!" Sally said from the porch. "You made your bed of sh—poop, now lay in it."

Careful not to let Stacy see, Sally turned and slipped an envelope into Norma's pocket. Norma shook her head and handed it back, whispering, "I can't take this."

Sally whispered back, "It's not for you. It's for my nephews, for Christmas. Hide it in the Bible. He'll never find it there." The two women hugged, and Melvin opened the passenger side door to get in. Quick as a rabbit, Sally slipped around him and sat down first. Confused, Melvin closed her door and went around to the driver's side.

"Look at that, Cole," pointed Frank. "Opening the door for our little girl. The kid's got class. It'll be useful to have a doctor in the family. We've got plans for Melvin Napier."

Chapter 20
Back Across the River

Once on the road, Sally reached into her tiny purse and pulled out her wallet, a pack of cigarettes, a lighter, and a half-empty bottle of cinnamon schnapps. She took a long, satisfying swig.

"What is that, a TARDIS purse?"

She shook her head as she lit her cigarette. "No, J.C. Penny. TARDIS, I think I've heard of them. Are they based out of Québec?"

"No, Gallifrey."

"Oh, that's right. I've thumbed through their catalog. Adorable stuff."

"I'll let The Doctor know you like it."

"You say the oddest things. Speaking of odd, I'm sorry about the way my uncles behaved. They can be downright pushy, but tonight was over the top. They've never treated Daddy like a lackey. Something's going on. And no matter what they said, you don't have to marry me." She paused dramatically, taking a long drag off her cigarette, gauging his response. Melvin said not a word. "*Obviously*," she was forced to continue, "I would never marry you or anybody at the point of a gun. I just can't believe how they acted."

"Yeah, pretty hardcore," he said. "Like something out of the Godfather."

"Whose godfather?" she asked, lighting her next cigarette.

"Famous Canadian movie. You'll see it one day. Could you crack your window?"

"Well, again, I'm sorry for all that." She pulled a flask of whiskey from her purse. "I appreciate you going today."

"That's what friends do. I'm still a little hungry. Got a ham sandwich in there?"

189

Melvin paced the floor of his loft at 2 A.M. that morning. *Marry her or get murdered. I do care for Sally.* He shook his head. *Next, they'd demand children. As soon as we had kids, I'd figure out a way home. Then I'm the father who ran out on his kids if I leave, or I'm the father who doesn't go back for his kids if I stay.* Melvin sighed. *I need a vasectomy.* His eyebrow shot up. *Words you thought you'd never say.*

He continued to pace. *I just have to get out before the wedding. That starts by getting back across the river. I can't believe she wants a damn yellow car. Why not put up a flashing neon sign that says, Look at me! I'm trespassing on military property. Please shoot.* He sighed again. *Even when I make it to Maumelle, I don't know what to do once I get there.*

Melvin took a deep breath. *What's important is that the boys have a father who loves them, even if it's another version of me. Destroying the letter is off the table.* He glanced at his loft. Nothing changed with his decision. *Okay, so now either Alexis got the letter, and I'm stuck in the old timeline, or she never gets it. If she doesn't, it's not because I destroy it. So, we're back to square one. Either I buried it in the wrong spot or depth, or it decomposes. I need to dig it up, check it and rebury it. Wait, I buried it almost five months ago. It might take some digging to find. The longer I'm there, the more likely I'm seen. A lot of disturbed ground could draw attention. That could lead to someone else finding it. Maybe the only way this works is not to dig it up.*

With no sleep in sight, Melvin put on a pot of coffee. *The intelligent thing would be to bury a second letter in a different spot at a different depth. That would be quicker and would double our chances. All I need now is for Donnie to deliver Sally's new lemon.*

Unfortunately, Uncle Donnie was a no-show. By mid-December, Melvin's patience had grown thin. "Sally, it's been almost three weeks. What happened to your uncle and the new car?"

She shrugged. "Sometimes their talk is just talk. When I was seven, they swore they'd buy me a pony for my birthday. Momma threw a fit, and Daddy tried to talk them out of it, but Uncle Jimmy insisted he'd have guys come down and build a fence around our backyard with a little stable. I cried for days when no one came. So, I can't say I'm surprised. It doesn't matter. There's nothing wrong with the one I have, especially since they fixed the transmission last week."

Melvin's shoulders slumped. Then his head snapped up. *Maybe their wedding talk was bullshit, too.*

By the weekend of the 15th, Melvin rolled the dice and borrowed her blue coupe again. With Christmas only ten days away, surely people had better things to do than worry about the spread of Communism in central Arkansas.

Just before sunrise that Saturday morning, he used the spare key Sally had given him and slipped into her loft. She'd given it in the event she locked herself out or if he needed to swing by late one evening—you just never know. He carefully lifted her car keys off the table, knowing she wouldn't arouse until the crack of ten. He paused. *What am I doing? Breaking and entering, theft—is that who I am now?* He quietly left, careful not to jingle the keys. *If she knew, she'd ask questions, and I'd have to lie. This way is more honest. I'll be back before she's up. And if the FBI comes around again, she can honestly deny knowing anyone used her car.* Soon, the three of them: Melvin, Sally's car, and Melvin's rationalization, were crossing the Main Street bridge on their way to Maumelle.

He pulled off the road into the woods on an old horse trail about a quarter-mile past where he'd stopped in July. The dense pines made it a decent hiding place from nosey neighbors in light green pickups. He could see his breath in the morning air as he hiked the quarter-mile back parallel to the road, staying hidden just inside the tree line. He scanned for cars in either direction and scampered across. The heavy coat Sally had bought him ripped as he hastily climbed through the barbwire fence. He rubbed his hands for warmth and disappeared into the dense woods.

He reached his backyard with his shovel, garbage bag, and sealed canister that protected his new letter. He carefully chose a spot in the yard. Despite all his planning, the master-thief-doctor-communist-spy had failed to consider one detail. Digging in the rocky soil of the Arkansas mountainside was hard enough during the summer. Digging here with temperatures below freezing was next to impossible. He recited every swear word he'd ever heard Sally say as his shovel barely penetrated the frost on the rock-hard ground.

Melvin cussed his way back to the car. Still angry when he arrived back at the Adams-Napier building around 9 A.M., he stomped up the stairs with his equipment a little too loudly. He'd only made it halfway up when Sally appeared.

"Did you take my car?"

"Uh, yeah. Had an errand to run this morning."

"What errand? What's with the shovel? What do you have behind your back?"

"I, uh, got this for you, for your garden. I was hoping you wouldn't see it yet. It was going to be a surprise. This other stuff is nothing."

"It doesn't look new. You bought it used?"

"Why not? It's a shovel. They don't go bad. You're up awfully early for a Saturday."

"I need my car. I needed it an *hour* ago. I thought someone had stolen it. I can't believe you took it without asking. You're lucky I didn't call the police."

"You gave me a key," he countered as he ascended the stairs, concealing the bag and ammunition box.

"A key to my loft, not my *car*, asshole."

"What's with the language? Why are you mad? We agreed last Thanksgiving I could borrow it anytime."

"Any time you *asked*."

Melvin cracked open his door, quickly tossed the ammo box and bag inside, and closed it.

"You tore your jacket!" she exclaimed. "How did that happen?"

Melvin shrugged. "I don't know. It's no big deal."

"No big *deal*? Do you know how long I saved up to buy that? I'm not some rich doctor who, by the way, helps himself to my food and liquor. And after two years, the first gift you buy me is a dirty-ass shovel that's been who knows where?"

"It's the thought that counts?"

"Give me my keys. Buy your own damn car. And give me back the key to my loft, too."

"Hey, I'm sorry I borrowed it without asking. I didn't think you'd care."

"You didn't *think*. That's your problem. You never think about anyone but yourself." She locked her door and stormed downstairs.

"Sally, I said I was sorry. Where are you going, anyway? Why do you have a suitcase?"

"Don't worry about it, *Melvin*. Don't give it a second thought. That's what you're good at, right? And while you're at it, why don't you take that shovel and stick it up your ass?"

"Well, that's not sound medical advice. First off, you could get a staph infection or a perforated bowel. Not to mention—*Sally*, wait! I'm joking. Don't go away ma—geez, she's in a mood this morning."

A voice from outside the building shouted, "I'm not in a mood, asshole!"

Melvin watched her pull away, slinging gravel as she went.

He intended to spend the day on research but worked on his apology instead. Settling on cooking for her, he hoped his limited kitchen skills would be enough of a gesture. Around seven, he knocked at her door, but she didn't answer. He called out to her, but she didn't respond. Thankful caller ID wasn't a thing yet, he phoned her loft, but she didn't pick up. By eight, he sat with fresh flowers on his table and had dinner with far too many leftovers.

When she didn't answer the next day, Melvin got the message loud and clear. As he lay in bed Sunday night, he stared at the ceiling. *No telling what's getting filed in the trash tomorrow. And ain't nobody getting a follow-up appointment. Who knew borrowing her keys without permission would piss her off this much?*

The next morning, she didn't come downstairs for work.

"Hey, Ronny," Melvin asked, "is Sally sleeping in today?"

"As a rule, I never turn down an opportunity to make a lewd joke about Sally in bed, but not today. Dr. Thomas said she left Saturday morning for a family emergency. Surprised you didn't know."

"Guess I was too busy being a jerk. We're not on the best terms right now."

Ronny grinned. "Trouble in paradise?"

"Something like that. Did she say who it was?"

"No, just that she'd be out for a while. Hey, have you seen Annette, the new temp girl? She's a total fox. I'm going to ask her to dinner, probably after lunch or maybe at the end of the day."

"Not for dinner with your mother, though, right?"

"What's wrong with that?"

Melvin shrugged. "Nothing, man. What do I know about women? Go for it."

After seeing his first patient, Melvin escorted her to check out. He was writing in her chart as they walked. "20/20 OU, emmetropia, ortho, slit lamp, posterior pole WNL."

"Here you go, Miss Cravits. I'm sorry—*Susie*. Our receptionist will make you an appointment for next year. Now, we'll dilate your eyes next time, so you'll need to go by the pharmacy three days ahead and pick up the drops. And thanks again for the offer, but unfortunately, I already have plans for the weekend. Perhaps another time." Noticing the new receptionist, Melvin said, "You must be Annette. Welcome. You look familiar. Have we met?"

"Uh, huh," she smacked her gum and smiled as she stared at him.

"Miss Cravits needs an appointment to return in one year. Can you do that for her?"

"Uh, huh."

"Well, okay, then. Carry on . . . I guess?"

"Uh, huh." Annette watched Melvin disappear around the corner.

"Excuse me," Susie said. "I'd like something around the first of next December. Could that be on a Friday?"

"Uh, huh," Annette replied. "I agree. He's a looker, alright."

With Sally gone, no car, and the frozen ground preventing anything from getting buried, Melvin turned his attention back to locating the crash site. He sat in the library on Saturday and searched back issues of the newspaper, looking for any reports of plane wreckage around the date of his arrival, but no luck. He considered a low-altitude flight along the curve to look for wreckage but decided to save his cash for warmer weather and a chance for storms. Melvin Napier was stuck until spring.

1952

Chapter 21
The Second Letter

I t was **Monday, March 31st, 1952**—three months, two weeks, and three days since Sally had left, not that he was counting. For the past three and a half months, no one had cussed at him, cooked for him, blew cigarette smoke in his face, called him a woman, or demanded he go on a picnic. There had been no banter trying to get follow-up appointments for his patients. The only words Annette seemed to know were "uh-huh" unless you were Ronny. For him, the answer was "No," and sometimes, "Hell, no." Melvin collected Sally's mail and had Ronny drive him to Conway. The Davis dealership had closed, and no one was home on Davis Street. From the unkempt lawn and flowerbeds, no one had been home in some time.

Although he'd sworn he wouldn't, Melvin had chartered two fruitless low-altitude flights searching for plane wreckage over the last three months. With the rise in temperature and the ground softening, he chomped at the bit to get back to Maumelle with his second letter. He considered buying a car but feared trying to get a driver's license without an ID, or a license plate, for that matter. Plus, having one car increased his chances of being identified. *If Sally were here, she'd be on her second new car since Thanksgiving.* But Sally wasn't here. For all he knew, she might never be.

Melvin sat in his office, tapping his desk with his fountain pen. *Ronny's car's in Cabot every weekend, and there's no way John allows anyone behind the wheel of his baby.* He rubbed his chin. *Annette has a car.* He casually approached her desk. "Oh, hey, Annette. Listen, I have an errand to do this weekend. Yeah, it's pretty important."

"Uh, huh."

"Do you think I might be able to borrow your car?"

197

"Uh, huh."

"Really? That's great. I appreciate it. Could I come by your place and pick it up early on Saturday?"

Her eyes widened. "You want to take me out?"

"No, I meant to pick up your car. Unless you'd rather meet somewhere else."

"You want to meet? At my place? This weekend?"

"Yeah, to pick up your car."

"Uh, huh."

"I only need to borrow it for a little while. Then I'll fill it with gas and bring it back to you. How does that sound?"

A smile spread across her face as she leaned forward. "That just sounds wonderful. Where are you taking me?"

"No, I just need to do an errand. It's doctor stuff."

"Uh, huh," she nodded. "You want me ready when?"

"Saturday morning at eight. You don't have to get ready or do any special. I'm just picking up the car."

"Uh, huh. Wear something special—got it. I can't wait."

"That's not what I . . ." he sighed. "Where do you live? Or you could pick me up, and then I could drop you off?"

"Uh, huh. You want to pick me up? Sure. What kind of car do you drive? Is it a convertible?"

"I don't have a car, Annette."

"Uh, huh. Oh, that's a drag. Hey, how about I pick you up instead?"

"There's an idea. How about you pick me up at eight Saturday morning?"

"Uh, huh. Hey, where do you live?"

"I live here, Annette. Haven't you noticed me coming down the stairs every morning?"

She winked. "Uh, huh, I've noticed you, alright."

"How about bringing your car to the office Saturday morning around eight? Would that work?"

"Uh, huh. You know, I've never been on a morning date before. Is that how they do it in your country?"

Melvin nodded. "Uh, huh."

As he finished his Monday afternoon clinic, Melvin's spirits rose. He wasn't sure how to handle Annette on Saturday, but that was a future problem. Today there was hope. After scheduling a follow-up for his last patient, Annette waved goodbye and said she couldn't wait for the weekend. Melvin headed back to his office, where he found Ronny seated behind the desk, glaring at him.

"Why are you in my chair, Ronny?"

"*Your* chair? Maybe it's mine. Maybe I'll just take what I want."

"It's no different than the one in the optical shop. You want to swap?"

"Do I want to *swap*? You son-of-a-bitch!"

"Excuse me?"

Ronny folded his arms. "I'm sorry. I meant to say, you *damn*, son-of-a-bitch. Going after my girl? *My* girl? Everything that walks in here wants to bear your children, and you go after the one woman you *can't* have? What kind of sick son-of-a-bitch are you? And you asked her out today just to beat me to the punch? Who the hell does that?"

"You talked to Annette?"

"Annette told me, Dr. Thomas, the patients, hell, I heard her outside telling the lamp post you two were going out. I thought we were friends. Well, pal, now it's on. When Sally gets back, I'm taking her from you, and there's not a damn thing you can do about it. You have no idea who you're messing with."

"Okay, let me point out six things wrong with everything you just said." Melvin held up a finger. "One, I didn't ask Annette out. I asked to borrow her *car*. She made it out to be a date. It's *not*. Two, even if I had, she's not your girl. You've asked her out how many times? Eight?"

"Twelve and a half. She's warming up to the idea."

"For three and a half months? Glaciers warm faster. Three, Sally's not my girl. If you want to take her out, go ahead. Also, you and I *are* friends, and that's not going to change. So, you're wrong about that, too. Finally, I didn't ask her out to beat you to the punch because A: she's already turned you down twelve times—"

"Twelve and a half."

"And B: I *never asked her out in the first place.* Got it?"

"No, I don't. You said six things. I only counted five."

"And you're ugly, too."

A grin broke out on Ronny's face. "Well, that's just inaccurate at face value. I'm quite the looker."

Melvin stroked his chin. "You are a looker, aren't you?"

"Uh, we're still talking about the ladies, right? You're making me nervous."

"I've got a proposition for you, Ronny."

"That's not making me any less nervous."

"Well, you're going to like this."

"That's what the last guy said."

"Just be here with your car at 7:30 Saturday morning and wear something nice. You're going on a date."

"Uh, huh. Where are we going?"

"It's with *Annette*, Ronny. You're going on a date with Annette."

"Oh, yeah, even better. Cool. Wait—she's expecting you."

"Tell her I got called away on a medical emergency, and you drove all the way here so she wouldn't have to be alone. She'll love it."

"Cool, cool. Wait—what'll I do then?"

"You take her to breakfast, walk in the park, whatever you normally do on a date."

"Oh, yeah, right, of course. I'll just, uh, do what I would normally do on a date. And what are you going to do?"

"I'm going to borrow your car and run an errand."

"Cool, cool. And when do I need to have her back here?"

"You're adults, Ronny. Whenever you guys want. You've got this."

"I've got this. Thanks, Melvin!"

Rejuvenated by the prospect of transportation, Melvin rewrote the second letter.

Dear Alexis,

I don't know if you're reading this letter first or second, but I buried the first one six paces East of the boulders in our backyard. East is toward the Meller house. If this is the first one you've found, then I need to explain. On my birthday in 2004, my plane crashed, and I awoke in Little Rock in 1950. I've been here for two years, trying to find a way home. I tried to contact you through your favorite movie by playing the ophthalmologist. I also took out an ad in the paper with our names, which I buried in the other box. I'm still searching for where I crashed to see if being in the air there will send me back home. But after two years, hope is dwindling. But you can still save me. If you find this before I leave, you must stop me. I miss you and the boys terribly and will do everything possible to get home. I love you more than you know. ~~But if I don't make it back, I want you~~ If something happens and this doesn't reach you in time, know I will survive the years and deliver this message myself. So, if you open our door one day and find an old man on the other side, please don't turn me away.

I will love you always,

Melvin

April 1st, 1952

When Saturday arrived, Ronny knocked at his door at 7:30. "Impressive, Ronny, right on time."

"Not really. I've been downstairs waiting for an hour. I don't have any fingernails left. I'm as nervous as a squirrel in church."

Melvin's eyes narrowed. "You mean a whore."

"Who's a whore?"

"That's the saying, as nervous as a whore in church. Not one of my favorites."

"No, it's a squirrel in church. Grandma used to say it all the time."

"That makes no sense. Why would a squirrel be nervous in church?"

"*Hello*, he could get stepped on. It makes no sense for a whore to be nervous."

"It's the point of the saying."

"Maybe in Canada, but not down here." Ronny bit his fingernails. "Man, I'm about as nervous as a deer in a room full of rocking chairs."

Melvin closed his eyes. "Not a deer. I'm officially done with this conversation."

Ronny's eyes lit up. "Hey, how about you come with us? That'd be fun. And when things start to steam up, I'll slip you the high sign, and you scram?"

"What are we, thirteen? The whole premise is that I got called away, and you're stepping in. You've got no reason to be nervous. You're just going on a date with someone fifteen years too young for you, way out of your league, and expecting someone else. What could go wrong?"

"You're an asshole, Melvin. When people don't call you an asshole, they're just being nice."

"Aw, Ronny, I'm just teasing you—mostly."

"Jerk. Still, no one's ever gone to the trouble to set me up before. I appreciate it. What's with all the gear?"

"Science experiment."

"What does a shovel, pickaxe, and ammunition box have to do with science? Why does a guy who lives in a loft even own a pickaxe?"

"You'd be surprised. Now, don't worry about Annette. I'm going to help you. Let me see those pictures of your dog."

"Great idea. It's always an icebreaker. I've got two new ones. Here's Ringo wearing a sweater Momma knitted for him. I picked out this particular pattern because—hey! What are you doing?"

"Getting rid of them. You can have them back on Monday. No pictures or talking about the dog or Momma or your living situation. Got it? Don't tell her stories about growing up, your favorite cousin, your pickle jar collection, or any of that crap."

"Well dang, Melvin, what the hell am I supposed to talk about?"

"You ask about *her*. Find out who she is, what she likes, where she's traveled. Be interested. Understand?"

"I guess. I wasn't going to mention the pickle jars, anyway. Not on a first date. You've got to keep a little mystery in the romance. Can I at least show her a picture of Mr. Pecker?"

Melvin clasped his hands and looked to the Heavens. "Dear Lord, *please* let that be a pet rabbit, squirrel, or chicken."

Ronny put his hands on his hips. "Ha-ha. You think you're so funny."

"Ronny?"

"Okay, he's a chicken. But he's cute as a button. When he hightails it around the coop, he does this thing with his head—"

"Ronny?"

"Yeah?"

"Hand me the clucking picture. Now, give me your keys. You look good, man. Just smile and let her do most of the talking. Oh, and have fun!"

He hopped in Ronny's car and pulled away, convincing himself this was the push Ronny needed. *Maybe it works out, or she rejects him, and he's forced to move on.* Either way, Melvin needed to get home.

He hid the car in the woods as he'd done a few months before and hiked until he was back in his future backyard. He pushed brush and saplings aside and selected his new spot. The pickaxe made short work of the hole. Lowering the wrapped ammo box down, he filled it in and carefully covered the area in pine straw.

Upon finishing, he felt pressure in his stomach. *This is it! I'm going home.* The sensation grew. He closed his eyes and tightened his body for whatever came next. As he crouched, he thought of Alexis, the boys, and all he'd been through over the last two years, all he'd missed at home. *The boys might be older now. Will I even recognize them?* The pressure in his stomach turned to outright pain. He clenched his fists. Then, all at once—a thunderous roar. Melvin passed gas.

The pain was gone. He shook his head with a smirk. The alteration of time was nothing more than last night's pinto beans and cornbread. The universe's warped sense of humor had slapped him once more. It wasn't the only thing hitting him. *Damn,* he thought, fanning the air around him, *was there cheese in that cornbread?*

Melvin turned to head down the hill when a gunshot rang out, exploding tree bark near his head. He hit the deck and held dead still as a warm sensation oozed down his neck. Silently reaching up, he pulled back a bloody hand. Applying pressure, he crawled under thick brush using his other hand.

A pair of boots rapidly crunched toward him through the forest. "Aw, man! Don't be dead, don't be dead, p-l-e-a-s-e don't be dead. I can't go through this again." The boots kicked Melvin's leg. "Hey, mister, you okay? Please don't be dead."

"Are you planning on shooting me again?"

"No, sir! I'm awfully sorry. Are you hurt bad?"

"Can safely say I've been worse, but you got my neck." Melvin crawled out and stood face to face with a wide-eyed kid in overalls looking not much more than nineteen. "No worries, kid," Melvin said. "You just nicked me, is all. The bleeding has almost stopped. See?" The boy's eyes rolled up, and he was out, hitting the ground hard before Melvin could catch him. Melvin secured his weapon, then propped the kid's head up and elevated his feet.

The young man slowly opened his eyes. "What happened?"

"You fainted. It's no big deal. What are you doing out here?"

"I'm deer hunting."

"In April? Is it deer season?"

"Well, yeah. I mean, it is, right?"

"Don't ask me. Never hunted anything but Pop-Tarts. So, you're hunting, but can't stand the sight of blood?"

"I ain't much of a hunter. What are Pop-Tarts?"

"Pure goodness wrapped in foil. So, if you're not a hunter, what are you doing in the woods with a gun?"

"Trying to learn. My daddy and my brothers hunt, even my little sister. They all call me sissy because I don't. I used to when I was little. Shot a squirrel right out of a tree with my 410 when I was eight. Then I threw up. Never hunted again till now. Thought if I could bring home a deer, they'd leave me alone. I've been out here since dawn. Ain't seen nothing till I heard a buck rutting—pretty loud, too. Then I saw movement and fired, but it was you. I'm awfully sorry for shooting you. You going to have me thrown in jail?"

Melvin rechecked his flatulence-related near gunshot wound and mentally crossed brown beans off the menu. "No, kid. Honest mistake. I should've been wearing orange."

"Did you see the deer? He was rutting pretty loud."

"No, but I heard him. I'm sure he's long gone."

The boy eyed him. "If you're not hunting, what are *you* doing in these woods, mister? It's not safe, you know."

Melvin pointed to his neck. "Your point is well made."

"No, I mean a Commy spy's been spotted around these parts. And they ain't never caught him. At least I come out with a rifle. All you brought was a shovel and a pickaxe. What are you doing anyway?"

"It's for my job."

205

"You get paid to wander out in the woods? What do you do?"

"I'm an Ophtha . . . archaeologist." Melvin put his hands on his hips. "Yup, I'm an adventurer. In fact, I'm a professor of Archaeology. My name is Dr. Jones, from the University of *Indiana*."

"I'm Clyde, from the town of Levy. I ain't never met an adventurer. What's an Ophtha-archaeologist?"

"You can just say, archaeologist. The other is an old French pronunciation. Archaeology is the study of the past, which I'm becoming more of an expert in every day."

"Well, what are you doing here? Ain't nothing around these parts."

"You couldn't be more wrong, Clyde. For centuries, the land around the Arkansas River was home to several Native American tribes."

Clyde's eyes widened. "You don't say. What's a Native American?"

"Indians."

"Oh. Why do you care about them?"

"Because Clyde, if we don't preserve our history and learn from the past, we're destined to repeat our mistakes."

"Wow, that's deep, Professor Jones. I want to learn about the past. Hey, want to see a burial ground I found after it rained hard?"

Melvin put on his superhero voice. "Sorry, Clyde, but my time here is up. I have to return to the university and tend to my neck. But you go ahead. And while you're at it, take a trip to your local library. You'll find a whole host of adventures right there in books." Melvin considered finishing with a School House Rock jingle but held off. He'd blown Clyde's mind enough for one day.

As Melvin drove home, his thoughts turned to Ronny. *Maybe it all worked out for him.* He shook his head. *No, it didn't. I'm such an asshole.*

Back at the Adams-Napier building, Melvin got supplies from the clinic and tended to his neck. Neither Ronny nor Annette were there. *Geez, I hope she didn't dump him somewhere miles away and make him walk back. I'm never going to hear the end of this.*

206

Evening came and went, and no Ronny. By Sunday morning, Ronny's car was still parked in the alley. Melvin fired it up and searched the downtown area without a clue where they could be. *Should I call his mother?* He shook his head. *He's a forty-year-old man. I am not calling his momma.* He parked back in the alley and hoped for the best.

The next morning, Melvin found Ronny whistling in the optical shop.

"You're in a good mood."

"Sure am," Ronny replied in a deep voice.

"Are those the same clothes you had on Saturday?"

"Sure are."

"What's with the Barry White voice?"

"Whatever, man."

"Well, are you going to tell me all about it?"

"Nope."

"Okay, dog, play it cool. Here are your photos back."

"Keep 'em."

"What?"

Ronny kept working. "Keep 'em, toss 'em—don't care."

"What about your car keys? Want those back?"

"For sure, daddy-o."

Melvin shook his head and walked back to clinic. "Oh, hey, Annette. Sorry I wasn't around Saturday. Medical emergency."

"Uh-huh."

"Did you have a good weekend?"

"Uh-huh. Like my new necklace? Ronny bought it for me."

"It's nice. So, you two had a good time?"

"Uh-huh."

"Okay, then. Good talking to you, Annette."

Chapter 22
Reunion

Three months later, Melvin got a knock at his loft's door. She was standing there, as beautiful as ever.

"Shit," he whispered as he grabbed and kissed her. Sally's eyes widened, then closed as she wrapped her arms around him. He stopped and backed up. She slowly opened her eyes and smiled. "I should leave more often."

"Yeah, sorry about that."

"My lips aren't. Always knew you'd be a good kisser."

"I'm sorry I ran you off. I didn't mean anything by borrowing your car."

"Oh, sweetie, I didn't leave because of you. You worried all this time you were the reason? Poor baby!" She reached for another kiss, but he pushed her back and wiped lipstick from his mouth. "Then, where the hell have you been for the past six and a half months? No calls, no letters? I even went to Conway looking for you!"

"You went all the way to Conway for me?"

He frowned. "Wasn't that far. Your whole family disappeared."

Tears welled up in her eyes. "They're gone."

His expression softened. "What do you mean?"

"Daddy, Stacy, all my uncles. They were murdered." She wiped her eyes.

He put an arm around her. "Come inside. Tell me everything."

Sniffling, she looked around as she sat down next to him. "Wow, you kiss me, and next thing I know, you've got me on your couch. Just what are your intentions, Dr. Napier? I wouldn't want a reputation."

"I'd say that horse has already left the barn."

"I'd pretend to be offended, but who are we kidding? You know, I haven't been in here since—"

"Since you broke in last year?"

"You need to stop saying that. No, what I meant was, I haven't been in here since before you moved in. This was our storage room, you know."

"Uh-huh." Melvin took her hand. "Sally, what happened to your family? Where have you been?"

Her tears returned. "You remember when Uncle Donnie never showed up with that new car?"

"You said that was typical."

"Yeah, but when Daddy called about it, he couldn't get a hold of them, so he took a trip up there. Come to find out that all of my uncles had mysteriously disappeared. Daddy was worried we'd be next, so we ran. I couldn't tell you for your own good."

"Holy crap. Where did you go?"

"Up to a little town in Missouri just north of Mammoth Spring. Daddy came across a little cabin out in the woods to rent. He and Stacy hunted and fished while Momma, Norma, and I cared for the kids. We only went into town once a month for groceries and didn't talk to anyone. We couldn't call or send letters. I wanted to call you so badly, but we couldn't risk it. Did anyone come around looking?"

"No. Well, maybe. There was a dark green sedan parked across the street for a couple of weeks. I thought they were visiting someone. No one ever came inside or asked about you."

"Good. I was worried about you.

"So, what happened?"

"St. Louis Cardinals."

"Birds?"

"No, sweetheart, baseball. We were fine for months, and no one bothered us. Well, no one but each other. It was a tiny cabin. Just the thought of having my own bathroom again is simply heaven. By the way, I don't *ever* want children. And don't even get me started on my mother."

"What does that have to do with baseball?"

"Dipshit slipped away to town one day, got drunk, and called his bookie. Had to gamble. Ever wonder how much your life is worth? Our family was worth fifty bucks on the Cards. They'd already found us by the time we figured out what he'd done. Daddy and Stacy shot at them from the cabin while we slipped out back with the kids and hid in the woods. We didn't even get to say goodbye."

"So, Stacy stepped up?"

"My brother was a dumbass, but no coward. When the gunfire stopped, we smelled smoke. That's when we knew. We heard them come for us next, stomping through the brush. We put our hands over the boys' mouths and didn't breathe. We lay in those woods all night, brushing off spiders and bugs, trying to stay quiet, trying not to cry. It was the longest night of my life. Everything was burned when we came out the next morning, even our car."

"Damn. Aren't you scared they'll come back?"

"Women and children aren't worth their time. Sure, they would've killed us that day out of convenience, but as long as we keep our heads down and mouths shut, Momma says we'll be fine."

"Where is she now?"

"Back home in Conway, weeding her flower beds like nothing happened. Norma and the boys left last night for New Mexico. She's got family out there. We're putting the dealership up for sale. We each took one new car off the lot—my last one." Sally began to cry.

He hugged her. "I'm so sorry. I can't imagine what you've been through. I'm just happy you're safe and back home. I know everyone at work will be happy to see you, too."

She wiped her tears and blew a hefty amount of snot into his handkerchief. She offered it back, but Melvin gestured she should keep it. "I'm glad to be back here, too," she said, still tearing a little. "Now, catch me up. Tell me everything that's happened since I've been gone. How did you get along without a receptionist?"

"We've had one. John hired a temp right after you left."

Her crying abruptly ceased. "Right after, huh? Where did he find an old maid on such short notice?"

Melvin shrugged. "The hospital, I guess. She used to work there."

"You seem to know a lot about her."

"Not really. I met her when I was a patient."

"So, you two have a history. How old is she? Is she pretty?"

"She's young. I guess you could say she's pretty."

"Prettier than me?"

"Well . . ."

"Of course, she is. Has she made a play for you? You didn't answer. She did, didn't she? Is that why you kissed me? Do you feel guilty about something? Ew, was it on this couch? What makes this girl so much more attractive than me? Does she have *special* talents?"

"You'd have to ask Ronny."

"Why the hell would I ask Ronny?"

"He's marrying her next week."

Sally shot up like a rocket. "What the hell? Ronny's getting *married*? To a *girl*? Bullshit."

"I'm the best man."

"*You're* his best man?"

"Yeah, apparently, I'm his best friend."

"Well, that's sad."

"I'm a good friend."

"You suck as a friend. I should know. Took my car without asking."

"You have a point."

"And his mother's going to let him bring a wife into her house?"

"They haven't spoken since he moved out."

Her eyes widened. "He did *what?*"

"He and his fiancée bought a little place over by Baptist Hospital. He's a different guy now. Even left his dog behind."

Sally's mouth fell open. "Shit-fire on a potato chip! I'm gone for a few months, and this whole place turns into one big shit show. This is utter *bullshit*. He is *not* getting married. Not to her." She slapped his arm. "How the hell could you let this happen?"

Melvin held his arm and half turned in defense. "You don't even know her."

She stuck a finger at him. "I know all I need to. She's either a grifter or an idiot. Ronny doesn't have money, so she's probably both. Either way, her ass is gone. First, I'm dragging his fat ass back to his momma's house. Then, I'm handling this little bitch." Sally clenched her teeth. "I hope to hell she puts up a fight."

She stormed out and slammed the door. It immediately reopened. "And *that's* what it means to be a real friend, dammit! Not this lolly-gagging, half-assed bullshit you've been doing. Best man—my *ass*."

The door slammed again and then reopened. "What did you say the address was?"

"Sally, I don't think you should—"

Her eyes went wild. "ADDRESS."

Melvin carefully handed it to the angry woman. She grabbed his shirt and kissed him hard. "Don't wait up, *buttercup*." The door slammed for the third time.

Melvin paused to see if it would reopen. When it didn't, he picked up the phone to warn Ronny and Annette they were in the direct path of a Sally-nado. Halfway through the dial, he considered that a Sally-nado could change direction in the blink of an eye. He put down the receiver and quietly made his dinner.

The next day, Melvin walked downstairs to find Sally, bright and early at her post, drinking coffee as if she'd never left. "Good morning, Sally. I've never seen you down here this early."

She blinked. "Don't know what you mean. This is when I'm supposed to be here."

"Yeah, but you're never—where's Annette?"

"Who, the little temp?" Sally shuffled some papers around. "Her services were no longer required."

"Ah, well, I'm sure that Dr. Thomas gave her a nice send-off. I guess he was pretty happy to hear you're back."

"I'm sure he will be as soon as he arrives. Coffee?"

"Yeah, thanks. What about Ronny?"

She returned with his cup. "Our optician? I suspect he's at his desk."

"So, how did it go? Did he make up with his mother?"

Sally sat back down. "I'm just the receptionist, Dr. Napier. I'll let you know when your first patient arrives."

Melvin made a beeline for the optical shop. "Good morning, Ronny."

"Good morning, Dr. Napier. Did you see the sunrise? It was spectacular."

"Yeah, I'm sure it was. Listen, about Annette—"

"Who, the temp? Water under the bridge, sir. Momma says it's best to let sleeping dogs go back to where they came from."

"Momma says, huh? So, how is your mother?"

"She's wonderful. Thank you for asking. Oh, and do you still have my photos of Ringo?"

"Sure, in my office. Okay, cut the shit, man. What happened last night?"

"What do you mean, sir?"

"You know what I mean. What happened with Annette?"

Ronny stared at him blankly and shrugged.

"You know, Annette, the girl who lives with you? The girl you're marrying next week?"

"Marriage? Oh, no, sir. That's not for me. Perhaps you are confused, sir. I did purchase a house as an investment property. This temp, her name was Annette, you say? She rented the property for a little while, but now she's moved on. Did I understand you to say Sally's back? That's wonderful news, sir. I'll have to swing by when I have a moment to say hello. Is there anything else I can help you with, Dr. Napier?"

"What is this, *The Stepford Wives?* What happened to Annette? Is she okay?"

"I'm sorry, sir, but I can't be held responsible for the current whereabouts of my former renters."

"I didn't ask *where* . . ." Melvin decided he didn't want to know more. He went to his office and hoped sleeping dogs really could go back to wherever sleeping dogs came from.

Chapter 23
The Capitol

Since her return, Sally had been in Melvin's ear to take her to brunch at the Capitol Hotel. According to her, it was *the* place to see and be seen. Paying top dollar for French toast didn't make much sense to him, but on Sunday morning, September 7th, 1952, he found himself on Markham Street, entering the beautiful hotel. Sally was in hog heaven with the fancy tablecloths, attentive service, great food, and high society. After the meal, she pleaded, "Let's go look at the hotel rooms, *please?*"

Melvin shook his head. "They're just rooms, and we're not guests. We have no business roaming the halls."

"Come on, I've always wanted to see what the hotel looks like, and we're here. Don't be such a fuddy-duddy." He relented, and they strolled past the attendant as if they belonged. Sally made him stop every few feet as she oohed and aahed over every little detail: the paintings, the window frames, the ornate woodwork around the ceilings, the carpeting, the hallway furniture—you name it. Melvin was sure that if Hell had a never-ending game of red light/green light, this was it.

She nodded toward a couple in their late twenties coming out of a room down the hall and looking a bit flush. "Someone got frisky this morning," Sally said with a smile. "What time is it, noon? Can't blame him. Just look at her. And by the look on *her* face, I'm guessing she got as much as she gave."

Melvin glanced their way. "She's a hooker. Look at the way she's dressed. Wonder how much that set him back?"

Sally slapped his arm. "Be nice," she whispered. "You don't know if she charged him. He could be her favorite regular."

215

As the couple headed their way, Melvin stopped cold. "Oh shit!" he whispered. "That's Norman McElhannon! He looks so damn young."

"Who's Norman McElhannon?" Sally asked with wide eyes. "Is he famous?"

"No. Growing up, he was kind of like my . . . I just know him. I've never seen him with a woman. Figures it'd be a hook—Oh, *shit!*" His face turned pale.

"What?"

"That's *Grandma!* She's so skinny. What's she doing in Little Rock? What's she doing with *him?*"

Sally squeezed his arm. "Quit your fooling. It's not funny." She whispered in his ear, "I don't know what they're doing *now*, but I can guess what they were doing ten minutes ago."

"Hey, son!" Norman hollered as he approached Melvin and stretched out his hand. Melvin almost passed out but managed to stay on his feet. *How the hell does he know me?*

The big man had a broad smile. "You look a damn sight better than the last time we saw you. Remember him, Mary? We took this poor man to the hospital a couple of years ago. Appears he lived."

"That's right!" exclaimed his 27-year-old grandmother with a bright smile. She gave Melvin a big hug that raised Sally's eyebrows. "We're so happy you're alive. Terrible accident. Thank goodness we found you on our way back from Memphis."

"Yes, very fortunate," Melvin said, avoiding eye contact with his grandmother he'd just accused of being a prostitute. *I was wrong about that, right?*

She smiled at him and moved her head until she caught his eye. "You were unconscious when we picked you up. What's your name, sir?"

"I'm uh, Calvin, Calvin Drapier. This is Sally Davis."

216

Sally's eyes widened, but she quickly smiled. "Pleasure to meet you. And thank you for saving my man."

"Pleased to meet you, too. I'm Mary Napier, and this is Norm McElhannon."

"*Napier*, did you say?" Sally asked as her eyebrows shot up again. She wrapped her arm inside Melvin's. "Did you hear that, honey? She said her name was *Napier*."

Mary cocked her head to one side. "Why do you say it like that?"

Sally patted Melvin's arm. "Oh, I just think it's a lovely name, don't you, *Calvin*?" Melvin nodded sheepishly.

Mary smiled. "Thank you, that's sweet. Are you two married?"

Sally's pupils dilated a little as she glanced at Melvin. "You know, he wants to propose, but the words just won't come to him. The doctor says it's an affliction and prescribed a ring and some knee-bending exercises, but so far, no luck."

Melvin looked at the floor and tugged on his collared shirt. Sally gave a devilish grin. "The truth is, we may not be married, but he makes love to me so often I can *barely* walk straight."

"Well,"—Mary blushed and looked lovingly at Norman—"I know just what you mean."

"I'm gonna be sick," muttered Melvin. Then it occurred to him his dad wouldn't be born until next year. He gave Mary a stern look. "Don't you have three children? Who's watching them right now?"

She backed up a step and stammered, "Why yes, my three sons are home with my sister. How on Earth did you know that?"

Remembering it was the '50s, Melvin replied, "I'm a doctor. We can tell."

"Oh, that makes sense," she nodded, her smile returning.

"Well, how about that!" exclaimed Norman. "We saved a doctor."

"You sure *did!*" replied Melvin, thinking of the lies his grandmother would one day tell. "Say, Mary, have you ever been to California?"

"Heavens, no!" she replied. "I don't think I could ever travel that far. It's funny you asked, though. I told everyone back home I was taking a trip out West for a couple of weeks. We've secretly just been hanging out here. We're so bad."

"Yeah," Norman chimed in, "first time we've come out of that room in a week."

Melvin cringed. *Norm's my real grandfather? I'm literally standing in front of my grandparents after they just got through screwing like bunnies. And they're still sweaty. Ew, she hugged me! She hugged me with grandma sex sweat! I will never be clean again.*

Norman's face lit up, "Don't know about you folks, but I'm starving!"

Sally smiled and squeezed Melvin's arm again. "I'll just *bet* you are."

The big man grinned. "We're about to have breakfast," he said, then glanced at his watch. "Actually, lunch. Why don't you two join us?"

Melvin held up a hand. "We don't want to intrude."

"What my courteous companion meant to say," Sally interjected, "was that it would be an honor, and thank you ever so much for saving my life. I would never have met this gorgeous woman standing next to me if you hadn't. The least we could do is treat you to lunch."

"Uh, yeah," Melvin replied. "That's pretty much what I meant."

"I've never turned down a free meal in my life," Norman said. "No point in starting now."

"Calvin feels the same way," Sally added with a smile. "Only he prefers free milk. All I can say is, moooo."

"We should be going now, Sally," Melvin said sternly. "Maybe we could all get together some other time?"

"You'll have to excuse my future fiancé," she grinned. "He gets nervous around new people. Terrible thing for a doctor, don't you think? Why don't you guys get us a table, and we'll be along shortly?"

Melvin jerked her to the side. "Sally, listen, we need to—"

"No, *you* listen, *Calvin*. I don't know who those people really are, or what's going on, or why you're acting this way. What I *do* know is that, for whatever reason, you don't want them to know your real name. If you want to keep it that way, we're staying because, frankly, my dear, I'm enjoying the *shit* out of this!"

So, off went Melvin and Sally to have brunch with his grandparents. "Look at this menu," complained Norman. "Mimosas and bloody Marys. Don't they have drinks for men?"

Mary blushed at the complaint. "Norman owns a drinking establishment back home in Subiaco. He's a bit of a connoisseur when it comes to alcohol."

"Drinking establishment? It's just a small bar, nothing more," Norman said. "And I'm no connoisseur. I'm Irish. I like beer and whiskey, not this Nancy-ass mimosa shit." He winked at Melvin. "Where I come from, no real man would be caught dead drinking that, right?"

The waiter stopped at their table and addressed Melvin. "Welcome back, sir. Shall I bring another whiskey for the lady and perhaps another mimosa for you, sir?"

"Uh, no, just two coffees. Cream for the lady but make mine black. Because that's the way I *drink* it. And whatever our friends want, put it on my tab."

"Oh, thank you," said Mary. "I'll have a couple of those mimosas. And don't be stingy with the champagne."

Melvin blurted, "Really? You drink?"

Norman laughed. "Does she drink? She may look skinny, but this little lady could drink you under the table."

Mary grabbed his arm as she lit her cigarette. "Norm, you're embarrassing me."

Melvin's eyes widened. "You *smoke*, too?"

"What's wrong with smoking, doctor?" she asked.

"It's just that we now know smoking affects not only your lungs but also your skin. Smoke long enough, and you'll look at least 15 years older than you really are. Nothing personal. I just always mention that to attractive young women."

"Hey!" Sally slapped his arm. "I smoke. How come you've never told me that?"

"Well, I—"

Norman dove in. "Sally, I'm sure Dr. Drapier feels you're so beautiful that you've got beauty to spare. And as for Mary's lungs, well, you can see she's got a healthy set of those!" Sally scowled at Melvin while Mary tugged on her sweater jacket to cover her chest.

Cringing at the anatomical reference to his grandmother, Melvin asked, "Maybe we could just change the subject?"

Mary nodded. "Yes, please. So, how many kids do you guys want? Assuming your man gets over his affliction."

Sally leaned in. "At first, I wanted four, but after seeing my sister-in-law deal with her four boys, I'm thinking just a dog."

"Oh, you've got that right," Mary said as she puffed away. "I can't keep up with my *three* boys. If I had another, I'd just shoot myself."

Melvin did the math on his father's birthday. The answer was nine months from now. "You know, Mary, these things do happen. You could have a fourth."

"Oh, I don't think so," she replied. "Besides, even if I did get knocked up again, I know a guy who can handle that sort of thing."

Melvin choked on his coffee.

Sally slapped his back repeatedly. "You okay, sweetie? Did I hit you too hard? Did you know that smoking not only steals your beauty, it also gives you incredible arm strength? Did I *fail* to tell you that?"

"Mary!" Norman protested. "You can't talk that way around a Catholic. Besides, it would be our love child."

"I didn't know you were such a romantic, Norm. You know I'm just joking." She put down her cigarette and kissed him.

Melvin stared at his drinking, smoking, abortion-talking, prohibitionist grandmother kissing the man he'd grown up thinking was just a family friend. Glancing down, he considered his father, Raymond, was probably there too, just below the tablecloth, only two or three cells old. He thought about the sacrifices his dad had made for him over the years and how he'd never asked for anything in return. As the server approached, Melvin slipped some cash into his pocket and nodded toward Mary. "No more alcohol in hers."

"So, Mr. McElhannon," Sally asked, "how long have you been in the bar business?"

"Please, call me Norm."

"Really?" Melvin asked, recalling the dozens of head slaps Norman had given him over the years for calling him Norm. "You're okay with that?"

"Why not? That's my name, and Mary likes it. I've had the bar since '45. We buy locally from the DeChambeau distillery here in town. I'm down here once a month and over to Memphis twice a year for the higher-end stuff. In fact, that's where we were coming from when we found Calvin." Norman's eyes lit up as he became animated. "It was a dark and rainy night on this little dirt road in the middle of nowhere. It was coming down in buckets, and I could barely see. Mary had fallen fast asleep to the rhythm of the wiper blades. Suddenly, I spotted this deer carcass in the middle of the road. I thought about running over it because swerving might put us in the ditch and bust our load. Then something whispered to me to hit the brakes instead, and I did."

"Was it an angel?" Sally asked on the edge of her seat. "Did an angel tell you not to run him over?"

"No, it was Larry."

"Larry?" Sally asked. "Who the hell is Larry?"

"He's a guy I know over in Clarksville. He once told me he ran over a deer, and it tore the shit out of his bumper and grill. Well, I couldn't have that. But as we got closer, you could see this was *no* deer.

221

It was a man. Ooh, it was a terrible sight—blood everywhere. I thought he was dead for sure!" Norman struck the table for effect.

Sally jumped like a little girl listening to a campfire story. "Then what happened?"

"I reached over to cover Mary's eyes, but she was *gone*."

"Gone?"

"She'd gotten out of that truck lickety-split and was tending to him as if he were family. We lifted him into the truck bed, and she doctored him all the way to Little Rock, pouring alcohol on his wounds and tearing strips off her shirt and skirt to bandage him up. She was half-naked by the time we got there. Honestly, I didn't think he'd make it more than a few miles, but she never lost hope. She somehow knew he'd pull through. Mary's the only reason he survived."

"Stop it, Norm." Mary blushed. "You're making me out like some kind of hero. We just did what any good Christian would do in that situation. When you find someone in that much need, you *should* treat them like family."

Norman looked at her and smiled. "You're too good for me, Mary." Melvin nodded in agreement.

Melvin reached across the table, took Mary's hand, and looked her in the eyes. "I owe you my life in more ways than I can say. *Thank you*." Sally began to sniffle. Melvin handed her his handkerchief. "What's wrong with you?"

"You almost died! And these wonderful people saved you. Now fate has brought us together so that you could thank her. I just can't get over it! If they hadn't been on that little road . . ." Melvin was no longer listening. She was right. He'd been focused on getting away from this horrible, awkward, unnatural family reunion and completely missed what a golden opportunity the universe had just handed him.

"Mr. McElhannon—"

"Please, call me Norman or Norm. You don't mind if I call you Calvin, do you?"

"Wouldn't bother me at all, *Norm*. You said you found me on your way back from Memphis? I had heard it was just outside Jonesboro. Can you tell me exactly where?"

"Well, it was on a little road, and it was raining. Mary, do you remember?"

"I'll never forget. We didn't come back on seventy because we went up to Marked Tree to find that barbeque restaurant, remember? We didn't like the traffic on sixty-seven, so we got off at Bald Knob and took some back roads. That's where we found you. It wasn't really at night, more like one or two in the afternoon. But it was raining pretty hard."

"Back roads around Bald Knob?" Melvin's eyes widened. "Do you remember which ones?"

"We got a little turned around," Norman admitted. "After we picked you up, we ended up on highway eleven, which took us back to sixty-seven. Do you remember the accident? When we found you, we never saw a car. I've always wondered about that."

"That's because I wasn't in a car. It was a plane crash—an explosion, really."

"Oh, my word!" exclaimed Mary. "A plane crash? That's so horrible. And you almost died. I never knew they were so unsafe. Norm and I were talking about taking a flight to Mexico one day. We've always wanted to try this avocado dish they have down there. They call it guacamole. Now, I don't think I could ever set foot on an airplane."

"You know," Melvin nodded, "I believe you."

Then she turned to Sally. "So, how did you two meet?"

Sally looked lovingly at her man and replied, "Well, Melvin just showed up in my life one day as if he'd dropped from the sky."

"Who's Melvin, dear?" Mary asked.

"Oh, right. I meant Calvin, of course."

"I'm afraid I don't understand."

"Yeah, Sally," Melvin added. "I don't understand *either.*"

"Melvin's just being—I mean, *Calvin's* just being funny. The truth is—"

"The truth is," Melvin interrupted, "last night, my name was Melvin."

"I don't get it," Norman said.

"We were role-playing."

"What's role-playing?" Mary asked. The three of them leaned in close to hear his answer.

"It's where—you have to understand that Sally and I have been together for some time. Occasionally we need a little spice, so I pretended to be Melvin, the mailman. Hey, did I mention she's an actress?"

"Really?" Mary asked excitedly.

"It's true," Sally nodded. "I played a major role in *The Accommodating Emmetrope.* Maybe you've seen it?"

"Oh, yes! I love that movie, and you're certainly pretty enough to be in pictures. You know, I thought I recognized you from somewhere."

"Yes," Sally nodded again. "I do look familiar."

"I don't get it," Norman said. "You pretended to be a mailman? So, what? Sally gets stirred up over getting a letter?"

"No, sweetheart," Mary patted his shoulder and whispered, "I think he was there to deliver his . . . you know, his . . ."

"His package," Sally said with a wide smile.

"Oh, I get it now!" the big man grinned. "Based on that look, Calvin, I'm guessing your package required a hefty postage."

Melvin felt the tips of his ears burn. *Could someone please shoot me now?* He glanced at Mary and realized it'd become a contest of which Napier could turn a deeper shade of red. "Well, I think Melvin's a swell name," Mary said in a small voice. "If I ever had another son, I might just name him Melvin."

"Or Raymond," Melvin offered. "Raymond's good, too. Just saying. It's a powerful, masculine name."

"Yes, now that I hear it, I like that name, too," she said with a smile.

"Yeah, me too," added Norman. "Hey Mary, let's try out Calvin's role-playing game tonight. I'll be Raymond, the handyman. Excuse me, miss. Is that table wobbly? Maybe you need a good screw."

Suddenly, Mary was the clear winner, turning five more shades of red. Melvin promptly stood up. "Sir, I think we're ready to order over here."

"I don't think he saw you, Dr. Drapier," Mary said. "So, Sally, you didn't say. Where did you meet? Hollywood?"

"Not exactly. Before I became a beloved movie star, I worked as the receptionist at his practice."

"Really? That's nice. Where do you practice?"

Before Sally could answer, Melvin blurted, "Batesville, just north of here."

"Yes, we've been through there," she replied. "Norman, remember that wonderful bed and breakfast in Mammoth Spring?"

"Do I? That bed was *sturdy*. She had me tied up like a calf. Don't remember making it to breakfast."

"Norm, stop!" Mary pleaded.

Yeah, Norm, Melvin thought. *Please stop.*

"We're all adults here. It's not like I'm telling them our routine or how flexible you are."

Mary buried her head in her hands. In a teary voice, she exclaimed, "You embarrass me so much! I could just *die!*"

Sally kissed Melvin's cheek and whispered, "Thank you for this. I'm having the *best* time!"

Mary regained her composure. "Once we were up and around, we did find it was a lovely area. Compared to Sugarfield, everywhere is. Did you two grow up near there?"

"No," Sally replied. "I'm from Conway, and Calvin's Canadian."

"Ooh," Mary grinned. "A foreign lover. How *exciting.*"

"Wouldn't know," Sally muttered.

"What was that, dear?" she asked.

"I said you can't imagine."

Melvin's eyes narrowed. "You guys have sure traveled a lot. How long have you been together?"

"A while," Norman replied, a little too evasively for Melvin's taste. "So, what kind of doctor are you?"

"I'm an ophthalmologist."

"That's eyes, right?"

He nodded.

Mary's eyes lit up. "Do you know Dr. Napier? He's an eye doctor here in town." Sally leaned forward on her elbows, eagerly awaiting his answer.

"No, but I've heard of him. Supposed to be a great guy."

Mary smiled. "I heard the same thing. Back home, all the girls talk about how good-looking he is, how he's not married, and how he is with the ladies, a real Dr. Casanova."

Melvin choked on his coffee again. Sally slapped his back hard.

"You should drink more slowly, honey. Now, Mary, are you talking about Dr. *Melvin* Napier?"

"Yes. Now that you say it out loud, it sounds a lot like your name, Dr. Drapier. With you both being eye doctors, I suppose people could find that confusing."

Sally nodded. "And how. Same sounding name, same profession, it's almost as if they were the *same* person." Melvin kicked her under the table, spilling her coffee. She apologized for her clumsiness and continued. "Well, I've spent some time in Little Rock, and *I've* met Dr. Napier. I have to say, I've seen better."

"Oh, that's too bad," replied Mary. "If Norm ever lost interest, I was thinking of getting blurry vision." The women giggled as the men sat unimpressed.

Then Mary leaned over to Sally. "I don't mean to pry, but that lady over there's been staring at Calvin. The one in the bright red dress."

Sally glanced over her shoulder. "That's no lady. That's Francis Moore."

Melvin choked again. He turned and caught Francis ogling him, making subtle gestures with her mouth. He quickly turned from the mischievous stare of his young grandmother, only to lock eyes across the table with the puzzled look from his other grandmother. His cheeks flushed once more, and he looked down.

Without missing a beat, Sally continued, "See that man beside her? That's her father, Buford. He'd be the state's richest, most powerful man if it weren't for the DeChambeaus. You know *their* story, right?"

"No, not really," Mary replied. "Do tell."

"Well, they founded this city after striking gold somewhere down by the river back in the day. Moore's have *always* played second fiddle, and from what I hear, it drives them nuts. And sitting across from Buford is our governor, and the man with the red tie is the attorney general whom I'm sure owes Buford favors as well."

"Goodness," said Mary. "You sure know who's who around here."

"Wish I didn't. I've had a few run-ins with daddy's darling little slut. She's only looking at Calvin because he's with me."

Mary whispered, "If it makes you feel any better, her dress is hideous."

"It is, isn't it? And with all that makeup, she looks like a clown. I wonder where she bought that dress, Barnum and Bailey's? It's like a big red flashing sign: Look at me! I'm a whore. I'm a sad, slutty, clown-whore."

"Well," Mary replied, "that's one way to look at it, I suppose."

"You're right, Mary. Saying it out loud does feel pretty *damn* good."

"Well, that's not exactly what I—"

"I'll admit, it's a little junior high, but still, feels pretty damn good. Do you know what would make me feel even better?" Before Mary could guess, Sally grabbed Melvin and dramatically made out with him, throwing in a bit of moaning, then looked back to Francis, who pretended not to notice.

Mary whispered in Norman's ear, "I take it back. You don't embarrass me."

After the public display of affection, the table sat in awkward silence while Sally straightened her dress and Melvin wiped lipstick from his face. Then he offered, "Coincidentally, my grandmother's name was Francis. She died before I was born."

"I think it's a lovely name," Mary said.

"Too bad it's wasted on that *bitch*," Sally added, just a little too loudly.

Melvin stood. "And with that, it's time for us to go." He motioned again for the waiter and handed him some cash. "Whatever these nice people would like to eat. And bring this man some real whiskey, no more of this Nancy-ass mimosa shit you've been forcing on us."

As Norman and Mary thanked them, Melvin replied, "I owe you guys my life. But Norm, if I may, I do have one request. One day, when you have a son and then a grandson, especially the *grandson*, promise me you won't go easy on him. Don't give him an inch. Trust me on that. Kids need direction and discipline."

"Uh, sure, Calvin. Whatever you say."

"And Mary, if that fourth does show up one day, go easy on the booze. New medical research says it's not good for the baby. Not good to smoke around them either."

With a concerned look, she nodded. "If you recommend it, doctor. I'll quit both, just in case. Maybe we all should."

As they walked out, Francis gave him a small wave and a wink. Sally pointed her nose in the air and jerked Melvin along until they were back out on Markham Street. Shoving him up against the hotel wall, she opened her mouth, but Melvin got in the first word. "Now, look, Sally, we talked about this. When I kissed you the night you returned, that was out of impulse. We can't be doing that."

"What, that back there just now? That had nothing to do with *you.*"

"I just wiped off a ton of lipstick that says otherwise."

"You are so clueless. Now, why was that loose slot machine in there was so hot and heavy to have you pull her lever? And what the hell was this Dr. Drapier from Batesville shit? And who *were* those people in there, and why does Mary have your last name?"

"The truth is, I'm a time traveler. I've wanted to tell you for a long time. Francis is my grandmother, and Norm and Mary are my other grandparents. They were probably conceiving my dad this morning, which creeps me out."

"I told you that shit wasn't funny. I swear I can't tell when you're joking. For all I know, you could be some lunatic who believes it. When are you going to take me seriously?"

"You're right. I met Francis when I first arrived. She made a play for me, but I turned her down. She didn't take it well."

"Bullshit. Nobody turns down Francis."

"Well, then I was the first. Believe what you want."

Sally stared him in the eye and finally nodded. "And the bed bunnies?"

"Don't call them that. She's a distant cousin who grew up here and writes letters to my family in Canada. After my wife's incarceration, I came here to escape all that. I never thought I'd run into her."

She backhanded his shoulder. "*Thank* you. Was telling the truth so hard? So, that's how you knew about her three sons. That also means she knows your granddad died from an avocado, and she still wants to try one? That's perverse. I was just starting to like her. Was your grandmother's name really Francis?"

Melvin nodded. "Yeah. She and my mother had some sort of falling out before she died. It was never spoken of."

"I get it. What are the odds the people who saved your life turn out to be relatives?"

"Have to say, I didn't see that one coming."

She shrugged. "Guess there's only one thing left to do."

"Yeah, what's that?"

She put her arm to her head and pretended to swoon as she fell into Melvin's arms. "Take me home, Dr. Casanova, and show me how you got your reputation."

"In your dreams, reception girl."

Chapter 24
The Girl from Georgia

Melvin didn't know how his grandmother had heard about "Dr. Casanova" all the way over in Sugarfield but didn't have to wait long to find out. On September 26th, only a couple of weeks after brunch with Sally, he crossed paths with a woman he'd seen in clinic two months earlier, a woman with an agenda, a woman who would track him down.

Back in July, a few days after Sally's return, Melvin met a new patient named Grace Moultrie, an attractive woman in her mid-twenties with a thick southern accent, more than you usually heard in Arkansas. Grace had been more interested in asking questions about Melvin than in answering questions about her vision. When she had gotten nowhere with her inquisition, she had proceeded to talk about herself. She was from Northwest Georgia and had explained how Northern Georgians shouldn't be confused with Georgians who lived below the gnat line. If you're wondering what the gnat line is, Melvin didn't ask. Grace had heard how wonderful he was, as a doctor, that is, and just *had* to come to see if he could help her. And, by the way, she was new to the area and wondered where people relaxed in this part of town with adult beverages. Not that she was a drinker, but on the other hand, she didn't want people to think she wasn't social because that simply wasn't the case. Far from it, she was a delight to be around, and Melvin had been invited to ask anyone who knew her regarding that point. After an eternity of one-sided dialogue, she had not mentioned one visual complaint. Her exam had been equally unrevealing, 20/20 without glasses, and perfectly healthy eyes. She had thanked him profusely for his time and expertise, emphasizing how much better she'd sleep at night, knowing she was under him, *under his care*, that is. When she had asked when they should see each other again, Melvin had suggested returning when she had an eye problem.

September 26th, 1952 was a comfortable 77-degree evening as Melvin relaxed at McKeen's after a busy Friday clinic. Sally had other plans for the evening, and he sat alone. She hadn't mentioned what those plans were, and he hadn't asked. Any possession he held over Sally's time was in her head, not his, although her company bothered him less with each passing day.

As he sipped his beer, he wondered if Mary had taken his advice about putting down the booze and cigarettes. For Raymond's sake, he hoped so. His thoughts were broken when heavy perfume engulfed him from behind, and the warm breath of a thick southern drawl tickled his ear.

"Well, hello, there," Grace said as she helped herself to the barstool beside him. "I thought that might be you. How's my favorite eye doctor?"

"Oh, hello, Mrs. . . ."

"It's Ms. Moultrie, of course. But you can call me Grace—or whatever you like." Melvin's eyes narrowed at that last part.

"Well, Ms. Moul—*Grace*, it's nice to see you again. What brings you here?"

"You, of course. What I mean is, the last time we were together, that is, in your office, I inquired where people go to unwind. And you said McKeen's just down the street. Your words have been on my mind for the past couple of months. What, with all the stresses in life, I deserve to relax and let loose a little. And here I was in town to do some shopping and thought I would be remiss not to follow my doctor's expert advice. So, here I am." She brushed her hair from her face and threw back her shoulders a little. "You were so right. This place is charming. It has everything a girl could want."

Despite her repeated efforts to invade his personal space to touch his hand or arm as she spoke, Melvin let her talk, partly for amusement and slightly out of loneliness. What harm could it do? She was just another attractive, single patient with no idea he was married or that this was going nowhere. Grace bought the next round and then the next and suggested they'd be more comfortable at a nearby table. As Melvin sat down, Grace soon joined him, bringing two more drinks from the bar. Soon, he got the whole story.

She'd been raised in Georgia beauty pageants, winning the titles of Little Miss Gainesville, then Miss Carrollton, and after that, Queen of the Winter Festival and, naturally, prom queen. Melvin learned her parents wanted her to attend college, but instead, she'd followed a boy to Arkansas. As the drinks flowed, it wasn't entirely clear what happened to that boy, but there was talk about his secretary. We didn't like the secretary, who was clearly the bad guy in the story. He also learned that Georgia peaches had nothing to do with fruit. He may have learned other things, but it turned into a blur.

The conversation shifted to Alexis. Someone was talking about her quite a bit. He tried to listen intently to what was being said, then realized he was the one talking. A couple of drinks more, and Alexis began talking back to him. She told him how much she'd missed him, that he was a wonderful doctor and damn gorgeous. Alexis didn't sound much like Alexis, but who cared? She had somehow found him. Melvin and Alexis made out a little in the bar, then stumbled down the street. They somehow made it up the stairs to his loft for a passionate reunion after two and a half long years of forced separation.

Early the next morning, Melvin awoke to a beautiful feeling. His struggle had only been a dream, a nightmarish ordeal, now melted away. He turned to snuggle with his bride but found only Grace, propped up on an elbow, watching him sleep.

Melvin scrambled out of bed and covered himself. Grace sported an amused smile.

"In my experience, most men are happy to wake up with me."

"What happened?" he asked, hastily putting on clothes.

"Well, you got what you needed, and I got what I wanted. You can still call me Alexis if you want. I'm sure she'd like to be taken out for breakfast."

"No! I mean, I don't remember after the bar. Did we . . . ?"

She climbed out of bed and stood with her hands on her hips. "Well, we didn't come up here to play cards."

"Could you please put something on, Ms. Moultrie?"

"Oh, this embarrasses you, does it? You were in such a hurry to get them off last night. I guess round three is out of the question?"

"No, I need to—three?"

"Oh, relax, doctor. I'm just playing with you. And my name's not Moultrie. Not anymore, anyway. It's Grable, Mrs. Grable." She reached into her purse and put her wedding ring back on. "Oh, don't look at me like it's a sin."

"Actually, it is. The Bible's crystal clear on that point."

Grace didn't look impressed. "Well, then maybe you should preach a sermon to my husband and that little tramp of a secretary who's only too happy to receive his dictation. Everyone in Sugarfield's talking about it. It's more than I can bear."

"You're from Sugarfield?"

"I know, you've never heard of it. Nobody has."

"So, I was revenge?"

"Oh, no, darling. You were *sweet* revenge."

Melvin walked into the main room and sat down on the couch with his head in his hands. *What have I done?* Now dressed, she sat beside him and put her arm around him.

"Relax, you're not the one to blame. Truth be told, none of this was your fault."

"How's that?"

"Let me tell you a story. My granddaddy was a rather famous pharmacist in Atlanta. And when Grandmomma couldn't give him a son, he taught my momma the family trade. In turn, she taught it to me from a young age. She wanted me to go to school to become a practicing pharmacist, but I met a boy. I was only fourteen and didn't have a shred of common sense. We wrote letters all during the war and married when he got back. He promised me a life of love and excitement. Instead, he gave me *Sugarfield*, Arkansas. Then he traded in this twenty-five-year-old for a newer model. He denies it, yet the whole town's talking about it. I am many things, but stupid isn't one of them."

"Sorry your husband's cheating on you. How was last night not my fault?"

She stood and continued in her syrupy southern accent. "Well, I was hoping you'd be a little more agreeable last night. Most men would. Despite my best efforts, you were a perfect gentleman. And I'll have you know it was quite a blow to my ego the way you droned on about that Alexis girl. Oh, I tried to overlook it, but as a young, healthy, well-figured American woman practically throwing myself at you, it was hard not to take it personally. I will say this, if your Alexis thought a spoonful of you the way you do for her, she'd be here. No matter what."

Melvin's expression lightened. "So, you're saying we didn't . . ."

"Oh, no, we did. We most certainly did. Based upon the thickness of these walls, I'm quite certain your neighbors can attest to it. What I'm trying to say, and mind you, I'm not particularly proud that I had to resort to such measures, is that I had to help you along."

"Help me along?"

"You just needed a little loosening up, is all."

"So, you got me drunk."

"I did. But it wasn't enough. So, I slipped a little something into your drink. I am a pharmacist, after all. Well, close enough. After that, I became your Alexis, and you became quite the little engine that could.

235

You know, all the girls back home are talking about this new bedroom game they're playing in the city. It's called role-playing. Perhaps you've heard of it. I was anxious to give it a try. I must admit, I do like it."

Melvin stood and put his hands on his hips. "What exactly did you drug me with?"

"Nothing, really—just a mild hallucinogen. I couldn't have you falling asleep on me. I needed your full attention, so to speak. And I got it. Oh, don't look at me that way. You didn't die."

His eyes widened. "Was that a risk?"

Grace put a finger to her lips as she thought about it. "Let's just say it was one I was willing to take."

He pointed to the door. "Get out."

"Calm down, Dr. Napier."

"Get out before I have you arrested."

"Arrested? And what would you tell the authorities? You got drunk, made out with a woman in a bar before several witnesses, and then took her to bed? I'm sure they'd investigate immediately—right after they laughed you out of the station. But if that's how you feel about it, I'll go."

Melvin pointed at her. "Don't move."

"Make up your mind, doctor. This indecisiveness doesn't suit you."

Melvin searched the bedroom, then called out from the bathroom, "Grace, what measures did we take last night to prevent pregnancy?"

"Refusing me breakfast and now worrying about our potential love child. I suppose the gentleman ship has sailed."

Melvin marched back into the main room with a frown. "Grace?"

"Relax. John and I have never been able to conceive. My plumbing won't allow it."

"How do you know it's not him?"

She shrugged. "Well, you *are* the doctor. I suspect we'll just have to watch my belly and the tramp's to solve that little mystery."

The blood left Melvin's face as he plopped back down on the couch. Grace took a seat next to him and reached for his hand, but he jerked it away. "I know you're cross with me, Melvin, but let's be clear. I'm never coming back here, and you'll never be in Sugarfield. Surely you realized I didn't need an eye doctor when I came to see you. You must have deciphered why I was there. Most men would've taken advantage or at least enjoyed embarrassing me for being so forward. Not you. You were a gentleman and played along. That's what made you so attractive. You were on my mind for two solid months. I was honest when I said I was stressed and deserved to relax. Things are just horrible at home. Of course, that's not your cross to bear. I'm sorry I resorted to nefarious methods to get what I wanted. As I've said, my husband and I are childless. If our little rendezvous results in a blessing, then I've evened the score with my husband and have a beautiful gift to remember our time together. I believe that's called a two for one, a twofer, if you will."

He stood once more. "There's the door, Grace."

"I'm going. I hope you have a wonderful life, Dr. Napier. I realize I'm in no position to offer constructive criticism, but consider dumping this Alexis and finding someone better. Believe me, it's miserable when you've chosen the wrong one. Oh, and I'm curious about that bulletin board in your bedroom with all those numbers and diagrams. What is that? Are you writing a book?"

Melvin's eyes widened, and he opened the loft door for her. "Uh, yes, I am."

"Well, isn't that impressive! Such a cerebral pursuit. Here I was content in the belief your greatest asset was a little further south." She winked. "Goodbye, Melvin." She tried to kiss his cheek, but he pulled away. She shrugged and sashayed out the door.

As she left, Melvin heard someone coming up the staircase. *Oh shit.* It had to be Sally, likely in her clothes from last night. With his door still open, he could easily hear the conversation. "Well, hello. Aren't you the cute little receptionist who works downstairs? You look like the cat who got the cream last night. Are you coming up here for more? Bravo." Grace's voice got a little louder. "Dr. Napier, I now understand why you were so adamant I leave. It appears you have a revolving *door* of beautiful women. I do admire a man with stamina. And at this early hour. You truly *are* amazing."

Melvin heard a raspy, hung-over voice say, "Moultrie, right?"

"Why, yes. You have a wonderful head for recollection on top of such a gorgeous figure."

"What are you doing here?"

"Well, a lady doesn't speak of such matters."

"Maybe not. Like I said, what are *you* doing here?" Melvin heard the click of Sally's lighter and could smell the cigarette.

"No need for unpleasantry. I suppose I was here for the same reason as you. I'm afraid you're a little late, though. As we say back home, you can't grow corn once you've run out of seed, no matter how badly you wish to plow."

Melvin heard Sally unlock her door. "Yeah? Well, I'm here because I *live* here." Sally paused. "Funny, though, seeing you outside his door on a Saturday."

"I'm afraid I don't catch your meaning, dear."

"Melvin tosses the trash out on *Tuesday*." A door slammed, followed by angry footsteps down the stairs. Melvin quietly shut his door.

Sally wouldn't make eye contact for the next two weeks, much less talk to him. Finally, she knocked on his door late one evening, barefoot in her nightgown and three sheets to the wind. "Her? And after all that bullshit: Oh, I miss my bitch ex-wife who's in prison and can't go on with my *pathetic* life or even look at another woman? But the minute the Georgia Express rolls in, you can't wait to board that hussy?" She tried to flip him off but used the wrong finger. She stared at it, trying to figure it out, then gave up. "Explain that shit to me." She tapped on his chest. "Explain it!"

Melvin blocked his door and didn't invite her in. "We talked about this. You and I are friends, not lovers. I don't owe you an explanation." He sighed. "But you mean a lot to me as a friend, so I'll tell you the story." She opened her mouth and pointed at his face but had no words. She paused in thought, raised her finger again, but again, nothing. Her eyes narrowed. "You piss me off. You know that?" She staggered back across the landing and opened her door. "Well, get your ass on in here, then."

Once inside, they sat on her couch. Melvin explained how Grace had stalked him to McKeen's, drugged him with who knows what, and then convinced him she was Alexis. He'd had no idea he'd slept with her until the next morning, at which point he'd abruptly kicked her out. Sally listened with big eyes. Each time Melvin paused in the story, she'd interject, "That bitch!" When he'd finished, she hugged him.

"Seeing as how you were drugged and could have died, I'll give you a pass." Then she pointed at him. "This time." Melvin considered reiterating he wasn't asking forgiveness but chose to let it go.

She waggled her finger at him once more. "You are so naïve. Have you never read a fairy tale? When an evil witch gives you something to drink, you walk away. You pull your head out of your ass, put that shit down, and walk away." She curled up beside him on the couch and purred. "Oh, and you should avoid Conway for a while."

"Why?"

"I sort of cried on the phone to Momma about you."

"That should worry me?"

"You remember how good a shot Daddy was?"

"Balls off a squirrel at a hundred yards?"

"Yeah, well, from a hundred and fifty yards, Momma could give that squirrel a vasectomy." She grinned and pretended to point a pistol at his groin. "Pew, pew. No more baby Melvins."

"You are so drunk."

She giggled. "Yes, I am." Then she asked to hear again how much she meant to him. Before Melvin could answer, she was gone. He carried her to bed and tucked her in. Locking her door and then crossing the landing, he stopped in front of his door. *I can't reach the woman I love, and the woman who loves me feels I cheated on her while she was out sleeping with someone else. I hate this decade.*

1953

Chapter 25
Gypsies of Las Vegas

On Friday, February 13, 1953, Melvin awoke from a dream about Alexis. He wondered what she was doing and how she would spend Valentine's Day tomorrow as he lingered in bed a little longer than usual. Getting up meant facing yet another day in his 1950s prison. Since getting intel from Mary and Norman, every escape attempt via flights over Bald Knob had failed. With no chance of parole, Melvin stared at his bedroom ceiling and debated getting out of bed at all.

For the past couple of weeks, he'd successfully dodged the topic of Valentine's Day around Sally. He knew she'd have her usual expectations. But a few days ago, she'd briefly mentioned she had a date in Conway that evening. Welcome news at the time, but now that it was the day before, Melvin wasn't so sure.

His patience had worn thin in clinic. A patient had become argumentative, and Melvin raised his voice, telling her exactly what he thought without a care who heard it. Ronny pulled him aside.

"I need your help, buddy."

"What is it, Ronny? I'm busy."

"I need a partner."

"What? Why?"

"My doctor says I shouldn't fly to Vegas alone. I need you, buddy."

"Man, I can't go to Vegas."

"Pal, look at you. You've moped around here for three years since your wife got put away. You can't afford *not* to go. I've already bought the tickets. Don't worry. I'll protect you from the sharpies." Ronny's eyes twinkled. "Pack a bag, 'cause we leave tonight. Valentines in Vegas, baby!"

That evening, Melvin found himself back at Adams Field, but this time with no private pilot, private plane, or hopes to be crushed. This time, he had a well-intentioned, potbellied optician with a flask of whiskey to "get things started."

They landed in Las Vegas around nine, and Melvin hailed a cab for the new Riviera hotel. Ronny shook his head emphatically, "Screw that. Take our bags to the hotel and drop us at the nearest nudey show!" Melvin followed Ronny into the first smoky nightclub they came across and grabbed a seat in the corner while Ronny sought out lap dances.

Melvin glanced up from his mandatory two-drink minimum and spotted Ronny trying to get his attention from the other side of the room. Melvin shook his head. *Dude, don't wave at me while she's doing that. Yes, I see her. You don't have to point. Well, at least he's not giving me—nope, there it is, the double thumbs up.* Melvin hung his head. *Is he showing her pictures of his dog? I can't watch this.*

Next, Ronny wanted to hit the casinos. As they stepped out onto the sidewalk, a lady in a turban approached them. "Tell your fortune?"

"Beat it, gypsy," Ronny said. "Unless you're throwing in a striptease, we've got better ways to blow our cash."

"I'm not a gypsy. I'm Lebanese. And I know who you are, Melvin Napier."

"How do you know my name?"

"She overheard us, man. Don't fall for that shit. All gypsies are scam artists."

"I know who and what you are, Dr. Napier. You're a fraud. You were a fraud as a young man, and you're one now. Shall I tell your fat friend your secret?"

"Ew, Melvin, what's your secret? And I'm not fat, sister. I'm solid."

She pointed at Ronny. "You are a fat and rude little man. This is no secret."

"Yeah? Let me guess, sweetheart. Melvin's secret is that he's about to lose money to a shyster?"

"Come inside, doctor. My shop is right around the corner. I give a special discount to Arkansans."

"Alright, Ronny, how did she know where we're from?"

"She must have lifted our wallets. No, mine's here. Well, she's good with accents. It's her job. But you missed the mark with Melvin, lady, by like a thousand miles. He's Canadian."

She shrugged. "Is he?"

"This is bullshit, Melvin. Let's hit the bricks."

"I know where you're from, doctor. And I know from when."

"I want to hear her out, Ronny."

"Don't be so gullible, dude. I know *when* you're from? What does that even mean? She speaks in riddles because she doesn't know anything."

"Come inside, Dr. Napier. For you, it's free. Your friend can wait here." She gave Ronny a stern look. "I'll get to you next. For ten dollars, I'll tell your future. For twenty, I won't tell Dr. Napier your secret."

Ronny pointed his thumb at himself. "Sweetheart, I ain't got no secrets."

"I know two big ones," she replied. "Want to hear them?" Ronny slipped her a twenty.

She took Melvin around the corner and opened the glass door to her shop. Inside, the walls were tastefully draped in curtains and tapestries. The smell of incense filled the room. She sat him at a reading table. "My name is Yara."

"Hi, Yara. I don't believe in any of this. So, how do you know my name?"

"My father told me."

"Is he my patient?"

"No, but my mother was."

Melvin nodded. "That figures. Tell your father nothing happened between your mother and me. Wait, she's not from Georgia, is she?"

"No, they're both from Lebanon. I can't truly tell anyone's future except yours. And even then, I only know the past."

"You do like riddles. What do you mean?"

"My past, your future, it's all relative. I've been waiting for you for a long time."

"What do you mean?"

"I was sent to find you."

"Sent by whom, your father? How did he know I'd be here?"

"He told me the story years ago. Told me about your trip here."

His eyes widened. "Years ago? Do you travel through time?"

She smiled. "Yes. I travel as Allah intended, one day at a time. You, of course, are another matter."

"I don't understand, but you have my attention. Why are you staring at me?"

"I have waited so long for this. I can't believe my task is finally at hand. For a long time, I questioned if you were even real."

Melvin nodded. "I hear that more than you'd think."

"You saved my mother. You saved us all"—she closed her eyes and slightly bowed—"I am honored to meet you."

"You sure you have the right guy? Who are your parents?"

"I'm not allowed to tell you."

"Well, what can you tell me? What was your task?"

"To deliver a message. Your knowledge of the future is more powerful than an atomic bomb, yet you wield it like it's nothing. You gave my father the gift of future knowledge without a second thought. It haunted him until the day he died."

"I'm sorry."

"Don't be. It saved me from a childhood of misery. Besides, that wasn't the message. Here it is. One day you will find yourself with a gun in your hand and a terrible decision to make. My father wanted

245

you to know you always have a choice. We believe those who shed the blood of others are farther from God. He didn't want that for you. Even as he was dying, he prayed for your soul more than his. He made me swear to find you and deliver this message."

"And you knew the date I'd be here?"

"I knew the city and the approximate years. I've been waiting here for a long time. The gypsy routine pays the bills."

"Why not just find me in Little Rock?"

"The knowledge you gave my father has been passed on to me. I can never return to Arkansas. I must preserve the timeline at all costs."

"Thank you for the message. And don't worry. I'm not a killer."

"Not yet." She stood. "Now, you must go. Your friend has a surprise for you."

"Really? What is it?"

"You understand I can't tell you, right? Basic causality?"

Having polished off his third scotch less than twenty minutes ago, Melvin stared at her blankly, his mouth partially open.

Yara sighed. "If I tell you, then it doesn't become a story worth telling my father, who then doesn't tell it to me, and then I can't locate you outside of Arkansas." Melvin's expression didn't change. She shook her head. "You don't understand how any of this works, do you? You were so much wiser in my father's stories. I'm beginning to wonder how you even got into medical school."

"Oh, that's a long story. Could be a whole novel. But since I've been back here, I'm a lot brighter than I used to be."

She nodded. "I'm sorry to say I believe that."

"Ronny's surprises aren't that memorable. Tell me what he has planned, and maybe by knowing what it is, it becomes a story worth remembering."

Her eyes narrowed. "Perhaps. He's going to get you drunk and have you wake up in the morning with a prostitute."

"Typical Ronny. That's so uninspired, even for him."

"Then you'll discover the prostitute is dead, and the FBI will knock at your door."

"What?"

"It turns out the FBI agent is in love with the prostitute and convinced you're the killer."

"Holy shit!"

"Then he puts a gun under your chin and cocks the trigger."

"Holy shit! And then?"

"You soil yourself."

"Yeah, that part would never happen. But it sounds like Ronny's stepped up his game. Damn, boy."

"Now, you must leave."

"Wait, no. Why am I here? Do I ever get home?"

She took his arm and led him to the door. "I'm not here to answer those questions. I've said too much. I must protect your timeline in as much as it protects my family. You should have patience and faith."

"Faith, patience, and don't shoot anyone? That's the message? Really? At least tell me your last name."

"This is the age of the atom, Melvin. And that is who I am." She pushed him out the door and locked it. Immediately, the lights inside went out.

Melvin knocked on the door. "Yara?"

"How long are you going to take?" Ronny asked, peeking his head around the corner.

"I've just got a couple more questions for her. Yara! Come on, open the door."

"Who the hell is Yara?"

"The mysteriously cryptic gypsy girl draped in foreshadowing."

"Gypsy girl?"

"You're right. Technically she's Lebanese."

"Who the hell are you talking about? I thought you just stepped back here to take a piss?"

"No, I was talking with Yara, the girl who just took twenty bucks off you."

Ronny shook his head. "Buddy, what did they slip in your drink? Oh, wait! Was she that redhead at the club? Yeah, man, she got my cash. Believe you me, she earned every dollar."

"No, we met her here on the street. The girl in the turban."

"Turban? All this for some broad with a scarf on her head? We're in Vegas, man. There are thousands of women willing to take those scarves off and everything else. Come on!"

"No, I'm grabbing my bag from the hotel and catching the red-eye home. Hey, I want to thank you for this, Ronny. I feel a lot better. We'll square up on the airfare back home." Melvin hailed a cab.

Ronny threw his arms up. "You can't leave. We just got here. No telling what debauchery lies ahead."

Melvin climbed into the cab. "You go ahead. If I stay, I'll just get drunk and probably wake up next to a dead hooker with a distraught FBI boyfriend who thinks I killed her. And then I'd be in a pickle."

As the cab pulled away, Ronny stood on the sidewalk, mouth open. "How the hell did he . . . ? Hey, at least give me a ride!"

After getting his bag, Melvin took the cab back to Yara's shop. The door was still locked, the lights out, and all the signs in her window were gone. He shoved on the door in frustration. The lock creaked. Another push, and he was inside. He hit the light switch, but no power. Stepping back outside, he noted the other shops had electricity. He borrowed a flashlight from the cabbie, claiming he'd lost his keys here earlier in the evening.

His eyes widened as he shone the light inside her shop, illuminating nothing but cobweb-encrusted bare walls. *Didn't take her long to get out of Dodge.* A stench hit his nose, and he spotlighted dust-covered trash in the corner with decomposing rats. He looked behind him and saw his footprints in the thick dust on the concrete floor, the only ones there. *What the hell?* He stepped outside and looked up and down the block. This was the place. He was sure of it. *How did she do that? And all that bullshit about me and my future? But the look on Ronny's face with the prank. She was dead on.* He rubbed his head. *I've got to stop drinking.*

Chapter 26
The Gift

It was Thursday, April 30, 1953, and Melvin had just finished clinic, showered, and put on a clean suit. Today was his birthday, yet another without his family. Sally had insisted on taking him to dinner and a movie. There was no getting out of it this time. Straightening his tie, he looked himself over in the mirror. Like getting on an airplane, everyone dressed for the movies as if going to church in this crazy decade. He sighed and longed for the good old days when no one batted an eye at sandals and a worn-out t-shirt.

Sally knocked on his door. As usual, he didn't invite her in. She smiled and caressed his face. "Geez, how old are you today? Cause I'm starting to see some wrinkles, old man. Is that a gray hair?" She reached up and plucked it.

He rubbed his scalp and gave a dirty look. "I'm only 36. And the way your mother tells it, I'm only slightly older than you—old woman."

Sally shrugged. "How would she know how old I am? I'm twenty-nine. But you, oh my gosh, thirty-six?" She patted his chest. "Where did the time go? You'll be dead soon." Her grin widened. "Come to think of it, I look so damn good in this outfit that a warm-blooded man would faint at the sight of me. You haven't even noticed. Maybe you're dead already. Let's see." She grabbed his arm and pretended to check his pulse. "Nope, you're still with us. Must be your vision. They say that's the first to go." She got close to his face to examine his eyes. "I'd recommend an eye doctor, but I don't know anybody good. Well, in my medical opinion, you might live, at least for a while. Any plans for your twilight years?"

He looked at her wryly. "I thought I'd seek out nicer friends."

"That's not a bad plan. Ronny can be a real ass."

"Well, you're not wrong," Melvin replied. "Being an ass is contagious, and you two *have* spent a lot of time together."

"Oh, no, doctor!" she exclaimed, raising her hands to hide her face. "Are you saying I'm suffering from a case of assitis?"

"Cute," he replied as her hands formed a butt crack, and her tongue came through, simulating the emergence of something else.

She dropped her hands. "Hey, when you die of old age, can I have your . . . never mind. You don't own anything good."

"You're a bit of a shit today, aren't you?"

She hugged him. "Aw, come on, it's your birthday! You can't be blue. Smile. Have some fun." She twirled, her skirt momentarily increasing in circumference. "You get to spend it with a *beautiful* woman." She quickly pointed at him. "And if you ask, when does she get here—I'll sock you!" He grinned. "Finally, there it is," she said. "Now, come downstairs. I have a surprise for you." He reluctantly followed, doubting Sally could do anything at this point that would surprise him.

Melvin was stunned. Parked next to her car was a beautiful, brand-new 1953 sedan. Dark blue exterior with chrome bumpers, the interior sported leather bench seats and wooden accents. She popped the hood and started talking up the engine's high points and latest technology. Melvin just smiled and nodded. She then pointed out the roomy and well-padded back seat.

"I can't believe you bought me a *car!* This is amazing. You shouldn't have. I can't accept it. It's too much."

"Sorry," she replied with a smile. "I can't return it. It's customized." She pointed to the dash. Melvin slid in behind the large steering wheel and ran his fingers over the shiny brass plate mounted to the console, "With love, Sally." In his thirty-six years, he'd never owned a new vehicle. Even when he and Alexis started to do well, they'd always bought used. He didn't know what to say. As usual, Sally was happy to help in that regard and slid in beside him.

"If you're looking for something to say, you could always start with: Thank you, Sally. You're as generous and thoughtful as you are beautiful."

"Thank you, Sally. And the rest of what you said. I can't believe it. You spent way too much."

"Not really," she admitted. "The guy who bought our lot was a friend of the family. I've been talking with him for a while. Even let him take me out on Valentine's. Anyway, a customer ordered this car in green, but when it arrived in navy, they wouldn't take it. So, he gave it to me at cost."

"You went out with this guy just to get me a car? How old is he?" Melvin's eyes narrowed. "What did you do?"

"I'm sure I didn't do anything you wouldn't have done for me. Now, don't just sit there gawking. Start her up! You finally got your driver's license, right?"

"Well, of course," he lied.

"So, what are you waiting on?"

"I don't know. There's something about this car. It feels, I don't know, familiar."

"Well, I promise you, it's brand new. Sometimes a car is so right that you feel comfortable the moment you get in."

He nodded. "That must be it. I love it!" The engine purred. He pushed in the clutch, shifted, and slowly backed out onto the street. Going through the gears as they reached the highway, the car performed beautifully—nothing like the cars from her dad. They drove the Arkansas highways well into the evening, putting the sedan through her paces, stopping only for a late supper at a roadside diner in Sheridan—the perfect ending to a beautiful evening.

Returning home, Sally led the way up the stairs. All night Melvin had thought about the three long years he'd fought for his family. For three years, the universe had denied him. On the other hand, it had given him Sally, the girl who'd been there for him, lied for him, had a government official's life threatened for him, and even survived a gun battle to get back to him. She was the girl he kept pushing away. How much longer would she wait? The universe was shouting, "What does it take to get through to this guy?" He gently spun her around as they reached the top of the stairs. "Hey, you." Melvin caressed her face and kissed her.

She smiled. "Hey, yourself." He kissed her again. Soon, they were making out with her back against his door. He fumbled for his keys and unlocked it. As it opened, she fell backward, giggling, and caught herself in the doorway.

"I want you to come inside," he said.

Her eyes grew large as she turned to look inside his loft behind her. Then she looked into his eyes, kissed his cheek, and said, "I'll see you tomorrow."

"What?"

She kissed him again, skipped over to her loft, and closed the door.

Melvin shook his head and watched her go. "Thought I understood women." He shook his head again. "Nope."

Sally was all grins at work the following day but not a word about the night before. That afternoon she casually mentioned plans in Conway for the weekend and left early. Melvin sat in his office, tapping on his desk. *Two years ago, she sneaks into bed with me. Now she's pretending last night didn't happen and avoiding me? What the hell?*

He picked up the phone. "Hey, David, it's Melvin. What's up? No, I didn't mean literally. It's just an expression. Really, never? I don't know . . . Bugs Bunny? Bugs Bunny—the rabbit. I realize they can't, but he's a cartoon. It doesn't have to make sense. It's a cartoon. You've *never* heard of Bugs Bunny? I don't know how to respond to that. Anyway, I could use your expertise. Have time for a beer this evening?"

As they drank at a corner table at McKeen's, Melvin pushed him hard on time travel.

"What's with the twenty questions?" David asked. "Are you writing a book?"

Melvin nodded. "It's a story I've been trying to write for three years until yesterday."

"What happened yesterday?"

"I gave up. I realized the universe was telling me to stop."

David folded his arms. "Well, unlike your cartoon rodent, the universe doesn't speak. It consists only of facts, matter, actions, and consequences. If you've given up, why are we having this conversation?"

"First, Bugs is a universally adored wise-cracking bunny, not a rodent. Second, maybe deep down, I don't want to quit on the story. Maybe it could still happen. Maybe I just need hope and inspiration."

"You're an odd man, Melvin. But I'll bite. What's it about?"

"In the story, a guy from the distant future, let's say, 2004, gets sent back to 1950. Now, he's having a beer with a physicist and wants to know how to get back home. I'll be the future guy, and you be the physicist. It'll be a stretch, but I think we can pull it off."

David smiled. "Yes, I've heard of that recently. They call it role-playing. But we're a couple of guys in a bar. I don't think you quite understand the nature of that game."

"Will you just play along? Now you're the physicist. What would you tell me?"

David slowly nodded. "So, that explains why you asked me about theoretically building a time capsule to reach 2004. Okay, I enjoy a good farce. How did you get here?"

"No idea."

"What do you mean you have no idea? You're the writer."

"I mean, the character has no idea. I got on a plane in 2004. Midway through the flight, it shook horribly, and I woke up severely injured in a hospital in 1950."

"Well, that's odd."

"You're damn right, it's odd. And I've been trying to find a way back home for the last three years. I have, or will have, a wife, two kids, and a dog. I'll do anything to get back to them."

David studied his eyes. "Is time travel common in the future?"

"No, don't be ridiculous. That's just Sci-Fi."

"What's Sci-Fi?"

"That's what we call science fiction in the future."

David chuckled. "So, if you know the future, prove it to me. The heavyweight championship is this Friday. You should already know who wins and in what round. So? Rocky or Jersey Joe?"

Melvin shook his head. "No. My character never watched sports, and his knowledge of history sucks. Wait, Rocky was a real-life boxer?"

"Wow, Melvin, you *don't* know sports, do you?" David rubbed his chin. "It's clever writing. It's either very convenient if you're character's lying about being from the future or very inconvenient for him if he's telling the truth. Still, I would ask your character for any future knowledge he could offer to prove his story."

Melvin scratched his head. "I could tell you all about the technology of my time, but wouldn't it change things if my character told the physicist about the future?"

"There's a high probability the physicist doesn't believe a word your character is saying, so let's risk it." Over the next forty minutes, Melvin told David every technological advancement, every historical event yet to happen, and every pop-cultural reference he could remember. When he'd finished his tale of the future, the two sat in awkward silence for some time, sipping their beer. Finally, David asked, "Did I tell you about my trip to Ft. Smith last month? I was driving these back roads and crested a big hill. The car got completely airborne. For the life of me, I can't recall the name of that little town on the road to Ft. Smith where that hill was."

Melvin replied, "Charleston. What does it have to do with my book?"

David's eyes narrowed. "Everything. I'm from Indiana. Between college, grad school, and working here, I've lived in Arkansas for twelve years, yet I still can't name most places outside of Little Rock. You're from Canada, and after only three years, you know the name of every little town in the state. You even know the hill I'm talking about on a road in the middle of nowhere."

"Well, I'm—"

David held up his finger. "You went to school in Québec, right?"

"Yes."

"Name five towns within 50 miles of Québec."

"What are you saying?"

"And another thing. I have a trained ear for dialects. You hide it well, but for a guy from Canada, you have an Arkansas drawl. It's subtle, but it's there. So, it's been clear to me for a while that you're from here. At first, I thought you were a fraud, pretending to be a physician. As I've gotten to know you, I realized you truly are an ophthalmologist and surmised you simply changed your name, although the reason wasn't clear. Listening to you now, it all makes sense. There is no book, is there?"

"Montmagny, Charny, Saint-Nicolas, Boischatel, and Loretteville."

"What?"

"Five towns near Québec City."

"That doesn't prove anything. If you were smart, you would've read a book about Canada."

Melvin smiled. "You think I'm from the future?"

"It'd explain a lot. You told me 50 years of future history. Anyone could make up a story. The problem is, when you ask a detailed question, the storyteller has to stop and figure out an answer that works with what they've said. Your story fits together perfectly, and when pushed on details, you didn't hesitate. Either you are the world's greatest storyteller, or it wasn't a story. Those were memories."

The awkward silence returned. Finally, Melvin said, "Damn, that's pretty smart. I can't believe you figured it out."

"You mean, you believe you're from the future?"

"Well, yeah, you just figured it all out."

"No, I was hypothesizing. You're serious, though, aren't you? You believe you're from the future?"

Melvin laughed. "No, man. I'm just screwing with you. Want another beer?"

"You do believe it. And what's more, I believe you."

"You do?"

"Let's be realistic. Who in their right mind would believe you're from the future?" He put his hand on Melvin's shoulder. "No one— except a *physicist*. Let's head over to my office. I want to hear everything. And pay the tab, would you?"

Melvin revealed the whole story, his family, the plane ride, waking up in the hospital, how he'd gotten his job, his experimental flights, everything. When he finished, he released a long breath. "You cannot imagine how cathartic it is to tell a secret you've held for three years. I still can't believe you believe me. If this were reversed, I'd say you were nuts."

David looked up from his notes and lit a cigarette. "That's because you're a physician and not a physicist. We don't consider human behavior in the equation. We look at evidence objectively without preconception. The data determines the conclusion. To dismiss your story as untrue without proper investigation would introduce personal bias. Plus, it's improbable to believe you're making it up."

"Why is that?"

"Because you have to assume technological progression has a somewhat linear function."

"Well, yeah," Melvin shrugged. "That goes without saying. Just for fun, could you explain it?"

"You have to figure technology will always improve over time. Dictating what future technology could or couldn't exist is pure hubris. Yet most non-physicists do just that. For example, if I traveled back to 1850 and tried to tell a layman about a future machine that could fly across an ocean, they'd say I was crazy. Or try to explain a car in 1750. A physicist, on the other hand, would listen. It's reasonably probable that someone will develop a device to manipulate time and space in the future. You're telling me that occurs in or around 2004. Who am I to argue? You're here, after all. After hearing your story, I do have a question."

"Fire away." Melvin took a breath, knowing this would be either a detailed technological question he probably couldn't answer or an existential one about future societal morality.

"Why would you want your telephone to play music? Isn't that the purpose of a radio?"

Melvin smiled. "I'm glad we're talking, David. When I first arrived, I was this close to tracking down Einstein but chickened out. I never thought anyone would believe me."

David's jaw dropped. "Thank goodness you didn't. That would've been a monumental error in judgment."

"Bad idea to contact one of the greatest geniuses of our time who knows more about time travel than anyone on the planet?"

David crushed his cigarette. "Dr. Einstein is one of our government's top assets. They've got eyes on him around the clock. You may not recall, but a Cold War is going on. Anyone within 100 yards of him gets, at a minimum, a full background check. What would yours show? Nothing, because you don't yet exist. Do you know where guys who don't exist end up? With all the other communist spies. And do you know where that is?" Melvin shook his head. "Neither does anyone else."

"So, how do I get back?"

"Well, to find the solution, we must understand the problem. We have to focus on how you arrived. Tell me again everything you can remember about that day." Melvin told him everything once more. David looked at him while he rubbed his chin. "Okay, let's start by considering everything we know. For example, you're on a plane and, therefore, in the air." Melvin looked at him like he was an idiot. "I'm saying that you're at a certain altitude, meaning less effect of gravity, decreased temperature, less air mass outside. You have cabin pressure, meaning decreased humidity, and you're moving forward at a certain speed. What kind of plane was it?"

"Single engine, six-seater, prop-plane." Melvin began to pace.

"When it started to shake, were you ascending, descending, or had the plane leveled off?"

"We leveled off not too long after takeoff." He snooped through David's bookcase.

David raised an eyebrow. "Please leave those alone. I'll examine models that fit that description and learn their average cruising altitude. A friend at the airport can tell us where you should have been after leveling—will you please stop that? My books are arranged in a particular order. We can also learn the temperature and humidity levels for the day you arrived."

"How does that help? Do you have any scotch around here?"

"No, this is my office. The more pertinent data we collect, the more accurate our calculations will be. Try to recall as much about the weather that day as you can. What were you wearing? Were you sweating or a little cold? Did you have an umbrella?"

Melvin took a seat and recalled as much detail as he could.

"Now, let's talk more about what you felt."

"Pain. And lots of it. Everything shook violently like the whole plane was going to explode."

"Hmm. That could happen for three reasons. First, it could have been something structural, meaning something was wrong with the plane and created small vibrations which successively propagated into larger ones. However, we have no evidence a structural weakness in the plane could alter the fabric of time. Second, something on board generated the vibrations, or third, the source was external."

"You mean like lightning or a tornado?"

"Doubtful. Lightning has struck many planes, and to our knowledge, none have resulted in time travel. Although, an upper atmospheric disturbance could produce vibrations. Did you feel a sudden change in cabin pressure or hear a roaring sound?"

Melvin nodded. "The pressure built up like crazy, but no roar."

"Hmm. Your pilot likely would have tried to steer around bad weather. We have no workable hypothesis for high wind speed creating a condition so abnormal it could alter time."

"So, you're thinking something on board?"

"It's certainly a variable we need to explore. Perhaps a piece of technology was onboard you weren't aware existed—something that could explain all this. Did you notice anything suspicious in the seating area?"

Melvin shook his head. "Just snacks. You don't happen to have any of those, do you?"

"Again, this is my office. I don't want roaches. Did you get a glimpse of any sort of cargo area?"

"I didn't notice one. Most normal people keep one or two snacks in a desk drawer—just saying."

"Well, I'd have to imagine anything capable of sending you through time would have to be quite large."

"Not necessarily. We've made a concerted effort in my time to make everything smaller, computers, phones, cars, you name it. This thing could have fit in your back pocket."

"If that's true, it could have been stowed in one of the seat pockets."

"Who would smuggle a time-traveling device to Jonesboro, Arkansas? It all sounds far-fetched."

"Says the man from 51 years in the future."

"Touché. So, you think the pilot was just flying me as a cover?"

"Assuming the pilot was involved. For all we know, anyone could have left a device there, intentionally or unintentionally, before the flight."

"Why intentionally?"

"Perhaps you were an alpha test. Suppose the device only worked under certain conditions, such as at a particular altitude. Put the device on the plane and see if it arrives in Jonesboro. Have your buddy then retrieve it."

"That's a lot of speculation. How do we sort all this out?"

"Why not talk with the pilot?"

"Sure, want to write him a letter and wait 51 years for a response?"

David shook his head. "If you were both subjected to the same device, then why not presume he's here as well?"

"Damn, I never thought of that."

"And more importantly, the device is likely here, too."

"Shit, you might be right!"

"Based upon your level of injury, if the pilot survived, he would have sought medical care."

"True. I'll pull records from that date at University Hospital and call Memphis and Jonesboro."

"As for the device, we simply need to locate the wreckage and hope the device has gone unnoticed."

"That's a problem. I haven't found any reports of plane crashes in the papers."

"Interesting. What if you, the device, and the pilot landed in the same place but in different times?"

"What?"

"It's possible the effect of the device is dependent upon your proximity in the plane. In other words, the device and the plane could have landed where you did, but twenty years earlier, or will crash there next week or next year."

"Wow, that's a lot to take in. I'll also check the asylum."

"The asylum?"

"Yeah. I had enough sense to keep my mouth shut when I woke up. If I hadn't, that's where I'd be right now."

"Good point," said David. "As for the device, it's imperative we determine exactly where you landed. Do we know who found you?"

"My grandparents."

"You're joking. What are the odds of that?"

"Apparently, pretty damn good."

David rubbed his chin. "That's a problem. That occurrence alone may have already disrupted the timeline. Fortunately, you were unconscious, so your interaction was limited."

"Yeah,"—Melvin looked away—"It's not like I caught them just after sex and joined them for brunch."

David laughed. "Holy cow! How disastrous would that be? You're hilarious. How do you come up with this stuff? Seriously though, we need to ask them where you landed. I should do it. With only a minimal knowledge of the future, I can minimize their timeline changes."

"No need. I landed near Bald Knob. Can you really get me home?"

"Melvin, I promise you, the solution to all this is right in front of us. We just have to clear away the nonrelevant data to see it."

"Oh, man," sighed Melvin as his head went down.

"What's the matter? Isn't that good news?"

"I'd given up real hope until just now."

"So, what's with the long face?"

"I thought I could never get back. I almost cheated on my wife."

David put his hand on Melvin's shoulder. "I don't know about 2004, but around here, lots of guys brag about girls on the side. It might just be our national pastime."

"That's not me."

"Well, the keyword is almost. Speaking of your wife, I presume the time capsule was to communicate with her?"

"I wrote her a letter a couple of years ago and buried it in our future backyard. I buried a second one last year for added insurance."

"And it's reasonable to assume she'll know where to dig?"

"We do extensive landscaping in 2004." David squinted at him. "Oh, that's what we call digging in the future. Calling it landscaping allows contractors to charge more."

David nodded. "I see. Exactly what did you tell her?"

Melvin cocked his head to one side. "Everything. The day I came here, what's happened since, everything."

"You were clear she shouldn't share this with the future you, right? You made it clear she shouldn't attempt to prevent this from happening?"

"Hell, no. I told her to stop my ass from ever getting on that plane. Why wouldn't I?"

"Melvin, what do you think happens to you here if she prevents you from getting on the plane in the future?"

"I don't know. I'm hoping none of this would have happened, and I'll disappear from here and go on living there."

"You understand the paradox you've created?"

"Dude, I've seen the movie. If I'm never here, I can't send the letter telling her to keep me off the plane. Don't worry. Nothing changed after I buried it. I think I may have created a new timeline and might simultaneously be here and there."

263

"Fascinating. Or another possibility: time could be repeating."

"A time loop? How?"

"Time loop? I've never heard that term, but it's appropriate. The first time through, you had this same idea to communicate with your wife. You told her to stop you. The moment she did, a paradox was created because the letter was no longer written. Now let's consider the moment after the paradox."

"Do you have any coffee?"

"Because there is no longer a letter to discover, the moment she prevents you from getting on the plane never happens. You then board the plane, arrive here, and, again, have the idea to write a letter. The cycle repeats."

"Is that a no on the coffee? It almost sounds like this is my fault."

"We have a saying in 1953. If the shoe fits—"

"Yeah, we have that one, too. So, I should tell her not to stop me?"

"That would be better. The best thing would be not to communicate at all. Better to find another way home."

"Are you suggesting I go back to Maumelle and dig up the letters?"

"Maumelle River?"

"No, the Marche area."

"I'd be careful over there. They spotted a communist spy."

Melvin hung his head and raised his hand. "That was me."

"You're a communist spy from the future? I didn't need to know that."

"I'm not a spy or a communist. I was burying the first letter when someone spotted me. The whole story blew up from there."

"No, that can't be. It was in the paper."

"We have a saying in *my* time. Don't believe everything you read."

"I've heard that one. I'll grab a slide rule and dig into the data while you grab a shovel and dig up those letters. Let's meet again in a week or so."

Chapter 27
The Invite

The following Saturday, Melvin found himself in his future backyard with shovel in hand. He paused over the area where he'd buried the first container. *What am I doing? What if David's wrong? What if the letters never worked because she never got them? And it wasn't about location, depth, or disintegration. What if it was always because, on May 9, 1953, I come here and dig them up?* He shook his head. *Back to this nonsense again.* He stared at the ground a little longer. *Okay, once again, I'm making a decision not to dig these up.* He closed his eyes and waited for something to happen. He opened one eye. *Okay, I mean it this time. I'm not going to dig these up—ever.* Once more, nothing. *So, either David's right, or maybe I just come back later and dig these up. Damn.* He stared a while longer, then snapped his fingers. *Got it! Oh, this is brilliant.*

Back in his loft, Melvin wrote a new letter:

My dearest Alexis,

Today is May 9, 1953. If this is the first letter you've found, this will sound confusing. Three years ago, I arrived here after a plane crash on a flight to Jonesboro on my birthday in 2004. I've missed you guys terribly. I've tried my best but haven't found a way back to you. But I have a new idea. In my other letters, I asked you to stop me from getting on the plane. When nothing changed, I spoke to David, my physicist friend. He thinks that stopping me creates a paradox leading to a time loop. I don't understand it either, but he insists you shouldn't tell me and let me go. He believes I can come home another way.

265

But physicists in 2004 surely know more than David. Take these letters to them and ask if you should stop me or not. You'll have to keep it from me. Also, I'm opening up an interest-bearing savings account in Grandma's name at Arkansas Bank. Why not? She won't know about it, so just take her over there to withdraw it for you and the boys.

Life here has been something else. Despite being intimidated by organized crime, accused of espionage in the papers, interviewed by the FBI, and suspected of government fraud by an agent who may or may not have been murdered by our receptionist's father, it hasn't been all bad. I've made friends here who care about me. You and the boys are my whole world, and I'm ready to come home. I'll do whatever it takes. I love you more than you know. Now, find a physicist and bring me home.

Love,

Melvin

P.S. Tell Grandma I know all about the Capitol Hotel, and shame on her.

By the following weekend, Melvin had a new container containing the third letter in the ground, fourteen paces east of the boulders. With no immediate change upon burial, he hoped David would come up with something. Unfortunately, David soon called to say his work had gotten hectic and the calculations would take a few more weeks.

Melvin hoped it wouldn't be too long because things with Sally were getting weird. Ever since his birthday, she cooked for him almost every evening. Despite the abundance of food on her table, she was never hungry. Plus, she no longer smoked, and the walks of shame had stopped. Even her drinking had decreased. Dr. Thomas expressed concern with her change in behavior, noting she had become downright pleasant. A few patients even mistook her for a new employee, telling her how glad they were that the crabby girl had been fired. Despite all this, Sally still hadn't made a single romantic gesture toward Melvin since that night. But he knew the clock was ticking.

On Saturday evening, June 13, 1953, he took Sally to the opening of the Riverside Drive-In. Laughter could be heard from the other cars as a cartoon kicked off the show.

"You know who that is, right?" Melvin asked.

"Bugs Bunny. Everyone knows that," she replied as she giggled at Elmer Fudd.

"Just checking. You know who should be here to see this? David."

"You want another guy here on our date? What kind of girl do you think I am?"

He stole some of her popcorn. "Do you ever think about the future?"

"Not really. Whatever happens, happens. No one knows the future."

"Unless you're a Lebanese gypsy in Vegas," he muttered.

"Vegas?" she asked. "When were you ever in Vegas?"

"Last Valentine's Day. I never told you the story about almost waking up with a dead hooker?"

"Whoa, whoa, *whoa!*" she exclaimed as she slid across the front seat as far from him as possible. "The night I was cozying up to a smelly old man to get you this car, you went to bed with a hooker in *Vegas?*"

As she commenced to slapping the patooties out of him, Melvin turned his head to avoid an eye injury and caught a glimpse of a man looking their way with concern. "Quiet down and stop hitting me! It wasn't my fault."

"It never is!" She slapped him harder.

"Stop it! I said *almost.* It was a prank set up by Ronny."

"Oh," she said, and then punched him in the arm.

"What the hell was that for?"

"Going to Vegas without me. And I'm pissed at Ronny, but he's not here. So, you didn't Grace Moultrie her?"

"No, I never even met her. I found out about it ahead of time and came right back home."

"His prank was to have you wake up with a dead hooker? That's kind of uninspired, even for Ronny."

"He was going to have an FBI guy bust in as her boyfriend and threaten to kill me."

She giggled. "Oh, that's kind of hilarious. You would've shit your shorts."

"You and Ronny are sick puppies." Melvin glanced over again, but the concerned man had disappeared. "Let's back up. You were concerned I slept with a hooker, but it didn't bother you she had somehow died?"

Sally shrugged. "Saves me the trouble."

"And what the hell did you mean, you got cozy with an old man to get my car? I thought all you did was go out?"

"Hey! It's Abbott and Costello. I've never seen this one."

"Sally?"

"Shh, Melvin. We're watching a movie."

She snuggled under his arm and dozed off as *Lost in Alaska* ended, and *The Lawless Breed* came on to complete the double feature. Having a little too much RC cola, Melvin gently pushed her aside and headed to the john. As he washed up, a kid slipped a note in his pocket and ran. He was long gone before Melvin could admonish him for approaching strangers in the men's room. Melvin pulled out the paper.

I know who you are and what you're after. Brown can't help you. 20th and Woodrow, 10 P.M. tomorrow. Show up alone or not at all. David W. Carroll.

Melvin fell back against the wall, remembered he was in a public restroom, and quickly stood up. He looked outside for the boy, but no luck. He stuffed the message in his pocket and walked back to the car. A truck in the back row started up and pulled away.

"Where did you go? I missed you. I got cold." Sally snuggled back under his arm.

"Well, you know, nature calls. And sometimes she leaves you notes."

"What?"

"Old Canadian saying. Shh, watch the movie."

Melvin closed his eyes and thought, *Who the hell is David Carroll? A patient? Someone from the bar? Someone from Detroit? What could he know? How does he know David? Did David tell someone? Am I being blackmailed?* His shoulders relaxed. *This has Ronny written all over it. Got to be. But how would he know David? Could it be Agent Smith? Did he survive the woods? With Cole gone, maybe he's back on my trail. Maybe I'm his great white buffalo. Smith couldn't know about David unless he's been following me. And he's just the type to do it.* Melvin slipped the note out and read it again, careful not to let Sally see. *Please let this be Ronny.*

"Hey, what's that?"

"Nothing, just my grocery list." He stuffed it back into his pocket.

"Yeah? Well, let me see it. If you're going to the market, I need some things."

"No, it's all crumpled up. Why don't we make a new list later?"

Her eyes narrowed. "Do you have another woman slipping you secret notes?"

"Don't be ridiculous. Do you think I'm the kind of man who could handle two girlfriends?"

Sally's eyes widened. "You've never called me your girlfriend before." She reached up and kissed him.

"What I meant was—"

"Melvin?"

"Yeah?"

"Stop talking."

"Okay."

"And Melvin?"

"Yeah?"

"When you're on a hot date with your girlfriend and have a choice between kissing or looking at your damn grocery list—choose wisely."

After kissing Sally goodnight, Melvin slipped down to the clinic and searched patient records. He found three David Carrolls, none of whom he'd seen in clinic, and none were David W. Carroll. *Who is this guy?* He looked at his watch. *I guess I find out in 19 hours, thirty-two minutes.*

He went to bed, but falling asleep was a table reserved for the unworried, and he wasn't on the list. By 4:30 A.M., he was sipping coffee and rereading his board. Then he organized his books, washed dishes, and scrubbed his bathroom. Next, he climbed to the roof and weeded Sally's garden as the sun greeted Sunday morning. He went for a run at the school, then returned to sweep the clinic floors, organize the exam rooms, and vacuum his office. Walking up the stairs, he heard a commotion in Sally's loft.

"Sally? You okay in there?"

She opened the door, her sleepy eyes and bed-hair betraying her. "Yeah, just tripped over the windowsill coming back in. Couldn't sleep. Did you hear all that noise downstairs? Did Dr. Thomas hire a cleaning crew, or was I dreaming?"

"Probably dreaming. You were up on the roof in your bathrobe?"

"Yeah, I go up there for a morning smoke."

"I thought you quit?"

"I know you did. That's why I do it on the roof, silly. This morning I discovered some damn squirrels got in my garden last night and pulled up all my tomato plants. Bastards!"

"Those were tomato plants, huh?"

"Yeah. Guess I'll have to put up some chicken wire—furry little sons of bitches. I had fun at the movies last night. Why are you so sweaty and dirty?"

"Just working."

"At this ungodly hour?"

"It's nine A.M."

"Exactly. I'm going back to bed. Why don't you go shower? Then we can snuggle."

"No, my car needs an oil change."

"Well, I'm a little tired right now," she said, yawning. "Maybe I'll do it this afternoon."

"I'll handle it."

"No, it's silly to pay someone. I'll do it later."

"No, *I'm* going to do it," Melvin said.

"You? Change the oil? In a car?"

"I'm not completely helpless, you know. How hard could it be? I'm just going to crawl under there and loosen the thingy on the . . . other thing."

"The cap nut on the oil pan?"

"Exactly. Then I put the new oil in the other thing. Piece of cake."

"Wait a minute." She reached inside her closet and gave him a bucket. "You'll need this."

"For what?"

"Oh, geez. You're the dumbest smart guy I know. Hang on, let me put on a shirt. Good thing you're so damn cute. Do you at least have a crescent wrench?"

Melvin looked at the ceiling. "Crescent wrench . . . crescent wrench. I'm going to say, no?"

She shook her head. "I feel completely safe in believing that. What oil weight did you buy?"

"There are different kinds?" He shrugged. "Once I reach that step, I'll get an expert opinion at the station."

271

"Hold up." She closed one eye and yawned. "So, your plan is to drain the oil, then drive to the station to buy more?"

"Well, not when you say it like that."

"Make the coffee while I get dressed. Today we're going to learn basic car maintenance. Then you're going to buy me the nicest lunch I can imagine. And I've got a *great* imagination."

Melvin repeatedly checked his watch all day. By six, he was sweating as Sally kept making plans for the evening, each of which he shot down, but he was running out of ammunition.

"You know," she finally said, "it's starting to sound like you don't *want* to spend the evening with me."

"Of course, I do. And I appreciate the automotive tutorial this morning. Now I could flip the lid off that rectangular canister and refill the transmission fluid with my eyes closed."

"Well, if you did, you'd be putting it in the brake fluid compartment. I guess I suck eggs at teaching. So, what's the deal? Are you meeting someone tonight?"

"No. I mean, yes."

She put her hands on her hips. "Yes?"

"I mean, no, not another woman. At least, I'm pretty sure it's a man."

"Usually, I'd tell you to stop talking about now. This is *not* one of those times."

"It has to do with David. I promised not to tell anyone. I have to meet with someone at ten to get some information, that's all."

"What information?"

"I promised not to tell anyone. Do you even listen when we talk?"

"I hang on your every word, sweetie. And you can tell *me* because I'm not just anyone."

Melvin shook his head. "I can't."

"So, you don't know this person?"

"No, just a time and an address."

"That's nuts. I'm going along for backup. Let me grab my pistol."
She picked up her purse.

"You have a gun?"

"You don't? Here, you can carry mine. Just be careful with it. I filed it down to a hair-trigger, and there's no safety."

"Geez! How does it even fit in that tiny purse?"

"I cut back on the booze, so now I have more room." She rummaged through her purse. "Let me see if I have some extra bullets. You can never have too many of those."

"Put that away."

"Are Canadians uncomfortable with guns? That explains a lot, actually. No problem. Here, just strap this knife to your ankle and—"

"No."

She reached back into her purse. "Brass knuckles?"

"I don't need a weapon. How much more could you possibly have in there?"

"Just the essentials. It's kind of a small purse, you know. You don't want anything?"

"My mind is my best weapon."

"Oh, sweetie, then I'm afraid you'll always be out-gunned."

"Ha, ha. If they wanted to hurt me, they would've done it already."

She raised an eyebrow. "They? How many of them are there?"

"I don't know. Look, I'm just getting information, that's all."

"In the middle of the night? At least tell me where you're going."

"They said I have to come alone."

Sally shrugged. "Well, that's not suspicious at all. Not even sure why I was worried."

"It'll be fine. Maybe they just spook easy. They said alone, so I can't show up with anyone else."

"No problem. I'll stay out of sight and cover you with my long gun. Just have to find it. I think it's in the back of my closet somewhere."

273

"You *think*? So, it's like your ironing board, broom, bowling ball, and sniper rifle might be somewhere in the closet, but who knows?"

"Are you making a crack about my ironing? Maybe a few of my skirts have had wrinkles, but there's only so much time in a day, Melvin."

"I'm commenting that you have a high-powered rifle with your prints on it and no idea where it might be."

"Don't be so dramatic. I have some idea." Opening her closet door, she put her finger to her lips. "Geez, that looks pretty full. It's got to be in there. It didn't just get up and walk away. However, I might have put it under the bed. If it is, I'm not crawling under there, not with those dust bunnies."

"You can survive a gun battle and lay in the woods all night with snakes and spiders, but you draw the line at dust bunnies?"

She shivered. "Dust bunnies give me the willies. Let me just dig in here for a minute." She maneuvered her leg partway into the closet. "Look, see? My ironing board is right back there. Let me just pry that out." She wrestled back and forth. "Damn, it's wedged. Oh, hey, I found my broom! Now let's see, long gun, long gun. Oh, I haven't worn that in a while."

"Who *are* you? I'm going alone. No guns, knives, poisons, or candlesticks in the library. I'll be safe and let you know when I get back."

"Candlestick? You really don't have a clue."

"I'll be fine."

"Okay, but if all this is bullshit and you're going on a date, just remember—hair-trigger."

Chapter 28
The Night of the Dead

Around 9:30 P.M., Melvin drove around the city, convinced Sally was following. He made several turns through the small neighborhood streets to lose her. He thought about her feeling the need to carry all those weapons. Before, he'd searched her purse to take away her liquor and had never found anything more dangerous than cigarettes. Of course, that was before she'd witnessed half her family slaughtered and set on fire. Now she was willing to put herself in harm's way for him without a second thought. *Would Alexis have done that for me? Maybe. No, probably she would. No, she would. Of course, she would.*

He turned on 20th until he found Woodruff Street. From his headlights, Melvin could see it was a cemetery. *Now what?* He shut off the car. *Do I wait here?* He got out and peered out into the darkness. *A smart guy would've brought a flashlight. Yup, that's what a smart guy would've done, dammit.* He recalled Sally mentioning she'd stocked his trunk with roadside supplies. He popped it open, finding a flashlight and loaded handgun. *I love that woman.*

He hopped the fence and slowly made his way through the headstones. *Zoinks, man, like this is some creepy shit. Wish Velma were here. Or better yet, Daphne. Yeah, she'd be into me. I could totally pull off an ascot.* Bugs hit his face as they raced toward his flashlight. He clicked it off and scanned around, listening. *Nobody? Is this a prank? Get me out here in the middle of the night?* He called out, "I'm tired and have to work tomorrow, Ronny. If you're going to jump out and scare me, could you just do it? Come on, man, what are we, teenagers?" If Ronny were hiding, he was hiding well. "This is pretty junior high, dude." He listened, but only crickets replied.

He shined the light on his watch, 10:12. "Alright, you've had your fun. I'm out of here." He felt his heart stop. Something was behind him.

Melvin spun around with his light. "Clyde? What are you doing here?"

"Hey, Professor Jones. I was crawdad fishing in the creek over yonder." He held up a bucket as proof. "Just cutting through here on my way back home. What's an ophtha-archaeologist doing in a graveyard at night?"

"I study the past, Clyde. You can learn a lot here. Guess I lost track of time. And you can just call it Archaeology."

"Naw, I prefer the French pronunciation. Well, I'll let you get back to it then. Have a good evening."

"Yeah, you too. Say, Clyde, you weren't the one who sent me the note, were you?"

"Note, Dr. Jones?"

"Never mind. Have a good night."

Feeling silly about the whole thing, Melvin headed back to his car. Weaving through the graves, he stopped stone dead. Right before him was David W. Carroll, or at least his headstone. He shined the flashlight all around but saw no one. He shut it off and listened. Again, nothing. In almost a whisper, he said, "Okay, Mr. Carroll, you haven't sent anyone a message since 1905. Why did you bring me here?"

A deep voice from the darkness replied, "Sometimes the dead have need of the living."

As Melvin slowly turned around, all he could think was how lucky it'd been he'd performed number two before leaving the loft. With eyes as wide as his bony orbits would allow, Melvin Napier stared at a shadowy figure. Trembling hands fumbled to click on the flashlight. Finally, he illuminated a dead man's face. Melvin could barely speak. "Cole? You're . . . you're dead."

"Yes, I am. So, there's no need for that."

Melvin looked down and realized he'd drawn the pistol. He tucked it back into his waistband.

"Point it a little more to the right," Cole said. "In case you want another child one day. As I recall, Sally filed it down to a hair-trigger."

"You can't be here. You're dead. This isn't sci-fi." Melvin reached out and poked his chest. "Sorry, sci-fi means—"

"I know what sci-fi means, Melvin. Cole Davis *is* dead. I'm not Cole Davis, never was."

"Who are you, then?"

"Who are any of us? I've been many things over the years: mobster, car dealer, family man, stock market speculator, and before that, a flying ace in the first war."

"I never knew you were a pilot."

"Ever since I was a kid. Tell you, though, it was tough getting used to no avionics."

"How are you here? How did you survive the shootout?"

Cole took a seat on a headstone. "Slipped out through a tunnel under the cabin."

"How lucky was it you found a tunnel? And dead or not, it's disrespectful to sit on a grave."

Cole gave a nonchalant shrug but didn't move. "I had the tunnel dug when I built the cabin."

"Sally said you were renting a cabin you'd found."

"I know."

"Is Stacy alive?"

"Yeah, he's fine."

"So, you built a secret hideout, just in case? Lucky you did, considering that's where they found you."

Cole shook his head. "You haven't figured it out yet, have you? There are no coincidences, no accidents. We make our destiny. I had Stacy place that bet."

"You *wanted* your family in a shootout?"

277

"Dying was the only way to save them."

"Did you count on them setting fire to the cabin with you inside?"

"We set that fire. Harder to ID the bodies."

"You had bodies?"

"It's the 1950s. Bodies aren't hard to come by."

"You knew all this was coming. Did the uncles tip you off?"

"The uncles," Cole scoffed, "bunch of greedy bastards. They took a bigger cut from my lot every year and didn't care how tight things got for us. Then to show up unannounced at Thanksgiving, expecting my family to act as servants? And the way they spoke to my daughter. Any man who does that forfeits the right to walk upon this Earth. Not to mention the plans they had for you."

Melvin's eyes widened again. "What plans?"

"Sooner or later, they would've had you doing things you never thought you would. You wouldn't survive prison, Melvin. It was time for them to go."

"Cole, are you saying that you—? What exactly are you saying?"

"I'm saying you were wise not to go duck hunting that day. The woods can be a dangerous place."

"Weren't you worried Detroit would come after you?"

"We had a head start. The family in Detroit assumed another family was making a move. But sooner or later, someone would be sent our way. Cole had to die, and he did."

"Where's Stacy now?"

"New Mexico with his family—under a new name."

"That's a hell of a story, but damn risky. What if they'd found the women and children in the woods?"

"We stuck around long enough to make sure. And we'd played enough games of hide and seek so they'd know where to go."

"I still can't believe it. Sally's going to faint when she sees you."

"No, she's not. Because you're not going to tell her."

"Why not?"

"Listen to what I'm telling you. Cole and Stacy Davis are dead. Sally and her mother are safe as long as that's true."

Melvin slowly nodded. "I get it. But why tell me?"

Cole stood and put a finger in Melvin's chest. "You need to know I'm still around watching over my family. You need to understand how far I'll go to do what's best for them."

Melvin took a step back. "What do you mean, what's best for them?"

"It's time for you to go, Melvin. I want you out of Sally's life."

"What? I care about your daughter, and she loves me. You and Kate even said I was the best thing she'd ever brought home."

"That was three years ago. Did you marry her and give her children? Or did you string her along? She's almost to the age where having kids is dangerous. You blew your chance. And why? Because you selfishly cling to the notion you're already married and have two children. None of whom you'll ever see again, and you know it. So, what gives you the right to deny my daughter everything you've enjoyed? It's time for you to go."

Melvin stared at Cole's cold gray eyes. *How could he know about the kids? Did he follow me and find the letters? Is that why it didn't work, because of him?* "How do you know about me, Cole? Who are you?"

"Just a guy who knows you're about as Canadian as Kenny Rodgers."

"Kenny Rodgers *is* Canadian."

Cole folded his arms. "No kidding? Never would've guessed that. Talented guy."

"Yeah, no doubt. Wait, you're from the future? Who are you, really?"

"In my old life, I flew rich assholes from point A to point B. Then one day, my charter is some rich douche-bag doctor. He's too busy on his cell to acknowledge I'm standing there. And when he finally does, this asshole puts up a finger for me to wait like a servant. So, to screw with him, I tell him I'm the doctor from *Star Trek*."

"Holy shit! You're my pilot, Leonard McCoy! I didn't recognize . . . you've gotten . . ."

"Older? Yeah, that happens. I've been here a lot longer than you."

"What happened to us?"

Cole shrugged. "Skies were clear, nothing on radar, then the whole plane shook."

"I know. I was there."

Cole snapped his fingers. "And then you weren't. Next thing I knew, I was on the ground, barely alive. A nearby family cared for me until I healed. Said it was 1916. I searched for you and the plane—mostly the plane—but you were both gone. So, I took a job on their farm. After the war, I came back and started a car dealership and bought that little house on Davis Street. Changed my name to Cole Davis and told people the street was named after my family, and we'd been here for generations. After a while, it just became fact."

Cole released a heavy sigh. "I was content to leave my past life behind, but then my daughter brought that same douche-bag doctor home one Thanksgiving, and he hadn't aged a day. At first, I thought you'd come to take me back to 2004. With a family and a better life here than I ever had back there, I wasn't about to let that happen. But you didn't recognize me." Cole smiled. "And why would you? I was just the hired help." His eyes narrowed, and his voice deepened. "I'm a fair-minded man and tried to tell you to settle in and build a life here, but you wouldn't listen. You just strung Sally along while you took plane rides and worked with Brown to find a way back. You planned to abandon her, right? I'm sure a man of your education considered what it'd be like for her if she turned up pregnant." Cole's jaw clenched. "Single mom in the 1950s, you thought about that, right? You selfish prick."

"I won't apologize for loving my wife and missing my children. So, yeah, I'm still trying to find a way back."

"Then you'll have no trouble doing as I ask, being in love with your wife and all."

Melvin looked at the ground. "No, I suppose not."

"Good." Cole reached behind his back. Melvin heard the uncocking of a pistol. "I'm tired of killing, Melvin. I'm too old for it."

Cole sat back down on the headstone, grunting as he did. "You'll let her down easy, though, right? And she's not pregnant? Because that would change everything."

Melvin held up his hands. "No, no chance of that. I'll do it the right way."

As Cole nodded and turned to leave, Melvin said, "Hey, why bring me to a cemetery? What was so important about this grave?"

Cole gave a half-grin. "This fellow was a state court judge. I thought it appropriate to see how your verdict would go." He shrugged. "Truth be told, I already knew."

"Because I'm a family man?"

Cole looked him in the eye. "Because you're a coward."

"I'm doing this for my family."

"Bullshit. Deep down, you know there's no way back. A real man would've stood his ground and fought for my daughter. You gave her up without hesitation. You're spineless. She's better off without you." Cole faded into the darkness. From a distance, his voice called back, "Disappear, Melvin, tonight. Don't make me help you."

Chapter 29
Decision Time

Safely back in his loft, Melvin locked his door and propped a chair against the doorknob. He sat down and placed one hand on top of the other to stop the trembling. He managed to pour a scotch, but halfway along its journey to his mouth, the phone rang, and the carpet enjoyed his drink instead.

"He-hello?"

"Melvin? It's David."

"David?"—he caught his breath—"You can't imagine how glad I am to hear your voice. I need some good news in the worst way. What do you have?"

"You were correct."

"About what?"

"It was an external device, likely hidden in a compartment in the passenger section of the plane."

"Are you sure?"

"The math pointed to a 94.6% probability of your landing site. I went up there and found the remains of the device. I was able to repair it and recreate the event in my lab. I sent my neighbor's cat twenty minutes into the past."

"A cat?"

"I needed to test a living organism, and I despise cats. So, if the outcome was detrimental . . . c'est la vie."

"But how would you know? Do you recall a cat unexpectedly appearing? Did it travel back twenty minutes or twenty years? Did it even survive?"

"Pertinent questions." David tapped his fingers audibly over the line. "Well, c'est la vie."

"What did your neighbor say?"

"She has several cats, so I doubt she noticed. Even if she does, she's not a good neighbor, so—"

"C'est la vie? Yeah, I get it. But can it send me the other way?"

"I adjusted the electromagnetic flow and attempted to send myself into the future. I'm pleased to report it worked. It made me nauseated, put a sizable rash on my chest, and some of my hair fell out, but I successfully arrived in the future. That's why you haven't heard from me. You had to catch up to me here. Melvin? Are you still there?"

"Yeah, I'm still here. I don't know what to say. You really did it. You can send me home."

"Yes, anytime you like. I'd recommend bringing a hat."

"David, you're a genius! You'll get the Nobel for this."

"That would be acceptable. I planned to place a clock on my mantle, but a Nobel prize might carry more visual interest. Shall we grab a beer at McKeen's to celebrate?"

"If it's all the same to you, I'd like to come to your lab, maybe in an hour? I have a couple of things I need to do first. You know, say my goodbyes."

"Oh, of course. Every traveler should. Seriously, though, want to get a beer tonight?"

"No, man, I'm ready to go. It needs to be now."

"You never fail to impress me, Melvin. Your seriousness is quite convincing. I wish I could get into this role-playing as much as you have. I have to tell you, the whole thing has been exhilarating—the math, the concept, the way we kept it going. I'm sorry to see it conclude. Would you like to start a new game?"

Melvin nearly dropped the receiver. "Game?"

"Yeah, I've told several of my colleagues, and they all want in. Perhaps this time, you could be an alien or someone who falls through a passage between worlds, and we're doing the math to get you home.

This time around, we'll have a whole team working on it. Wouldn't that be grand?"

All the air left Melvin's lungs. "You thought we were playing a game?"

"Well, I know I'm stepping out of character, but it's over, right? I mean, I got you home."

Melvin squeezed the bridge of his nose. "So, you never found a device, never did all that research you were talking about, never did any real math?"

"Oh, I did the math. That was the fun of it for me. I'd like to thank you for asking me to play. You know, you had me going when we started. I genuinely thought you believed it. I was this close to calling for a padded wagon when I figured it out. Did you study theater in school?"

"Yeah, I studied a lot of different things back then." Melvin shook his head and laughed the joyless laugh of a man who'd lost everything. "Just a game. What did the math actually show?"

"As expected, nothing."

"What do you mean?"

"No correlation, not even a suggestion allowing for higher P values. Without additional data to input, the results were conclusive in finding no correlation with any of the variables we've considered. In other words, the math says that your character will remain here in 1953. There's no evidence that will change. And since time travel doesn't functionally exist, that's exactly what it should show."

"Yeah, I suppose that's true. You're right, David, it was all great fun. I appreciate the dedication you put into it. I think I need a break from role-playing and will pass on the beer. But thanks again, and thanks for calling. Take care."

Melvin poured another scotch and picked up pen and paper one last time.

Dear Alexis,

This is my last letter. A dangerous killer from our time is stalking me, and if he finds where I'm burying these, then it risks none of them getting to you. He's been here much longer than I and has convinced me that whatever technology brought us here is long gone. My physicist friend just told me the same. After three long years, I'm afraid they're right.

I don't know how long I've been gone from your standpoint, but when you're ready, you need to live your life. I hope you remarry, find happiness, and provide a good life for our boys. If I survive long enough, I'll come and find you, but if you haven't seen me by the time you read this, then I didn't make it. Know that I tried everything imaginable to get back to you. Even if the universe keeps us apart, it can't keep me from loving you. Tell the boys I will always love and be proud of them and will watch over them from Heaven. Hug and kiss them for me. I will always be with them. I'll always be with you.

love,

Melvin

June 14th, 1953

Two hours later, he jumped at the banging on his door. Had Cole or McCoy, or whoever he was, changed his mind? Gun in hand, he removed the chair and stood to one side as he slowly unlocked it. The door burst open, "You didn't tell me you were back! It's been four hours! How long have you been home? I've been wearing a trail on my carpet, worried sick about you!"

He held up his hands. "I'm fine. It was fine."

"I see you found my pistol." Sally snatched it away.

"Uh, yeah, I appreciate it."

285

"So? What happened? Where's all your stuff? Why is your suitcase out?"

"I have to go. Some things I need to take care of. Things I need to do alone."

"I don't understand. Where are you going?"

"I can't say. It's for your own good. You, of all people, should understand."

She grabbed his arms. "You're wrong. I completely *don't* understand. Explain it to me."

"I can't say."

"When will you be back?"

"I can't say."

"Can't or won't? Are you even coming back?"

He pushed her off. "Don't make this any harder than it has to be. I have to go."

"Back to Canada? Back to her? Did she contact you? What's with the ammunition box? Those hold rounds for a machine gun. Secret meetings and guns?" She folded her arms. "What the hell is going on, Melvin? Are you in trouble? Is this about that communist spy? Are you trying to hunt him down? I know you, Melvin, and you'll get killed for sure. You're not a go-out-and-capture-a-spy kind of guy." She put her arms around him and buried her head in his chest. "If you're doing all this to impress me, you don't have to. I didn't fall for a big strong man who could handle himself. I fell in love with *you*."

Melvin pushed her away and picked up his bags. "Goodbye, Sally." Without a look or a kiss, he walked out.

1954

Chapter 30
Homecoming

It was Friday, December 24th, 1954. A year and a half had passed since that night in the graveyard, the night a dead man came back to life, the night Sally's man had walked out on her, the night a part of her had died. She heard a knock at the main door downstairs. "It's 10:30 at night. Who the hel—*heck* could it be?" As she partially opened the main clinic door, her eyes grew wider than the crack in the doorway.

"Merry Christmas."

She slammed it shut. Then she reopened it. "You son-of-a-bitch!" She slammed it again. Then she threw it open and hugged Melvin tightly. Then she slapped his hairy face. "Where the hell have you been?"

"Everywhere."

A voice from the top of the stairs called down, "Who is it, hun?"

Melvin nodded. "I should have guessed you'd have company."

Sally turned red and was about to reply when a man came bopping down to join them in the doorway. "Who's your friend, Sally? My goodness, he looks just like me! With the exception of your beard, sir, it's like I'm looking in a mirror. I'm Brian, and you are?"

Melvin stared at him. "I'm nobody, just an old friend passing through. Apologies for the late hour."

Brian gave a broad smile and a handshake. "Well, how about that? Won't you come inside and join us? I can't get over how much we look alike. Were we separated at birth?"

"No," Sally said. "I'm sure this man has business elsewhere, don't you?"

Brian looked at her incredulously. "At this hour, on Christmas Eve? Show some mercy on your old friend here. He looks cold and skinny. When's the last time you've eaten, sir?"

Melvin scratched his beard. "Can't quite recall. I wouldn't want to intrude."

"Nonsense! We have plenty. Have you ever tried Sally's cooking? She's the best cook in three counties." Brian patted his belly. "I've put on ten pounds since we met."

"That's kind of you, Brian, but Sally's right. Maybe another time."

"You heard him," Sally said. "Dr. Napier said another time. Now let's respect his—"

"Wait a just minute." Brian leaned against the doorway with his arms folded. "You're not the Dr. Melvin Napier who used to work here, are you?"

"Depends. Do you work for the IRS, FBI, DOJ, or any other commonly abbreviated governmental agency?"

"No, but I was a member of FFA back in school."

"FFA?"

"Future Farmers of America."

"I'll allow it. Yes, I'm Melvin Napier."

Brian shook his hand again. "I've heard quite a lot about you. Sally, I didn't know you two were friends."

She looked away. "Friend is a strong word. We worked together briefly before he disappeared. Dr. Napier was just saying he's here to see if any of his old belongings were still around. I can't think of anything here that could be considered *his* anymore. Tell me, Dr. Napier, was it anything in particular? Perhaps something you regret leaving behind?"

"Sally, it's freezing outside," Brian pleaded. "At least let the man step inside for some dessert while we look for his things." She looked at Brain, rolled her eyes, and stepped to one side, allowing Melvin to enter.

"You're in for a treat, Dr. Napier," Brian enthusiastically said as he led the group up the iron spiral staircase. "We have some left-over apple pie that will knock your socks off. I'll put on a pot of coffee. Tell me, sir, how long has it been since you left?"

Sally rattled off, "One year, six months, and ten days."

"Wow! Isn't she a peach, Melvin? A beautiful woman with a mind able to calculate that quickly is something to behold."

"Yup," Melvin replied, bringing up the rear. "She's a keeper. Man would be a fool to let her get away."

Sally scoffed.

"What was that, sugar bear?"

"Nothing, Brian. I just think it's a little late to invite someone in from off the street."

Brian turned around just short of the door. "He's not just someone off the street, sugar pie. He's your friend."

She released a long sigh. "You're right—as usual. He *was* a co-worker. Let's go inside. I'll get the pie."

"No, sweetheart. It may be women's work, but it's Christmas Eve, and he's your acquaintance. You two have a seat and catch up. I'll serve *you* for a change."

Sally and Melvin sat opposite each other in her living room, avoiding eye contact as Brian clattered around the kitchenette. Finally, he turned and served coffee and pie.

"This sure is a quiet group," he said, taking a seat on the couch next to her. "Nothing to say after a year and a half?"

"It turns out there isn't much to talk about," she replied, looking anywhere but straight ahead. "Interesting how you can work with someone and not really know who they are."

"Sometimes you don't even know yourself," Melvin added, now gazing at her. "Sometimes you have to hit the road to find out."

Her jaws clenched as she reached for her coffee. "And sometimes everything you need is right in front of you."

290

Melvin nodded. "Sometimes it is. Sometimes it takes losing what we need most to appreciate how much it truly meant to us."

"Goodness, that's deep, Melvin," Brian said. "You sound like a philosopher at heart."

"Sounds pure hippy-dippy to me," Sally grumbled as she sipped coffee.

Brian frowned. "Language, hun!"

Melvin's eyes danced in amusement and shot a glance from Brian to Sally.

She fiddled with her cup and saucer, pretending not to notice. "You're right, Brian. I apologize for my strong language. For all I know, Dr. Napier, you could be one of those hippies I've heard about in California. I didn't mean to offend."

"No offense taken. I did meet some wonderful people involved in that movement."

"Did you?" Her eyes narrowed as she now looked directly at him. "I can only imagine the places you've been, the people you've met, and all the things you must have done with them. I wouldn't know, you never having called or even bothered with a postcard. At least that's what the other employees told me. You must have been somewhere that didn't have phones or postal service. Bora Bora, perhaps?"

Melvin adjusted in his seat. "Yes, Ms. Davis, I traveled extensively. It still is *Ms.* Davis?"

"Oh, it is," Brian confirmed with a grin and a mouth half full of pie. Then he pointed at Melvin. "And please don't get the wrong idea about her having a man over at this hour. Sally's a respectable girl, as I'm sure you know from working with her. As for her current surname, it's simply ground we haven't covered—yet."

Melvin nodded slowly. "Interesting. Tell me, Brian, how did you two meet?"

Sally set her cup down and stood up. "It's getting late, and—"

Brian gently touched her arm, lowering her back onto the couch as his eyes came alive. "It's the *greatest* story. I was in the produce section at Ward's Market sizing up some cantaloupe when a shopping cart came out of nowhere and hit me."

"Hit you, you say?"

"Indeed. As I looked up from the floor, I saw the most beautiful woman running toward me, apologizing."

Melvin took a bite of pie and smiled. "Running? How far away was she?"

"I don't know. I suppose she was coming from the tomato section. Yes, that's correct. The cart had gotten away from her and just happened to smash into me."

"Really, at Ward's Market? I don't recall the floor having any significant degree of slope."

Brian scratched his jaw. "No, now that you mention it, I don't believe it does."

"And unless they've changed, the tomatoes are a good distance away from the cantaloupes. That's a long way to lose a cart on level ground. Based on the physics involved, I'm surprised—"

"The details aren't important, Dr. Napier," Sally interjected. "You're missing the point of the story. Go on, Brian."

"Well, she helped me up and tore off part of her dress to stop the bleeding."

Sally patted his thigh. "Let's not be overly dramatic, Brian. It was just a small scratch."

"No, hun, I had to get stitches, remember?" He lifted his shirt. "I still have the scar, see?"

"The point *is*,"—her volume shot up—"it was a happy accident, and that's how we met."

"Exactly." Brain grinned. "Now, it may have been the morphine they gave me in the emergency ward, but the more we talked, the more we discovered we had in common. I found out she likes the same foods

I do, the same hobbies, same taste in movies and music. And to top it off, it turned out we went to the same church. Doesn't that just beat the band?"

Melvin slurped his coffee. "The Episcopal down the street?"

"No," Brian's smile faded. "First Presbyterian on Moore."

"Is that right?" Melvin smiled at her. "Funny then, that you never met her before that day."

"It's getting awfully warm in here," Sally said, fanning herself. "I'll crack a window."

"No need, sweetie-bear." Brian immediately stood up. "Let me turn down the heat. You do look a little flushed. And you, sir, make an astute point. You'd think I would have noticed a girl as pretty as Sally at church. Big dumb me—Mr. Oblivious."

"Don't say that, Brian," she defended. "It's a large congregation. You're smart and kind and have *mountains* of integrity. Certainly not the type to run out on a girl."

"Ms. Davis," Melvin stated in a prosecutor's voice, "I could have sworn you said you attended the Episcopal down the street. When did you switch?"

"I've *always* attended First Presbyterian, Dr. Napier," she replied nonchalantly. "I guess you made a mistake. Perhaps it wasn't your only one. Why would you even remember that? I'm just the receptionist."

"Don't say that, honey pie," Brian scolded. "Sally basically runs the practice. She schedules, files, answers the phone, and puts patients in the rooms. The place would fall apart without her. Having worked here, I'm sure you'd agree, Melvin."

Melvin smiled. "Who in their right mind would argue?"

Brian finished off his pie. "So, tell us, Melvin, where did your travels take you for the past—what was it dear, one year, six months, and ten days? I'm still amazed you could just rattle that off like you didn't even have to think about it. I would've had to use all my fingers and take off my shoes to figure that out."

293

Melvin leaned back. "It's a long story, could be a whole novel, and it's getting pretty late."

"Yes," she hastily agreed, "he should be on his way. I believe you're experienced in finding your way out, Dr. Napier?"

"Now hold on," Brian protested, sitting down his coffee. "I take it you just rolled into town and, my apologies, sir, but it looks like you don't have a penny to your name. Where are you staying tonight?"

Sally smiled. "I hear under the Twelfth Street bridge is nice."

Brian frowned. "I'm disappointed in you, honey bunches. What a cruel thing to say, and on tonight of all nights. What's gotten into you this evening? Melvin, you are more than welcome to come and stay with me."

"I couldn't do that, Brian, but thank you. The Thomases have graciously offered to have me stay with them tonight."

Sally's eyebrows shot up. "So, you've already seen Dr. Thomas?"

"Yeah, we had some things to discuss."

"So, this wasn't the *first* place you stopped after being away a year and a half?"

"And ten days," Brian cheerfully added. "As you so elegantly calculated, honey-pie."

"Well, I suppose I should be going." Melvin stood. "Thank you for the hospitality, and thank you, Ms. Davis, for the apple pie. I can't remember the last time my lips touched anything that enjoyable. Truly delicious."

Sally folded her arms. "Oh please, Dr. Napier. I'm sure your lips have touched *plenty* of deserts better than mine in your travels."

Melvin looked her in the eyes. "No, Ms. Davis. Nothing even came close."

"You shouldn't argue with him, dear," Brian happily advised. "When a man compliments your cooking, you should simply say, Thank you."

"Thank you, Dr. Napier. And Brian's right, it's getting late. The Thomases will be asleep by the time you make it over there." She opened a drawer and pulled out a key. "You can stay in the loft next door. I'll get you a pillow and a blanket and phone them that you're staying here."

"That's the right thing to do, dear," Brian said with a smile. "I knew the real Sally would come around."

"Yes, Ms. Davis, your kindness is . . . unexpected."

"Don't get too excited, Dr. Napier. I used that loft to house chickens six months ago."

"Chickens?"

"Yes, I needed eggs for breakfast and fertilizer for my roof garden. I'm afraid I haven't had a chance to clean in there. Okay, pillow and blanket. Here you go." She sported a satisfied grin as she opened the door to let him out. "You might crack a window for the smell. Awfully cold out, though. I suppose you could light the heater, but then it'd smell like hot shi—chickens."

"Oh, dear," Brian said, putting his finger to his lips. "We've been so busy visiting that we forgot to look for Dr. Napier's things."

Sally put her hands on her hips. "You know, I do recall a box of things he left behind when he walked out . . . on the practice. We burned it. Have a good night!"

"Well, it's getting pretty late for me, too. I'll walk you out, Melvin. Good night sweetheart. See you tomorrow morning for church?"

"Wouldn't miss it for the world, Brian. Merry Christmas." She reached up and kissed his cheek.

"Yowzers, that's the ticket!" he exclaimed as he snapped his fingers. "Say, do you have anything to carry up, Melvin? I'm going your way."

"Not necessary. You're too nice, Brian. I sincerely mean that."

As Melvin pulled a bag from his dirt-covered sedan, Brian peered inside. "That's a swell brass plate on the dash: With love, Sally. I'm guessing there's an interesting story behind it?"

"The car was a gift from my cousin, Sally . . . Struthers."

"You must be close. It's an awfully nice gift."

"Yeah, she's great. Spends a lot of time in other countries helping poor children."

"She sounds fantastic."

"She is. She didn't need her car and giving it to me was just a way of keeping it all in the family."

Brian nodded. "Now, is this everything you own? Pardon my saying, but it's not much."

Melvin's eyes narrowed. "I don't need much."

"Oh, look at that. Is there a guitar in that case?"

"Just an old six-string from a five and dime."

"Are you pretty good?"

"I do a little Travis-picking. Met a few guys in my travels that helped me along."

Brian smiled and blew into his hands for warmth. "I don't know what that means, but I've always found guitars fascinating. May I?"

Melvin stepped aside. "Whatever floats your boat, dude."

Brian gently pulled the guitar from the case and examined it under the streetlamp. "Looks like she has some miles on her, but still serviceable. It's a shame people have written on it. Previous owners?"

"No, that's Johnny Cash, Elvis Presley, and Buddy Holly."

"I see." Brian carefully placed it back in the case. "Friends of yours?"

"Musicians—all pretty handy with a guitar."

Brian shook his head. "I'm afraid I've never heard of them. No disrespect to your buddies, but I suspect not everyone makes it in the music industry."

Melvin shrugged. "Care to wager?"

296

Brian chuckled and shook his head. "No, my friend, I don't drink, gamble or swear." He motioned his hand forward. "It's just the straight and narrow for me."

Melvin looked him over. "I can see that."

As he ascended the stairs, Brian followed close behind, happily chatting. "Have you ever heard of the Crew Cuts or the Chordettes? I have all their albums. They're pure gold in my book."

Melvin turned the key to his old loft and pushed hard. The door partially opened, scraping dried excrement as it went. Brian covered his mouth and nose. "My word! Did those chickens die in there? You can't possibly sleep with that odor. Come home with me, brother."

"I've slept in worse."

"You're a better man than I, Melvin Napier."

Melvin's eyes narrowed again. "Doubt it."

Brian went down three steps. "Well, I'd stay and chat longer, but the truth is, that smell is about to bring up Sally's apple pie. Probably not as good the second time around. Good night. It's been great meeting you. And Merry Christmas to you, sir!"

"Merry Christmas, Brian."

Melvin threw his shoulder into the door to get inside. He cranked up the heat and cracked a window to get some airflow. After beating chicken feathers out of the old mattress, he spread Sally's blanket on top and collapsed, smiling in his old bed's soft and wonderful familiarity. As he lay his head down for a long winter's nap, he was disturbed by a gentle wrapping at his door.

"Holy shit, it stinks to high Heaven in here," Sally said, covering her mouth and nose.

"That's what happens when you keep chickens indoors. I can't believe John okayed that."

She shrugged. "What he didn't know didn't hurt him. And it was just one chicken. One really big-ass chicken."

"Where did you get a live chicken?"

297

"Look around. Where *can't* I get a live chicken? This one happened to be a gift from my cousin in Georgia."

"Cousin on your mother's side?"

"How did you know that?"

"Just did. From the looks of it, your big-ass chicken had one hell of a digestive system."

"Yeah, he shit everywhere," she giggled. "It's on the ceiling, too, see? How does that even happen?"

"Oh, shit, you're right. No idea."

"Guess Dr. Thomas will have to replace every bit of that ceiling tile."

"No rush. I'd say the parts of the carpet your chicken didn't eat should be the first to go."

Sally stepped back out onto the landing. Melvin followed in step and looked into her eyes. "So, how's everything around here?"

"Nothing ever changes . . . except that you came back," she said, staring back, then looking away. "Oh, we did have the clinic floor retiled."

"Yeah?" he asked as he regained her gaze and moved closer.

"Yeah," she replied, searching his eyes and moving in closer still. "Dr. Thomas hired Dwiggins and company. They're local."

"Local, huh?" He caressed her face. "Local's good."

"I love local," she softly replied, closing her eyes as they kissed.

Then she pushed him back. "Hold on! So, you think you can just show up here, and everything goes back to the way it was?"

"No, I didn't think that at all."

One of her hands went to her hip. The other pointed a finger. "You thought I'd just be sitting around for over a freaking year pining for you?"

"No, not at all."

"Then why are you back?"

He looked deeply into her eyes. "Why do you think?"

Sally turned to hide her smile. "Well, you're a few months too late. Brian's my boyfriend now. I didn't mean to kiss you."

"Yeah, I know." He gently spun her back around, and she kissed him again.

"I didn't mean that, either. So, are you back or just passing through?"

"I start back to work right after New Year's."

"Sticking around long?"

"Planning on it." They made out a little more.

"Ew, I can't get used to that beard. When's the last time you had a haircut or a bath? Brian's such a great guy. We shouldn't be doing this."

"I agree." They passionately kissed again.

Sally put her hand on his chest. "We should stop. This is wrong."

"Yes, very wrong."

She kissed him again and then pushed him back. "I'm not inviting you over tonight. I'm with Brian."

Melvin raised an eyebrow. "Who are you trying to convince?"

She shook a finger. "This is your fault. You need to stop kissing me."

"You knocked on my door."

"I was just checking on you. That's all. Just being neighborly." She kissed his neck and began unbuttoning his shirt, whispering, "Maybe I should invite you over. That *would* be the neighborly thing to do."

He pushed her away. "I may be an asshole, but you're not."

Her eyes widened. "What? No! I'm completely an asshole. Ask anybody."

"I don't think so," he replied. "For all the talk, deep down, you're decent and better than this. Good night, Sally. Merry Christmas."

1955

Chapter 31
After Five Long Years

Melvin sat in bed sipping a beer for breakfast on New Year's Day, 1955. Having cleaned the last chicken leftovers from his loft, he stared at the bare wall where his board had been. *Guess Sally chunked it to make room for her big-ass chicken. Can't believe she gave it free rein in here. Must have been one of those free-rein chickens I've heard about.*

As it often did in the quiet hours, his mind drifted to his family. *It's 2009 for them. Jake won't remember me, and Daniel hates me for leaving. Let's see: I'll be 38 this year. 2004 minus 1955—that'd be 49 years plus 38. Damn, I'll be 87 if I live that long. I guess she's remarried by now. Boys have a father. That's good.* He looked up and sighed. *Only one thing left to do.*

He stood on a chair to reach the ceiling tile, which still reeked of chicken goodness. Holding his breath and closing his eyes, he pushed it aside and pulled down two dust-covered boxes. *It was stupid to keep these.* Opening the first box, he thumbed through stacks of research and leads that never panned out, shaking his head at the wasted time and energy. *If anybody had found these, my only friend would be a psychiatrist. Couldn't get any worse than that.*

That evening, Melvin stood in the alley below, tending the fire in a burn barrel as he sipped a bottle of bourbon he'd stolen from Sally's loft. He'd lost his wife and children and was now risking his life returning for the one woman alive who cared for him, a woman now in the arms of another man. He tossed another stack of fruitless research into the fire, wondering what the hell else the universe could take from him. Blue and yellow flames enveloped and turned black years of misplaced hope. His thoughts turned to the crazed, murderous, overprotective, dead father who didn't know he was back in town—not yet anyway. *How long before he finds me? Maybe he's out there now, adjusting his rifle sights, accounting for wind and distance.* Melvin took another swig, closed his eyes, and spread his arms wide to give his assassin an easy target. He was startled by an energetic voice.

"Hi, Melvin! Got some hot dogs for that fire?"

"Oh, hey, Brian. *Sally.* What are you two kids up to this evening?"

Brian's eyes sparkled. "We're just back from a hot date. It was fantastic. Wouldn't you agree, Ms. Davis?"

"Yes, of course." She grinned. "Dr. Napier, is that a cigar? Since when?"

Melvin shrugged. "Since a nightclub in Galveston."

Brian looked concerned. "Does the smoke bother you, hun? We can leave."

Sally shook her head. "I'll manage. Wouldn't want to be rude."

"No offense, Melvin. As a doctor, I'm sure you'll understand the intolerance to tobacco smoke non-smokers like Sally and I can have."

"None taken." Melvin took an extra-long drag and exhaled smoke rings in Sally's direction. "So, you've never been tempted by the evils of tobacco, Ms. Davis?"

"Nope," she answered, deeply inhaling his second-hand smoke and closing her eyes in ecstasy. "Never have."

"Me neither," Brian added in his chipper voice. "Never have, never will. Right, sweetie?"

"What? Oh, yes, of course, they are. I once heard that smoking ages your skin by 15 years."

"Fascinating, honey bear!" Brian exclaimed. "Where did you pick up that nugget of wisdom?"

She shrugged. "Might have been over brunch at the Capitol Hotel three years ago. Who knows?"

"Golly, dear, for a guess, that's oddly specific."

She nodded. "Yeah, weird, right? So, Dr. Napier, what potentially incriminating evidence are you destroying in this poor barrel?"

"Ghosts of Christmas past. So, going out two nights in a row, huh?"

"No, sir. I didn't call on Sally last night."

"Not on New Year's Eve?"

"Brian doesn't believe in going out that night. It's too dangerous."

"And you agree, right, hun? What, with all those party-goers drinking hooch, using all kinds of profanity, swerving on the roads, and shooting guns in the air, it's pure madness. Those bullets have to come down somewhere."

Sally's face went blank. "Yes, Brian, a party would be too much excitement for us. Who needs it?"

Melvin took a drink and then cocked his head to one side. "So, you guys went out tonight instead. And you're already back by nine?"

"Of course," Brian explained. "I wouldn't want to tarnish Sally's reputation. I know it doesn't mean much to alley cats like you and me, Melvin, but women folk around these parts take it pretty seriously. Now, if you don't mind me saying, you seem to be celebrating a little yourself. I'm guessing what you're holding isn't exactly a bottle of RC cola."

"Nope, it is not." He held out the bottle. "Would you like some, Brian?"

"No, sir, and I believe you know that Sally and I don't go in for that sort of thing. Right, sweetie bear? Clouds the mind and fogs the soul."

Melvin's eyes lit up. "Is that true, *sweetie bear?*"

"Absolutely," she replied, staring longingly at the bottle. "You don't know what it's like, Dr. Napier, to go for a good long while without alcohol. Not that I would know, never having tried it. Don't know what I'd do if I did—probably relax, get a good night's sleep, maybe *enjoy* dinner for a change." She hugged Brian. "I'm just kidding. I'm sure it would make me go crazy. Goodness, the look on your face right now!" She forced a giggle, but it came out creepy.

303

Quickly, Sally pointed at Melvin. "It looks as if *you're* no stranger to alcohol, Dr. Napier. You've almost finished half that bottle. One would assume you purchased it and not borrowed it from someone else. Because that would be *very* rude."

Melvin eyed her as he took a long swig. "Since you and Brian don't drink, one would assume that's no concern to you."

"True. I'm thankful for Brian's positive influence. He's always thinking of what's best for me."

"Yeah," Melvin nodded, "he's something, alright."

"Enough, you guys!" Brian protested. "You're making me blush. Ms. Davis, may I have the honor of escorting you to your door? And good night to you, kind sir. If I had any marshmallows, I'd sure give them to you."

As the couple walked away, Melvin called out, "You know, Brian, you're an honest man. And honesty is always the best policy. Wouldn't you agree, Ms. Davis?" He saluted with her bottle and took another swig.

"Good night, Dr. Napier," she called back. "And go easy on that bourbon. I'm sure it wasn't cheap."

On Monday, a clean-shaven Melvin was back in the office seeing patients. His younger female patients were excited to have him back, and his older female patients resumed their parade of single daughters and granddaughters who bestowed offerings of baked goods and accompaniments to church and Sunday lunches. To their delight, this time around, he happily accepted.

Sally resumed her position on the offensive line, blocking as many pretty young women from getting into his clinic as possible. Still, as Dr. Casanova's reputation grew, she feared too many had slipped into the backfield. Ultimately, Sally had one play left. She just couldn't decide if she was willing to call it.

Melvin drank most every evening and lived off a fridge packed with the hopes of daughters and granddaughters in the form of casseroles and bunt cakes. John counseled him about dating patients or their offspring. Melvin casually argued this was not considered unethical by 1955 standards. John conceded his curiously stated point but suggested it might not be the best business practice and urged him to seek companionship elsewhere. Melvin nodded. He was way ahead of him.

On Monday, February 14th, 1955, Sally floated around the office. Ronny had never seen her so happy. When asked, her responses were coy and evasive. Finally, she revealed Melvin had offered to cook dinner for her tonight. Ronny replied, "You're spending Valentine's at home with your next-door neighbor? Isn't that a little pathetic, even for you? Besides, shouldn't you be spending it with your boyfriend?"

"Who? Oh, Brian has to work. Even if he didn't, he doesn't believe in Valentine's Day. He says it's just an excuse to get hopped up on chocolates, and who knows where that could lead? He may have a point."

Ronny rolled his eyes. "Well, that's just stupid. I can see why you're cheating on him."

"It's not cheating." She held up her left hand as exhibit A. "As long as this finger has no jewelry, I'll date 50 people if I please."

Ronny nodded. "They do say history repeats itself."

"Screw you, Ronny. You can't ruin my beautiful mood."

"You know it's not a real date, right?" he scoffed. "After five years, he's suddenly interested? Think about it. He knows your drama, bad habits, and all your secrets—except one. He's just taking pity so that you're not alone tonight. You know I'm right."

"You don't know what you're talking about."

Ronny shook his head. "Denial, it's so sad. Why don't you avoid the embarrassment and come over to our house and watch our new TV? Momma's making her famous chicken and dumplings."

Sally looked at him incredulously. "Thank you, but pass. Tonight is different." And she knew it. There had been signs. He'd kissed her passionately the night he returned and then respected her relationship with Brian. Despite all the women he was seeing, he still made time for her, finding excuses to touch her arm or put his arm around her. He'd even once moved her hair off her face while talking with her. He'd never offered to cook before, and now he wanted to—on *Valentine's Day?* It couldn't get any more romantic.

Melvin closed his eyes as he cooked that evening and savored the rich smell of his marinated steaks. He tapped his foot to the blues record on his turntable and uncorked a bottle of wine. He glanced in the mirror again and adjusted his collar. He'd known her for half a decade. Why was he nervous? Was it a date? Should he try to kiss her? She'd made it clear Brian was working tonight, and that's why she agreed to stop by if she had time. *She damn well better make time,* he thought as he downed a glass of merlot. *These sirloins cost two dollars!*

A knock came at his door, and a knot formed in his throat. As he opened his door to find his best friend smiling at him, the nerves vanished. She looked amazing. He told her so and invited her in. It must've taken her hours to get ready. Damn straight, this was a date. Even though she'd been in his loft for over a year tending to a big-ass Georgia chicken, Sally fussed over what a lovely place it was. Melvin played along, giving her the tour and telling corny jokes, to which she laughed a little too loudly. She pointed at the red box on his table. "What's that?"

"It's Valentine's Day. I thought you might like some chocolates."

"Oh, that's so sweet! I really shouldn't. Maybe just one since you went to the trouble." She closed her eyes and allowed it to melt in her mouth. Then she asked, "Is that wonderful smell, steak? When did you learn how to cook?"

"I learned a few things on the road."

"Don't take this the wrong way, but it smells so much better than your Canadian dishes. You should check on it." No sooner had his back turned than another piece of chocolate disappeared from the box. The other little chocolates trembled as the five-fingered monster soon returned to devour more of their brethren.

Melvin worked the skillet. "Wine's on the table, too. I don't know if you're into it anymore with your new lifestyle, but it's there if you"—he turned around—"I see you've helped yourself."

Sally smiled and wiped her mouth. "Didn't want to be rude."

Melvin examined the bottle. "Wow, only a quarter left. That was quick. At least you used a glass."

She shrugged. "I started out using a glass."

"Did you even taste it on the way down?"

She took his hands. "Dance with me."

As they danced, ate, talked, and laughed, there was no mention of what's-his-name. A third bottle lost its cork, and they fell together onto the couch in laughter. Sally gave him a serious look. She had the one play left in her playbook, and this was the moment. "What?" he asked.

She sat up. "There's something I want to tell you."

Melvin sat up as well. "If it's about the candy, I already know. You wiped out the whole box."

"It's true," she replied with a salute. "Those poor little chocolate bastards never stood a chance."

"Language, hun!"

"Shut up," she giggled and playfully slapped his arm. "I'm trying to be serious. No, I want to tell you something, something about me."

"Really? That's cool because I've also wanted to tell you something . . . for a long time. I just didn't know how. You first."

Her pupils dilated as she softly shook her head. "Mine is really nothing, nothing at all. Can't even remember what it was now. What do you want to tell me?"

He adjusted on the sofa. "I don't know how to say it. Can't believe I'm so bad at this. When I was on the road, maybe even a long time before that, I figured out I liked Pina Coladas, and now I don't care if it gets me killed."

She shook her head. "You are the strangest man I've ever met."

"I know."

Her eyes lit up. "Oh, I get it." She put a finger to her lips. "Let's see. I like pearl-handled .45s and toast with my coffee. Your turn again."

"No, you don't understand."

"We're not playing a game?"

"No. Geez, Sally, how do I tell you our story is like a John Hughes film from the '80s?"

"That's ridiculous. They weren't making movies in 1880."

"Point taken. What I mean is, you know how sometimes your heart tells you that you want something so bad that you'd do anything for it, but no matter what you do, you come up short?"

She cut her eyes at him. "I think I have some idea."

"Then, one day, you realize that the very thing you've been looking for has been right in front of you the whole time?"

She smiled. "I don't know your friend . . . John Hughes? But he sounds swell."

"He is. Did I mention how pretty you look in pink?"

"Thank you." She playfully slapped his face. "Stop. Why are you laughing?"

"I'm sorry. That was so cheesy."

"Cheesy? You think I look cheap?" She slapped him harder.

"Not at all. Where I'm from, cheesy means something different." He rubbed his cheek. "My face feels numb. Slap me again."

Sally wound up and walloped him. Melvin adjusted his jaw and giggled. "Nope, nothing. How much wine have we had?"

"Want me to hit you again? I can get my rolling pin."

He held up his hands in defense. "I'm good. Listen, what I mean is, I know I've been away, and I know the situation has changed, but what I want to know is, what are *you* thinking?"

Sally placed her hands in her lap. "Well, I'll put it this way. I haven't had a cigarette in six months."

Melvin smiled. "I'm proud of you—again. I know it's been hard."

"Thanks. I'm also watching what I eat and going on walks. You know what mother says, If you don't watch your figure, no one else will. Plus, I've been more helpful to patients lately. I try not to get up for coffee as much when they're waiting. I mean, at least now I think about it when I do. Until tonight, I haven't had a drink in forever."

"That all sounds great. He's had a positive influence on you."

"Who? The guy who happens to look like you? The guy I stalked to the grocery store and rammed with my shopping cart so I could meet him?"

"Sounds like you hit him pretty hard."

"Yeah," she snickered, "who knew he was a bleeder? I did it because of you, Melvin. Even before you came back, I thought about you every day. And now you're here. You make me want to be a better person. And you get me, like no one else. You see through all my bullshit and know all the craziness of my family, and yet you're still here."

"I ran out on you."

"I know, for a year and a half . . . and ten days—ten *long* days. They were all long."

"I'm sorry."

"But you came back for me—for *me*. I've never met anyone like you. Do you know what it's like to meet someone and they just make you feel . . . ? I mean, I shouldn't feel this way, but I do."

He nodded. "I know exactly what you mean. When I got here, I didn't know anyone. You were there for me. You looked out for me. I

309

don't know how I could have survived without you. You mean so much."

She wiped away a tear. He leaned in to kiss her, and she didn't pull away. The affections grew heavier as the wine and the evening continued to flow. By the end of the last bottle, Sally finally got the night that had been on her mind for five long years.

⚖

Melvin woke first and wrapped his arm around her as she snuggled against him for warmth in the chill of the morning hour. He stared at the ceiling as waves of nausea and guilt washed over him. This was wrong. He was a cheater.

Was he? His mind went to court to consider the evidence. First on the stand was the pseudo-pharmacist from Georgia who'd drugged and had her way with him. That didn't count. *If anything,* the defense argued, she should've been arrested. Next up was Heather, his devoted college girlfriend he'd cheated on with her roommate, Jenny, the aspiring drug addict. Okay, that was pretty bad. Before that was Casandra, his high school sweetheart who was on the verge of becoming one of the most brilliant, recognizable, and wealthy musical performers in the world, but not before he cheated on her with "Top-10" Christina, a girl with an IQ equal to the rocks in Charlie Brown's Halloween bag. The defense stipulated that move was just plain stupid. So, maybe his track record for decision-making wasn't perfect, but he was a dumb kid back then. And he wasn't married. And none of those girls had been Alexis.

On the other hand, a lot had happened on the road and, more recently, with the eager women from his clinic. None of these had caused him any remorse—not like this. The verdict was in. His family in 2009 was now his past or future, or whatever you wanted to call it. Getting back wasn't possible. It never was. He'd moved on and was living life again. So, why the guilt this morning with Sally? Why did it feel so wrong?

She awoke and kissed him, immediately noticing the look on his face. She covered her mouth. "Do I need to brush my teeth?"

"No," he replied as he kissed her, "just lost in thought."

"Whatcha thinking about, handsome?"

He took a deep breath. "Last night. This was all so fast."

She propped up on an elbow. "It took five years. We have very different definitions of speed. It's good, though, right?"

"I couldn't be happier."

"Me neither." She kissed him again and got up. "I'm going to make some breakfast before work."

"I was hoping you would."

She slipped on his bathrobe. "Are you sure nothing else is on your mind?"

"Did you buy that for me just so you could wear it?"

She smiled. "Sure is nice and warm. Tell me what you're thinking."

"Just wondering how it took us so long to get here."

Sally waved in derision. "That's easy. It was your fault."

Melvin sat up. "My fault?"

"Hey, I've known from day one that we'd be great together. You're the one who's wanted to jump off a bridge for the last few years. You finally look happy. But I see something else, too."

"What?"

"I see worry in your eyes."

His head went back. "Worry? Me?"

She sat beside him. "It's okay. I know she hurt you, but she's gone. She's your past." She took his hand. "I'm right here, right now. You have no *idea* how much I understand the fear of getting hurt again. But you have to know that I'm not her. We're together, and you could never say or do anything that would drive me away. I love you."

He took another deep breath. "I . . . I . . ."

"Want breakfast? Yeah, I know," she winked and got up. "Relax, Napier. You're not the first to come up short at the goal line. Don't

311

worry. You've got three more downs. At least you're finally on this end of the field."

Melvin didn't get her baseball analogy but knew she was right. This *was* his life, right here. She wasn't the love of his life before, but maybe she was now. After all, he'd come back for her, right? Well, that and because he was flat broke. But he'd come back for her, right? That must mean something. She clearly had no doubts about him and what she wanted. Maybe it was time to drop the L bomb.

That evening, he pulled her close and whispered the words she longed to hear. He promised he was living for the here and now, and what he wanted was in his arms. She cried and bear-hugged him until he thought a rib snapped. He felt fortunate to have her, fortunate to have a chance at a normal life, and fortunate she didn't have a shopping cart to hurl at him.

Throughout the month and into March, they were together most evenings. Melvin emotionally committed, but the two A.M. guilt trips returned nightly. Sally, on the other hand, was downright pleasant to everyone. Once again, patients mistook her as "the new girl," and once again, Dr. Thomas subtly questioned her regarding substance abuse.

During this time of bliss, Melvin never asked how Brian took being dumped, and Sally never brought it up. He often thought about Brian, a moral, ethical, straight-shooter who'd bent over backward to show him kindness, a man clearly in love with the woman Melvin was taking to bed. Brian had committed to her without compunction. And the way they'd kept him in the dark about their past on Christmas Eve didn't sit well either. Melvin tried to put it out of his mind and hoped she'd let him down gently. He already had enough guilt for two lifetimes. *Why couldn't Brian have been an asshole like everyone else? That would've been the considerate thing for him to do, right? Would've made this whole thing a lot easier—asshole.*

Chapter 32
Baseball and the Confession Stand

By Saturday, April 2nd, 1955, Spring had arrived. Melvin had settled back into practice, to John's great relief. He wasn't thrilled Melvin was seeing their receptionist, but at least he was no longer dating patients. And who could argue with Sally's disposition? She showed up on time, patients liked her, and she found room on the schedule for *everyone*. She'd even adopted a new filing system that involved an actual filing cabinet.

Melvin kissed her good morning. "Want to go to a Trav's game today over at Ray Winder?"

"A what?" she asked.

"Arkansas Travelers. It's a minor league baseball team here in town."

"You mean the Little Rock Travelers at Traveler's field?"

"Yeah, that's what I meant."

She squinted at the thermometer through the window. "It's like 50 degrees outside. Besides, you don't like sports."

"Things change."

"Why did you call it Ray Winder? Isn't he an owner? It's not like they named the field after him."

"Oh, right. Who knows? Maybe one day they will."

"Doubt it. Nobody goes to those games anymore. Besides, they're moving the team to Shreveport and talking about expanding the zoo over there."

"I can guarantee you neither of those things will ever happen."

She shook her head and kissed him. "You are so Canadian."

When they returned from the game that evening, Melvin noticed a light from the clinic's back hall. "I'll go check that out. See you upstairs."

Melvin knocked on the door to John's office. "You okay?"

John looked up from his desk. "Oh, hey, Melvin. Hope I didn't disturb you."

"No, just rolling in. What are you doing here on a Saturday night?"

"Just thinking about today."

Melvin sat down across the desk from him. "Tough day?"

"Every year."

Melvin picked up the bottle. "Looks like you've been hitting it pretty hard. Want to talk?"

"No, thanks, I—you know, why not? I suppose I can tell *you*. You may not show the best discretion, but you know how to keep a secret."

"What do you mean?"

John smiled. "Come now, Melvin, what you were doing with all those flights to Jonesboro wasn't hard to figure out." He poured Melvin a scotch and slid it over.

Melvin took a sip. "You knew about that?"

"Everyone knew. You're a young man and entitled to look around. I was perfectly fine with you carousing outside of our catchment area. But since you've been back, you've taken liberties with the daughters and granddaughters of our patients. And now our receptionist? Good gravy, man, stop playing musical beds and settle down!"

"You don't hold back when you're drinking, do you?"

John pointed at him. "And what's more, you've never said anything about your ex-wife or your past since joining us. You've never mentioned what you did for the last year and a half. And you've never said anything about your accident. Others have talked about the Canadian Miracle for five years, but you've never said a word one way or the other. Most people would be dying to tell how they cheated death. Not you. It's as if more is going on than you want people to know."

"Well, I would have to say—"

John leaned back in his chair. "And another thing. When the military rolled into town looking for that spy, everyone panicked. Everyone except you. You were cool as a,"—he searched for the word—"cucumber, like it was any other day, like you knew something the rest of us didn't. Explain that."

"How much have you had?"

"Not nearly enough." He leaned forward and tapped on his desk. "Cards on the table, Melvin. Who are you, really?"

He shrugged. "I'm your partner from up North."

"That's right. I keep forgetting you're French-Canadian. By the way, vous ne parlez pas un mot de français n'est-ce pas?"

"Look, John—"

"It's okay, Melvin. Most Arkansans don't speak French."

"My mother was French, but we grew up only speaking—"

"Please stop lying to me."

"John, you've had a little too much to drink. It's me, Melvin. I'm just the guy who responded to your ad five years ago."

John downed his scotch and poured another. "There was no ad."

"What?"

"We needed someone, yes, but I was searching by word of mouth. It's below the dignity of our profession to advertise, even for help."

"You knew, from day one? Why did you offer me a job if you knew I was lying?"

"You must have had your reasons. Our practice was busy, and you were the first to apply in two years."

Melvin shook his head. "You wouldn't hire someone off the street with no credentials when you knew they weren't honest. Not you."

"You weren't just anyone. I knew your father."

Melvin folded his arms and leaned back. "I kind of doubt that."

"I owed him a debt. When I found his son in need, I did what anyone would."

"How drunk are you?"

"Just enough that I may not remember much tomorrow and definitely enough that Mrs. Thomas will be disappointed."

"Alright. Tell me about my father. When did you meet him?"

"Were you in the war, Melvin? I've noticed you rub your finger where a ring used to be. I knew a lot of guys who wore them to remember their wives and children."

"No, I never served. Where I'm from, the Army wanted you to be all that you could be. Back in those days, all I could be wasn't enough."

"Failed your medical? Wanted to do your part, but they wouldn't let you? At least you tried. I fought in France for the first. Tried to serve in the medical corps for the second, but the board rejected me. Said I was the only EENT in town and needed me here."

"I'm sorry, John. But about my father—"

"Just a polite way of saying I was too damn old."

Melvin reached across the desk. "Why don't you let me have that glass? I think you've had—"

"My father fought in Cuba before I was born. Did I ever tell you that?"

"No, but we were talking about—"

"Was certain my son would sign up like his friends after Pearl. He had ROTC training. Could've easily received a commission. But when he showed no such inclination, being the *outstanding* father I am"—John shook his head—"I sat him down to straighten him out. He tried to tell me his ideas about war and morality and what it means to be an American, but I refused to listen. We had words." John's head sunk to his chest. "Haven't seen him since. I got so angry the night he left that I threw out his things, except that old suit we gave you and a single photo Mrs. Thomas had hidden from me, thank goodness. We hired a detective after the war to find him, but nothing. Mrs. Thomas likes to believe he went to California and has a family of his own, and maybe one day he'll forgive me and pick up the phone." John looked Melvin in the eyes. "But that'll never happen. Truth is, the detective found him. I'd shamed my son so deeply that he'd enlisted under another name and got killed. I never told her. What kind of man casts out his own son? Lies to his wife? Ever wish you could go back in time and stop yourself?"

Melvin slid the glass of scotch back to him. "Maybe once or twice. Sometimes a lot of hardship follows a decision. Best we can do is learn from it and grow."

"Do you believe that?"

"Some days. What else can you do? It's not like we can really travel in time." Melvin smiled. "Unless you know something I don't."

John stared at him, then smiled back. "No, I suppose not. Time travel is just fantasy for the H.G. Wells of the world. But if you ever figure out a way, I'd appreciate it if you'd go back and stop me."

"Given the opportunity, you have my word."

"Thank you, Melvin. I would forever be in your debt."

"Of course, John. That's what friends are for. Let's get you home. How about I drive?"

Chapter 33
Old Dog, Old Tricks

On Friday, April 8th, 1955, Melvin scrubbed for his next cataract surgery. He purposely slowed down and savored the moment. In his hectic world of clinic and surgery, scrubbing in was often his quietest time of the day. His first six surgeries had gone well, and aside from a remote history of trauma, nothing was special about the next one. With the patient prepped, draped, and topical cocaine applied, he drew a deep breath and made his initial incision for the day's final surgery.

Everything proceeded as usual until he attempted to express the cataract. Suddenly, it disappeared down into the back of the eye. Melvin froze. In 2004, he would have sutured up his incision and sent the patient to a retina surgeon. But here, he *was* the retina surgeon.

Beads of sweat ran down his temple. The room began to spin. The scrub nurse asked, "Dr. Napier, would you like another instrument? Dr. Napier?" But he couldn't hear her. His mind was desperately reaching back five years to the textbooks he'd read while recovering in the hospital. Lost in his thoughts, he heard the nurse's voice suddenly deepen, "Is there a problem, Melvin?"

He looked up to see his friend scrubbed in and standing next to him. Melvin breathed a sigh of relief. "What brings you to the OR, John?"

"Oh, I was just rounding on a couple of patients when I heard scuttlebutt that the most skilled surgeon in the hospital finally had a real case on his hands. I had to see it for myself. Hope you don't mind. If it bothers you, I can leave."

"No, you stay right there. The entire lens just did a nosedive into the deep end of the vitreal pool. History of trauma, and I'm guessing just enough zonules not to show me how loose they were at the slit lamp."

John nodded. "Uh, huh. Seen it more times than I've wanted. So, what's the hold-up?"

"Because I have no clue what—your preferred procedure is here in the States."

"Probably no different than in Canada. What did you do up there?"

"Closed up and called a retina specialist."

John smiled through his mask. "Ah, the specialists for the specialist system. Well, we don't have any of those around here, now do we? Guess we're just going to have to fix this ourselves. Now I'm just an old country surgeon, but I'd be happy to give you my opinion." No sooner had he uttered those words than Melvin stepped aside to allow him full access.

"Well, we have two schools of thought. One states it's so detrimental to root around down in the vitreous that you should just leave it. Maybe it'll resorb. You keep him dilated in a face-down position and hope it falls forward. Then you constrict the pupil to capture it and take it out. Of course, the patient could suffer significant inflammation, glaucoma, and retinal separation with that plan."

Melvin winced. "That sounds just awful. What's plan B?"

"You could do this. Cindy, hand me that lens loop."

"Here you are, doctor. And my name is Mary Ann."

"Of course, it is, dear."

Melvin watched in amazement as John confidently retrieved the sunken lens and sutured up the wounds. "Wow, John, that was so straightforward."

"Not much to it, really."

"You weren't afraid of damaging the retina?"

"You weigh the risk of the procedure against leaving it there. Just remember to avoid removing too much of the vitreous, so the eye doesn't collapse."

319

"I can't thank you enough for stepping in."

"Nonsense. Happy to do it. You've been so quick and so slick with your surgeries and taught this old dog so many new tricks that I feared I had nothing to offer in return." He winked. "This made my day." John shared his thoughts on post-operative instructions and headed back to the clinic, almost skipping as he went.

By 5 P.M. that afternoon, Sally had left for Conway to spend Easter weekend with her mother, and Melvin went to McKeen's to relax after his stressful day. The regulars greeted him as he claimed his favorite bar stool. Mrs. McKeen poured his usual.

"Thanks, Ethel. Where's Walter this evening?"

"Seeing his brother over in Clarksville."

"You didn't go with him?"

She shook her head. "I've seen his brother. Besides, somebody's got to work." She smiled. "Did I tell you how much we missed you while you were away?"

Melvin smiled. "Thanks, Ethel. I missed you guys, too."

She winked. "Hey, where's your cute professor friend? He hasn't come around since you left."

"David's in Kentucky. He's the new chair of Physics at the university. Big promotion."

"Well, I'm happy for him, but it's a mistake if you ask me."

"You have experience as a university chair, Ethel?"

"No, but administration is administration. All I have to mess with is Walter and a handful of employees, and that's enough. It's smarter to be like you, in charge of no one but yourself."

Melvin sipped his beer and considered her words when a voice boomed behind him. "Calvin? Calvin?" He felt a slap on his back.

"Norman?"

"Hello, doc! I was beginning to think you didn't know your own name."

"Yeah, sorry. I was lost in thought. Tough day at the hospital. What brings you up from Suby? On a run here or coming in from Memphis?"

"Neither. Came down for some fly-fishing in the morning with an old friend. Hey, Ethel! Where's that sorry-ass husband of yours?"

"Oh, my! I'm sorry, Norman. He went off to Clarksville and forgot all about your fishing trip."

Norman shook his head. "He didn't forget. He owes me five dollars. That's what it is."

She opened the register, but Norman waved her off. "Thank you, sweetheart, but it needs to come out of his pocket and into my hand. A bet's a bet. The good doctor and I are going to sit over at that table. Would you mind sending a couple of beers our way?"

"Okay, sugar. He's our adopted son, you know, all the way from Canada." She pointed to the miniature maple leaf flag on the bar.

"Really? Well, you couldn't have picked a better one than ole—"

"Thanks, Ethel," Melvin interrupted. "Lead the way, Norm."

Norman grabbed a chair. Melvin picked up his beer and reluctantly joined him at the table where Grace had drugged him almost three years ago.

Norman pointed. "Are you toting Sally's purse? Is she around?"

"No. This is my satchel." Melvin stuffed it into his windbreaker. "Just for essentials. It's a doctor thing."

The big man grinned. "Got lipstick in there? A little powder for the cheeks?"

"It's good to see you, too, Norm. Sorry about your fishing trip."

"It happens. So, Ethel's adopted son, huh? You must be in here a lot. Drive all the way down from Cave City just for this bar?"

"I like this bar. We're in Batesville, not Cave City."

"Yeah," Norman nodded in satisfaction, "you did say Batesville, didn't you? Cave City is a little south of there, right next to Bald Knob."

"No, it's north of Batesville. Maybe you're thinking of Pleasant Plains."

"Maybe I am. For a Canadian, you sure know Arkansas."

Melvin shrugged. "I'm sure when you came down here from New York, you knew the area after a while."

Norman rubbed his chin. "Yeah, I sure did. How'd you know I'm from New York? I never mentioned it."

Without missing a beat, Melvin replied, "Same way I know you're Catholic. I can hear it in your voice."

Norman leaned forward. "And just what the hell does a Catholic sound like?"

"They sound a lot like that."

Norman slapped his knee as his deep laugh thundered off the bar walls. "Damn, you're right! I'm sure glad I ran into you, Calvin. I could use someone to talk to outside of Logan County."

Ethel sat their beers on the table. "Here you go, boys." She winked. "Don't believe a word Norm says, Melvin."

Norman's eyes widened as he watched her return to the bar. "She just called you—"

Melvin hung his head. "Look, I know what you're thinking."

"You've been role-playing—with *Ethel?*"

Melvin's eyebrows shot up. "Okay, maybe I didn't know what you were thinking."

Norman stared with wild eyes. "Isn't she a little old for . . . ?" He shook his head. "Walter's one of my dearest friends. Does he know that she, you know,"—he leaned forward and whispered—"calls you Melvin?"

Melvin took a deep breath and nodded. "Technically, yeah. He's usually around when she does. Sally, too."

Norman rocked back in his chair and looked at the ceiling. "Holy shit, Calvin. A group thing? *This* is why I don't live in the city."

Melvin winced. "Feel free not to mention this to anyone—ever."

Norman downed half his mug. "Believe me, I won't."

Melvin released a long breath. "So, what's going on in Logan County that you can't talk about?"

Norman slowly smiled and lowered the front two legs of his chair back to the floor. "I'm a father."

"Congratulations!" Melvin cringed. "Who's the unlucky woman?"

His grin grew wider. "Mary, the same one you met at breakfast."

"That's wonderful. I liked her a lot. Lousy taste in men, but otherwise seemed pretty smart. When did you guys get hitched?" Melvin asked, knowing they never would.

"We didn't. It'd be a scandal and ruin her good name. I can't even tell anyone he's mine. It's killing me."

"Wow, that's tough, dude. Who does she say is the father?"

"She says it's you."

Melvin spewed his beer. "What the fu—what?"

"Yeah, your questions about going out West gave her the idea. She says she was out in California and fell in love with a Dr. Drapier. They quickly married, but he choked to death on an avocado a few days later. Kind of a stupid story, but she's sticking to it."

Melvin shook his head. "Don't I know it."

"What do you mean?"

"She strikes me as that kind of girl. Once she puts something out there, she's never going to back up."

"Damn, Calvin, you sure have her pegged." He downed the last of his beer. "You always that good at reading people?"

"I'm a doctor. So, what's his name?"

Norman reached for his wallet. "Raymond. He's a great-looking kid, smart as a whip. Take a look."

Melvin examined the photo of his father, the toddler he was rumored to have sired. "Yeah, good-looking kid. What is he, two?"

"Almost." Norman held up the photo next to Melvin. "You know, if I didn't know any better, I'd say he takes after you. And you seem to know Mary pretty well." Norman's expression soured as the big man rolled up his sleeves, revealing massive arms. "Has Mary ever called you Melvin? Is she part of your *group?*"

"Whoa, hey!" Melvin held up his hands in defense. "She is absolutely, categorically not, okay? He's your kid. Just look at those features. That's all you, man. If anything, you and *I* kind of favor."

Norman reached across the table and slapped his shoulder. Melvin teetered in his chair in reverberation. "I'm just busting your balls, Calvin. But to be honest, there was a time when I wasn't so sure. The way she carried on about you for months after that breakfast, I thought maybe you'd slipped into town and stuffed her turkey. But when Raymond arrived with those McElhannon eyes, I just melted. Oh, and you'll be happy to know she quit drinking and smoking on your orders. Quit swearing, too, although damned if I know why." Norman's eyes softened as he looked at the picture. "This little guy is my whole world. It just kills me I can't be around him more."

"What are you going to do?"

"Be his father, as best as I can." Norman cracked his big knuckles. "And no one will ever know he was born out of wedlock, not Raymond, not anybody. Got it? No son of mine is growing up being called a bastard."

Melvin held up his hands again. "Yeah, man. I'm cool. But why not propose? Tell people you adopted him?"

Norman caught the last drip from his mug. "She's Protestant, and I'm not. Around there, Protestants teach their little spawn to throw rocks and beat up the Catholic kids. Just the way it is. If we married, her older brothers would come at me for a beating, and I'd give 'em one. But no matter how it went, they'd have nothing to do with Mary and Raymond. Getting hitched would just be selfish on my part. Plus, I served with her husband and was there when he died. His ghost would haunt my ass every day."

"You had a kid with his widow. Dude, that ship has sailed."

Norman waved a dismissive hand. "That's just fooling around. Marriage is forever. I should get going. If I can't fish, I might as well open the bar." He winked. "The good Baptists will be parched by now."

Norman stood and pulled out cash for the beers. Melvin waved him off. "On me, big guy."

Norman smiled. "Thanks. You take care, Calvin. But do me a favor. I want you to kick Ethel and Walter out of your sex club. That whole thing,"—he winced—"you need to stop. It's unnatural."

Melvin nodded. "Will do."

"Good." He shook his hand. "And if you're ever passing through Subiaco, first round's on me."

Melvin smiled. "Oh, I will be in your bar one day, Norm. Count on it. And take care of that baby. He's liable to give you a grandson."

"Grandchildren? Heaven help me!"

Chapter 34
You Had to See This Coming

Once Norman had gone, Melvin stood to leave the Grace table when a voice behind him ordered, "Sit back down, Doctor."

Melvin didn't need to turn to know who it was. "Cole, or whatever your name is, so great you're here. I was expecting you sooner."

Cole took a seat across from him with a smug grin. "Judging me for using different names, *Calvin?*"

"Speaking of judgment, Sally's in Conway with your widow." Melvin finished off his beer. "The holidays have been tough ever since her shitty husband died."

Cole feigned concern. "And you didn't go? Didn't want to sit around and reminisce about me?"

Melvin shrugged. "Nothing personal, but it's people like you I'd rather forget." He put his hand to his mouth. "Oh, I guess that was kind of personal."

Cole's eyes narrowed. "You can't forget, though, can you? Ever since you've been back here, you remember everything. It's like your mind works overtime. You can't shut it off. Hey, how was gramps? Did you spill the beans?"

"Who?"

Cole threw his thumb over his shoulder. "The big guy who just left, about your age, looks like you? You know, the guy who doesn't know your real name."

"What do you care?"

"Ballsy talking to your relatives—stupid, but ballsy. Change their mind, change your future. And you can't predict what those changes will be. Do you remember any changes? You don't, do you? Now, is that because you can only remember the change or because it hasn't happened yet? Mind-blowing, isn't it?"

"Your point?"

"Being in the past can be deadly. Change one thing, and someone doesn't get born. That's murder. How many innocents have you killed so far, Melvin?"

"What do you want?"

Cole shook his finger. "Tricky thing about being in the past and knowing the future, you're powerful yet vulnerable. For example, see that guy over there? To kill *him*, I'd have to, I don't know, shoot him with this pistol." Cole lifted his shirt, exposing the gun in his waistband. "But to kill *you* is so much easier. All I have to do is alter a relative's future, like your grandpa, and you end before you even start."

"Is that it, Cole? Are you going to kill me by killing my family, just like you killed that agent, your mob buddies, and anyone else you didn't much like the looks of? Where are *your* relatives, Cole? Is this what your future mom hopes you'll grow up to be? How do you sleep at night?"

"You think I killed Agent Smith? Why would I kill someone so useful? Did you know that after our hunting trip, the FBI was finally persuaded to accept his application? Today, he's part of the anti-communist task force. Quite an impressive career, wouldn't you say?" Cole slid a manila folder across the table.

"What's that? A list of everyone who owes you a favor?"

He grinned. "You'd need a whole filing cabinet. Open it."

Melvin's face went pale as he examined the documents. Some were in English, others in Russian, but they all had one thing in common, Melvin Napier. He looked up at Cole. "What the hell is this?"

Cole motioned to Ethel to bring drinks. "I thought about killing you. I thought about it a lot. I was disappointed when you tucked tail and ran, but you're a selfish coward, so it was predictable. Thought about tracking you down, but I'm a man of my word."

Melvin waved off Ethel.

Cole shrugged, then leaned forward. "But imagine my surprise when you came back. I had a bead on your skull so many times, but a thought kept creeping into my brain. If I kill you, then you miss out on everything 1955 has to offer—like the penal system." His cold gray eyes lit up. "With prison reform just a few decades away, imagine experiencing it firsthand. I couldn't deny you the gift of suffering. Until you've been locked up, you just don't know what kind of man you really are." Cole tapped on the file. "Forgery is so simple in this time. People will believe anything. But I don't have to tell you, the Canadian Miracle, master of deception. Imagine when these documents come to light. A stranger from another country shows up with no identification and no past and is spotted sneaking around Army property. It's your origin story, comrade. Aren't you excited? I'm excited. This will make Will Smith's career. He's going to be *thrilled.*"

Melvin folded his arms. "Bullshit. You haven't given it to him yet. You want something."

Cole nodded like a proud parent. "Good for you. You're a little less stupid than I remember. Let's take a ride."

Melvin scoffed, "I'm not going anywhere with you."

"Yes, you are." He pulled up his shirt again. "I'll kill several of these people and get away with it. I'm dead, remember? Perfect alibi. But you? Someone will remember the shots coming from this table and find the folder. Do you like gas? I hear they have a whole chamber of it."

Melvin sighed and stood. "Where are we going?"

"Let's take a little walk to your car."

"Then where?"

Cole gave a sly grin. "Where else? We're going home." As they headed for the door, Ethel waved. "Goodbye, son, come by the house for Easter dinner."

"More relatives, Melvin?" Cole shook his head. "That's unfortunate."

"No, she's crazy. She calls everyone her son. I just come here too often. I drink too much."

"Yeah, you do. Never understood why Sally wanted to date an alcoholic. Guess opposites attract."

As they headed down the sidewalk, a toddler scurried up behind Melvin and grabbed his pant leg. "Daddy, Daddy, Daddy!"

A woman chased after him. She pulled him back and, in a thick Georgia accent, said, "No, sweetheart, that's not your daddy." Melvin locked eyes with a startled Grace Grable and then looked at the child. Neither said a word. She whisked the boy away, saying, "Well, Matty, I suppose you just never know. Come on. I heard the Easter Bunny's in the department store. Let's see if we can catch him before he hops away."

Cole put his hands on his hips and laughed. "Damn, Napier. You get around."

"That was just some kid on the street. Made a mistake."

"A mistake was made, but it wasn't his. I saw how the mama looked at you. No doubt where that boy got his eyes." Cole shook his head. "You are one arrogant son-of-a-bitch. Don't you realize you can't jump back in the past and screw every girl you meet? Kids grow up and have families. It starts a new timeline—everything changes. How irresponsible can you be? And you think *I'm* the bad guy in this story?"

Melvin started back down the sidewalk. "Let's get this over with."

"Alright, stud, you drive. Try not to run over any of your bastard children."

Cole directed him toward Marche near where Melvin usually climbed through the fence. "Now, this is where that spy was spotted, right? Let's go have a look for ourselves." Cole unlocked the trunk and pulled out a shovel.

"How did you get keys to my car?"

"I was a car dealer for thirty years. It's 1955. Wasn't that hard."

Melvin put his hands on his hips. "Have to say, I'm a little disappointed in the lack of automobile security in this decade. Want me to carry that shovel for you?"

Cole smiled and shook his head. Melvin ducked through the barbwire and led him over the hill and down to the river.

Cole scanned the area. "So, this is it, huh? This is where the future Dr. and Mrs. Napier have a house and raise a family, right here on the banks of the river? S-h-o-o-o-t. Premium view? What'd that set you back, four, five hundred K?"

"Something like that."

"Something like that!" Cole shouted as he raised his hands and addressed the congregation of oaks and pines. "He's so humble, ladies and gentlemen. Let's give it up for the rich doctor. Let's all hand over our daughters. Do you promise to marry them, Melvin? Is that how it goes? Girls grow up with next to nothing, and the rich doctor promises to marry them if they hop in his bed?"

Melvin's jaw tightened. "You don't know what you're talking about."

"How about that hot southern belle back there with your kid? Did you marry her?"

"Shut up, Cole. You have no idea."

Cole extended his hands as a prosecutor to a jury. "So, clear it up for me. You came back for my daughter, knowing what I'd do, and then you proceeded to screw around on her. Did that make you feel like a man, or are you just stupid?"

Melvin pointed a finger of condemnation. "You want to talk? Okay. You say having kids in the past is wrong, yet you've had two. And you're not exactly father of the year, are you? You say by changing the past, I might kill someone, but you've killed plenty." Melvin threw his hands up. "And what sane person fakes their death and hides from their family? You want to talk about your daughter? Let's talk about *her*. You're upset when I'm with her, and you're upset when I'm not. I don't know what the hell happened to you all these years, but dude, you're certifiable."

Cole held up the folder. "Big talk from a fellow whose future I hold in my hand."

Melvin's shoulders slumped. "Cut the shit. You never intended to give that to Smith. It's not why we're here."

Cole tossed the folder aside, pulled his revolver, and aimed at Melvin's head. "You truly have gotten smarter. You're right. I promised to kill you if you ever came back, and unlike you, I'm a man of my word. Plus, I killed Agent Smith back on that hunting trip. Some men can't be bought. Unlike you, he had my respect."

"Think you'll get away with killing a doctor in 1955? They'll never stop looking for you."

Cole shook his head. "They'll never start. The Army will spot your car back there and search the area. They'll find your body in a shallow grave along with that folder. The city will celebrate that the Commy spy was put down by local justice, and they won't care which good ole boy did it. More importantly, Sally will see you for the liar you are." He sighed. "I should've killed you when you first stepped on my property five years ago. I invited you to my dinner table, to become part of my family. With the knowledge between us, we could've done anything. Could've had anything. That whole time I sat there worrying you'd come to take me back, to take away everything I had." He cocked the hammer. "Well, look at me now, Melvin, because that's exactly what you did. You asked me how I sleep? Tonight, I'll sleep like a baby."

"Up every two hours and wetting yourself?"

Cole laughed and let the hammer back down. "Damn, that was pretty funny. Last time we met, you were shitting yourself. Look at you now. You're about to get your head blown off and cracking jokes like Cool Hand Luke. Were those seriously your last words?"

Melvin turned a pretend crank on his hand, slowly flipping him off.

Cole shook his head with a smile. "You've changed. In another time, I might have liked you. Tell you what, I'll make you a deal. I'll take out four bullets and spin it—a little Russian roulette. Get the irony, comrade?" He pulled the pin and flicked the gun to expose the cylinder. "Now, if you can convince me—"

Before Cole could utter another word, Melvin pulled a knife from the satchel hidden in his jacket and threw it into Cole's thigh. Cole's eyes widened as he looked down. In a flash, Melvin covered the ground between them and hit him with an uppercut with Sally's brass knuckles. Cole hit the ground hard on his back. Melvin jumped on him, reached for his knife, then froze, staring down the barrel of Cole's revolver once more.

"No, no, no, Dr. Napier. You don't win. There's no happy ending for you. Back it on up, dipshit." Cole got to his feet, rubbing the cut on his chin. He wiped the blood on his shirt and examined his leg, all the while keeping the gun aimed squarely at Melvin. "Drop the knuckles. Damn, you're fast. Probably fast at everything, aren't you? Run fast and do things faster than everyone else? Wasn't that way back in 2004, was it? Ever wonder why? Problem is, now you're messing with your own kind." He pulled the knife from his leg and tossed it aside. "Knife throwing, huh? They didn't teach that in med school. Worst throw I've ever seen." Cole put a hand over the bright red blood. "Tear your shirt and bandage my leg."

Melvin shrugged. "Why? You're already dead. You're just too stupid to know it."

"What the hell does that mean? I'm holding the gun, idiot." The blood seeped around his fingers.

Keeping his distance, Melvin slowly tore the bottom of his shirt. "I should thank you for sending me out on the road, Cole. I got a lot out of it. Met and learned from anyone who would teach me—you know, Sarah Conner style. Some were even famous, just not yet. I went pretty much everywhere. Then one morning, I woke up in the Rockies.

And as I sat there wondering where to go next, all I could think about was that night in the graveyard. I've been a lot of things in my life. Screwed up plenty. Neglected things I shouldn't have. Still, I'd never run from anything or anyone until that night. To make it worse, I hurt people who cared about me. You were right. I was a selfish coward. But that morning in the mountains, I decided I was done running. I sought out someone to teach me how to throw a knife with unbelievable precision."

Cole waved the pistol at him. "What the hell was that? A bad guy monologue? Stop the damn chatter and get to work on my leg. And don't brag about precision, slick. You missed my chest by a mile."

Melvin shook his head and smiled. "Wasn't aiming for the chest. Feeling a little light-headed? The sun's going down. Getting cold?" He licked his finger and held it up. "I feel a nip in the air."

"Get that on my leg before I blow your head off!" Cole weakly grabbed for the bandage, but Melvin easily backed out of his reach.

"Isn't that your plan either way? Just use your belt for a tourniquet. Tough to do that with a gun in your hand. Want me to hold it for you?"

"You think I'm stupid?"

Melvin shrugged. "Little bit, yeah."

"You have to help me. You're a doctor."

Melvin rubbed his chin. "That's true, I am. And you're right. Medical school never taught me how to throw a knife, but they did teach me the location of the femoral artery and how long it takes to bleed out, which is why I'm stalling. By the way, thanks for pulling the knife out. That really helped to speed things up." Melvin glanced at his watch. "Good news. I think I'll get home in time for dinner. Nothing better than Sally's home cooking." He winked. "I think you know what I mean."

"Doesn't have to be this way, Melvin. Tend to my leg, and we can work together. You and I are the same, not like these 50s schmucks.

We're faster, smarter, and we know the future. Think of what we could do."

Melvin blinked hard. "Hold up. Are you suggesting I trust you, let down my guard, and we become a team? That's so cliché. Why do all bad guys say that? Do you take a class? Are you a classically trained antagonist?" He pointed at him. "Get this straight. You are a raving lunatic and a murderer. We are nothing alike. I will never—son-of-a-bitch, I'm giving the clichéd response."

Cole's eyes narrowed. "Still high and mighty, thinking you're the smartest guy in the room. You forgot one thing. We heal faster, too. You think you're stalling? I'm just waiting for this bleeding to stop so I can enjoy kicking and killing your punk ass."

Melvin shook his head. "You won't heal fast enough."

"I can still shoot you."

"Don't see how that helps. You look pale. Gun getting heavy?"

Cole looked at him with pleading eyes. "Come on, Melvin. You took an oath."

"The Hippocratic Oath says nothing about saving lives, just relieving suffering. We've all suffered from you, Cole. That suffering is about to end."

"If you don't help me, it's murder. Can you kill someone? Can you live with that?"

"Technically, it's not murder. You're already dead, remember? But you're right. I'm not a killer." Melvin looked at his watch. "At least not for the next two minutes, thirty seconds. Sally gave me this watch. Do you like it? Hey, you don't look so good. Want to sit down?"

Feebly, Cole took his left hand off his leg to help keep the gun up. The bleeding had slowed. "See? Healing already."

Melvin shook his head. "That's not why."

Cole nodded in understanding. "Then, you first." Birds scattered as the shot rang out. Melvin's body slumped to the ground.

Chapter 35
Da Svidania, Idiot

Melvin slowly sat up. Cole's body lay motionless, a bullet wound to his head.

"Professor Jones? You okay?"

"Clyde? You shot him?"

"He was aiming to shoot you. Did you faint?"

"Who me?" Melvin stood and brushed off the dirt. "Of course not. What are you doing here?"

Clyde bent down and picked up the folder. "What's this?"

"Oh, hey, that's nothing, just a misunder—looks like you're reading it anyway."

"According to each of these documents, your true name is Dr. Napier, and you are a Soviet agent."

"Clyde, you can put down the rifle. I'm not a—what happened to your voice? What do you mean, every document? You can read Russian?"

"We can stop playing games, Dr. Jones. We know you are a government agent. We just do not know from where."

"I don't belong to any government. I'm Canadian."

"No, you are not, and you are not from Indiana. You arrived in town with no papers, no verifiable past, and you have at least two aliases. The question is, who do you work for?"

"Whom."

"I am not familiar with that abbreviation. What does it stand for?"

"No. You asked, who do you work for? It should be whom. Whom is the object of the preposition *for*. It's really a question of using the proper pronoun. But I'm sensing you're not up for a discussion on grammatical semantics."

"Very funny. English is not my first language, and I suspect not yours either. These papers are a poor attempt at forgery meant only for blackmail. We would know if you worked for the Americans, and obviously, you do not work for us. Out of professional courtesy, who sent you?"

"Holy shit, you're an actual communist spy?" Melvin's eyes widened. "We had one, after all? How about that? What the heck are you doing in central Arkansas?"

"My government received reports of a large-scale investigation of espionage here, and they dispatched us to discover who, or *whom,* and why."

Melvin smiled. "Let me wrap my head around this. People around here are paranoid over the Cold War. Someone sees me here, assumes I'm a communist spy, they investigate it, and then the USSR sends an actual communist spy to investigate the investigation, confirming the original paranoia?"

Clyde rolled his eyes. "For a grown man, you see things with the simplicity of a child."

"It's a gift."

"It is not a compliment."

"But you're just a kid."

Clyde shook his head. "Not for a long time. My boyish face is my cover."

"And you think I'm a spy, too?"

"That is debatable. When we first identified you, I was convinced you were a complete amateur, a buffoon, a bumpkin, an idiot, a simpleton, a—"

Melvin held up a hand. "I get it. Move on."

"I asked permission simply to kill you and come home. But when my superiors read your reports, they believed it was deeply encoded, and no one could be this stupid. They believe you are a seasoned professional. So, I was given permission only to wound you for interrogation."

"You shot me on purpose?"

"I shot a tree near you. The bark cut your skin—three years ago. Stop whining."

Melvin rubbed his neck. "Still hurts. You said my reports. What reports?"

"The reports to your handler, code name, Alexis."

His eyes widened. "Alexis?"

"Come now, Dr. Jones, a little respect, please. I am good at what I do. You, on the other hand . . . We have never experienced agents burying correspondence for anyone to find. It is either very stupid or quite ingenious."

"You *dug up* my letters?"

"Of course. They were sent back for analysis. My superiors wish to pass along their compliments on your presumed brilliance. They believed it to be the perfect cover to write letters of fantasy. On the surface, it appears you're nothing more than a coward asking permission to end your assignment and return to your country. They suspected a deeper message. I, however, stood by my initial assessment."

"Which was?"

"Idiot."

Melvin nodded and pointed at him. "Right. Thanks for that."

"I will admit, we could not figure out how Alexis was supposed to retrieve the reports. He frequented this area but never directly to the burial site."

"What do you mean?"

Clyde pointed at Cole's body. "Obviously, that's Alexis. We identified him after we spotted him performing overwatch. His dedication was admirable. He spent several evenings with a rifle on your position to protect you. And you cannot deny he passed you

337

instructions at the drive-in for your cemetery rendezvous, where he gave you further orders, which you immediately followed. Like you, he has no verifiable past. But unlike you, he has been here considerably longer and used many aliases. Why was a termination order given? Did you refuse an assignment? Why did Alexis bother with a forgery file?"

Melvin put his hands on his hips. "I can not *believe* you dug up my letters and sent them to Russia." He shook his head. "Son-of-a-bitch."

"Why do you care?" Clyde asked, lowering his gun. "You have spoken to him directly. Those reports are now meaningless."

Melvin shook a finger. "For months, I sweated bullets over those letters. Should I dig them up and destroy them? Should I dig them up and put them in a better container? Should I bury copies or bury new ones? And this whole damn time, THIS WHOLE DAMN TIME, it was Russians. Russians stole my letters. Son-of-a-bitch!" He shook his head. "I did *not* see that coming."

Clyde stiffened. "I am not Russian. I am Ukrainian. And you should thank me."

"Thank you? I buried those letters for a damn good reason. Why the hell should I thank you?"

"After our experts failed to decipher your code, they were released to the public as approved reading. More eyes equal a greater chance of seeing hidden information. It is a controversial technique but occasionally effective. The Letters of the Arkansas Traveler were extremely popular and widely read throughout the Soviet Union. Your reports are now required reading at our training facilities. And they have become the basis of three popular Russian novels."

"So, I'm a hit in the USSR?" Melvin rolled his eyes. "That sounds about right."

"Yes, there is even an interpretive ballet. It's called Pis'ma Russkogo Puteshestvennika. It means—"

"Letters of a Russian Traveler?"

Clyde nodded. "You speak Russian. Why am I not surprised?"

338

"Not really. My wife got us tickets for my birthday."

"So, you have a mission in the Soviet Union and plan to attend our ballet. I find this disturbing."

"Not as disturbing as actually attending a ballet."

"My superiors are still interested in learning the true meaning of your reports. If you are the expert agent they believe you to be, no amount of torture should get you to talk. But if I am correct, it will not take long. Shall we begin?"

Melvin held up his hand. "Or, we could just go with what your superiors believe. They are your superiors for a reason. You don't want to waste time with a bunch of useless torture. You know what *might* work? Bribery. I say, let's give that a try."

"You mock me, Dr. Jones. You have deduced I do not have permission to torture you."

Melvin glanced away. "Yes, that's exactly right."

"It does not matter. We already know your mission. You are here for conversion of ideology. During your time away, you met with many people, some of whom are only now growing in notoriety and influence. We are familiar with these techniques. Our governments share the same goal. That is why I saved your life."

Melvin cocked his head to the side. "But did you, Clyde? I had him right where I wanted."

"Pointing a loaded .38 at your head?"

"No, bleeding out." Melvin pointed at the body. "See where I hit him with the knife? That's precision."

Clyde folded his arms. "That was dumb luck. I watched you. You aimed for the chest and missed."

"Missed my ass. I'm an expert with that thing."

Clyde picked up the knife, carved out a small circle on a tree, and handed it to him. "From where you're standing, an expert could easily hit that."

"An expert doesn't have to prove anything. My work speaks for itself." Melvin tossed the knife hard into the ground, missing his own foot by mere inches. "You know, I had this whole thing timed to the minute. I was set to say a cool line right before he passed out. And then you went and shot him in the head like some barbarian."

"You have my apologies, Dr. Jones. If you like, you may say your cool line now."

"No . . . now it would sound all rehearsed and stupid."

Clyde examined the sky. "It's getting dark. Perhaps we should stop wasting time, dig a grave, remove the hands and teeth, and burn the remains along with the file?"

"Well, yeah. Why do you think I brought a shovel and a knife?"

"Alexis brought the shovel."

"Just like I planned."

Clyde rolled his eyes. "You are a master of our craft."

Once Cole's charred remains had been buried, Melvin tossed his hands and teeth into the river. "You can tell your superiors, if you're looking for converts, you'll have no luck here. Arkansans are as patriotic as they come."

Clyde nodded. "What will you tell the daughter of the man you have killed? Is she part of your organization?"

Melvin pointed sternly. "She's an uninformed civilian and off-limits. Understand?"

Clyde shook his head. "You have wasted three years of my life, Dr. Jones. I have no interest in allowing you to waste more. I am obligated to point out that since your government has issued a kill order, you are a man without a country. My superiors would like to offer you a position."

"I'm retiring from the game, Clyde. I've done my part."

"On behalf of every Soviet agent, we are overjoyed to hear it. Da svidania, *idiot*."

Fortunately, it was a full moon, and Melvin found his way back to the car. As he drove home, he considered Clyde's words. In a couple of days, he'd face the daughter of the man he'd killed or would have if he'd lived another thirty-eight seconds, a man whose body he'd just burned and buried, a man who'd raised, loved, and watched over Sally, a man now reduced to a charred skeleton with no hands—a ghost of the Arkansas River. Melvin looked at his hands on the steering wheel and released a long and uneasy breath. He'd survived. It was a Good Friday.

Late Easter Sunday, Sally returned home and knocked at his door. Melvin had spent the day at home, uncomfortable going to church two days after attempted murder, even if it was self-defense.

"Hey, sweetie!" she greeted him with a kiss. "How was church this morning?"

"Everything you could imagine," he lied, adding to his list of spiritual iniquities. "How's your mom?"

"Not great. Norma stopped sending letters a couple of years ago. Did I tell you that? It's like they just disappeared. Now she's lost her and all her grandchildren, too. We put flowers on Daddy and Stacy's graves. I think it helped. We'll never see another like those two."

"Not unless he comes back as a ghost," he muttered, "a ghost with no hands or teeth."

She stuck her head in his fridge. "Anything interesting happen around here while I was gone?"

"Nope. I had a beer at McKeen's with my granddad, got abducted, ran into my illegitimate son, then took a nice drive out to the countryside, where I tried to commit justifiable homicide. After that, I solved an international mystery and learned I'm famous in Russia. You know, the usual crap."

"Uh-huh." She twisted the top off her beer and snapped her fingers, zipping the bottlecap across the room. "Do you remember the last time you saw Daddy?"

"Would have to say—yes."

"Do you remember what he said to you?"

Die, you smug bastard? But Melvin replied, "We were sitting in the kitchen with your uncles. It was terrible."

"Yeah, he was protecting you. He liked you. He always did. So did my dipshit brother. Did I ever tell you how much he respected your beer move at that first Thanksgiving?"

"You're joking."

She giggled. "I wish I was. After that, he made people throw beer cans at him while he tried to catch and drink them at the same time. It was the stupidest damn thing. Norma said he ruined four good shirts and got forehead stitches twice. Dumbass. But he liked you." She kissed him. "I like you, too. Guess it runs in the family." She sighed. "Do you think Daddy's looking down on us right now?"

"Up, down—yeah, I'm sure he's looking."

"Well, I'm exhausted. Let's go to bed. Maybe I'm not all *that* tired."

"You want to sit up a while, then?"

She grabbed his shirt. "Nope."

Chapter 36
Lies, Deceit, and Blackmail

Whatever grief Melvin's conscience was dishing out melted away over the next few days as he poured into his work. It was Friday, April 15th, 1955. His complicated surgery patient showed steady signs of recovery, and everything was returning to normal. As he escorted a young lady to check out, he declined her invitation to Sunday brunch. Sally gave her a scornful look. "The doctor told you he was busy that day, Missy. Looking at his schedule, he's busy every other day, too. You can wait right over there until I'm ready for you. Well, hello, Dr. Napier. Are we still on for dinner this Sunday?"

"Sally, please check her out."

She took a long sip of coffee from the Detroit Lions mug Melvin had bought her through the mail-order catalog. "Have a seat, Missy. I'll get to you when I finish talking with my fiancé." Sally gave Melvin a look that said, Can you believe this lady?

Melvin mouthed back, "Fiancé?" Sally smiled and shrugged.

After clinic, the twosome walked down to McKeen's and chatted with Walter from their favorite barstools. Melvin turned and scanned the room a few times but found no future relatives or homicidal maniacs hell-bent on his demise. He relaxed a bit, and it hit him. With all the recent commotion, he'd given no thought to Grace or her son. *What did she call him—Matty? There was a Matt Grable in Sugarfield, Dad's old boss.* Melvin shook his head. *She got her little souvenir, after all.* When he turned back to the bar, his date was gone.

"Walter, where's Sally?"

Walter seemed not to hear him. "Brian, my boy! Welcome back. You're my favorite customer who doesn't drink. You are also my only customer who comes to my bar . . . not to drink."

"Ah, hello, Mr. McKeen. Not your only one. Don't forget about my best girl. I can't seem to find her. Have you seen Sally?"

Walter's smile melted. "I have customers. You know Melvin? Maybe he's seen her."

"Thanks a bunch. When you get a moment, I'd like my usual."

Walter sighed. "Rum and coke, hold the rum."

"You know me so well." Brian extended his hand. "Melvin! Great to see you, old friend." Brian pointed to the glass next to Melvin. "Keeping company tonight? Hot date?"

Melvin glanced at Sally's beer. "Oh, that's mine. I drink a lot." He reluctantly downed it, knowing this would incur her wrath. "So, Sally's still your best girl? That's great. How are you two kids getting along?"

"Couldn't be better. We went on a whirlwind road trip this past weekend."

"Oh, really."

"Oh, yes. I introduced her to my family, and then we headed down to Conway to spend Easter with her mother. Such a tragedy about the car accident that killed her father and brother. Fog can be so dangerous. That's why I never drive in it—ever. There's no place that important I need to be."

Melvin raised an eyebrow. "Yes, very tragic. I've heard several versions of the story. No telling what really happened. In the end, I suppose the result is the same."

"Astute point. I've noticed she talks a lot about *you*."

"She does?"

"Oh yes, the way your patients all love you, bring you food, and invite you to lunch. You must be one heck of an eye doctor. Some days I even think she's sweet on you."

Melvin's eyes cut sideways as he buried his mouth in the other beer mug. "What? That's crazy."

Brian nudged him. "I'm just teasing you—a little give-and-take between buddies. You look a little pale. I'm sorry if I upset you, but I

344

suspect that look isn't about my sweetheart. Want to talk about it?" Brian sat on the stool where Sally had been. "I'm a great listener."

Melvin stared at him a moment. "Have you ever done something terrible? Maybe two things? Something that would hurt others if they ever found out?"

"Yes, Melvin, I understand regret. You know, I never had a great relationship with my father. My older brother looked out for me my whole life. He was so proud when I got accepted into the University. So, on my first day of college, I called home. He answered, and instead of chatting with him, I immediately asked to speak with my mother. I know it's horrible, and I'm embarrassed about it to this day. So, I know how you feel. I doubt whatever is haunting you could be worse than that."

"Wow, Brian, I don't exactly know how to respond to that."

"Glad I could help. So, what have you done? Couldn't hurt to get it off your chest."

"Let's see. I've murdered my girlfriend's father, cheated on my wife multiple times, lied to my grandparents, and fathered a son out of wedlock with a married woman I don't intend to support. Plus, I'm sleeping with a woman who's dating the world's nicest guy and single-handedly responsible for bringing a communist spy into our state. And did I alert the authorities? Nope. I chose to put my personal interests over those of our community."

Brian patted him on the shoulder. "Okay, big guy, I get it. You don't have to tell me if you don't want to."

Walter came back over. "Here's your coke. Need to start a tab?"

"No, sir. One's my limit. I like to keep a clear head." Brian shot-gunned the soda and placed the glass on the bar with authority. "Well, gentlemen, if my girl's not here, logic dictates she must be elsewhere. I'm afraid I can't stay here carousing and drinking all evening."

Walter shook his head. "Of course not. It's a *bar*."

"See you gents another time!"

345

"Bye, Brian."

"Come back soon." Walter sighed. "One day, I'll slip him some rum just to see what happens."

Melvin shook his head. "No, you're not."

"No, I'm not. Such a nice boy." Walter poured another beer. "Melvin, you're like a son to us, and we love Sally, but what you kids are doing behind his back isn't right. You should marry her or cut her loose."

"Well, as usual, you're not wrong. Let me clear my tab—and hers."

"Hers too? Do you know how much that is? You're not leaving again, are you?"

Melvin shook his head. "I just need to do one good thing today."

Back at the loft, Melvin put his ear to Sally's door to listen for Brian's voice. All he could hear was Sinatra playing, so he knocked.

Sally opened the door with her bathrobe open, revealing a thin nightgown. "Care to come in, handsome?"

"You ditched me at the bar."

"I didn't ditch you. I was due for a visitor today and needed to get home. Fortunately, that didn't happen, which is a little odd. Normally, it shows up like clockwork. Anyway, I took the opportunity to slip into something more comfortable for you."

"You wanted to slip out of something *uncomfortable* is more like it."

"Potatoes, *potätoes*."

"You never told me you were still dating Brian. Tell me again about Easter weekend."

She closed her robe. "He told you about that, huh?"

"So, every time you've been busy, that's why?"

A scowl spread across her face as she held up her left hand. "Notice anything missing? Do you know how old I am? Maybe I'd like to have a family. We've known each other, what, five years? And we're just now getting serious? Are we even serious? And you're upset that

I'm making time with a man who moves things along at a normal pace? Well, mister, if you want to be upset over that, then you need to ask yourself, what are you prepared to do about it?"

"I don't like demands."

"It's not a demand, sweetheart. It's reality."

"Fine. You do what you need to, Sally. You always do."

Over the next two weeks, they hardly spoke. Ronny felt it all the way over in the optical shop. "Damn, Melvin, did the temperature just drop? Could you two be any colder? What's going on?"

"Not much—just lies, deceit, and blackmail."

"You mean a relationship? Been there, partner. When I was with Annette, that vinyl played over and over like a . . . record, I guess, because it's a vinyl. Take it from me, sometimes you just need to move on. Can't get caught hanging out in the past. I tell you what, if I could go back and tell myself to stay the hell away from her—"

"What did you just say?"

"I just said that if I could go back in time and tell myself—"

"Deliver a message." Melvin snapped his fingers. "That's what *she* did and then disappeared."

"Well, I guess. I mean, she disappeared because I stone-cold dumped her ass. I was like, Hey, babe, I can't be strapped down with some whiney, skinny, little—"

"Ronny, do you remember when we took that trip to Vegas?"

"Do I? It was epic! You and me on the strip, girls galore."

"Do you remember the gypsy we met that night, the one you paid twenty bucks not to reveal your secrets?"

"This again? Never happened. I don't have secrets, bro. When did you make it with a gypsy girl?"

"Exactly. You don't remember her."

Ronny shrugged. "We drank a lot that night. I do remember getting hot and heavy with this red-headed pole dancer. Remember her? I was shelling out dollar bills like they were going out of style. Classic."

"Do you know what this means? You can't remember her because everything changed. She was never there. She disappeared."

"Broads do that, man. Sometimes, it's a good thing. I remember this one time, I was talking up this chick in the grocery store, I mean, she wasn't really a looker, but she wasn't *not* a looker—"

"The letters, Ronny. It means the *letters* will work."

"Are you saying I should send Annette a letter? I don't know, man. You don't know what went down when Sally showed up. You weren't there."

Melvin grabbed his shoulders. "I can go home, Ronny. *Home!*"

"You are home. You live upstairs." Ronny sniffed him. "Have you been drinking? It's the middle of the day, dude. Not cool."

"Thanks, Ronny. I can't tell you what this means to me."

"Sure, anytime." As Melvin walked away, Ronny called after him in an ever-softening voice, "That's why I'm here, all alone in the optical shop, where no one ever comes. You'd think a damn eye doctor could occasionally prescribe a pair of glasses."

Melvin strode up to the reception desk. "Ms. Davis, could I please see you in the break room?"

"Of course, doctor."

"Sally, I'm sorry. You're right, I haven't given you everything you deserve and have no right to be upset over Brian."

"No, it's my fault for sneaking around. You've never kept secrets from me, and I was wrong to keep one from you. I've loved our time together. You've given me more than you know. Look, tomorrow's your birthday, and it's Saturday. Let's go on a picnic. I know a lovely place. How about I cook for you tonight?" She smiled. "I bought that new Johnny Cash album."

"You're the best, but I have something I need to do first."

Chapter 37
The Last Letter

After work that day, Melvin went shopping—ammunition box, solder gun, pickle jar, all the usual suspects. This was it. Yara, the Lebanese gypsy daughter from the future or past, or whenever, had proven the immediate causality of time manipulation. She'd spent years waiting to tell Melvin about killing someone with a gun. And just twenty-two days ago, he'd chosen to pack a knife into his man purse instead of Sally's gun, presumably because of her message. As a result, he didn't kill Cole. He wasn't a killer. It was no longer a story he would one day tell her father, who would now never send his daughter on a mission to Vegas. Yara was now somewhere else, having lived a different life. And the change had been immediate. Either that or she'd quickly packed her shit and left. No, her little shop had been vacant for a good while.

With a wide grin, he sat at his kitchen table. *This is it. My letter plan would've worked if it hadn't been for those meddling Russians, and now they're gone. Cole's gone, and Agent Smith is gone. No one's left to screw this up. All I need is to bury one last letter, and this all ends.*

Melvin picked up his pen, but all he could think of was her. *Brian's a better man than I'll ever be. He loves her. That's got to be enough.* He sighed. *I'll break up with her at the picnic, then drive out and bury the letter tomorrow evening. He'll marry her, and they'll have a loving family and never have to see me again. If this works, she won't even remember I was here.* He wiped his eyes. *It's best for everyone. Once I get back, I'll find her and make sure she's cared for.*

He stared at the blank page. *What if, by writing the letter, the decision becomes final enough to ensure I bury it tomorrow and disappear right now?* He dropped his head into his hands. *Why is this so hard? Maybe I should go over there, and—no, I'm writing this now and going home. I'm going home!*

Dear Alexis,

"Shit!" Melvin hurled his pen across the room. He kicked his chair back and stood at the window, staring out at 1955 Little Rock. This wasn't his Little Rock, and he knew it. He wasn't meant to be here, wasn't supposed to have met her, wasn't supposed to have been part of her life. Then his face went pale. *I'm the reason Cole came back in time. I'm the reason she was born. If I write this letter, will she be erased?* A potential ghost knocked at his door. The letter wasn't in the ground—not yet.

"I thought I heard something. You okay?"

He shook his head. "I lost my pen."

"I brought you some baked chicken. It's cold, but—"

Melvin snatched the plate. "I love your cold chicken."

She reached up and wiped his face. "Have you been crying?"

"What? Hey, know what goes great with chicken? Beer. Why don't I grab a couple, and we'll climb up and sit by your garden?"

"That'd be nice. Are you writing a letter?"

Melvin flipped the page over. "Yeah. Some new information became available, and the long-term prognosis changed. I need to give someone bad news, and I don't know how."

"Is it someone I know?"

"It's someone you've never met."

"I know everyone in your clinic."

"They came to my clinic in a time when you weren't there."

"Oh. Well, the best way to give bad news is just to say it. You shouldn't put it off. They have a right to know. Anything else is less than honest."

He nodded and looked into her eyes. "So, the thing is—"

"Ready to go to the roof?"

He wiped his eyes. "Yeah."

Melvin chowed down on the last drumstick as they cuddled on her bench. "Your garden looks great."

"Yeah, those squirrels never came back. It made all the difference."

"And they never will."

She pulled back from him. "How do you know? Does Melvin Napier speak for all squirrel-kind?"

"No, I'm just saying they're probably scared of you. I know I am."

"You better be."

Melvin pointed at her lap. "What's up with your beer? I've never seen one survive that long."

"I'm just not in a beer mood."

"Are you sick?"

"No, just don't feel like beer."

He shrugged. "First time for everything, I guess. Hey, how did you hear me toss a pen from all the way over in your loft? I swear you have better hearing than anyone I know."

"It's just something I was blessed with, along with other attributes, as you might have noticed. Did I ever tell you people say I look just like Marilyn?"

"You mentioned it once, a long time ago. But you didn't have to. I noticed it right off."

Sally laid her head on his shoulder as he wrapped his arm around her. She softly said, "Isn't the last of the sunset the most beautiful? Some people prefer sunrises, but not me. I like the tail end of a sunset. It has the most fascinating colors, like the sky is painted. What do you think that says about me?"

"I think *you're* fascinating, Sally. I've never known anyone like you. I think there's so much to you that it takes getting all the way to the end of the sunset to get to know who you really are. And the more you get to know, the more beautiful you become."

"I don't know what to say," she replied, wiping away tears. "Look at me. I'm such a wreck."

"No." He gently pushed the hair from her face. "You're the most together person I know."

"You're such a liar. I smoke, drink, swear, speak my mind, and I'm unmarried and over thirty. I'm just a hot mess. Maybe women can be like that somewhere in the future, but not here. I know what people think of me. I've never fit in. It's like I was born too early, you know, like I'm somehow lost in time. Do you ever feel that way?"

He nodded. "You mean like you're in the wrong place but can't leave—until you can, but then it feels like you're right where you're supposed to be, even though you know you're not?"

Her eyes narrowed. "Melvin?"

"Yes?"

"You are a *very* odd man."

"You've mentioned that."

She reached up and kissed him. "But you're cute, so we tend to let these things slide." She took his hand. "I don't know what tomorrow holds, but whatever comes our way, I want you to know I will always love and be there for you, Melvin Napier, no matter what."

He looked into her eyes. "If anything ever separated us, I promise I would find you, even if it took fifty years." He caressed her hair and kissed her.

She pulled back. "But what if I don't make it fifty years?"

"Then, I'll still find you and reverse haunt your ass."

Her eyes searched his. "What's that?"

"I don't know. I just made it up."

"It sounds kind of horrible."

"I know. It really does."

"I suppose I'd better not die."

He squeezed her hand tightly. "You'd better not."

She kissed him again. "Let's turn in early."

He looked at his feet. "No, I need to finish that letter. It's time."

"Okay, come over when you're finished?"

"Yeah, if I can."

"Of course, you can—if you really want to."

Chapter 38
Moving On

Melvin awoke the next morning on April 30th, 1955, his thirty-eighth birthday. Considering he would be born in 1971, his cake would have negative sixteen candles. Sally knocked at his door. "Ready?"

"Sure, but why so secretive about where we're going?"

She playfully flicked him on the forehead. "Because it's a surprise, dummy."

Melvin's eyes narrowed. Every day he had known her, Sally had dressed to the nines with a good deal of attention to her appearance. But today, she wore a simple dress, hair in a ponytail, and bare minimum makeup and perfume.

"What's in the basket?"

"You'll see," she said, leading them to his car. "I missed you last night. Did you finish your letter?"

"Yeah, took longer than I thought. I wondered if things would be different once I finished it, but they weren't. Didn't want to wake you."

"I'm sure it just takes time. I was pretty tired, anyway. Pop the trunk."

"Have a seat," he replied, opening the door for her. "I'll take care of those."

"Such a gentleman today. Are you ill?"

He placed her basket and quilt next to the ammo container with Alexis's name and closed the trunk. Soon, they were across the river and onto highway 365 toward Conway.

"Are we going to see your mother?"

She shook her head and smiled as they passed through the small settlement of Palarm and continued onward. Near the town of

Mayflower, Melvin's engine made a crunching noise. Sally's eyes narrowed. "When's the last time you had her serviced?"

He shrugged. "September?"

"Really? September of '53 or '54?"

"No, last September, so '54." He paused. "This September will be *1955.*"

She snapped her fingers. "Is that how a calendar works? *Finally,* someone has cracked the code."

"No, September 30th, 1955. It hasn't happened yet."

"What are you talking about?"

"The day James Dean dies in a car crash. I remember the movie. It's called *9-30-55.* I remember because they filmed it in Conway."

Her eyes widened. "James Dean's dead?"

"No. It's only April. That's the point."

She slapped his arm. "Don't be cruel. You know how much I love James Dean. Besides, there's no way they filmed in Conway and didn't call me after my near-Oscar nomination for the *Accommodating Emmetrope.*"

Melvin cut her a side glance. "When were you ever nominated for an Oscar?"

Sally straightened in her seat. "I said *near*-nomination." She sighed heavily. "Honestly, I think the problem is my agent."

"You don't have an agent."

She pointed at him. "Exactly, and that's the problem. Now, tell me they haven't come out with a new James Dean movie I didn't know about. Tell me you're just screwing around."

Melvin put on his best James Dean voice. "Well . . . maybe I am." As Sally pretended to swoon, he thought, *I could change it. I could go to California and stop him from dying.* His eyes widened. "Sally, why are we here?"

"You mean in Mayflower? It's on the way."

"No, I mean on Earth. Do you think it's for a reason?"

She nodded. "I'm sure of it."

"I think I'm here, in this place, in this year, for a higher purpose."

"What do you mean?"

"Back in school, an old girlfriend tracked me down in a bar. She said she and her friends were here for a higher purpose and wanted me to join them. I was too immature to understand it then, but I get it now. I was put here for a purpose. Sally, for reasons you wouldn't believe, I can fix a lot of problems. If you had the knowledge to make the world a better place, wouldn't you?"

Her eyes narrowed. "What old girlfriend?"

Once they reached Conway, she pointed north. "Keep going."

"Do we have enough gas?"

"Aw, are you worried?" She gave an evil grin. "I'll help you. You may not know this, but see that dial on your dash? You judge how close the little arm is to the letter E, because E stands for—"

"Enormous smartass?"

When they reached the small town of Greenbrier, she directed him down a dirt road, and another, and then another. Eventually, they came upon a picturesque farm with large fields surrounding a white two-story home with a wrap-around porch. A large red barn sat off to the right.

"Turn in here," she pointed. "Drive right on out into the field."

"Who lives here?" he asked.

"No one right now. It just sold. I know the owner. We can have a picnic over by that big oak."

"Kind of a long trip for lunch."

She playfully grabbed his chin. "Aw, always the romantic. What happened to Dr. Casanova?"

"You're right. It's beautiful out here, in the middle of nowhere, where we could be murdered, and no one would ever know."

They spread her great-grandmother's quilt under the shade of the oak tree. Birds happily chirped as he uncorked a bottle of white wine. They nibbled on egg salad sandwiches and chit-chatted about work, the weather, local politics, and nothing really.

He reached over and wiped egg from the corner of her mouth. "I've never seen you in a ponytail. Trying something new?"

"Oh, not really," she undid her ponytail and fluffed her hair. "That better?"

"I think it looks great either way."

She smiled. "It's peaceful here, don't you think?"

"Yeah, quiet and relaxing," He leaned back on his elbows and flicked at the quilt. "Ants sure look happy."

Sally gazed across the field. "What would you think about living here?"

"Way out here? Why?"

She turned and looked into his eyes. "Why not?"

He sat up. This was the moment, the moment where he had to let her down gently somehow, to tell her they were finished, to explain that he was leaving—without explaining why. It would crush her, the woman who'd done so much for him, who had given everything she could. Her pain would be on his hands. There were no words.

Sally turned her gaze back to the field and sighed. "It's unfair to ask you for something you're not ready to give. I've spent a lot of time waiting, a lot of time with Brian, thinking about you, wondering if you could be the guy. But you can't. I've always kind of known that." She sniffed. "None of this has been fair to him. He's such a good man."

Melvin nodded. "He is a good man."

"At our house in Conway, we have a bell on the porch."

"Yes, I've seen it."

"It was a gift from my great-great-grandfather to my great-great-grandmother on her 35th birthday. I was named after her. He wrote an inscription saying he would always take care of her. She died only a month or two after that. I've often wondered about her life and how it must have been. She was so lucky to have someone to always be there for her. I turn 35 in November. By then, she'd already been married twenty years, had a house, and raised four boys. What have I done? Nothing."

"Sally, you shouldn't compare—"

"Brian asked me to marry him, and I said yes."

Melvin blinked at her. He opened his mouth, but the words wouldn't come. She turned to see his eyes, her eyes holding out hope he'd tell her not to. Melvin's eyes widened as he now understood. She'd brought him here under the pretense of telling him goodbye, but it was actually an ultimatum, a last chance at happiness together. Speak now, or forever hold your peace.

Finally, the words came. Melvin hated the man who said them. "I think that's the smartest thing I've ever heard you say, Sally. And I've heard you say a lot."

She smiled and turned away to brush a small tear. "He bought this place for us. We'll get married and move in. I won't be around after that, Melvin. I won't drive to Little Rock every day for that crummy job just to see you. I won't."

He took her hand. "You shouldn't. You have your life. You should live it." She reached up and kissed him for what felt like the last time. They sat on the quilt in silence, looking at the field. A red-tailed hawk dove, then flew off with something in its mouth.

"Look like lunchtime for all of us," Melvin said. "What do you think that was, a mouse?"

"I don't know."

He sighed. "One day, you're just a mouse trucking along in a field, thinking everything's going your way, and then bam. It didn't matter if you were a good mouse or a bad mouse. Someone, somewhere, decided your time was up. Do you think his family will miss him? What do you think his name was? I'll bet it was Steve."

She turned and looked at him. "Will you come to the wedding?"

"You couldn't keep me from it. I'd bring Steve as my plus one, but at this point, I think he'd just fall to pieces."

She softly punched his arm. "You are so goofy. Just because I'm getting married doesn't mean we can't still be friends. We could hang out now and then." She gave him a look but bit her lip.

"What is it? Is it about our time together since I've been back? You're worried it'll make things awkward? I swear I'll never say a word to him. And by him, I mean Steve, the mouse. Brian, on the other hand, I'm calling him as soon as we get back."

She looked down. "I know you'd never say anything. It does have to do with our time together."

"You have to do what's right for—"

"I'm pregnant."

"What?"

"You're a doctor. I shouldn't have to explain it."

Melvin snatched the wine glass from her hand. "You're done with that."

"It's only wine. I stopped the hard stuff, even beer."

"You can't drink *any* alcohol. How far along?"

"Just a few weeks."

Melvin shoved the hair back from his forehead. "You're sure?"

"I'm late, and I'm never late."

"I've never known you to be on time for anything."

"With this, I'm the freaking tower of Big Ben. The doctor confirmed it."

"Does Brian know?"

Sally continued to look down at her hands. "I told him a couple of days ago."

Melvin gazed off into the distance. "Well, congratulations, then. I imagine he's pretty happy."

"Not so much. We've never been together."

Melvin shot her a look. "Wait—what?"

"Brian's a devout man. He believes in abstinence until marriage."

Melvin's eyes went to her belly. "So, then it's—"

She looked up at him and nodded.

"I thought you were on the pill?"

Sally cocked her head to one side. "I'm not sick. Why would I be on pills?"

No oral contraceptives in the 1950s. Add that to the list of Shit That Would've Been Good to Know.

"I know what you're thinking," she said.

"I doubt it."

"I know it's yours because you're the only man I've ever been with."

He shook his head. "Hang on. I'm your next-door neighbor. You've taken the Walk of Shame up those stairs more times than I can count. You can't expect me to believe—"

Sally looked down at her hands again. "I said you were the only *man*."

"That doesn't make any—*oh*. Really? How come I didn't know that? I'm your best friend. Why didn't you tell me?"

She looked away. "Maybe it's something you can talk about in Canada, but not in Little Rock. Not yet anyway. Maybe in another 20 years."

He shrugged. "Or slightly longer. When did you know?"

She sighed and avoided his eyes. "I fooled around with a boy in college enough to figure out what I'm not."

"Wiles with the neurological tic?"

Her head snapped around. "He didn't have a tic!" Her expression softened as she shrugged. "At least not at first. And no, it wasn't him. After that, I figured my fantasy of being the small-town schoolteacher in the cute little house with the white picket fence wasn't happening, so I quit school and moved to Little Rock. That's where I met Francis

Moore. She helped me understand who I really was. I thought we were soul mates until she dumped me like I was nothing—*bitch.*"

"You don't say?" Melvin cringed, confident he was going straight to Hell for the image of Sally and his grandmother now in his head. "If you're—" he paused, unsure of the appropriate 1955 term, "that way, then why me? You've never been reluctant when we're together, and you've flirted with me from day one."

She smiled at him, then looked away. "You've always been easy on the eyes. At first, it was good cover around the office. Then I kind of fell for you. I shouldn't have, but it just happened. There's something about you. I don't know . . . you're kind of goofy."

"And Brian? Is he goofy?"

"Don't judge me, Melvin. You no longer have that right. He's a good man, and he loves me."

Melvin nodded. "Does he know about your . . . preferences?"

"Yes, it was only fair to tell him. He says he doesn't care."

Melvin's eyes widened. "Wow. Now I want to marry Brian. Does anyone else know?"

"Just you two—and Ronny, of course. He and I have always looked out for each other. It's not easy. There aren't many of us."

"That's why you went bat shit when he hooked up with Annette."

"No! Annette was a cheap, opportunistic, dumbass, gold-digging little hag. He was lonely, and she took advantage. He never would've been happy, not in the long run. Anyway, bitch got what she deserved."

Melvin put his hand on her stomach. "And this? Does Brian know about us?"

"I came clean about everything. He says he forgives me and still wants to get married."

Melvin shook his head. "What a guy. So, when's the wedding?"

She rubbed her belly. "Soon. You know how people like to talk. It'll be okay for a while. Everyone knows how much I like beer."

"Yeah, you've got that going for you. You can't smoke while you're pregnant, either, or around the baby afterward."

She glanced up to the sky. "This just keeps getting better and better. What else can't I have, chocolate?"

"No, you can have as much chocolate as you want."

"Good, because that was going to happen anyway." She took his hand. "You can't come to the wedding. I just asked to see if you would. Oh, and you might want to watch out for a while. After I told Brian, he put a bat behind the seat of his truck." She sighed. "I wish Daddy were here to walk me down the aisle. He would've been so happy. Not with you, of course. He would have *shot* you."

Melvin nodded. "That was his plan."

"What do you mean?"

"There's something I should tell you something about your dad."

"What is it?"

He looked into her searching eyes, the eyes of a little girl who still idolized her daddy. "He loved you as much as anyone I've ever seen. He would have done absolutely anything to ensure your happiness."

"Thank you for saying that, Melvin. I think that's why I fell for you. You remind me of him."

Melvin cringed and adjusted on the quilt. "So, Brain wants to marry you and raise our child. How would it work? Where would I fit in?"

"What do you mean? You should be relieved. You're off the hook."

"This is my child, too."

Her eyes widened. "I didn't know men ever felt that way. Okay, once things settle down, we'll decide how you can be a part of our child's life. How about a family friend?"

Melvin nodded as he shifted his gaze off into the field. Thoughts of Norman flooded his head. He and Mary must have had this same conversation, forcing him to the sidelines for years to come.

"We could call you something like, Uncle Melvin. In return, we have your word that you'll never tell our child the truth. You must give me your word."

Reflexively, Melvin nodded again. But as he did, his heart thumped hard against his chest wall. Maybe Grace's son was his, but she wanted nothing to do with him. This was Sally, and she was having their child. He now had a family here. Would burying the letter kill them? And what if the gypsy had just packed up and left? What if burying the letter doesn't work, and he'd just agreed to give up his child and the woman he loved for nothing?

The field and the tree overhead began to spin as nausea overwhelmed him. The only thing he knew for sure was that he didn't want to be Uncle Melvin and lead the life of Norman. Screw that—screw Brian.

Melvin climbed up on a knee and took her hand. As he gazed into her eyes, the spinning and nausea melted away. "Sally, I love you. Will you marry me?"

She cried through her smile. "I've waited so long to hear that." She got up on her knees and hugged him. "Thank you, Melvin. No."

His eyes widened, and he pushed her out of the hug. "What? We're having a child."

She stood and wiped tears from her cheek. "It's not enough. You may love me, but you're not in love with me—not like you are with Alexis. Since we've been together these last three months, it's been Heaven for me. But Heaven's not Heaven if you're the only one there. I deserve more. I know you, Melvin, the real story."

His eyes widened again as he looked up at her.

She took his hand. "I know you're not divorced, and your wife was never in prison. I read your board."

Melvin shot up, his eyes as wide as they would go. "You saw my board?"

She sighed. "I *may* have broken into your loft a couple of times a few years ago and tried on your clothes and laid in your bed."

"A *couple* of times?"

Her voice grew indignant. "Oh, big deal. Most men would take that as a *compliment!*"

"Most men would have you *arrested!*"

"Well," she said, lowering her voice, "let's not dwell on the past. The point is, I may not have understood all the math, but I learned something bad happened to you in Canada that prevents you from returning to your family in Maumelle. That's why you went so crazy when we met your cousin at the hotel. You're hiding here to protect them. They must be devastated without you. At one point, I even thought about contacting them with a letter or postcard or just anything to let them know you're alive and alright. But I couldn't figure out where to send it, and no one at the post office had any idea. I even went to the library one day to find Maumelle on a map of Canada, but I guess it's too small." She snickered. "Can you imagine? Me in a library?"

"You knew this whole time, and we became a couple anyway?"

She nodded, her eyes turning red once more. "Not my finest hour. I thought I could be okay with it, but I can't." She wiped her tears. "You need to return to them if it's safe."

"I don't know if I can."

"You're not listening. There's nothing for you here. I deserve someone who's in love with me and only me. I deserve a man like Brian." She was quiet for a moment, then said, "I've changed my mind."

"You have?"

"I don't want to get married without you. Before you leave, will you walk me down the aisle? It would mean everything to me."

He wiped away her tears. "Wouldn't miss it for the world." Then she reached up and wiped away his.

They gathered their things in silence and walked back to the car. Once more, he opened her door and put things into the trunk, momentarily staring at the ammo box, then slammed it shut. Once inside, he turned the key several times, but the engine wouldn't turn over.

"Stop doing that," she scolded. "You'll flood it." Sally got out and popped the hood, instructing Melvin to start it when she said so. He sat behind the wheel and waited, a little emasculated, but did as he was told.

As she worked under the hood, Melvin had one foot on the ground to prop the driver-side door open. "Are you in love with him? Are you going to be happy being Mrs. . . ? What's Brian's last name anyway?"

She emerged from under the hood, the late afternoon sun catching her summer dress. It struck him how beautiful she truly was, standing there, wiping her hands on a stereotypical mechanic's rag that had appeared out of nowhere. "Try turning it over now. Westfield. I can't believe you didn't know that. Mrs. Sally Westfield. It's a strong name." The car still wouldn't start, and she disappeared again under the hood.

Melvin paused in thought, then replied, "Westfield? No kidding? I went to school with a guy named Stanley Westfield. Smart son-of-a-bitch." He laughed at the thought of him, anything to push aside thoughts of pregnancy and a rejected marriage proposal. "Hey, did you know we even looked alike?"

"What did you say?" an irritated voice called back, a voice trying to focus on fixing the damn car.

"I said we looked just alike. He was a little shorter, but still. So, there was this one time when he took a test for me, actually, two times. That's how I got into college—and med school, for that matter. I've never told that to anyone." He shook his head and smiled. "Stanley drove this old piece of shit car. It had holes in the floorboard where you could see the road. He had a name for it. What was it he called it? Oh yeah, he named it Sal . . . "

"He named his car Sal?"

Melvin couldn't hear her. His expression had gone blank as he shifted further inside and stared at the brass plate on the console, the driver-side door closing as he did. He now recalled why this car, this particular car, looked so familiar. *Oh, shit.* More dots connected in his head. *Oh shit! That would make Stanley my grand—*

In the middle of his epiphany, the entire car began to shake. He reached for the key, but the engine was off. Sally screamed, jumping back just as the hood fell. Pressure built inside the cab as the vibrations worsened. Melvin jerked on the door handle, but it wouldn't budge. He tried to roll down his window, but it didn't move. The car rocked side to side, tossing him inside the cab. Nauseated, Melvin wished he hadn't eaten so much egg salad.

Sally jerked hard on the outside door handle. "No! Get back!" he shouted through the glass. She ignored him, trying to break the window with her elbow. The left front fender exploded off the car, narrowly missing her and wrapping around a tree like tin foil. "Get the hell away! I'll find a way out!" She refused and tugged on the rear door.

Thrown this way and that and struggling in the suffocating cab pressure, Melvin caught glimpses of her through the windows. The car's violent movements were slamming her and their unborn child. With all he had left, he shouted, "Sweetheart . . . get our baby . . . out of here!" In tears, Sally withdrew.

The car's increasing vibrations sounded like a freight train, giving a green glow in the fading afternoon light. Sally screamed his name, and a thunderous roar emerged as the vehicle exploded inside. She turned, covering her belly as glass shards sailed in every direction, narrowly missing her. For a moment, she thought she heard him scream, followed by . . . nothing. An eerie silence descended upon the farm. Sally rushed to the car, expecting the worst, but found no one. The inside was a bombsite: the dash bent forward, the seats bent backward, and the trunk blown open—all contents destroyed.

Hoping he'd been thrown from the car, Sally frantically scoured the area as darkness fell. Having heard the explosion for miles, people arrived and joined the search with flashlights and lanterns until dawn.

But Melvin was gone.

Chapter 39
Epilogue

The society section of the local newspaper reported, "In a wedding full of intrigue and surprises, Mr. and Mrs. Brian Westfield married on Saturday, June 4th, 1955, at the First Presbyterian Church on Moore Street. Mr. Walter McKeen, a family friend, walked the bride down the aisle to her position beside Mr. Ronald Roberts, an unconventional choice for maid of honor. Mr. Larry Westfield, brother of the groom, stood as best man. Of interest, Mrs. Eunice Westfield, widow, and mother of the groom, did not appear on speaking terms with her new daughter-in-law prior to or after the ceremony. Although she held her tongue during the vows, her dark charcoal dress spoke volumes. Also in attendance was a tall woman wearing a scarf and sunglasses, seated alone in the back row. She was rumored to have been none other than Francis DeChambeau, a nonpracticing attorney-at-law, wife of John DeChambeau, and well-known daughter of Buford Moore. However, the mystery woman disappeared before the ceremony's conclusion, and her true identity remains unconfirmed.

Champagne was served at the reception, but the new couple declined to partake per their strong convictions regarding spirits. Mr. and Mrs. McKeen, reception organizers and local bar owners near the bride's former place of employment, declined comment. The newlyweds happily departed for Paris, the one in Logan County, on their way to honeymoon with breath-taking views high atop Mount Magazine, where they'll stay at the beautiful lodge before moving to their new farm in Greenbrier, just north of Conway."

After the local midwife told Sally she was having a boy based on the way she was carrying, Sally spent hours compiling a list of possible names—names Brian never had time to review. After the honeymoon, he threw himself into learning how to be a farmer, spending his days in the field and evenings studying the almanac and other agricultural publications.

Busy as he was, he found time each day to watch his new wife walk out into the field to place fresh flowers on the damaged sedan. He couldn't tell from a distance, but she appeared to be talking to the car and would stand there for an eternity. Brian warned her about snakes under the car, that passing neighbors would think she was touched, and finally, that the car was leaching rust and ruining the soil. Undaunted, the vigils continued until the day the sedan disappeared. Sally pleaded, threw fits, and levied threats until Brian finally paid the man at the junkyard to haul it back. However, upon its return, he had it dumped behind the barn and covered it with a tarp, which he firmly anchored into the ground, a shrine no more.

At dawn on December 15th, 1955, sparse contractions awoke Sally from the little sleep the parasite in her belly allowed. She lay there a little longer until he played soccer with her bladder. She rocked side to side until she generated enough momentum to get out of bed. She looked over and noticed Brian hadn't come to bed. Nothing new about that. She'd slept alone for the last two months. He had a cot in the barn and slept there after late nights working on the tractor's engine. Last month, she'd gone out to tidy it up for him and discovered an empty whiskey bottle under the cot. She'd said nothing. He was a good man working hard to keep things afloat, and she was the last person on Earth to judge a little drinking. Or maybe she didn't bring it up because she'd licked the last drop out of the neck. She figured the baby could handle it. After all, it was *her* kid.

Another contraction said hello as she started a pot of coffee. Today was Kate's birthday, and Sally picked up the phone, knowing her mother would already be up. The party line for their rural area had been out the past few days, and still no dial tone this morning. She flinched with another contraction as she cracked an egg. With a few weeks to go, she wasn't concerned. The doctor had warned these might happen. With bacon, eggs, and pancakes on the table, she wrapped herself in a quilt and stepped out onto the porch to call Brian to breakfast, shivering as she met the chill of the morning. Her shivering came to an abrupt halt as she stared at the empty spot on their dirt driveway where his truck should have been. She looked with contempt at her useless car. The alternator had gone out two months ago, her belly too large for her to get in there and replace it. Brian had promised to have it fixed, but like a lot of things lately, it had been neglected. She hadn't seen him since dinner last night and wondered where he could be at this insane hour.

Her thoughts shot like an arrow to the check-out girl at the feed store. Rumors abounded that her fingers lingered when she handed Brian change. Sally had dismissed it as small-town gossip. Now, as she wrapped the quilt a little tighter, she wasn't so sure. She scanned the dirt road in front of the farm, hoping maybe he'd just gone for donuts. How wonderful would that be? Since quitting drinking and smoking, she'd lived on coffee, donuts, and chocolate. But as usual, nothing stirred on their desolate little road, the nearest neighbor over three miles away. The baby kicked in protest to the cold. She gently caressed her belly and, in breath she could see, told Mr. Calvin Drapier Westfield to settle down. Her eyes widened as a warm gush ran down her leg. Whatever adventures lie ahead for this little man, Calvin's story was about to begin.

1925

Melvin awoke to the warmth and softness of a mattress and pillow. *What a bad dream.* He slowly opened his eyes. A nearby nurse came over.

"Where am I?"

"You're in City Hospital, in Little Rock. Can you tell me your name?"

His eyes widened. "I'm where? What year is this?"

She smiled. "Why don't you just rest for now? No need to worry. You're getting the best care 1925 has to offer."

"Son-of-a-biscuit-eater."

The End

ABOUT THE AUTHOR

THE STORY BEHIND THE STORY

MN Wiggins is a husband, father, professor, musician, and surgeon who's lived and worked all over the Southern US. Originally authoring textbooks for his trainees and publishing research in the medical literature, he transitioned into fiction, debuting with *Magical Arkansas Tales,* a collection of children's stories co-written with his son. He soon followed with the first in the Arkansas Traveler series, *The Sugarfield Sugar Cookie: Sweet Southern Drama.*

Prior to the completion of *Sugarfield,* Dr. Wiggins wondered if modern physicians could adequately practice medicine without current technological advances, whether we were still teaching and emphasizing the age-old techniques of history and physical diagnosis or foregoing this in reliance on machinery. Having no volunteers to travel into the past to find out, Dr. Wiggins spent a year traveling back to the 1950s through medical textbooks of the era to get his answer.

We hope you have enjoyed this second installment of the Arkansas Traveler series, *Letters of the Arkansas Traveler: Lost in Time.*

Melvin Napier will return in *1925.*

Made in the USA
Columbia, SC
08 September 2023

22603002R00228